Romanticism, Sincerity and Authenticity

Romanticism, Sincerity and Authenticity

Edited by

Tim Milnes

and

Kerry Sinanan

First published 2010 by
PALGRAVE MACMILLAN

Palgrave Macmillan in the UK is an imprint of Macmillan Publishers Limited,
registered in England, company number 785998, of Houndmills, Basingstoke,
Hampshire RG21 6XS.

Palgrave Macmillan in the US is a division of St Martin's Press LLC,
175 Fifth Avenue, New York, NY 10010.

Palgrave Macmillan is the global academic imprint of the above companies
and has companies and representatives throughout the world.

Palgrave® and Macmillan® are registered trademarks in the United States,
the United Kingdom, Europe and other countries.

ISBN 978–0–230–20893–3   hardback

This book is printed on paper suitable for recycling and made from fully
managed and sustained forest sources. Logging, pulping and manufacturing
processes are expected to conform to the environmental regulations of the
country of origin.

A catalogue record for this book is available from the British Library.

A catalog record for this book is available from the Library of Congress.

10 9 8 7 6 5 4 3 2 1
19 18 17 16 15 14 13 12 11 10

Printed and bound in Great Britain by
CPI Antony Rowe, Chippenham and Eastbourne

Contents

Notes on Contributors

Daniel Cook is a Leverhulme Early Career Research Fellow at the University of Bristol. Before this, he worked as an AHRC-funded Research Fellow on the *Cambridge Edition of the Works of Jonathan Swift* and received his PhD at the University of Cambridge. He has recently completed a book entitled *Antiquaries and Romantics: The Rise and Fall of Thomas Chatterton.*

Alex J. Dick is Assistant Professor of English at the University of British Columbia in Vancouver, Canada. He is editor (with Angela Esterhammer of *Spheres of Action: Speech and Performance in Romantic Culture* (2009) and (with Christine Lupton) of *Theory and Practice in the Eighteenth Century: Writing between Philosophy and Literature* (2008). He is currently completing a book project on money and value in the Romantic period.

Angela Esterhammer is Professor of English at the University of Zurich. She is the author of *Romanticism and Improvisation 1750–1850* (2008) and *Spheres of Action: Speech and Performance in Romantic Culture* (co-edited with Alex J. Dick, 2009). Previous publications include *Creating States: Studies in the Performative Language of John Milton and William Blake* (1994) and *The Romantic Performative: Language and Action in British and German Romanticism* (2000). She has edited several collections of essays, the most recent of them being a volume of international, comparatist papers entitled *Romantic Poetry* (2002). Her current research interests include performance, print culture, and mediality during the late Romantic period.

John Halliwell is the Research Assistant for the Centre for Romantic Studies at the University of Bristol and is currently completing his PhD on Political Satire in periodicals of the Romantic period.

Sara Lodge is Lecturer in English at the University of St Andrews, UK. She is a specialist in nineteenth-century literature, with a particular interest in poetry, print culture, comedy and work produced between 1820 and 1850. She has published various articles on nineteenth-century poetry and periodical literature and is the author of *Thomas Hood and Nineteenth-Century Poetry: Work, Play, and Politics* (Manchester University Press, 2007) and *Jane Eyre: an Essential Guide to Criticism* (Palgrave, 2008).

Tim Milnes is Senior Lecturer in English Literature at the University of Edinburgh, UK. He is the author of *Knowledge and Indifference in English Romantic Prose* (Cambridge University Press, 2003) and *The Truth about Romanticism: Pragmatism and Idealism in Keats, Shelley, Coleridge* (Cambridge University Press, 2010). He has also published articles on Coleridge, Bentham, Hazlitt, Percy Shelley and Charles Lamb.

Dafydd Moore is Associate Dean and Head of the School of Humanities and Performing Arts at the University of Plymouth, UK. He is author of *Enlightenment and Romance in the Poems of Ossian* (Ashgate, 2003) and has edited and introduced *Ossian and Ossianism*, 4 volumes (Routledge, 2004). He has also written numerous book chapters and articles on Macpherson, including contributions to *Eighteenth-Century Life, Eighteenth-Century Studies,* the *British Journal of Eighteenth-Century Studies, the Review of English Studies* and the *New Edinburgh History of Scottish Literature.*

Margaret Russett is Professor of English at the University of Southern California, USA and has held visiting appointments at the Breadloaf School of English and Bogazici University, Istanbul. Her teaching and research focus on British Romantic literature, the gothic novel, literary theory and contemporary fiction. Her most recent work has addressed the relationship between literary imposture and Romantic aesthetics. She is the author of *De Quincey's Romanticism: Canonical Minority and the Forms of Transmission* (Cambridge University Press, 1997), *Fictions and Fakes: Forging Romantic Authenticity, 1760–1845* (Cambridge University Press, 2006), and articles published in such journals as *ELH, Studies in Romanticism, SEL, Genre,* and *Callaloo.*

Kerry Sinanan is Senior Lecturer in English at the University of the West of England, UK. She has published on the Atlantic slave trade, including 'Slave Narratives and Abolitionist Writing' for the *Cambridge Companion to Slave Narratives* (2007). She is completing a monograph, *Slave Masters and the Language of Self,* and is co-editing a collection, *Slavery and its Contradictions.*

Ashley Tauchert is Associate Professor of English at the University of Exeter, UK. She is author of *Mary Wollstonecraft and the Accent of the Feminine* (Palgrave, 2002) and *Romancing Jane Austen: Narrative, Realism and the Possibility of a Happy Ending* (Palgrave, 2005). She currently directs the Exeter English Studies MA Programme and coordinates the Eighteenth-century Narrative Project.

Jane Wright is Lecturer in English Literature at the University of Bristol, UK and is a specialist in nineteenth-century poetry. She is currently working on a project entitled 'Strains of Sincerity in Victorian Poetry', is co-editing and contributing to *Coleridge's Afterlives, 1834–1934* for Palgrave (forthcoming), and has published articles in *The Explicator* and *Victorian Poetry*.

Acknowledgements

The ideas behind this collection germinated in a conference organized by Kerry Sinanan, in conjunction with Bristol University's Centre for Romantic Studies, at The University of the West of England in July 2005, entitled 'Acts of Sincerity: Authenticity and Identity in the Romantic Era'. The editors are indebted to all of the delegates who attended this forum and who contributed to the lively discussions and debates that ultimately gave rise to the present volume. Thanks are also due to the anonymous readers for Palgrave for their time, care and helpful comments.

Introduction

Kerry Sinanan and Tim Milnes

''Twere better to be dumb than to talk thus'

One of the key passages in Wordsworth's 1800 politico-pastoral poem 'Michael' marks the point at which the eponymous and taciturn shepherd finally speaks for himself:

> Our lot is a hard lot; the sun himself
> Has scarcely been more diligent than I;
> And I have lived to be a fool at last
> To my own family. An evil man
> That was, and made an evil choice, if he
> Were false to us; and if he were not false,
> There are ten thousand to whom loss like this
> Had been no sorrow. I forgive him; – but
> 'Twere better to be dumb than to talk thus.
>
> ('Michael', 233–41)

Michael is reluctant to put words to his bitter experience, but the source of his discomfort, one suspects, is not confined to the painful subject matter; rather, it is located in the act of speaking itself. Michael is authentic to his fingertips, but feels compromised by the very words that express that authenticity; he is sincere, but his sincerity results in a muddle of confession and self-justification, such that ''Twere better to be dumb than to talk thus.' The problem for Michael (and indeed, for Wordsworth) is that muteness, the complete abdication of voice, is no more an option in pastoral than it is in everyday communication. Heeding this lesson, modern commentators have grown accustomed to the idea that a certain amount of failure is the price – and perhaps even

the condition – of success in the quest to understand 'authenticity' and
'sincerity'. Lionel Trilling, whose seminal work on the subject remains
a touchstone for many of the contributions to the present volume,
concedes that sincerity and authenticity are 'best not talked about if
they are to retain any force of meaning'.[1] Similarly, Geoffrey Hartman
hesitates before launching his own inquiries into 'authenticity' and
'spirit', wondering whether such concepts 'cannot be saved from their
own pathos. Perhaps we should not even try to sober them up.'[2]

Romanticism's preoccupation with authenticity and sincerity intensifies concerns and questions that had pervaded philosophy and literature throughout the eighteenth century. With the explosion of print,
literary forms flourished and genres were transformed, reaching new
networks of readers in the private and public spheres. The Romantic
period saw a heightened awareness of this dissemination, a concern that
focused on the authenticity of the selves who wrote such works as well
as the sincerity of the feelings they expressed. Allied to this concern was
a desire to discover a holistic self at the heart of writing, a hub at which
the *meaning* of a word might be connected with the *truth* of an intention. Thus, it is in Romantic literature and thought that 'sincerity' and
'authenticity' are fused – and thereby transformed – for the first time.

And yet, authentic selfhood remains elusive, disappearing even as it
is grasped. For Charles Taylor, this problem of realization is inherent in
the 'expressivist' turn of Romanticism:

> Fulfilling my nature means espousing the inner élan, the voice or
> impulse. And this makes what was hidden manifest both for myself
> and others. But this manifestation also helps to define what is to
> be realized. The direction of this élan wasn't and couldn't be clear
> prior to this manifestation. In realizing my nature, I have to define
> it in the sense of giving it some formulation ... A human life is seen
> as manifesting a potential which is also being shaped by this mani-
> festation.[3]

The problem of understanding the way in which Romanticism draws
together being and language is further complicated by the fact that
Romanticism itself is more than just the historical space or critical
medium in which this fusion occurs. Preoccupied with history and
intensely – sometimes cripplingly – conscious of its own becoming,
Romanticism, it can be argued, is the problematic *form* through which
modernity understands itself as self-inaugurating; indeed, some have
argued that modernity's 'repetitive compulsion' is itself Romanticism.[4]

As a result, the concepts of authenticity and sincerity first acquire their numinous character through Romanticism's investment in the discourse of origins. Accordingly, it is by negotiating their own complex and reflexive network of relationships with Romanticism that most of the essays in this collection attempt to rethink the histories and theories of sincerity and authenticity.

This endeavour is initiated by the decline of two broad critical movements that dominated the treatment of these ideas throughout the twentieth century: one existential and phenomenological (but increasingly sceptical), the other historical and dialectical. The first, encouraged by Heidegger's conception of authenticity as a mode of being that is achieved by Dasein rather than conferred upon it,[5] cast the Romantic struggle with authenticity as primarily a phenomenological problem (as in Hartman's own early work on Wordsworth), or at least as an important crux in the history of ideas (as in Meyer Abrams).[6] The second took its cue from Adorno's dismissal of Heidegger's 'preestablished harmony between essential content and homey murmuring' as 'a left-over of Romanticism'.[7] Alerted by Adorno and Benjamin to the links between irrationalism, capitalism and Romanticism, a number of critics submitted the concepts of authenticity and sincerity to the full force of the dialectical energy (the 'beauty of inflections', as Jerome McGann calls it) that they summon.[8] Unsurprisingly, each of these critical traditions rediscovered its prototype within Romantic literature. Thus, just as Hartman and Abrams seek to explore the phenomenological implications of Wordsworth's suggestion that Michael's being lies too deep for words, McGann identifies in Byron an embracement of the *negativity* within which discourse and social being are formed. It is this negativity, he claims, that enables the Byronic critique of Romantic totems in *Don Juan*:

> If people contradict themselves, can I
> Help contradicting them, and every body,
> Even my veracious self? – But that's a lie;
> I never did so, never will – how should I?
> He who doubts all things, nothing can deny.

> (*Don Juan* XV, st. 88)

Through Byron's tireless *performance* of selfhood, McGann argues, the paradox of authenticity is itself exposed as the 'contradiction ... at the core of Romantic self-integrity', through which Romantic poetry 'opens itself to the horizon of its antithesis, to the horizon of hypocrisy'.

It is this contradiction, Byron shows us, that sustains the 'illusion in the Romantic idea(l) of spontaneity and artlessness'.[9] Sincerity, *contra* Wordsworth, is parasitic upon hypocrisy, and authenticity, upon *not* being true to oneself.

There can be little doubt as to which of these two paradigms of sincerity and authenticity – what might loosely be termed the 'Wordsworthian' and the 'Byronic' – has enjoyed the ascendancy over the past 30 years or so. Even allowing that the enormous influence of McGann's approach, and others like it, owes as much to Derrida's deconstruction of Heidegger's notion of 'presence' as it does to the apparently irresistible rise of historicism, it remains the case that when commentators on Romanticism write of authenticity today, they are likely to be more aware of the insistent tug of negativity than the aura of Dasein. In other words, while many critics are prepared to celebrate Byron's staging of sincerity within a literary arena that responds to the diverse demands of his Regency audiences, few are inclined to accept Wordsworth's spontaneous outpouring as the fiat of 'authentic' selfhood.

Truthfulness, and being oneself

To see why, we first need to be clear about the conditions under which the concepts of authenticity and sincerity come together. On the face of it, their magnetic attraction for each other is puzzling. The question of authenticity, after all, is fundamentally a matter of being: as Hartman notes, authenticity contrasts with 'imitation, simulation, dissimulation, impersonation, imposture, fakery, forgery, inauthenticity, the counterfeit, lack of character or integrity'.[10] Sincerity, on the other hand, is described by Bernard Williams as one of the two main virtues of truthfulness. Truthfulness, he argues, implies a respect for the truth that involves both accuracy and sincerity: thus, 'you do the best you can to acquire true beliefs, and what you say reveals what you believe'.[11] Authenticity is a state, sincerity a practice. To inquire into the intersection of these ideas then, is to ask how an ontological question (how *real* is this thing or person?) came to be linked to a problem stemming from the pragmatics of communication (to what extent does this *expression* correspond to an *intention*?).

One clue as to how this comes about is provided by the concept of the 'genuine', which has both ontological and communicative connotations. A person can be genuine in the sense of being real or authentic; at the same time, he or she can be genuine in the sense of being honest or sincere. Etymology sheds light on the adaptability of 'genuine' to these contexts, in particular through the cognate 'genuflex-ion'. Both terms contain the key Latin prefix 'genu', or knee, but while in the latter this joint is bent in deference to authority, in the former it becomes the means by which paternal authority is exercised; the father acknowledges the child as genuinely his by placing it on his knee. Thus, the common element in 'authenticity' and 'sincerity' to which the idea of the genuine alerts us is the notion of an authorizing *origin*: just as the authenticity of an individual's everyday being is determined by his or her relation to an original, authorizing essence, the test of a poem's authenticity lies in its relation to the hand of the writer from which it originated. At the same time, what makes a verbal expression sincere is that it corresponds directly to the intention that it represents.

Identifying the concept of the origin as the point where sincerity and authenticity meet provides an indication of the historical context of this gathering. In his early work, Foucault identifies the 'origin' as part of the 'great quadrilateral' of the modern 'Western *episteme*' that sustains and yet confounds subjectivity with its constant retreat and return. From the nineteenth century it 'is no longer origin that gives rise to historicity; it is historicity that, in its very fabric, makes possible the necessity of an origin which must be both internal and foreign to it'.[12] In this way, he argues, the retreat and the return of the origin fig-ures an incommensurability within the modern self. Whether or not we accept the further implications of Foucault's argument, his observation suggests that it is through a discourse within which the status of the 'subject' is tied to an 'origin' that the ideas of sincerity and authenticity meet and branch out into recognizably modern formations.

The crucible for the modern conceptions of sincerity and authentic-ity, in other words, is Romanticism: it is in the language of the late Enlightenment that the transformation of the 'extended' self into a punctual subjectivity is politically and philosophically consolidated. Correspondingly, Hartman notes the change that occurs between pre-modern and modern conceptions of authenticity, whereby the allusion to an *external* source as authority disappears into its obverse, so that 'authen-ticity now signifies a moral strength *not* based primarily on formal or institutional authority'.[13] As modern subjectivity assumes an increasingly commanding position, authority moves indoors, an interiorization that has ramifications for the work of writing. The Oxford English Dictionary registers how in the early nineteenth century the frequency with which the term 'authentic' is applied to an original *work* declines as the word is increasingly connected to the idea of a work that can be *traced* to an origin.[14] This apparently minor semantic adjustment reflects a significant shift in ontological weight, as the origin in question moves from world to mind. In the period with which we are concerned, an authentic thing is becoming less a prototypical or original thing, and more a *genuine* thing, that is, something that really proceeds from its origin – in the case of writing, the intending consciousness of the writer.

This in turn touches on the concern that forms the core of this volume, for it is an important consequence of the realignment of authenticity that *sincerity's* role in discourse acquires a newly privileged status. As the idea of the authentic hardens around a core, internal self, and the social is increasingly experienced as 'other', so sincerity takes on the burden of maintaining and reinforcing intersubjective norms. Charles Guignon expresses this eighteenth-century predicament succinctly: 'If the social realm is inherently inhuman, the way to humanize it is to be sincere in your dealings with others: we need to say what we mean and mean what we say.'[15] Such a world, founded on perfect truth, is imagined by Godwin in *An Enquiry Concerning Political Justice* (1793): 'If every man to-day would tell all the truth he knows, three years hence there would be scarcely a falsehood of any magnitude remaining in the civilized world.'[16] This is not merely a whimsical hope that honesty would prevail: Godwin's goal is the protection of individual natural rights within an equitable society. The realization of this political ideal is paramount and depends ultimately on personal truthfulness: indeed, it 'is by no means certain that the individual ever yet existed, whose life was of so much value to the community, as to be worth preserving at so great an expence, as that of his sincerity'.[17]

What many writers of this period discover, however, is that saying what we mean and meaning what we say is easier said than done. In the face of Godwin's utopian vision of a society in which 'every man would make the world his confessional', the mediations of language can themselves appear as an affront to authenticity and sincerity.[18] This brings us back to Wordsworth: configured as a punctual and essentially private origin from which the spring of sincerity runs pure into discourse, Michael's authentic self resents the tax levied upon it by the pragmatics of communication. His muteness, a withdrawal from voice, is a consequence of seeing language and history as threats to, rather than the conditions of authentic being and sincere expression. This leads many to conclude that understanding how 'authentic' selfhood can adjust in the face of the contingencies of language and history requires a worldview fundamentally different from that of Godwin. As Williams notes, even Rousseau eventually came to suspect that 'one may be in the dark about what one most wants or most deeply needs'.[19]

Sentiment and sympathy

And yet, it is Rousseau whose discourse of sensibility epitomizes the Romantic impulse to return us to ourselves. For Rousseau, the Enlightenment's legacy was to remove us from our natural humanity and to divide us by prioritizing rational responses: 'It is Reason that engenders self-love and Reflection that strengthens it; it is reason that makes man shrink into himself.'[20] This shrinking into oneself is not a return to authenticity, however, but a contraction of feeling and virtue. Authenticity is diminished by reflection; civilization produces social institutions and structures that thrive on inequality, thereby engendering a level of self-interest that prevents us from feeling the natural pity which, for Rousseau, is the source of virtue:

> It is therefore certain that Pity is a natural Sentiment, which, by moderating in every Individual the Activity of Self-Love, contributes to the mutual Preservation of the whole Species. It is this Pity which hurries us *without Reflection* to the Assistance of those we see in Distress; it is this pity which, in a State of Nature, stands for laws, for manners, for virtue.[21]

Rousseau's pity contrasts with the theory of sympathy adumbrated by Adam Smith. For Rousseau, pity is spontaneous: it inheres within us and it is precisely its primacy that ensures its virtuous effects. For Smith, however, a willed and corrective self-control is vital to ensure that our passions contribute to the glue of social sympathy. Throughout his *Theory of Moral Sentiments* (1759), he stresses that our benevolent tendencies are improved by subsuming our selfish passions to our sense of the greater good: 'Self-command is not only in itself a great virtue, but from it all other virtues seem to derive their principal lustre' (VI.iii.11); indeed, 'passions are very apt to mislead' (VI.iii.1) us from fulfilling our potential for virtue. In this way, Smith implies that we are more true to ourselves when we circumscribe our primary impulses. Preromantic sympathy was not bound to an inner, authentic selfhood. As Dror Wahrman observes, 'Sensibility, in its eighteenth-century sense, did not originate in the heart; it originated in the surrounding environment, and only subsequently left its marks on the heart.'[22] Smith's map of the affections, then, is a model for how ideal sentiment is moulded by the external, by consideration for others, and by that 'other' self, the impartial spectator.

In Smith's world of social interaction, manners are a necessary refinement of feeling, the precondition of sincerity. Yet this in turn raises the question of how to read outward gestures and relate them to character. Steele and Addison's ideal spectator is taught to tell the difference between fake manners and those that denote genuine civility. Aware of how performativity can condition sociability, Addison recommends the *Spectator* to the reader who 'considers the world as a theatre, and desires to form a right judgement of those who are actors in it'.[23] On the contemporary stage, drama thrived on ridiculing hypocritical and insincere characters. As Marshall Brown points out in his assessment of Goldsmith's *She Stoops to Conquer* (1773), in this 'world whose meanings have all been backwards', sincerity itself becomes a projection: '[p]roperly speaking, neither a person, a work, nor a sign bares its inside or wears its heart on its sleeve. The face (or the surface) is the boundary, not the revealer of meaning'.[24] This view of the relationship between self and sincerity, while prevalent throughout the eighteenth century, is revolutionized in the Romantic period. In Wahrman's words, 'What made such views about the doubling, splitting, or transmigrating of identities possible ... was a non-essential notion of identity that was not anchored in a deeply seated self; which is what rendered it so different from what was to follow.'[25]

This is not to say that the perceived need for sociability to be underpinned by rationalized civility and manners is extinguished by the advent of Romanticism. Indeed, a 1778 contributor to the *London Magazine* suggests that being ourselves could threaten the very veneer of politeness that enables social intercourse: 'Truth, like Beauty, requires the aid of dress and appears the most amiable when most concealed,' she writes, adding that 'we may behave with politeness without forfeiting our sincerity'.[26] It is unlikely that this contributor would have been much moved by Godwin's exhortation to his reader to cultivate a level of honesty according to which 'the truth and the whole truth' would be spoken arising out of the 'uniform' 'commerce between ... tongue and ... heart'.[27] However, even Godwin allows that this 'truth' may be spoken with 'kindness' as well as with sincerity,[28] revealing the delicate negotiation within late-eighteenth-century discourse between Smith's model of sympathy, predicated upon an awareness of what Trilling terms the 'social circumstances of life', and a suspicion that 'mannering' sentiments makes sincerity itself 'not authentic'.[29]

The novel: doing in a manner nothing

Nonetheless, in certain modes Romantic discourse insists that '[i]t is social man who is alienated man'.[30] The intensification of interest in problems of sincerity and authenticity is driven and expressed through both the revolution of traditional literary forms and the circulation of new ones. As Markman Ellis notes, the novel is quickly recognized as an ideal form that can offer solutions to the rupture between civility and spontaneity. In particular, '[r]eading sentimental fiction ... was to be an improving experience, refining manners by exercising the ability to feel for others'.[31] Mackenzie's *The Man of Feeling* (1771) presents an ideal of sympathetic benevolence in the character Harley, whose responses to the plights of his fellow man become a paradigm of moral sentiment. But while his feelings enable sympathy in the novel, they are a threat to Harley himself. When, at the end of the novel he discovers that his love for Miss Walton is returned, Harley tells her his heart 'will, I believe, soon cease to beat, even with that feeling which it shall lose the latest'.[32] The very ecstasy he experiences upon realizing that his love is requited brings this love, and all other feelings, to an end, showing how dangerous the life of authentic sentiment could be. Mackenzie's Harley, moreover, is identifiably a 'man of mode', whose broader literary influence ends as abruptly as it began. As Wahrman observes of this genre, 'the novel and the type performed a striking vanishing act'. No longer considered authentically manly figures, Harley and his sentimental counterparts would give way to other characters that could influence because of their credibility.[33]

Instead, it was the realist novel that was to find new powers of appeal towards the end of the century. Marilyn Butler shows how the rise of realism is itself a response to political upheaval, offering a less subversive form of fiction at a time when stability was desirable.[34] Many see the presentation of life in a mode that appears to glean its content from observable facts about real life not only as more affecting than the idealized portrayal of sentiment, but also as more effective didactically. Through verisimilitude, the realist novel attempts to resolve questions about the sincerity of characters and the earnestness of the form itself. Early novelists had struggled to turn fictional lies into moral truths: is Richardson's iconic heroine, Pamela, a liar and a harlot as Fielding read her? Is her authenticity compromised by her reliance on her parents, or is she sincere in her own convictions? An even more controversial heroine, Roxana, had taken on a life of her own as early as 1724, forcing Daniel Defoe to give up attempts to have her sincerely repent. Instead, it is left to the reader to discern if any lessons had been learned when Roxana muses that 'my repentance seemed to be only the consequence of my misery, as my misery was of my crime.'[35] With the ever-theatrical Roxana, Defoe seems unable to reconcile either the lie of fiction with its moralizing potential or the inauthenticity of character with the potential sincerity of the form.[36]

By the Romantic period, such controversies had become the warp and weft of a genre flexible enough to be a vehicle for competing ideologies. The realist narrative mode of Austen, Edgeworth and Scott aims to depict an authentic version of life and to teach the reader to put 'society before self'. Realism does not deny that the individual has needs and desires, but 'its social ethic rebukes individualism', proposing compromise instead.[37] Indeed, the question of whether society *allows* one to live an 'authentic' life, even in the spirit of pragmatic compromise, is compellingly posed by Godwin in *Caleb Williams* (1793), which blends materialist realism with elements of Gothic to chart relentlessly the oppression of the individual by a corrupt and diseased state. In his novel Godwin demonstrates the devastating consequences, on both state and individual, of lying and insincerity. The root of the villain Falkland's corruption is his commitment to an inauthentic mode of living: having 'imbibed a love of chivalry and romance', his reputation takes precedence over honesty about his true nature, while his determination to conceal the murder he has committed causes Caleb's downfall. In contrast to the hero of realist fiction, Caleb is antisocialized, clinging to his individualism in the face of overwhelming odds. Given Godwin's emphasis on honesty in his *Enquiry*, he is, perhaps, a surprising advocate of the novel form. While romance has had a pernicious effect on Falkland, for Caleb, fiction offers access to truth:

> I was desirous of tracing the variety of effects which might be produced from given causes. It was this that made me a sort of natural philosopher; I could not rest till I had acquainted myself with the solutions of the universe. In fine, this produced in me an invincible attachment to books of narrative and romance.[38]

This contradictory appraisal of the value of romance reflects the paradoxes of the mode itself. The difference between Falkland and Caleb is that Caleb puts his individuality before the aesthetic imbibed from romance and so stays 'true to himself', despite enormous suffering. Indeed, when Godwin comes to assess Mary Wollstonecraft's *Mary* (1788), it is its sincerity above all else that he values: 'The story is nothing … But the feelings are of the truest and most exquisite class.'[39] Here Godwin echoes his own final assessment of *Caleb Williams*: 'When I had done,' he recounts, 'I soon became sensible that I had done in a manner nothing.'[40] In Godwin's 'doing' of 'nothing', it is tempting to read an almost Heideggerian sense of existential possibility: novels might not directly effect great revolutions of state, he suggests, but an active commitment to authenticity and sincerity is where power lies.

Poetry's 'second naïveté'

It is, however, in the realm of poetry that Romantic writers appear to engage most urgently with the problems of sincerity and authenticity. Thus, the *Advertisement* to Wordsworth and Coleridge's *Lyrical Ballads* (1798) presents poetry in the 'language of conversation' of everyday people, and, in the case of 'Goody Blake and Harry Gill', declares this poem to be 'founded on a well-authenticated fact'.[41] In the *Preface* of 1802, the authenticity of the collection is asserted as emanating from the simplicity of 'low and rustic life'. The value of such poetry is that it shows how the 'essential passions of the heart … speak a plainer and more emphatic language': the verses are composed of the sincere, 'spontaneous overflow of powerful feelings' vital to the emotional 'connection' between poet and reader.[42] The figures in these ballads are the disenfranchised, the lowly, unstable 'characters … belonging to nature rather than manners' and, in relating their struggles and dilemmas, Coleridge and Wordsworth aim to bring a new, authentic dimension to the genre. Accordingly, the speakers' voices in the poems are not educated or refined; their pitiful exclamations, plaintive apostrophes and urgent repetitions offer a stark contrast to the Augustan wit and polish of the century's earlier poetic modes. Sincere feeling is *in* the language before it is produced by reflecting *on* it.

In addition to striving for more authentic content, Romantic poetry attempts to articulate alternatives to rationality, placing itself as a form in 'contradistinction to directly analytical or purely conceptual modes of thought' and thereby accessing more authentic sources of the self.[43] As Taylor argues, for the Romantics, nature is that source that allows the individual to correlate and connect with the universal: 'a central part of the good life must consist in being open to the impulse of nature, being attuned to it and not cut off from it … the nature that speaks within me is the good that must be cherished'.[44] Taylor goes on to observe that it is through our sentiments, our feelings, that we can hear this voice of nature. Consequently, the need to know and articulate 'what we find within' becomes crucial.[45]

The problem, as Hartman phrases it, is that accessing that which is within has its attendant dangers, for 'every increase in consciousness is accompanied by an increase in self-consciousness'. The attempt to know oneself is dogged by the 'corrosive power of analysis', threatening poetry's status as an alternative to rationality.[46] As Wordsworth discovers in *The Prelude*, meditation does not always enable calm reflection but rather unearths disquiet and unease. Even the sincerest 'humility' may become 'an over-anxious eye/That with a false activity beats off/ Simplicity and self-presented truth.' (I. 243–9). From a Hegelian perspective, from the moment they are conceived by the intellect 'authenticity' and 'sincerity' announce their longing for, and thus the *absence* of, the very thing they denote. The same realization produces what Hartman calls Wordsworth's 'via naturaliter negativa',[47] a dialectical decentring of consciousness, which, like Hegel's phenomenology, suggests that the deepest 'truth' of the subject consists, as Trilling puts it, 'in its being *not* true to itself'.[48] In this way, communication with nature becomes the only means whereby a *reciprocal* awareness free from the obstacles of self-consciousness can be explored.

Such reciprocity is evident in Charlotte Smith's *Elegiac Sonnets* (1786). In her sonnet 'To Melancholy', the 'evening veil' of 'latest autumn' (1) offers a dreamy, liminal space in which the poet may commune with nature. This communication begins with the poet in the position of a receiver of nature's mysteries, listening to the 'sighs' that nature 'breathes'. The 'shadowy' but sensate world of nature in this threshold time voices 'mournful melodies' that evoke the pity of the listener. Stimulated by nature's lamentations, the poet achieves a meditative, melancholic state born out of mutuality with this authentic source of feeling:

> Oh melancholy, such thy magic power,
> That to the soul these dreams are often sweet,
> And soothe the pensive visionary mind! (12–14)

The poet here needs nature to achieve the balance of all the senses that is necessary to composing poetry, a balance which, as Coleridge maintained, 'brings the whole soul of man into activity' and 'blends and harmonizes the natural and the artificial'.[49] The speaker is an audience of nature, listening with pleasure to a source that will 'soothe' her heightened sensibility. In this way the poet needs nature as a maternal, calming force that allows her to sustain her creative powers.

Smith's poet, like Wordsworth's, needs nature to offer a cure for self-consciousness: listening to the breathing of the woods, poetry is possible once her 'pensive' mind is becalmed by melancholy. For Keats, in contrast, the problem is not simply that self-consciousness is a barrier to authentic poetry but that poetry should have little to do with 'self' at all. In his strident response to Coleridge and Wordsworth, Keats denounces the insincerity of poetry that is produced by the 'egotist': 'We hate poetry that has a palpable design upon us – and if we do not agree, seems to put its hand in its breeches pocket. Poetry should be great and unobtrusive, a thing which enters into one's soul, and does not startle it or amaze it with itself but with its subject'.[50] Not only, then, is one's true self – even if discovered through nature's power – not an authentic source of poetry, but a true poet has 'no Identity ... he has no self'.[51] Keats wishes to lose a kind of self-awareness that he feels blinds us to truth. He wants to inaugurate a state of 'negative capability ... of being in uncertainties, mysteries, doubts, without any irritable reaching after fact and reason'.[52] In this way, truth will not be a philosophic song. Rather, as McGann puts it, 'the naïve ... cannot be self-consciously achieved ... it must come (to the cultivating mind) as it were by accident'.[53] Like Wordsworth and Smith, Keats's poetry uses the power of negativity to figure authenticity as the synthetic destiny of the dialectical consciousness rather than as a paradise lost: on this conception, poetry signals, as Hartman puts it, 'a return, via knowledge, to naïveté – to second naïveté'.[54]

Modern criticism, however, has become suspicious of the recuperative energies of Romantic poetry, sensing the operation of what Marjorie Levinson calls a 'rigged dialectic: a subjectively privileged and armoured affair'.[55] According to McGann, it is Byron who, against Wordsworth, demonstrates that a providential narrative of consciousness cannot fully encompass alterity and difference. 'A writer', McGann's Byron maintains, 'cannot "possibly show things existent" and at the same time "be consistent" ... because the "process" of subjectivity is an existential and not a logical (or dialectical) process'.[56] Rather than sustaining the concepts of the authentic and the sincere 'negatively', through the manoeuvrings of Wordsworthian antiselfconsciousness, alterity opens up these ideas to new horizons of doubt. Such horizons, in turn, lead to limitless possibilities, including the indeterminacies of rhetoric, play and audience, within which Byron performs his pageant of selfhood.

Autobiography and the signature of sincerity

In no area of Romantic writing are these aporias more evident than in the consummate form of reflexivity signalled by the writing of the *self*. In Romanticism, autobiography becomes an exemplary mode of writing that purports to allow a correspondence with the self and, through sincerity, to forge a privileged connection with other human beings.

While eighteenth-century spiritual autobiography rehearsed specific formal tropes, assuring sincerity through repetition, the Romantic writer seeks to assert authentic individuality through originality. Thus, Rousseau opens his *Confessions* with the declaration: 'I am undertaking a work which has no example, and whose execution will have no imitator. I mean to lay open to my fellow mortals a man in all the integrity of nature and this man shall be myself!'[57] Here the form of autobiography and the self expressed are mutually dependent, the originality of the former in particular being assured by that of the latter. But while Rousseau offers a sincere self, composed as nature made him, Paul de Man argues that once the putative author of autobiography signs himself in this way, establishing a 'contractual promise' with the reader, it is in fact the reader who 'is in charge of verifying the *authenticity* of the signature'. Self-presence is relinquished at the moment it is claimed and the 'myself' Rousseau hopes to present 'is in fact no longer a subject at all'.[58]

The 'defacement' that de Man describes as the inevitable consequence of writing the self is also a risk in letter writing, where the signature of the author inscribes the letter with a putative authenticity. Within the unprecedented textual productivity of the Romantic period, the sincerity of the person writing is increasingly invoked as a touchstone of moral value and of the worth of the literature itself. In turn, this culture of authority led to the commodification of the signature, encouraging the 'validation' of forgeries and imitations that were popular because of their very claims to authenticity. Thus, the market for James Macpherson's 'collection', *Poems of Ossian*, was regulated by questions about the sincerity and morality of the author himself. Those like Henry Mackenzie, who believed the deception, felt that the poems 'did exist in the Highlands, and were collected occasionally not by him only but also by other people of the most undoubted veracity'.[59] Similarly, Hugh Blair asserts that the authenticity of the collection may be verified by the apparent sincerity of the author:

> Of all the men I ever knew, Mr Macpherson was the most unlikely and unfit to contrive and carry on such an imposture, as some people in England ascribed to him. He had none of the versatility, the art and dissimulation, which such a character and such an undertaking would have required.[60]

Blair and Mackenzie's uneasiness is apparent, and betrays a problem at the root of the relation of sincerity and authenticity. If authenticity ultimately depends upon sincerity, rather than being the bedrock upon which truthfulness is based, then *every* writer's authority is vulnerable within a system of truth in which everyone's sincerity is at stake and yet relationally dependent upon that of other writers. Within this cognitive economy, increasingly urgent testimonies on behalf of sincerity have the curious effect of unsettling it, in the same manner that stock can be undermined by overvaluation. Behind Blair and Mackenzie's edgy investments in the credibility of Macpherson's work, then, is an awareness not only that their shares will fall if it proves bankrupt, but that their own interventions may be hastening its collapse.

This anxiety even extends to self-expression. In her journal, begun in 1768, Fanny Burney raises the question: to whom can one trust one's own expressions?

> To have some account of my thoughts, manners, acquaintance and actions, when the Hour arrives at which time is more nimble than memory, is the reason which induces me to keep a Journal: a Journal in which I must confess my *every* thought, must open my whole Heart! ... to *whom* dare reveal my private opinion of my nearest Relations? the secret thoughts of my dearest friends? my own hopes, fears, reflections and dislikes – Nobody! To Nobody, then, will I address my Journal! since To Nobody can I be wholly unreserved – to Nobody can I reveal every thought, every wish of my Heart, with the utmost unlimited confidence, the most unremitting sincerity to the end of my Life![61]

In yearning to be honest with herself, to 'open [her] whole Heart', Burney acknowledges that she is simultaneously being insincere with others, breaking confidence with her friends by the very act of disclosing the feelings that she covers up in everyday life. Yet this confession is crucially different from Rousseau's. In Burney, there is an absenting of self in the mode of addressee that Rousseau masks. Burney's designation of herself as 'Nobody' presumes the erasure of self caused by self-inscription that de Man outlines. This erasure, however, is not the cul-de-sac one might imagine, for it is what enables the journal to be written; for Burney, it is the *sine qua non* of sincerity. Indeed, Burney almost seems to take delight in her own defacement, acknowledging the absence of which her correspondence with self is the cause.

Alterity and subjectivity

De Man is not alone among modern commentators in seeing sincerity and authenticity as originating in the abyss between self and inscription.

From this perspective, Burney's self-cancellation is merely the less palatable but inescapable side of Wordsworth's self-positing consciousness. And yet, as Jürgen Habermas has argued, the slippage from dialectic into aporia is itself instigated by Hegel's original radicalization of epistemological doubt. Hegel's ambition is to reinstall the authentic as *telos* rather than origin; dialectically, the self *becomes* authentic. And yet, Habermas argues, by restructuring human reason according to an overriding principle of negation, Hegel's initial critique of epistemology turns into a critique of knowledge itself, whereby scepticism's traditional mistrust of reason is radicalized into 'a mistrust of mistrust'.[62] Hypostatizing dialectic in the Absolute merely provokes the idea of an otherness that is *incommensurable* with the power of reflection and critique. For Habermas, modern theory's unhappy attempt to 'escape the strategic conceptual constraints of the philosophy of the subject merely by performing operations of reversal upon its basic concepts' is one of the long-term consequences of this hypostatization.[63] In other words, the radical alterity that returns to haunt the missions of theory and criticism (in Nietzsche's idea of 'power', for instance, 'différance' in Derrida, and Jameson's framing of history as 'what hurts') can be traced back to Hegel's decision to subordinate critique to negation.[64]

Accordingly, some commentators have detected in the postmodern, 'decentred' self an unhappy repetition-by-inversion (a chiasmus rather than a reconfiguration) of an Enlightenment totem that reproduces the shadow of consciousness stripped of critical resources. The current collection of essays contributes to this debate by seeking to explore possible configurations of authenticity and sincerity that lie beyond a spectrum limited by (at one end) the ideal of an unmediated expression for an original 'human' voice, and (at the other) the epistemological hypervigilance of de Man. As Habermas indicates, Hegel's role here is pivotal, for his is the first major break with the philosophical discourse of centred subjectivity. Postmodernism's eagerness to dispel Hegel's dream of an authentic future for alienated consciousness might seem, in this light, not so much premature as beside the point. The reasons *why* this dream ends have yet to be determined satisfactorily, and yet they have profound implications for what we perceive to be at stake in the concepts of authenticity and sincerity.

Indeed, in his own contribution to the unfinished project of modernity, Habermas attempts to recover a model of linguistic intersubjectivity in Kant, Schiller, Fichte and early Hegel that trades upon 'the paradigm of mutual understanding between subjects capable of speech and action', and works as a Romantic 'counterdiscourse' to the language of hypostatized subjectivity,[65] while Hartman's narrative of authenticity is predicated upon a Romantic revision of Hegel whereby the trials of sincerity and authenticity inevitably leave their indelible 'scars' upon the spirit.[66] In a similar vein, Taylor argues that if the inescapable frameworks that make human life intelligible are *truly* inescapable, they can only be understood through narrative, a form of 'Romantic expressivism', whereby authenticity is conceived to be a *process* that always involves 'the exploration of order through personal experience'.[67] Within this holistic economy of the real, there is no standpoint from which the role played by sincerity can be subjected to the scrutiny of a radically suspicious hermeneutic. As Williams observes, 'where the presence of other people is vital, sincerity helps to construct or create truth'; in such a manner, 'I become what with increasing steadiness I can sincerely profess.'[68]

None of this is to say that authenticity and sincerity cannot be theorized or historicized. On the contrary, engaging with the complex theoretical and historical narratives of these concepts forms an essential part of the rationale of this collection. Hence the centrality of Romanticism: by binding authenticity and sincerity, it raises the ontological and discursive status of the work of art to an unprecedented level. And yet, through its simultaneous discovery of the power of negativity, Romanticism also initiates the conflict between modernity's homesick longing for authenticity and its dogged pursuit of critique. Thus, while no single theoretical or methodological programme unites the essays in this collection, there remains, among the many family resemblances that run between them, an awareness of how this conflict continues to exercise modern criticism. Cast by the Romantics as a struggle between poetry and criticism, it is a predicament that forms both the subject and the framework of the contributions here.

Forging authenticity

It is tempting to think of authenticity, at once inconceivable and indispensable, disreputable and incorrigible, as an inherently paradoxical concept. In 'Genuity or Ingenuity? Invented Tradition and the Scottish Talent', Margaret Russett notes that even commentators who are sceptical of the notion of authenticity often find it impossible, in practice, to extricate the concept from their own researches. This raises a conundrum faced by all scholars who wish to problematize the notion of authenticity, but, encumbered by Romantic conceptions of the 'genuine', lack a compelling alternative to the term they critique.

Russett argues, however, that an alternative discourse of authenticity can be extrapolated from the careers of several Scottish (and canonically 'minor') antiquarians and ballad imitators who grounded their poetic practice in the philosophy of David Hume.

Russett's own 'alternative' history incorporates a case study of how Lady Elizabeth Wardlaw's nationalist ballad 'Hardyknute' (1719), recognized as a modern imitation almost from its initial appearance, is naturalized over the course of the eighteenth century: to the point that, in 1781, John Pinkerton is able to launch himself as a poet by claiming to have uncovered the lost 'second half' of the well-known ballad fragment. Once a more genuine version of 'Hardyknute' was eventually extracted from the variously 'padded' versions in general circulation, Pinkerton was discredited as a poet and condemned as an unreliable collector.

Pinkerton responds to his attackers, however, by launching a defence of forgery as a fictional practice. Against the orthodox ideology of authenticity, he develops critical, and historiographical principles that propose a Humean understanding of literary history, prefiguring Hugh Trevor-Roper's later account of Scottish cultural nationalism as an 'invention of tradition'. In this way, Russett forges her own links between the ancient artefact, the distressed imitation, and the modern original that realizes a sceptical, Humean vision of history as consensual fiction. It is this reflexive version of temporality, she concludes, that constitutes a *strong* – if not 'authentic' – counter-tradition to the temporality associated with the high Romantic lyric.

A different perspective upon the relation between Romantic lyricism and contemporary constructions of authenticity is offered by '"A Blank Made": *Ossian*, Sincerity, and the Possibilities of Forgery', in which Dafydd Moore explores how Romantic commentary upon James Macpherson's *The Poems of Ossian* (1761–1763) capitalizes upon the poems' ambiguous status as literary forgeries. Moore registers the tendency of recent commentary to downplay the 'fraudulent' nature of *Ossian* on the grounds that the absolute authenticity of the poems was not a matter of overriding concern for Romantic readers. Against this, he contends that the very ambiguity surrounding *Ossian*'s status, origin and authenticity as literary text is actively exploited by Romantic writers such as William Hazlitt, for whom the possibility that *Ossian* is a fiction constitutes merely another 'blank made' in the nihilistic, Ossianic universe. Accordingly, by outlining the reception of the poems in the early nineteenth century, chiefly in the works of Scott and Wordsworth, Moore accounts for *Ossian*'s symbolic value within Romantic poetics in terms of its role as an ontological 'hybrid' and a litmus test for the power of emotional and imaginative engagement.

Like Russett and Moore, Daniel Cook endeavours to extricate eighteenth-century languages of authenticity from more 'essentialist', Romantic conceptions of origins and temporality. In 'Authenticity among Hacks: Thomas Chatterton's "Memoirs of a Sad Dog" and Magazine Culture', Cook examines the relationships between sincerity, authenticity and antiquarianism in the work of the 'boy-poet' and forger, Thomas Chatterton. The long-standing interest in the authenticity of Chatterton's works, Cook claims, has been driven in large part by the assumption that the Rowley forgeries are *the* literary achievement in Chatterton's oeuvre, and that his 'modern' works are merely the by-products of a poet's need to earn a living. Behind this assumption is the idea that Chatterton was a genius led astray by the grubby profession of metropolitan writing, a notion Cook links to the Romantic faith in original genius. It is this faith, Cook claims, that must be extirpated if we are to understand the significance of works such as 'Memoirs of a Sad Dog' (1770).

Accordingly, Cook bypasses the dichotomy of Augustan rhetoric and pre-romantic feeling in order to trace the complex modulations of literary satire and literary sentimentalism in the reflexive performances of mid-century 'hack' writing. He argues that the confrontation between satiric and sentimental modes of writing in the prose and poetry of magazine writers provides the necessary context for understanding Chatterton's neglected modern works, as well as those of his hack colleagues in the magazines. Correspondingly, the danger Cook identifies is that, in their tendency to isolate Chatterton from the environs of the magazine culture with which he engaged in works like 'Memoirs of a Sad Dog', 'Romantic' literary histories and methods of individuating authors overlook how the 'intertextual piracies' of this culture develop a literary idiom that tests conventional notions of authenticity and sincerity.

Acts of sincerity

Godwin's vision of a society in which every man would make the world his confessional, and Wordsworth's call for a spontaneous overflow of powerful feelings, expressed poetically in the real language of men, usher in a new ideal sincerity at the dawn of the nineteenth century. Modern commentary has adopted different attitudes to this paradigm shift. As Angela Esterhammer notes, while late-twentieth-century critics, working within the legacy of New Criticism, faced the challenge of reconciling a definition of sincerity in poetry with scepticism about authorial emotion or intent, more recently this challenge has been magnified by a powerful critical focus on the well-developed dimension of theatricality and performativity in the public sphere of Romantic culture. In this light, in what sense can Romantic poetry be taken to exemplify sincerity, let alone a 'sincere ideal'?

In 'The Scandal of Sincerity: Wordsworth, Byron, Landon', Esterhammer attempts to answer this question by identifying two distinct discourses of 'sincerity' in English Romantic literature, the difference between which is reflected in the contrast between Wordsworth and Byron. While both poets associate sincerity with spontaneity (that is, with a natural, unmediated response to stimuli) Wordsworth insists, particularly in his 'Essays upon Epitaphs' (1810) and in his elegiac poems, that sincerity is the antithesis of acting. With Byron, on the other hand, and with other 'late' Romantics such as Letitia Landon, sincerity and spontaneity come to be associated with performance. Accordingly, Byron's explorations of 'sincerity' in the late Cantos of *Don Juan* (1819–1824) reflect a recognition that natural, unmediated responses must be registered in the body (through gesture, inflection and embodied expression, or even through more overtly theatrical conventions such as clothing) in order to be communicated and become socially meaningful. According to Esterhammer, this embodied version of sincerity, which is always on the verge of succumbing to parody or excess, reveals the aporia within sincerity itself, insofar as the latter implies an exact correspondence between the incommensurate frameworks of private emotion and public semiotics. Such incommensurability, in turn, gives rise to what she terms 'the scandal of the speaking body'.

Like Esterhammer's chapter, Tim Milnes' 'Making Sense of Sincerity in *The Prelude*' focuses upon Wordsworth in its attempts to account for the complexities of sincerity in Romantic writing. Unlike Esterhammer, however, Milnes characterizes the performative aspects of sincerity in Romantic writing in pragmatic rather than aporetic terms. For Milnes, 'sincerity' in Wordsworth cannot be understood in isolation from the poet's use of 'sense'. Both concepts are closely related to notions of truth and meaning, relations that modern criticism has largely sought to historicize and/or deconstruct. For Milnes, however, the nature of these links has been misconceived. Setting out from William Empson's observation that Wordsworth's 'sense *of*' reality vacillates between the empirical/epistemological and the semantic, Milnes argues that this blurring of the boundaries between truth and meaning need not be seen as obfuscation. His claim is that, notwithstanding Wordsworth's Rousseauian yearning for an alethic and semantic origin that might underwrite the sincerity of the poetic voice, *The Prelude* harbours an alternative discourse of *communicative* rationality. According to the latter, sincerity is tied not to an intentional logos, but to the pragmatics of communication and intersubjectivity that sustain truth and interpretation. Reading the 'Blind Beggar' episode of *The Prelude* in light of this discourse, he concludes, reveals how Wordsworth seeks to make 'sense' (out) of sincerity.

In their treatment of performativity and pragmatism respectively, Esterhammer and Milnes both suggest that there is more to 'sincerity' in the Romantic period than that outlined by Trilling's narrative of Rousseauian transparency overcome by a Hegelian concern with otherness. Kerry Sinanan further extends this line of inquiry to the contemporary debate over slavery. In her chapter, 'Too Good to be True? Hannah More, Sincerity and Evangelical Abolitionism', Sinanan takes issue with critical assessments that depict the anti-slavery interventions of Hannah More and ex-slave-trader John Newton as 'conservative', insincere and inauthentic. She places the correspondence between the two figures within the frame of a complex exchange between abolitionism, sensibility and evangelical discourse.

Drawing upon the ethical holism of Charles Taylor, Sinanan argues that the medium of the letter offers an important insight into sincerity as an *act*, one which does not presuppose the existence of a Rousseauian, 'authentic' self. This signals a shift away from sincerity conceived as introspective reflection, and towards a notion of sincerity as outward, practical and intersubjective. Accordingly, she sees the letters exchanged by More and Newton as articulations of authentic sources of the self that allow these selves to flex and change. In 'Sensibility: an Epistle to the Honourable Mrs Boscawen', for example, More's empathy is rooted in an evangelical sensibility that encourages the 'feeling' individual to empathize with his or her enslaved brothers and sisters and so promote their liberty. For Sinanan, More presents a dialectical view of self that must simultaneously interrogate the sources of the self for sincerity and participate in the world as 'it is now'. The true radicalism of this kind of sincerity, she contends, lies in its acceptance that such participation involves a fundamental transformation of self in the very act of transforming the world.

Never an easy act for the Romantics to accomplish, the performance of sincerity is, in many respects, even more testing for the

Victorians. Accordingly, in 'Sincerity's Repetition: Carlyle, Tennyson and Other Repetitive Victorians', Jane Wright offers insights into the changing significance of sincerity as a cultural and literary criterion of value during the first half of the nineteenth century. Writing against the demands of a burgeoning industrial world, Wright claims, nineteenth-century authors experience the burdens of literary sincerity inherited from their Romantic forebears in the form of a suffocating pressure that threatens the writer with speechlessness. Thomas Carlyle, in particular, is conscious that the means for addressing a public audience are limited if one wishes to speak with sincerity: neither poetic language, nor rhetoric, nor sermonizing will suffice. Through stylistic analysis, Wright shows why sincerity (the word and the spiritual ideal) is the cause of Carlyle's famously verbose inarticulacy. In so doing, she reveals that the unavoidable inconsistencies of human behaviour and linguistic self-expression are, for the early Victorians, both attested and compensated by repetition. For Carlyle, repetition lies at the heart of the difficult relation between sincerity and style, a principle mirrored in the poetry of Tennyson, whose explicit emphasis on repetition, Wright concludes, at once draws upon and skews the literary value of repetition established by Coleridge and Wordsworth.

Marketing the genuine

This fascination of a rapidly expanding reading public with sincerity goes hand in hand with an increasing interest in the early nineteenth century with bibliographical authenticity. As Sara Lodge notes, such interests drive the interplay between periodical literature – a larger and more powerful sector than ever before – and a revitalized interest in literature whose value might be supposed to lie in its opposition to mass-produced, ephemeral and public literary forms: the rare folio, the autograph letter, the hitherto unknown manuscript. By the 1820s periodicals are vying for glimpses into the private writing of Byron, while extracting from the juvenilia, albums and diaries of the famous. Through new technologies of print, such publications are able to produce in large numbers facsimiles of the autographs and early images of well-known authors – materials whose value to their audience lies largely in their apparent promise of contact with self-expression untrammelled by consciousness of public desire. Accordingly, the early nineteenth century witnesses a marked rise in the *market* value of authenticity, as seen in the celebrated Roxburgh sale (1812) of a rare edition of Boccaccio and the 'Chaldee manuscript' (1817), which helps to launch *Blackwood's Edinburgh Magazine*.

Lodge's chapter, 'By Its Own Hand: Periodicals and the Paradox of Romantic Authenticity', explores some conditions and consequences of the premium placed on authenticity by periodical literature in the early nineteenth century. It examines two case studies: first, the debate between the *London Magazine* and *Blackwood's* regarding the appropriate use of persona (which leads to the death of the *London's* editor in a duel with a representative of *Blackwood's*), and, second, the rise and fall between 1823 and 1840 of literary annuals, such as *Friendship's Offering*. In both cases, Lodge argues, the totemization of authenticity becomes a victim of its own cultural success. She describes how the *London* fights a battle over the lines between sincerity and disguise, legitimate masks and disingenuous blinds that is compelling but, in the context of a cutthroat and barely regulated market, ultimately unwinnable. The annuals, meanwhile, trade on Romantic authenticity with such success that, fatally, they draw attention to the gap between their knowing tactics and their 'innocent' self-image. In each case, Lodge maintains, the paradoxical status of the authentic as bearer of (on one hand) commercial and (on the other) emotional value, places it at the centre of the relation between Romantic discourse and its audience.

Other, more politically radical, forms of print culture, however, were already contesting notions of authenticity. In his chapter, 'Acts of Insincerity? Thomas Spence and Radical Print Culture in the 1790s', John Halliwell offers a reassessment of how concepts of sincerity and authenticity are reshaped during the politically turbulent 1790s. Halliwell focuses upon the work of the radical propagandist Thomas Spence, examining the latter's role in the creation of a radicalized and politically literate common reader. Through his work both as a publisher, and particularly as the editor of the periodical *Pig's Meat* (1793–1795), Spence circulates a huge variety of politically provocative material, from the first English translation of 'La Marseillaise', to essays by Richard Price and Joseph Priestley. In doing so, Halliwell notes, he makes expensive and inaccessible political writings available in the digestible form of a penny weekly, thereby educating his plebeian audience in the language of political discourse. At the same time, Spence deploys satire as a way of challenging standard constructions of authenticity and thus the key symbols and modes of state authority. Halliwell concludes that, by including a variety of satiric forms within the pages of *Pig's Meat*, from mock ballads to showmen's notices and parodies of loyalist anthems aimed to contest the forms of political discourse, Spence reshapes authenticity as a status authorized not by the state, but by the 'radicalised common reader'.

The case of Austen

The emergence in the late eighteenth century of a new idea of genuineness has far-reaching implications for the art of the novel. Nowhere are such ramifications more evident than in the work of Jane Austen, whose fiction engages with such issues both thematically and on the level of literary technique. Accordingly, the closing essays in this collection address different aspects of Austen's explorations of the many permutations of sincerity and authenticity in Regency England.

As Alex Dick notes in the first of these essays, Austen writes during a period in British financial history that witnesses a revolution in views of the fundamental principles of monetary economics. The gold standard, legislated in June 1816, grounds British economic orthodoxy for a century. Theorized by Henry Thornton, David Ricardo and others, the gold standard is seen by many at the time as an 'invariable measure of value', allowing finance to be flexible while protecting it from shock and disaster. The standard functions as an ideal: it defines how much gold there *ought to be* to keep the system true to itself. At the same time, the standard resonates with wider anxieties in contemporary culture. Many fear that the 'fictitious system' of paper credit that flourishes after cash payments are suspended at the Bank of England in 1797 will enfeeble the sincere and forthright British national character. More than guiding financial probity, then, the standard comes to offer a paradigm for measuring moral conduct.

In his chapter, 'Austen, Sincerity, and the Standard', Dick explores how the anxieties over trust and sincerity in Austen's fiction echo the instability of the new finance. For Austen, sincerity is an invariable measure of value, a measure that, just as in political economy, can only be *implied*. Austen's peculiarly ironic sincerity, Dick argues, constitutes an alternative standard to gold that inheres in writing (the medium of banknotes, political controversy and fiction alike). He identifies the 'standard' that operates in novels such as *Mansfield Park* (1814) as *embarrassment*, defined in the eighteenth century as an inability to pay debt, but understood here as a register of potential disruptions that also produces social cohesion. Embarrassment thus becomes a peculiarly modern form of sincerity, through which everything that is wrong can be acknowledged without jeopardizing the integrity of a social system;

effectively, as Dick contends, it becomes a way for individuals to register the fundamental insincerity of commerce without causing that system to falter. From this perspective, the genius of Austen's pioneering use of free indirect discourse is that it enables the narrator to pass judgements without doing so *sincerely*. In expressing her own embarrassment, Dick concludes, Austen articulates a new kind of sincerity, not only for realist fiction, but also for modern consciousness.

Austen's innovative handling of narrative voice reveals how, during this period, questions of sincerity and authenticity intersect with the problems of literary realism and its dynamic relationship with the object of representation. As Ashley Tauchert discusses in the final chapter of this volume, '"Facts are Such Horrible Things!" The Question of Authentic Femininity in Jane Austen', Austen's novels mark the high point in the wave of English literary realism that grew out of the eighteenth century. From the exposure of the realist heroine as a literary construct in *Northanger Abbey*, to the performative exploration of the complexity of competing perceptions in *Emma* and anxieties over the 'true' object of love in *Pride and Prejudice*, Austen's work is steeped in questions about authenticity and appearance, truth and fiction, realism and romance.

Tauchert examines Austen's particular mode of Romantic realism in the context of the novelist's experimental representation of reality through narrative in the very early works, 'Jack and Alice', 'Love and Friendship' (1790), and *Lady Susan* (1794), each of which foregrounds narrative form over realist content. Recent criticism has suggested that the shift between early and late Austen marks an adaptation to regulatory codes, an increasing diminishment of the earlier, anarchic voice into the later narratives of ordered restraint, and thus a slide into insincerity. This depicts Austen's transition from juvenile to mature novelist in terms of a shift in writing context from Enlightenment to Regency, one which constrains the early, more philosophical and experimental Austen, but which also makes her publishable as the writer of longer, safer and more 'respectable' works that would establish her as the peer of Fielding and Richardson.

Tauchert proposes an alternative model. This foregrounds the life of the writing subject in narrative. We can, Tauchert argues, understand Austen's narrative work as itself performing the trajectory of becoming-woman, analogous to the fictional development of her heroines, whereby the libidinal energies that run riot in Austen's early narratives are harnessed to produce the aesthetic transcendence of the later works. Thus, the heroines' various narrative performances of 'becoming-woman' incarnate the transition of the *writing* subject from girl into woman. In addition, by focusing on Austen's 'romancing' of reality, Tauchert makes a strong case for considering her work as a powerful and authentic form of *feminine* epistemology.

Notes

1. Lionel Trilling, *Sincerity and Authenticity: The Charles Eliot Norton Lectures, 1969–1970* (Oxford University Press, 1974), p. 120.
2. Geoffrey Hartman, *Scars of the Spirit: The Struggle against Inauthenticity* (Palgrave Macmillan, 2002), p. 1.
3. Charles Taylor, *Sources of the Self* (Cambridge University Press, 1989), p. 375.
4. Philippe Lacoue-Labarthe and Jean-Luc Nancy, *The Literary Absolute*, trans. Philip Barnard and Cheryl Lester (State University of New York Press, 1988), p. 17.
5. See Martin Heidegger, *Being and Time*, trans. John Macquarrie and Edward Robinson (Basil Blackwell, 1962), p. 78: 'Dasein exists. Furthermore, Dasein is an entity which in each case I myself am. Mineness belongs to any existent Dasein, and belongs to it as the condition which makes authenticity and inauthenticity possible.'
6. See especially Geoffrey Hartman, *Wordsworth's Poetry 1787–1814* (Yale University Press, 1964) and M. H. Abrams, *Natural Supernaturalism: Tradition and Revolution in Romantic Literature* (Oxford University Press, 1971).
7. Theodor Adorno, *The Jargon of Authenticity*, trans. Knut Tarnowski and Frederic Will (1964, London: Routledge, 2003), pp. 43, 46.
8. See Jerome J. McGann, *The Beauty of Inflections: Literary Investigations in Historical Method and Theory* (Oxford University Press, 1985).
9. Jerome J. McGann, *Byron and Romanticism*, ed. James Solderholm (Cambridge University Press, 2002), pp. 115, 117.
10. Hartman, *Scars*, p. 25.
11. Bernard Williams, *Truth and Truthfulness: An Essay in Genealogy* (Princeton University Press, 2002), p. 11.
12. Michel Foucault, *The Order of Things: An Archeology of the Human Sciences* (1966, London: Routledge, 2002), p. 359.
13. Hartman, *Scars*, p. viii.
14. 'Authentic', *Oxford English Dictionary*, 2nd edn., 3 March 2006 <http://dictionary.oed.com/>.
15. Charles Guignon, *On Being Authentic* (Routledge, 2004), p. 35.
16. William Godwin, *An Enquiry Concerning Political Justice*, vol. 1 (Dublin, 1793), p. 222.
17. Ibid., vol. 1, p. 260.
18. Ibid., vol. 1, p. 220.
19. Williams, *Truth*, p. 182.
20. Jean-Jacques Rousseau, *A Discourse on the Origins and Foundations of Inequality among Mankind* (London, 1761), p. 75.
21. Ibid., p. 76.
22. Dror Wahrman *The Making of the Modern Self. Identity and Culture in Eighteenth-Century England* (Yale University Press, 2004), p. 186.

23. Joseph Addison, 'The Spectator' No. 10, Monday March 12, 1711.
24. Marshall Brown, *Preromanticism* (Stanford University Press, 1991), pp. 187, 189.
25. Wahrman, *Making*, p. 176.
26. *London Magazine* January 1778 'Reflections of a Lady on Sincerity', p. 24.
27. Godwin, *Enquiry*, vol. 1, p. 253.
28. Ibid., p. 223.
29. Trilling, *Sincerity*, p. 11.
30. Ibid, p. 30.
31. Markman Ellis, *The Politics of Sensibility. Race, Gender and Commerce in the Novel* (Cambridge University Press, 1996), p. 17.
32. Henry Mackenzie, *The Man of Feeling* (W.W. Norton and Co., 1958), p. 92.
33. Wahrman, *Making*, p. 38.
34. See Marilyn Butler, *Romantics, Rebels and Reactionaries: English Literature and its Background 1760–1830* (Oxford University Press, 1981), p. 155.
35. Daniel Defoe, *The Fortunate Mistress* (London, 1724), p. 407.
36. See G. A. Starr, *Defoe and Spiritual Autobiography* (Princeton University Press, 1965).
37. Butler, *Romantics*, p. 156.
38. William Godwin, *Caleb Williams*, ed. David McCracken (Oxford World's Classics, 1982), p. 4.
39. Quoted in *Mary, Maria, Matilda*, ed. Janet Todd (Penguin, 1992), p. x.
40. Godwin, 'Preface', *Fleetwood* (1832), quoted in *Caleb Williams*, p. 341.
41. William Wordsworth 'Advertisement to *Lyrical Ballads*' (1798), *Romanticism, An Anthology*, ed. Duncan Wu (Blackwell, 1998), p. 191.
42. See Wu, p. 357.
43. Geoffrey Hartman, *Wordsworth's Poetry 1787–1814* (Yale University Press, 1971), p. 182.
44. Taylor, *Sources*, p. 372.
45. Ibid., p. 374.
46. Hartman, *Wordsworth's Poetry*, p. 180.
47. Ibid., p. xv.
48. Trilling, *Sincerity*, p. 44.
49. Samuel Taylor Coleridge, *Biographia Literaria*, eds James Engell and Walter Jackson Bate, vol. 2 (Princeton University Press, 1983), pp. 15–17.
50. John Keats, 'To John Hamilton Reynolds', 3 February 1818, letter 59 of *The Letters of John Keats 1814–1821*, ed. Hyder Edward Rollins, vol. 1 (Harvard University Press, 1958), p. 224.
51. John Keats, 'To Richard Woodhouse', 27 October 1818, letter 118 of *Letters*, vol. 1, p. 387.
52. John Keats, 'To George and Tom Keats, 21, 27 December 1817, letter 45 of *Letters*, vol. 1, p. 193.
53. Jerome McGann, *The Poetics of Sensibility*, p. 123.
54. Hartman, *Wordsworth's Poetry*, p. 181.
55. Marjorie Levinson, 'Introduction', *Rethinking Historicism: Critical Readings in Romantic History* (Basil Blackwell, 1989), p. 2.
56. McGann, *Byron*, pp. 116–17.
57. Jean-Jacques Rousseau, *The Confessions of J-J. Rousseau with the Reveries of the Solitary Walker*, vol. 1. (London, 1783), p. 1.

58. Paul de Man 'Autobiography as Defacement', *Modern Language Notes* XCIV (1979), p. 923.
59. Henry Mackenzie, 'To Samuel Rose', 27 July 1796, *Literature and Literati: The Literary Correspondence and Notebooks of Henry Mackenzie*, ed. Horst W. Drescher, vol. 1 (Peter Lang, 1989), p. 187.
60. Hugh Blair, 'To Henry Mackenzie', 20 December 1797, *Literature and Literati*, vol. 1, p. 199.
61. Frances Burney, *Journals and Letters*, ed. Peter Sabor (Penguin, 2001), p. 1.
62. Jürgen Habermas, *Knowledge and Human Interests*, trans. Jeremy J. Shapiro (1968, London: Heinemann, 1972), p. 9.
63. Jürgen Habermas, *The Philosophical Discourse of Modernity: Twelve Lectures*, trans. Frederick Lawrence (1985, The MIT Press, 1987), p. 272.
64. Fredric Jameson, *The Political Unconscious: Narrative as a Socially Symbolic Act* (1981, Routledge, 2002), p. 88.
65. Habermas, *Discourse*, pp. 295–6.
66. See Hartman, *Scars*, p. 43: '[T]he vastness of Hegel's totalising perspective does not succeed in envisioning history as a necessary and justified scene in which the agency of spirit leaves no scars.'
67. Taylor, *Sources*, p. 495.
68. Williams, *Truth*, pp. 203–4.

Part I
Forging Authenticity

1
Genuity or Ingenuity? Invented Tradition and the Scottish Talent

Margaret Russett

> Some Romanticisms are more Romantic than others:
> some are the real thing, while others are premature or
> belated, or simply false – anachronistic or fraudulent
> simulacra ... Scotland, neither English nor foreign,
> stands for an *inauthentic* Romanticism, defined by
> a mystified – purely ideological – commitment to
> history and folklore.[1]

Long before Hugh Trevor-Roper denounced the artifacts of Scottish
nationalism as "a retrospective invention," Scottish poets were notorious for "fraud, forgery and imposture, practised with impunity and
success."[2] This charge, coming from an architect of the Romantic
folklore revival, suggests why the demise of an authentically Scottish
literary culture has often been correlated with the genesis of *English*
Romanticism, or Romanticism proper.[3] For the antiquarian Joseph Ritson
and his late-eighteenth-century compatriots, Scotland was at once the
repository of a precious, though vanishing, oral tradition and a factory
of faux antiquities whose speciousness was synonymous with their infe-
riority to true remains. Ritson's attitude helped shape a literary history
in which Scotland still figures both as the spiritual homeland of that
most fetishized Romantic form and as the place where a *lyrical* balladry
conspicuously failed to develop. The ballad – now synonymous with
the origins of English Romanticism – was closely linked, during the late
eighteenth century, with the matter of Scotland. Ethnographic projects
like Walter Scott's *Minstrelsy of the Scottish Border* (1803) capitalized on
thematics and topography that were already prominent in anthologies
like Percy's *Reliques of Ancient English Poetry* (1765); indeed, Flemming
Andersen has argued that our "concept of the ballad genre ... reflects a

primarily Scottish tradition."[4] Beginning with Scott himself, however, the Scottish contemporaries of Wordsworth and Coleridge have more often been characterized as ballad imitators than as ballad innovators – as purveyors of "anachronistic or fraudulent simulacra" rather than as custodians of the real language of men.

A provisional explanation may be sought in the formal paradox of Romantic balladry, as exploited by its most influential practitioners. Wordsworth and Coleridge adopted the ballad as the antique vehicle for a conspicuously modern sensibility; the point was the disjunction between form and content. In Wordsworth's "Simon Lee," for example, the ballad stanza encourages readers to "expect/Some tale" (ll. 71–2) of the fallen House of Ivor – expectations which are, of course, abruptly punctured when Wordsworth's persona instructs them to "make" a tale from the barely narratable facts of Simon's decrepitude.[5] As against such trenchant irony, capitalizing on the perceived obsolescence of the form itself, late-eighteenth-century Scottish balladeers knowingly inherited a form that was, *like their nation*, "modern and archaic at once."[6] Popular ballads, revered from the mid-eighteenth century onward as the "reliques" of a lost feudal culture, were of course produced in great numbers long past the moment of their rediscovery; Susan Stewart notes that "the period of generation for the traditional ballad ... extend[s] from the middle of the sixteenth century to the end of the seventeenth; those appearing on broadsides and in broadside style reached their peak in the period 1750 to 1850."[7] The efflorescence of the ballad, in other words, coincides with what is now called "Early Modernism." Scotland, for its part, was identified with the backward, fading culture of the Highland clans and the lost cause of the Stuarts, but also with the theorization of modernity known telegraphically as the "Scottish Enlightenment." The catachresis of ancient and modern that defined Wordsworthian balladry was the *sine qua non* of the Scottish ballad, in which the modernity of traditionalism was both more overt and less insistent. Scotland was thus the obvious site for the manufacture of "novel antiquities" – James Macpherson's Ossianic epics being the most notorious, but far from the sole, eighteenth-century examples. By the end of the century, indeed, Ritson could describe forgery as a national vice: "Why the Scotish literati should be more particularly addicted to literary imposition than those of any other country, might be a curious subject of investigation," but it was certain that "the forgeries of Hector Boethius, David Chalmers, George Buchanan, Thomas Dempster, Sir John Bruce, William Lauder, James Macpherson, and John Pinkerton, stamp a disgrace upon the national character, which ages of exceptional integrity will be required to remove."[8]

This chapter recounts an especially byzantine episode in the forging of the Scottish ballad tradition and, from that episode, extrapolates a genealogy of Scottish Romanticism that differentiates it in kind, and not merely in quality, from the "authentic" Romanticism that developed south of the border. In doing so, I mean to emphasize the simulacral quality of the Scottish tradition, while suggesting that its anachronisms can be understood in terms of a capacious and peculiarly national sense of the word "fiction." My story has three parts. The first describes the making of a modern antique, the heroic ballad of "Hardyknute." The second establishes the philosophical context for that invention through a short biography of John Pinkerton, the latest culprit in Ritson's catalogue of infamy, and a figure who straddles the domains of literary and empirical history. The third section speculates on the legacy of invention inherited and carried on by two working-class Scottish poets, James Hogg and Allan Cunningham.

I

What becomes a legend most? Now an obscure entry in the history of folklore, "the noble ballad of Hardyknute" was among the best-known Scottish poems of the eighteenth century. It has been said to com-memorate the thirteenth-century Battle of Largs, during which forces marshaled under Scotland's King Alexander III beat back an invasion by Norway's King Haakon Haakonsson. But as Scott notes in his "Remarks on Popular Poetry," the story related in "Hardyknute" is "irreconcilable with all chronology, and a chief with a Norwegian name is strangely introduced as the first of the nobles brought to resist a Norse invasion."[9] The name recalls that of the eleventh-century English king Hardicanute, but this hardly explains why it was "feird at Britain's Throne" or why it would adorn a Scottish warrior who "livit quhen *Britons* Breach of Faith/ Wroucht *Scotland* meikle Wae."[10] Such idiosyncrasies were variously regarded by eighteenth-century commentators as the indubitable proofs of the poem's modernity and as evidence of the wear and tear sustained during its long currency in oral tradition. Popularized in the wake of the 1715 Jacobite uprising, "Hardyknute" was both an ideological and a textual curiosity: an ancient ballad unknown till after the Union; an anti-Celtic paean to Scottish independence; a "fragment" that was also an "epick"; a taut tale of battle and a convoluted love story; an anony-mous work that boasted no less than five named authors, and whose variants were as few as 120, or as many as 785 lines long.[11] Above all, it was a "mystery" whose plot ended in "dreadful Uncertainty" and whose provenance was just as obscure.[12] A patent example of invented tradition, "Hardyknute" nonetheless gradually acquired an anthemic status over the course of the eighteenth century. It was, as Scott later recalled, "the first poem I ever learnt, the last I shall ever forget," having by the 1770s long since passed back into "the mouths of old women and nurses" from its first appearance in print five decades before.[13] What interest us here are the stages by which "Hardyknute" accrued its patina of antiquity even while it became a byword for Scottish literary imposture.[14]

"Hardyknute" was first published, by most accounts, in an anonymous twelve-page folio of 1719, although two slightly different versions may have appeared earlier.[15] The question of how it came to be printed has been controversial since at least 1761, and what exactly *constitutes* the poem is even less clear. Beginning with the second problem, we find the shortest early version to be a simple tale of military valor, in which the aged but still vigorous Hardyknute is recalled from his peaceable retirement to vanquish the Norse invader. This poem contains only two stanzas unrelated to its martial plot: one lamenting the fatal beauty of Hardyknute's daughter, "Fairly fair," and another that describes the hero's brief encounter with a languishing stranger knight. The ballad ends with Hardyknute's defeat of the Norse king and a rousing peroration: "Let *Scots*, whilst *Scots*, praise *Hardiknute*,/let Norse the Name aye dread,/And how he faught, and aft he spar'd,/shall latest Ages read."[16] Despite its designation as a "fragment," there is little here to suggest that the poem is incomplete or that its theme is anything more complicated than a celebration of Scottish might. Mel Kersey has identified its contemporary appeal with the desire for a "Unionist" hero and a consolidation of British identity in the face of a foreign enemy.[17] But neither this version nor the slightly longer (232 lines) 1719 Edinburgh folio was widely known during the eighteenth century: the poem familiar to most readers, and reprinted in numerous subsequent collections, was a 336-line version that appeared five years later in Allan Ramsay's influential 1724 anthology, *The Ever Green, Being a Collection of Scots Poems, Wrote by the Ingenious before 1600*. While praised for its "remarkable Turn of Brevity," Ramsay's version was embellished with 14 additional stanzas and a new conclusion. In this rendition, the hero achieves his victory and turns homeward, only to find that:

> Loud and chill blew westlin Wind,
> Sair beat the heavy Showir,
> Mirk grew the Nicht eir *Hardyknute*

> Wan neir his stately Towir,
> His Towir that usd with Torches bleise
> To shyne sae far at Nicht,
> Seimd now as black as mourning Weid,
> Nae Marvel sair he sichd.
> Thairs nae licht in my Ladys Bowir
> Thairs nae licht in my Hall;
> Nae Blink shynes round my *Fairly* fair,
> Nor *Ward* stands on my Wall.
> Quhat bodes it? *Robert, Thomas* say,
> Nae Answer fits their Dreid.
> Stand back, my Sons, I'll be zour Gyde,
> But by they past with Speid.
> As fast I haif sped owre *Scotlands* Faes,
> There ceist his Brag of Weir,
> Sair schamit to mynd ocht but his Dame,
> And Maiden *Fairly* fair.
> Black Feir he felt, but quhat to feir
> He wist not zit with Dreid;
> Sair schoke his Body, sair his Limbs,
> And all the Warrior fled. (ll. 313–6)

It was this version – longer, but more emphatically fragmentary – that was construed by mid-century commentators, schooled by Joseph Addison, as "the first *Canto*" of a "Heroick Poem" whose author had "form'd to himself a more extensive Plan than that which we find executed. Love and the tragical Effects of that unbridled Passion, were in all Probability design'd to be the chief Ingredient in the Texture of his Fable." The final stanza, which "intimate[s] nothing less than the Rape of *Fairly Fair*," raises "our Curiosity to the highest pitch; and whets our Appetite for the succeeding Canto, where it behov'd him to reveal that Mystery of Horror."[18] While answering to the "epic" need for a unifying national myth, by 1740 "Hardyknute" had also become a mystery that solicited imaginative completion: "The reader perceives that the spirit of the poem requires, that he should supply many intermediate ideas," noted another editor, who supplied copious notes to fill in the gaps.[19] These ideas had something to do with the presumed historical backdrop, but even more with the salacious details of the subplot. The mystery of *how* the story was to have ended, and *what* was missing from the existing text, entwined with another, hardly less enticing: *who* wrote the poem in the first place? Assuming, probably on Ramsay's authority, that the ballad was ancient, mid-eighteenth-century editors were free to devise a myth of the author: one who was familiar with Homer but also ahead of the curve in his appreciation of Gothic aesthetics and the psychology of suspense.

Although the point may have been less to answer such questions than to ask them, an answer emerged with the publication of Percy's *Reliques*, in which "Hardyknute" appeared as a "Scottish fragment" – albeit a "meer modern" imitation of the manuscript fragments Percy had famously rescued from the fire. By this point, "Hardyknute" had already been republished several times, both on its own and in anthologies like Warton's 1753 *The Union, or, Select Scots and English Poems*. The version that appeared was usually Ramsay's 336-line text with its cliffhanger conclusion. According to Percy, there was:

> more than reason to suspect, that it owes most of its beauties are of modern date; and that these at least (if not its whole existence) have flowed from the pen of a lady, within this present century. The following particulars may be depended on. One Mrs. Wardlaw, whose maiden name was Halket ... pretended she had found this poem, written on shreds of paper, employed for what is called the bottoms of clues. A suspicion arose that it was her own composition. Some able judges asserted it be modern. The lady did in a manner acknowledge it to be so. Being desired to shew an additional stanza, as a proof of this, she produced the three last beginning with "Loud and schrill, & c." which were not in the copy that was first printed.[20]

This story, as tantalizing in its way as the ballad's ominous conclusion, discredits one learned myth of authorship only to erect another. Why should the composer of a new stanza be regarded as sole author of the poem? By this reasoning, Percy might have claimed authorship of the ballads he so liberally "puffed" and "pomatumed."[21] Like earlier editors of "Hardyknute," the genteelly English Percy assumes that the ballad must have *an* author, even if more than one writer is known to have had a hand in it. Lady Wardlaw's spontaneous addition is hard to distinguish, in kind, from the stanzas added by Ramsay, who also took it upon himself to archaize and Scotticize the spelling – the better to suit a date of origin "before 1600." One might speculate that the ballad's ascription to a *female* author, and one with no other literary reputation, left it quasi-anonymous and thus available for creative adaptation. In fact, according to one source, Lady Wardlaw based her poem on "fragments" which he "had heard ... repeated in his infancy," long before the 1719 version ever surfaced.[22] The poem was less the discrete, temporally bound production of an individual than it was an evolving series of performances. Stewart remarks that for mid-century collectors like Ramsay and Percy, "authenticity was not a value in itself," but it might be truer to say that the kind of authenticity they claimed for folk artifacts could accommodate a measure of editorial virtuosity.[23] The mode of composition they shared is not too distant from the ethos of oral balladry, even if Ramsay's additions tended toward the classicizing (for example the amplification of battle scenes and the insertion of epic similes) and the curatorial – that is, toward an "aesthetic" rather than a "political" version of Jacobitism.[24] Later anthologies published musical settings of "Hardyknute" – at least two melodies survive[25] – so it seems clear that the ballad circulated orally as well as in print, quickly attaining the currency that helped it, in Percy's phrase, to "pass for ancient" even while its modern touches were generally recognized.[26]

This brief sketch suggests how the career of "Hardyknute" anticipates the problems of authentication and documentation that would later dog Macpherson's Ossianic poems, supposedly translated from extant Gaelic manuscripts and undoubtedly based on orally transmitted songs and legends. The textual history of "Hardyknute" mimed the collaborative style of oral transmission, even while the logic of supplementarity – neatly inverting Percy's conjectural history of bardic composition – transformed a short ballad into a long relic. The added stanzas converted a terse martial narrative, suitable for recitation or singing, into an episodic tale of lawless passion and imperiled virginity – a plot more in line with contemporary *literary* tastes, especially south of the border. The expanded "Hardyknute" fit right in with the "lewd themes of [Percy's] ballads," which, as Nick Groom has commented, are "excessively violent and brutal," marked as primitive by their incessant rehearsal of "rape, pillage, and carnage."[27]

As the poem grew, stories of its provenance multiplied. The most elaborate authorial mystification and the most ornate version of the ballad both date from 1781, when a young Scot, recently translated to literary London, published his slim volume of *Scottish Tragic Ballads*, featuring a two-part, 785-line "Hardyknute," audaciously described as "Now First Published Complete." Dismissing Lady Wardlaw as no more than a transcriber, the youthful editor assigned a date "near the end of the fifteenth century" to the verses he claimed to have "recovered" from "the memory of a lady in Lanarkshire." "Now given in it's original perfection," the poem was surely, he declared with Chattertonian braggadocio, "the most noble production in this style that ever appeared in the world."[28] In this version, Hardyknute returns from the battlefield to find his castle strewn with corpses, including that of his son Mordae, whom he had sent back to escort the lovelorn stranger knight they encountered on their way to battle. His wife, deranged with grief, tells him that the knight was his enemy Lord Drassan, and that Drassan has abducted Fairly Fair. Hardyknute and his remaining sons set off in pursuit. Lord Drassan resolves to meet them in combat, but in response to Fairly's pleas for mercy, declares that the man who dares harm Hardyknute will be killed in turn. A bloody battle nonetheless ensues, and two more of Hardyknute's sons are slain. Finally Hardyknute and Drassan meet one-on-one; Drassan tells Hardyknute that he has married Fairly; Hardyknute challenges him to a duel; Drassan's page, remembering his master's vow, stabs him; and the poem concludes with Hardyknute mourning the demise of his rogue son-in-law.[29]

Its prolixity, even in outline, suggests how sharply this oedipal drama – ornamented with lengthy speeches and gothic scene-painting – deviates from the spare narrative of the "mutilated fragment" first published in 1719.[30] Owing something to both *Clarissa* and *The Castle of Otranto*, it makes good on earlier editorial speculations with a mini-epic of sex and violence that caters to sensational tastes. Its Gothicism bears witness to the modernity of "antiquity," even while its bulk strains the theory of oral transmission well past the breaking point. The lengthened poem did in fact win some acclaim, and was reprinted in several subsequent collections, but it gained little credit as a discovery: one sympathetic reader told its editor that "I have made up my mind with respect to the author of it. I know not whether you will value a compliment paid to your genius at the expense of your imitative art; but certainly that genius sheds a splendor upon some passages which betrays you."[31] This reader, it seems, could wink at a device like that used by Allan Ramsay when he published his own poem "The Vision" with a note dating it "anno 1300, and translatit 1524."[32] But while Ramsay's embellishments to the poems in *The Ever Green* passed with comparatively mild censure, by 1781 a two-part, souped-up "Hardyknute" was too much for most readers to swallow. Joseph Ritson – himself at work on a collection of *Scotish Song* – pounced, and a heated periodical exchange followed. In a 1784 review for the *Gentleman's Magazine*, pointedly addressed "To John Pinkerton" and signed "*Anti-Scot*," Ritson charged:

> This ballad has been substantially proved an artful and impudent forgery: but whether *Mrs. Wardlaw* were the *mother* or the *midwife*, is of very little consequence; the *bantling* is certainly *spurious*. There is not,

I readily acknowledge, any great degree of criminality in reprinting a fine and popular ballad; even though, from a defect in judgment, or a sturdy adherence to what Dr. Johnson might call Scotch morality, you did not believe, or thought proper to deny, its true origin. But what excuse can you have for the publication of a *second* part, or continuation, of this poetical fraud? Not ignorance surely! No; the composition must be altogether your own. Neither the lady, nor the common people of Lanerkshire [*sic*], from whom you pretend to have recovered most of the stanzas, will deprive you of the honour of its procreation. The poetry is too artificial, too contemptible; the forgery too evident.[33]

If Lady Wardlaw was indeed the primary author of "Hardyknute" – and modern scholars have generally assumed, in the absence of certain proof, that she was – only in 1784 did she and her fellow suspects became "forgers."[34] The logic is evidently that of guilt by association: it was the opportunistic publication of Part Two that provoked Ritson's denunciation of the "fine and popular" ballad of *The Ever Green* and the *Reliques*, along with its sequel.

His hand forced by Ritson, Pinkerton publicly acknowledged Part Two when, a few years later, he issued a more sedately scholarly collection of *Ancient Scotish Poems* (1786). In the preface, he averred that when he wrote his sequel to "Hardyknute," he truly believed in the poem's antiquity: a less preposterous claim than it first seems, if we grant that old ballads were regarded, by Percy and others, as fair game for editorial improvements. Now admitting his mistake, Pinkerton produced yet another theory of the ballad's authorship, ascribing it to Lady Wardlaw's brother, Sir John Hope-Bruce, who pretended to have found it "in a vault at Dunfermline ... written on vellum, in a fair Gothic character, but so much defaced by time, as you'll find that the tenth part is not legible."[35] On this evidence, Pinkerton concluded that "Sir John was the author of Hardyknute, but afterwards used Mrs. Wardlaw to be the midwife of his poetry, and suppressed the story of the vault."[36] From her quasi-authorial status in the *Reliques*, the woman has been demoted to a figure of slippage: slippage from historical to fictive discourse, from legendary to modern time, and from genuine to fake artifact. Thus the disciplinary task of assigning provenance correlates, for both Pinkerton and Ritson, with the proliferation of genealogical metaphors. The literary work, conceived as a fixed and immutable object, must have a single father. The forgery or faux antique is thus a bastard: in Ritson's unsubtle terms, "the illegitimate

offspring of Mrs. Wardlaw, by Sir John Bruce." In the guise of defending the poem's true author, Ritson dismisses materiality and history at
once; Pinkerton, for his part, assigns authorship to the (Scottish) *nation*
by linking "Hardyknute" with an eminent modern Scot.[37]

Among the ironies of this episode is that even while Ritson demo-
lished any lingering belief in the antiquity of "Hardyknute," his
attack on Pinkerton's sequel helped to strengthen the "authenticity
effect" of the Wardlaw/Ramsay version.[38] Although Ritson declines
to itemize the telltale signs of Pinkerton's forgery, Scott later noted
that "the poetry smells of the lamp," that "the glossary displays a
much greater acquaintance with learned lexicons, than with the
familiar dialect still spoken by the Lowland Scottish," and that "in
order to append his own conclusion to the original tale, Mr Pinkerton
found himself under the necessity of altering a leading circumstance
in the old ballad."[39] Apparently Scott *could* hear the accents of the
peasantry in the version he learned as a child. It is unclear which
"original tale" he means, but it seems he has simply subtracted Part
Two from the 336-line poem that appeared in his beloved *Reliques*,
and which thus becomes venerable by default.[40] Scott has almost
forgotten that Lady Wardlaw, although female, was hardly one of the
illiterate "milkmaids" evoked by his reference to Lowland dialect.[41]
No doubt the older poem's "Turn of Brevity," a trait often stressed
in ballad scholarship, made it seem more faithful than its bloated
sequel to the tradition of anonymous composition. Even so, we may
note in passing that Scott's object of veneration is (in its shorter as in
its longer versions) emphatically a *narrative* poem, more plot-driven
than Percyan ballads like "Sir Patrick Spence," whose abruptness and
ellipses influenced the formal reflexivity of Wordsworth's *Lyrical
Ballads*. Thus while narrative was attenuated in Wordsworthian balladry, and Coleridge spoofed its machinery in "The Ancient Mariner,"
story remained central to the Scottish ballad tradition.

The dispute over "Hardyknute" cemented Ritson's reputation as a
fanatical proponent of textual purity and widened the gap between
those who, like himself, regarded the ballad editor's task as that of
fixing the earliest version and those who, like Ramsay and Percy, saw
the ballad's actual *or* apparent antiquity as a license for creative adaptation.[42] As Pinkerton jibed in his retaliatory review of *Scotish Song*, Ritson
"spared no pains" to:

> restore [the poems] to error and imperfection ... None of your
> improvements and conjectures! All must be facsimile. No other

simile will go down ... But do give us a little touch of the black letter, you understand: and by all means supply not a word, a syllable.[43]

According to Ritson, representing one pole of eighteenth-century practice, "tradition ... is a species of alchemy which converts gold to lead."[44] Taken to its logical extreme, as Pinkerton implies, this assumption would yield pristine works that had never been read or heard of, and hence to an evacuation of *all* literary tradition, not merely that of "vulgar poetry." Tradition, for Pinkerton, is a matter of *simile* – of perceived resemblance and imaginative extension – rather than the naked letter of *facsimile*. Ritson's attack and Pinkerton's reply thus also mark the divergence of two schools of thought about textual authenticity: an "English" school (even if some of its adherents were Scots) that identified authenticity with origins, and a "Scottish" school that emphasized the poem's popularity as evidence of its authentically national character. The English view can be summarized in two anecdotes, drawn from the late-eighteenth and mid-nineteenth centuries respectively. The first concerns a practical joke on the Society of Antiquaries perpetrated by the Shakespeare editor George Steevens, who in 1790:

> had a coarse marble stone inscribed with *Saxon letters*, importing it to be part of the *sarcophagus of Hardyknute*, and describing the manner of his death, which was that of dropping suddenly dead, after drinking a gallon flagon of wine at the marriage of a Danish lord.
>
> This stone was carried to a founder in Southwark, who was in the secret, and a private buz whispered about, that such a curiosity was found.[45]

For Steevens, by 1790, "Hardyknute" was so obviously modern that only a fool could be deceived by it. In the wake of their paired "forgeries" – Steevens's mean-spirited hoax, Pinkerton's jejune self-promotion – "Hardyknute" became virtually synonymous with literary fakery: so much so that, 50 years later, its spuriousness had infected the entire canon of Scottish popular balladry. In 1848, Robert Chambers dolefully announced to the readers of *Chambers' Edinburgh Journal* that "the high-class romantic ballads of Scotland are not ancient compositions – are not older than the early part of the eighteenth century – and are mainly, if not wholly, the production of one mind ... [that of] Lady Wardlaw of Pitreavie."[46] Chambers "arrived at this conclusion" after noting verbal parallels between "Hardyknute" and others like "Sir Patrick Spence" – although previous commentators had noted the same echoes and drawn the opposite inference.[47] Indeed, Chambers arrives at *inauthenticity* by the same route that led others to affirmation: by assigning "Hardyknute" to a determinate – if fictional – author. Although his opinion was not widely shared, "Hardyknute" lost much of its appeal for English collectors after the Pinkerton affair: the Victorian ballad editor Francis James Child, for example, dismisses it in one sentence as "a modern production, and ... a tame and tiresome one besides."[48]

But as a member of the Society retorted to Steevens: "it is not to the impeachment of sagacity a thing with the marks of genuity is admitted to be such."[49] The felicitous word "genuity," in which we may hear a whisper of the postmodern "simulacrum," suggests why Scott and his fellow Scots could admire "Hardyknute" as "a most spirited and beautiful *imitation* of the ancient ballad," without insisting on a literally ancient pedigree.[50] For Scott, and for the other Romantic-era Scots I discuss in a following section, the line between original and imitation is less the sharp ontological divide associated with high Romanticism than it is the mark of a historicizing fold, the turn by which the modern *constitutes* the past. Scott himself, as is well known, began his career as an imitator of literary ballads, earned his credentials with a folk ballad collection, expanded into verse narratives like *The Lay of the Last Minstrel*, and proceeded to "invent" the form of historical fiction: each stage in the series nuances the modern's reinvention of tradition. As the first poem he learned by heart, and as the utterance of a collective national voice, "Hardyknute" defines Scottishness for Scott – even if its hero is fictional, its text unstable, and its antiquity a mere matter of convention. I next consider how John Pinkerton, Scott's predecessor and alter ego, both exemplified and theorized the paradox I have described.

II

Pinkerton's small niche in literary history rests mainly on his work as an editor – in such anthologies as *Ancient Scotish Poems* and his later collections of travel narratives – as well as the eccentric theory of Scottish racial origins for which he earned the distrust of other Scots and the belated approval of Trevor-Roper, who cites it in his controversial essay on the Scottish Highland tradition.[51] (It seems clear that Pinkerton valued "Hardyknute" partly for the anomaly that troubled Scott: the hero's name was Danish, suggesting that the ballad could be read as a "Pictish" or "Gothic" rather a Celtic myth of Scots identity.)[52] But though he ended his career as an editor and historian, Pinkerton began as a poet, publishing his first effort, *Ode to Craigmillar Castle* (1776), in his teens and following this with volumes of *Rimes* (1781), *Two Dithyrambic Odes* (1782) and *Tales in Verse* (also 1782), as well as several plays, both performed and unperformed. When he published *Scottish Tragic Ballads*, the "Hardyknute" volume, he was apparently hopeful of making his reputation as an original poet. Thus he may not have been utterly dismayed when Ritson exposed his "forgery" of Part Two, especially since this gave him an opportunity to claim the authorship of several other poems in the volume, amounting to almost half its total contents. The publication of "original" poems as the "ancient" sponsors of a modern editorial persona suggests how much Pinkerton learned from Thomas Chatterton's Rowley forgeries, the reigning literary controversy of the 1780s, when Pinkerton was first trying to get noticed.

Unlike Chatterton, however, Pinkerton lived to enjoy the mixed blessings of his notoriety. The measure of celebrity he won for Part Two of "Hardyknute" did not boost the reputation of his acknowledged poems, and once branded a forger, he never rid himself of the stigma. Among the delectable ironies of his career is the fact that his major, perfectly genuine, contribution to ballad scholarship – *Ancient Scotish Poems*, 1786, based on the collection of Sir Richard Maitland – was widely considered a forgery for at least 100 years, apparently because its premise evoked the tried-and-true forger's gambit of the "found manuscript."[53] In his *Biographical Dictionary of Eminent Scotsmen*, Robert Chambers marveled at how "Pinkerton maintained that he had found the manuscript in the Pepysian Library at Cambridge ... The forgery was one of the most audacious recorded in the annals of transcribing. Time, place, and circumstances were all minutely stated – there was no mystery."[54] But although this accusation happened to be false, it was a peculiarly fitting response to the work of a man who not only first tasted fame as a ballad forger but who defended the practice even in this more respectable sequel. In the preface of *Ancient Scotish Poems*, where he admitted writing Part Two of "Hardyknute," Pinkerton added that his "imposition ... was only meant to give pleasure to the public; and no vanity could be served, where the name was unknown." Neither could there have been "any sordid view," since he had refused the publisher's offer of half of the future profits. "Perhaps," he conceded, "like a very young man as he was, he had pushed one or two points of the deception a little too far; but he always thought that novel and poetry had NO BOUNDS of fiction."[55]

This is an unusually expansive early use of the word "fiction," to include not only prose and verse narrative, but also the editorial paratexts Pinkerton adapted from Chatterton.[56] It is also obviously disingenuous; Pinkerton may have refused payment for *Scottish Tragic Ballads*, but only after he tried to foist his faux antiques on Percy, then compiling materials for a new edition of the *Reliques*.[57] And this defense of "fiction" sits oddly with Pinkerton's aspersions against Macpherson, whom he considered "a man of genius" but whom he censured for mixing history and romance (a feint; Pinkerton's hostility to Ossian was motivated by his own peculiar style of anti-Celtic Scottish patriotism).[58] In fact, Pinkerton was to become noted, as a historian, for his strict adherence to manuscript sources and his insistence that, as he told Percy, "ancient history can only rest upon ancient authorities."[59] But if Pinkerton's career, like that of Scott's *Waverley*, suggests a relinquishment of youthful "romance" for the austere pleasures of "real history," it also clarifies the ideological trajectory of such a narrative. Pinkerton's early experiments in forgery, and his gloss on the practice in his pseudonymous *Letters on Literature*, outline a specifically Scottish understanding of fiction – and its role in the empirical discipline of literary history – which was less superseded than abandoned in his later work.

Letters on Literature was published in 1785, after Ritson denounced the "Hardyknute" volume and before Pinkerton's attempted rebound with *Ancient Scotish Poems*. It appeared under the pseudonym of "Robert Heron," which, as it happened, was the real name of another young Scot who, like Pinkerton, was then at work on a history of Scotland and who claimed that the odium inspired by the *Letters* irreparably damaged his career.[60] The volume is a strange combination of erudition and adolescent posturing, in which, as Chambers commented, Pinkerton appeared "guilty of affecting strangeness for the purpose of attracting notice."[61] Among its more startling entries are a scornful critique of Virgil and a proposal for amending the English language by forming plurals with *as* instead of *ss*. None, however, is more audacious than Letter XLIV, "On Literary Forgery," in which Pinkerton attacked the Ritsonian "innocents who call ... forgery criminal" and asserted, on the contrary:

> that nothing can be more innocent; that the fiction of ascribing a piece to antiquity, which in fact doth not belong to it, can in no sort be more improper than the fiction of a poem or novel; that in both the delight of the reader is the only intention ... Perhaps nothing can be more heroic and generous in literary affairs than a writer's ascribing to antiquity his own production; and thus sacrificing his own fame to give higher satisfaction to the public.[62]

Manifestly partisan, this is still hard to refute. Its contemporary resonance speaks to Pinkerton's "postmodern" status among the generation of Scottish intellectuals who inherited the most radical insights of Scottish Enlightenment historiography before these tenets found an acceptably *fictional* form in nineteenth-century historical romance. Situated, as Ian Duncan has described Pinkerton's contemporaries, "on the far threshold of an identifiable historical stage of modernity," Pinkerton was the "Scot" to Ritson's "Anti-Scot" not because he was a Jacobite or Covenanter (he was neither), but for his early, and scandalously explicit, view of tradition itself as "a fiction, founded not in metaphysical properties, in causal connections, but in the shared associations ... of its participating subjects: in other words, a reading public."[63] Thus his defense of forgery was matched by the equally bald assertion that:

> there is no such thing as truth of fact, or historical truth, known to man. History is merely a species of romance, founded on events which really happened; but the bare events as stated by chronologists are alone true; their causes, circumstances, and effects, as detailed by historians, depend entirely on the fancy of the relater. Of other truths none are positive to man, save those subject to his senses; and even these are fallacious, tho the truths they affirm are positive, *as to us* ... From this observation, however, a certain species of truth, which consists in the relation and connection of things, must be exempted; providing this may be called positive truth. I mean, truth of nature, or that universal truth to be found in poetry and works of fiction. This consists in the propriety and consistence of event, or character, or sentiment, or language, to be found in such works.[64]

We may be reminded here of Catherine Morland's *faux-naif* complaint, in *Northanger Abbey*, that "a great deal of [history] must be invention. The speeches that are put into the heroes' mouths, their thoughts and designs – the chief of all this must be invention, and invention is what delights me in other books."[65] Pinkerton's authority for his conflation of "history" and "romance" is indeed none other than David Hume, to whom Pinkerton dedicates a eulogistic chapter of the *Letters on Literature* and who, in his *Treatise of Human Nature*, resolved the antinomy of history and romance into modes of reading differentiated only by degrees of "belief." "If one person sits down to read a book as a romance, and another as a true history," Hume observes:

> the latter has a more lively conception of all the incidents. He enters deeper into the concerns of the persons: represents to

himself their actions, and characters, and friendships, and enmi-
ties: He even goes so far as to form a notion of their features, and
air, and person.[66]

Pinkerton's variation on the Humean theme implies that historical
"truth" inheres in the *literary* qualities of "relation" and "connection"
which Pinkerton, like Austen's heroine, finds to be better exemplified
in poetry and fiction than in "real solemn history." The history reader's
"belief," for Hume, is grounded on nothing more than "the fidelity
of Printers and Copyists," which assures that "one edition passes into
another" without significant "variation."[67] By this account, the history
of nations rapidly collapses into the history of textual transmission.
Scott, less sanguine than Hume about the fidelity of copyists, points out
that – just *like* "a poem transmitted through a number of reciters" – a
"book reprinted in a number of editions, incurs the risk of impertinent
interpolations ... unintelligible blunders ... and omissions equally to
be regretted" – a moral underlined by the career of "Hardyknute."[68] It
follows, if history is but a more "lively" narrative genre than romance,
that *literary* history, without even the barest of events *d'hors texte*, has
no more or less authority than the texts it purports to document. Thus
a piece "ascrib[ed] ... to antiquity" may readily be absorbed into the
"long chain of causes and effects, which connect any past event with
any volume of history"; and the invented Hardyknute may possess
more "force and vivacity" in the minds of modern readers than even
the real Julius Caesar.[69]

The consequences of this discovery, for the literary heirs of the
Scottish Enlightenment, were twofold. On the one hand, as Duncan
has argued, Scottish cultural identity assumed the form of a "collective
fiction" sustained by the republic of letters. On the other hand, fictions
of origin – whether of nations, of families, or of ballads – may well
have held less allure for post-Enlightenment, post-Union Scots than
they had for the generation of English writers nurtured on Young's
Conjectures on Original Composition and Ritson's belief that "genuine
and peculiar natural song" was "to be sought ... in the productions of
obscure and anonymous authors, of shepherds and milk-maids, who
actually felt the sensations they describe," and who were "perhaps
incapable of committing the pure inspirations of nature to writing."[70]
(Myths of) origin and tendency may indeed be co-relative, but here
epistemology recapitulates nationality. Pinkerton disavowed his own
youthful indiscretions (not his irascibility) in later life, but they persisted to shadow the cultural anthropology of his greatest successor,

Walter Scott. Scott concluded his survey of Scottish popular poetry by invoking the names of three fellow practitioners who had "honoured their country, by arriving at distinction from a humble origin," and "under whose hand the ancient Scottish harp ... sounded a bold and distinguished tone."[71] Are these ballad practitioners, ballad imitators, or forgers? Scott declines to say, but it is to two of them – James Hogg and Allan Cunningham – that I turn for a Pinkertonian conclusion to my own survey.

III

Cunningham was working as a stonemason and had gotten no further as a poet than a few unpublished verses when in 1809 he met one Mr. Cromek, a London engraver with intellectual aspirations, then visiting Scotland to collect materials for his portentously titled *Reliques of Robert Burns*. Cromek was uninterested in Cunningham's poems, but lit up when the young man mentioned "the old songs and fragments of songs still to be picked up among the peasantry of Nithsdale." According to Cunningham's later account, "the idea of a volume of imitations passed upon Cromek as genuine remains flashed across the poet's mind in an instant, and ... a few fragments were soon submitted."[72] In this parodic iteration of the encounter between English antiquarianism and protean Scottish ingenuity, Cunningham's credibility as a native informant carried him through the triumphant appearance of *Remains of Nithsdale and Galloway Song: With Historical and Traditional Notices Relative to the Manners and Customs of the Peasantry*, published "by R. H. Cromek" but written entirely by Cunningham, who, according to his biographer, composed not only the ballads but also the introduction and descriptive notes, and even corrected the proofs.[73] Although Cunningham was only mentioned (in the introduction written by himself) as assisting with Cromek's "research," readers including Hogg, Scott, Francis Jeffrey, John Wilson of *Blackwood's Edinburgh Magazine*, and the younger Thomas Percy averred that the poems were "too good to be old," and Cunningham's authorship became an open secret.[74] The volume was to prove the foundation of Cunningham's long and varied career as a contributor to *Blackwood's* and, later, a regular columnist for its rival the *London Magazine*; a historical novelist in the manner of Walter Scott; an epic poet and dramatist; a respected editor and folklorist; a journalist for *The Athenaeum*, contributing essays on literature and the fine arts, as well as biographical studies of writers and artists; and author of the magisterial six-volume *Lives of the Most Esteemed British Painters, Sculptors, and Architects*.[75]

Cunningham's ethos as forger/collector is a curious mixture of Pinkertonian flamboyance and Ritsonian conservatism. On the one hand, he boasted to his brother James that "I could cheat a whole General Assembly of Antiquarians with my original manner of writing and forging ballads."[76] His biographer notes with some dismay that Cunningham "was not alone in this kind of literary imposition," but that two of his compatriots – William Motherwell (1797–1835) and the revered Robert Burns – "did something of the same kind," presenting as "old verses" what were actually "original composition[s] of [their] own."[77] In this sense, the *Remains* was merely one more entry in Ritson's "series" of Scottish "fraud, forgery and imposture." On the other hand, Cunningham cast himself as the elegist of an archaic and vanishing culture; Scotland, he wrote, "is an age or two behind [England] in corruption, and she has hitherto preserved her ancient character" with ballads "floating on the breath of the people," whereas "in no district of England are to be found specimens of this simple and rustic poetry. The influence of commerce has gradually altered the character of the people: by creating new interests and new pursuits, it has weakened that strong attachment to the soil which gives interest to the localities of popular ballads."[78] Having just bragged of "these songs and ballads ... written for imposing on the country as the reliques of other years," he informed James that he had "begun a work of Poetry and Criticism. I mean to restore all our Scottish songs to their uncorrupted purity, to alter and amend others, where correction is necessary, and to produce upwards of a hundred original ones of my own to be sown among them."[79]

Perhaps indicative of his position on the margins of both Scottish and English literary culture, these contradictions anticipate the discordant styles and personae – from the folksy "honest Allan" of the *London Magazine* to the learned biographer of British painters – that proliferated throughout Cunningham's miscellaneous career. Just as it is hard to distinguish the earnest from the opportunistic in his pose as custodian of Scottish folk culture, it would be difficult to characterize his "voice" in a way that might satisfy, for example, the Coleridge who averred of his friend's poetry that "had I met these lines running wild in the deserts of Arabia, I should have instantly screamed out 'Wordsworth!' "[80] Versatility was doubtless partly a matter of survival, given that Cunningham did not enjoy Wordsworth's degree of financial independence, and so leapt at whatever publishing opportunities came his way. Yet his polyvocality not only recalls the stereotype of the "protean Scot"; it suggests a corollary, at the level of individual psychology, with the Humean/Pinkertonian view of history as consensual fiction. For according to Hume, even "the identity, which we ascribe to the mind of man, is only a fictitious one," and "the same person may vary his character and disposition, as well as his impressions and ideas, without losing his identity."[81] The familiar hypostasis of a continuous and inimitable subjectivity is the supreme fiction devised in response to such Humean skepticism. Here, then, we can glimpse how the eighteenth-century discourse of *historical* authenticity – of temporal origins – intersects with the discourse of authentic *subjectivity* more often associated with Romanticism. And while it might be a stretch to claim that Cunningham modeled his career on Humean principles, it is less implausible to suggest that the ideal of selfhood as "something invariable and uninterrupted, or ... something mysterious and inexplicable" had less cachet for post-Enlightenment Scots than it had for their English contemporaries.[82]

Be that as it may, Cunningham's proteanism is nothing compared to the wild oscillations, uncanny doublings, and abrupt volte-faces that marked the career of his early hero, James Hogg. Its divagations make that career hard to summarize, but Hogg's publications include a manual on sheep farming; several epic poems; collections of ballads and folksongs; a neo-Addisonian periodical; novels and "anti-novelistic fictions"; short stories; three versions of a memoir; and the pseudo-Biblical "Chaldee Manuscript." He wrote in standard English and in lowland Scots dialect, and in voices ranging from the man of the world to the country bumpkin, from the pedantic to the boisterously funny.[83] Matters are further complicated by the fact that, for the last decade of his life, Hogg's own writings were overshadowed by the fame of the "Ettrick Shepherd," his persona in *Blackwood's Magazine*. Critics both in his own time and more recently have agreed in finding Hogg's work uneven at best, incoherent or even "crazy" at worst; it is, at any rate, so discontinuous that even Hogg despaired of "imitat[ing] [him]self."[84] Indeed, he had tried to do just this in the 1816 hoax publication *The Poetic Mirror*, where he posed as the editor of a collection of new poems by Britain's greatest living poets, including Byron, Wordsworth, Coleridge, Scott – and James Hogg. In a volume whose contents were, in fact, all written by Hogg, although many were mistaken for the genuine article, the least recognizable may be "The Gude Greye Katt," the poem ascribed to Hogg.

Were Hogg intending to repeat a familiar role or a recent success, we might expect to encounter the dialect songster of *The Mountain Bard* (1807) and *The Forest Minstrel* (1810), or a Spenserian narrative in the style of *Mador of the Moor*, published about six months before *The*

Poetic Mirror. But "The Gude Greye Katt" is a supernatural tale in ballad meter, told in flamboyantly faux antique language that suggests a
Scotticized Chatterton, replete with doubled consonants and terminal
"e"s. Its feline heroine lives in a laird's castle and appears at will in the
shape of a beautiful woman. Accused as a witch, she is interrogated by
a lascivious bishop whom she spears with a claw and then carries into
the sky. The spelling and supernaturalism loosely recall "Kilmeny"
and "The Witch of Fife," two of the twelve verse tales that make up
The Queen's Wake (1813), Hogg's best-known publication to this point.
A narrativized anthology, *The Queen's Wake* tells the story of a contest
among seventeen bards for Queen Mary's Harp. Each bard sings a song
in a characteristic style. Several contestants were intended as portraits of actual present-day poets; the sixteenth, for example, is Allan
Cunningham, and the tenth, "the poor bard of Ettrick," is clearly
Hogg himself.[85] But while one might expect that Hogg's entry in *The
Poetic Mirror* would echo his persona's song in *The Queen's Wake*, neither "Kilmeny" nor "The Witch of Fife" is sung by the bard of Ettrick.
These two poems in "Hogg's mock-medieval 'ancient stile'" – one
a mystical tale of a virgin translated to another world, the other
the boisterous story of a husband punished for spying on his wife's
coven – were among the most popular in the volume, despite one
reviewer's complaint that "gothic beings" such as "ghosts and brown-
ies, and vampires, and grim-white women are grown as familiar as
cats and dogs that sleep upon the parlour rug."[86] In "The Gude Greye
Katt" Hogg evidently took a page from this hostile reviewer, spoofing
the "mountain an' fairy school" he claimed as his purview (in contradistinction with Scott's "school o' chivalry") – but choosing for his
"own" voice the most transparently artificial style of the many he had
mastered.[87] "The Gude Greye Katt" could as plausibly be taken for a
parody of "Hardyknute" as of Hogg.
    Despite featuring a heroine with "that within her ee/Quhich mor-
tyl dochtna bear," and despite its mystically unresolved conclusion,
"The Gude Greye Katt" is less spooky than silly, less mysterious than
carnivalesque. When, for example, the bishop in the warmth of his
zeal "press[es] the cumlye dame," he finds that her "breste of heuinlye
charm,/Had turnit til brusket of ane katt,/Ful hayrie and ful warme!"[88]
Pitting a "masculine" desire to possess and classify against "feminine"
(or feline) virtuosity, the poem reads something like a comic version
of *Lamia*. Its mixture of gothic, folkloric, satirical, and sentimental
elements, with genuine as well as pseudo-Scotticisms like "Filossofere"
(philosopher) used to amusingly deflationary effect, recapitulates the

generic and tonal instability that make Hogg's work seem alternately brilliant and inept. Whereas, therefore, the "Wordsworthian" entries in *The Poetic Mirror* sound uncannily like Wordsworth, "The Gude Greye Katt" suggests that Hogg has either *no* individual voice, or so many that parody is impossible. It seems in fact that not all readers even grasped a parodic intention; "The Gude Greye Katt" was the only poem from *The Poetic Mirror* to be reprinted in the 1876 "centenary edition" of *The Works of the Ettrick Shepherd*, where it was in no way distinguished from Hogg's other verse.[89]

A satire on the pretensions of "high" Romanticism, *The Poetic Mirror* subverts the authenticating criteria it also reaffirms; and it does so in a peculiarly Scottish way. From this point of view, Hogg's failure to "imitate [him]self" is a strength, and his wild careerings a Humean lesson in the "fictitious" basis of the author function. We may be reminded at this point of how Hume envisions "personal identity":

> One thought chaces another, and draws after it a third, by which it is expell'd in its turn. In this respect, I cannot compare the soul more properly to any thing than to a republic or commonwealth, in which the several members are united by the reciprocal ties of government and subordination, and give rise to other persons, who propagate the same republic in the incessant change of its parts.[90]

If Hogg's "soul" seems less a peaceable republic than a collection of feuding fiefdoms, Hume's political analogy suggests how the conception of the individual intertwines with that of the nation. Insofar as an authentically Romantic poetics has been identified with continuous history (the authority of origins) and a continuous selfhood (the authority of "personal identity") we may infer the national bias of an "English" Romanticism constituted, in part, by the repudiation of Scottish Enlightenment philosophy and practice. By constructing a genealogy that links the fortunes of two "minor" Romantic poets with a forged tradition, I mean both to imply that other criteria for authenticity might be imagined, and to demonstrate by hapless or eccentric example that they will be difficult to square with more conventional historiographical practice. The history of "Hardyknute," I have argued, suggests that "genuity" might be reimagined as the *ingenuity* by which a verbal artifact is renewed and remade for successive generations. That protean text allegorizes, or is allegorized in, the careers of Pinkerton, Hogg, Cunningham, and other such exemplars of "Scottish morality." Lacking, or eschewing, the self-similarity that guaranteed Wordsworth's authority, they suggest – in sometimes attractively unsettling, sometimes disconcertingly opportunistic ways – that, just as antiquity can be forged, so can the capably ingenuous poet ventriloquize his imagined community.

Notes

1. Ian Duncan, with Leith Davis and Janet Sorensen, "Introduction" to *Scotland and the Borders of Romanticism* (Cambridge: Cambridge University Press, 2004), p. 1.
2. Hugh Trevor-Roper, "The Invention of Tradition: The Highland Tradition of Scotland," in Eric Hobsbawm and Terence Ranger, eds, *The Invention of Tradition* (Cambridge: Cambridge University Press, 1983), p. 15. Joseph Ritson, *Scotish Song* (London: J. Johnson, 1794), 2 vols; vol. 1, p. lxx.
3. Duncan et al., *Scotland*, pp. 1–10.
4. Quoted in Nick Groom, *The Making of Percy's Reliques* (Oxford: Clarendon Press, 1999), p. 28.
5. William Wordsworth and Samuel Taylor Coleridge, *Lyrical Ballads and Related Writings*, William Richey and Daniel Robinson eds (Boston: Houghton Mifflin, 2002), pp. 66–7.
6. Duncan et al., *Scotland*, p. 14.
7. Susan Stewart, "Scandals of the Ballad," in *Crimes of Writing: Problems in the Containment of Representation* (New York: Oxford University Press, 1991), p. 108.
8. Joseph Ritson, *Scotish Song* (London: J. Johnson, 1794), 2 vols; vol. 1, pp. lxii–lxiii, lxx.
9. Walter Scott, "Introductory Remarks on Popular Poetry, and on the Various Collections of Ballads of Britain, Particularly those of Scotland," in *The Poetical Works of Sir Walter Scott, Bart.* (Edinburgh: Cadell and Company, 1830), 11 vols; vol. 11, pp. 18, 65.
10. Here and elsewhere, except when noted otherwise, I quote from the version of "Hardyknute" that appeared as the last item in Allan Ramsay's *The Ever Green, Being a Collection of Scots Poems, Wrote by the Ingenious before 1600* (Edinburgh: Thomas Ruddiman, 1724), 2 vols; vol. 2, pp. 247–63, ll. 5–6, 228.
11. See Mel Kersey, "Ballads, Britishness and Hardyknute, 1719–1859," *Scottish Studies Review*, 40–56, for a persuasive account of the way "Hardyknute" figured in debates over British identity during the eighteenth century; I have also relied on Kersey's essay for corroboration and amplification of the textual history recounted below. The shortest version of "Hardyknute" is that printed in the 1877 compilation *Songs of Scotland*; the longest appears in John Pinkerton's *Scottish Tragic Ballads*, discussed below.
12. From the anonymous editorial postscript to *Hardyknute: A Fragment. Being the First Canto of an Epick Poem; With General Remarks, and Notes.* (London: R. Dodsley, 1740), p. 35.
13. David Masson, *Edinburgh Sketches and Memories* (London: A. & C. Black, 1892), pp. 111–12. Old women were the proverbial custodians of ballad lore; the reference here is to an 1855 edition of "Gil Morrice" which was advertised, according to Ritson, as having been "carefully collected from

the mouths of old women and nurses." ([Joseph Ritson], *Scotish Song* [London: J. Johnson, 1794], 2 vols; vol. 1, p. lxx). Kersey notes that although a version of "Hardyknute" may have been published as early as 1710, this has not been conclusively shown; its first dated publication is 1719 (Kersey, p. 52 n. 12).

14. The word "genuity" was evidently coined to describe authentic-*looking* artifacts such as, in this case, the "sarcophagus of Hardyknute," described below. See John Nichols, *Illustrations of the Literary History of the Eighteenth Century* (London: J. B. Nichols, 1828; rpt. New York: AMS Press, 1968), 8 vols; vol. 5, p. 431.

15. Kersey discusses the evidence for and against versions earlier than the 1719 edition (pp. 43, 52 n. 12).

16. I quote here from an 8-page chapbook in the Bodleian Library, conjecturally dated to 1724 but perhaps as early as 1710, titled *Hardiknute. A Fragment of an old Heroick Ballad* (p. 8, ll. 201–4).

17. See also Albert B. Friedman, *The Ballad Revival: Studies in the Influence of Popular on Sophisticated Poetry* (Chicago and London: University of Chicago Press, 1961), pp. 135–7, on the particularly Scottish vogue for ballad collecting in the early eighteenth century, as well as Allan Ramsay's role as editor/expander of "Hardyknute." Friedman comments suggestively that "the delight the [English] metropolis took in pseudo-Scottish song helped to teach Scotsmen the value of the real thing in their midst ... too ... this was the period when the Union was being debated and effected, and it was natural that Scotsmen should emphasize their cultural distinctness the more as their political independence lessened" (p. 135).

18. *Hardyknute: A Fragment*, (1740) pp. 4–5, 35.

19. [Anon., ed.] *Hardyknute. A Scottish Fragment. See Percy's Ancient Ballads, Vol. 2, p. 94, Edit. 2. NB Modern Spelling is substituted for the ancient* (1793), pp. 20–1.

20. Thomas Percy, *Reliques of Ancient English Poetry*, intro. Nick Groom (London: Routledge/Thoemmes, 1996), 3 vols; vol. 2, pp. 87–8. See also Percy's 1761 letter to Thomas Warton, informing him that "Hardyknute is neither more nor less, than a Modern piece" (quoted in Kersey, p. 43), and his application to Lord Hailes for corroboration that "Hardyknute" was "a meer modern composition" (Harriet Harvey Wood, ed., *The Correspondence of Thomas Percy and John Pinkerton* [New Haven and London: Yale University Press, 1985], p. ix).

21. John W. Hales and Frederick Furnivall, eds, *Bishop Percy's Folio Ms. Ballads and Romances* (London: N. Trubner, 1868), vol. 1, p. xii.

22. *Percy's Reliques*, p. 88. According to one story about Lady Wardlaw, recounted in Wood, ed., *Correspondence of Percy and Pinkerton*, she claimed to have transcribed "Hardyknute" from "the recitation of an old woman" (p. 3n).

23. Susan Stewart, "Scandals of the Ballad," in *Crimes of Writing: Problems in the Containment of Representation* (New York: Oxford University Press, 1991), p. 112.

24. That "Hardyknute" was read as Jacobitical seems clear from Lord Hailes's dismissal of Sir John Hope-Bruce as a candidate for the ballad's authorship, on the grounds that Bruce "was a steady Whig" (Hailes to Pinkerton, December 2, 1785, in *The Literary Correspondence of John Pinkerton, Esq. Now First Printed from the Originals in the Possession of Dawson Turner* [London: Henry Colburn and Richard Bentley, 1830], 2 vols; vol. 1, p. 104.

25. See *The Paisley Repository. Being a Collection of Poetry, Original and Selected* (Paisley: J. Neilson for J. Millar, n.d.); Oswald, ed., *Curious Collection* (1742); Herd, *Ancient and Modern Scottish Songs* (1776); *Scots Musical Museum*; *Songs of Scotland* (1877); C. H. Maver, *Scottish Melodies*, vol. 2, p. 143.
26. *Percy's Reliques*, p. 347.
27. Groom, *Percy's* Reliques, 41.
28. [John Pinkerton], *Scottish Tragic Ballads. [Containing] Hardyknute, An Heroic Ballad, Now First Published Complete; With Other More Approved Scottish Ballads, And Some Not Hitherto Made Public, In the Tragic Stile.* (London: J. Nichols, 1781), pp. xxxv, 106–7.
29. Pinkerton, *Scottish Tragic Ballads*, pp. 1–34, 107.
30. Pinkerton, *Scottish Tragic Ballads*, p. xxxv.
31. *Literary Correspondence of John Pinkerton*, vol. 1, p. 25.
32. Harriet Harvey Wood, ed., *The Correspondence of Thomas Percy and John Pinkerton*. Vol. 8 of Cleanth Brooks and A. F. Falconer, gen. eds, *The Percy Letters* (New Haven and London: Yale University Press, 1985), p. 8n.
33. [Joseph Ritson], open letter "TO MR. PINKERTON," in *The Gentleman's Magazine: And Historical Register*, vol. 54. (London: John Nichols for D. Henry, 1794), p. 812.
34. For a dissenting view, see G. Ross Roy, "Hardyknute – Lady Wardlaw's Ballad?", in *Romanticism and Culture: A Tribute to Morse Peckham and a Bibliography of his Work*, ed. H. W. Matalene (Columbia, SC: Camden House, 1984), pp. 133–46.
35. [John Pinkerton], *Ancient Scotish Poems, Never Before in Print. But Now Published from the Ms. Collections of Sir Richard Maitland ...* (London: Printed for Charles Dilly; and for William Creech at Edinburgh, 1786), p. cxxvii. Pinkerton published his theory that Sir John Hope-Bruce wrote "Hardyknute" in spite of Lord Hailes's assurances to the contrary (*Literary Correspondence of John Pinkerton*, p. 104).
36. Later editions of the *Reliques* adopted Pinkerton's theory; see *Percy's Reliques*, p. 347.
37. Ritson's misogyny was neither unusual nor extreme. Pinkerton was even more dismissive of women authors, once remarking that Sappho was "the only female who ever wrought anything worth preservation" ([John Pinkerton], *Select Scotish Ballads. Volume II. Containing Ballads of the Comic Kind* [London: J. Nichols, 1783], p. xv). Like Pinkerton, Ritson went out of his way to discredit Lady Wardlaw, though he proposed Sir Alexander Halkett rather than Hope-Bruce as the true author (*Letters from Joseph Ritson, Esq. to Mr. George Patton. To Which Is Added, A Critique by Mr. John Pinkerton, Esq. Upon Ritson's Scotish Songs* [Edinburgh: John Stevenson, 1829], p. 8).
38. I borrow the phrase "authenticity effect" from Ian Duncan, in "Authenticity Effects: The Work of Writing in Romantic Scotland," *South Atlantic Quarterly* 102.1 (2003), 93–116. Duncan, in turn, borrows the term from James Buzard.
39. Scott, "Remarks on Popular Poetry," pp. 66–7.
40. Scott's admiration for the *Reliques* is noted by the editor of the Everyman edition, who cites Scott's recollection that "the first time ... I could scrape a few shillings together, I bought unto myself a copy of these beloved volumes; nor do I believe I ever read a book half so frequently or with half the

enthusiasm" (*Percy's Reliques* [London: Dent, n.d.], two vols; vol. 1, p. vii). While Scott may have heard "Hardyknute" recited before he encountered a printed version, it seems reasonable to assume that Percy's text was the one with which he was most familiar.

41. Ritson ascribed the "genuine and peculiar natural song of Scotland" to "shepherds and milk maids" (Ritson, *Scotish Song*, vol. 1, p. lxxix).

42. It was apparently his animus toward Pinkerton which inspired Ritson's notorious remark that "a man who will forge a poem, a line or even a word will not hesitate, when the temptation is greater and the impunity equal, to forge a note or steal a guinea" (quoted in *Correspondence of Thomas Percy and John Pinkerton*, p. xxxvi). Pinkerton, in turn, was partly responsible for the characterization of Ritson as a pedant who "spared no pains to reject any improvement, and to restore [poems] to error and imperfection" (quoted in *Letters from Ritson to Patton*, p. 45). Scott characteristically splits the difference, dismissing the view of "poor Ritson" of literary forgery as a "crime," while generally siding with Ritson against Pinkerton ("Remarks on Popular Poetry," p. 58).

43. [John Pinkerton], review of *Scotish Songs* in *The Critical Review*, January 1795; quoted in *Letters from Ritson to Patton*, p. 45.

44. Ritson, *Scotish Song*, lxxxi.

45. George Steevens, letter to the *General Evening Post* (October 25, 1790), quoted in John Nichols, *Illustrations of the Literary History of the Eighteenth Century* (London: J. B. Nichols, 1828), 8 vols; vol. 5, p. 431.

46. Quoted in Norval Clyne, *The Romantic Scottish Ballads and the Lady Wardlaw Heresy* (Aberdeen: A. Brown, 1859), p. 36.

47. A more recent (and plausible) twist on Chambers's hypothesis is offered by David C. Fowler, who suggests in *A Literary History of the Popular Ballad* (Durham, NC: Duke University Press, 1968), that Percy's correspondent and collaborator David Dalrymple, Lord Hailes, may have written or substantially rewritten "Sir Patrick Spens" and several other Scottish ballads which were "completely unknown to the world before their publication in the *Reliques* in 1765" (p. 254).

48. Francis James Child, ed., *English and Scottish Ballads* (Boston: Little, Brown, 1860), 8 vols; vol. 3, pp. 148–9.

49. Nichols, *Literary Illustrations*, p. 431.

50. Scott, "Remarks on Popular Poetry," p. 37.

51. Pinkerton contended, beginning with the preface to *Ancient Scotish Poems* and continuing with his *Dissertation on the Origin and Progress of the Scythians or Goths* (1787) and *Enquiry into the History of Scotland Preceding the Reign of Malcolm III* (1789), that the Celts were a congenitally inferior race and that the true ancestors of Lowland, English-speaking Scots were Pictish – which, Pinkerton believed, meant Danish or Gothic. Trevor-Roper cites Pinkerton, "a man whose undoubted eccentricity and violent prejudices cannot rob him of his claim to be the greatest Scottish antiquary since Thomas Innes," for a refutation of the belief that early Caledonians wore plaid ("The Invention of Tradition: The Highland Tradition of Scotland," in *The Invention of Tradition*, eds. Eric Hobsbawm and Terence Ranger [Cambridge: Cambridge University Press, 1983], pp. 15–41 [27–8]). On the significance of Pinkerton's historical opinions, see Colin Kidd, *Subverting Scotland's Past: Scottish Whig*

Historians and the Creation of an Anglo-British Identity, 1689–1830 (Cambridge: Cambridge University Press, 1993).

52. See *Scottish Tragic Ballads*, p. 87, for Pinkerton's gloss on Hardyknute's name.
53. On the "found manuscript" and its place in the eighteenth-century forgery narrative, and on the Chatterton case specifically, see Margaret Russett, *Fictions and Fakes: Forging Romantic Authenticity, 1760–1845* (Cambridge: Cambridge University Press, 2006). See also Nick Groom, *The Forger's Shadow: How Forgery Changed the Course of Literature* (London: Picador, 2002).
54. "John Pinkerton," pp. 245–8 in Robert Chambers, *A Biographical Dictionary of Eminent Scotsmen*. New edn, rev. Thomas Thomson. (New York: George Olms Verlag, 1971 [rpt. 1870]), 3 vols; vol. 3.
55. Pinkerton, *Ancient Scotish Poems*, pp. cxxvii–cxxxi.
56. The 1786 edition of Johnson's *Dictionary* lists the following definitions for "fiction": "1. The act of feigning and inventing. 2. The thing feigned or invented. 3. A falsehood; a lie."
57. See Wood's introduction to *The Correspondence of Percy and Pinkerton*, p. x, and Percy's rejection of Pinkerton's offer, pp. 2–3.
58. On Pinkerton's opinion of Macpherson, see e.g. *Ancient Scotish Poems*, pp. xlv–li.
59. Pinkerton to Percy, 19 November 1785, in *Correspondence of Percy and Pinkerton*, p. 59.
60. See Wood's introduction to *Correspondence of Percy and Pinkerton*, in which she also quotes Cowper's verse condemnation of the *Letters on Literature* (p. xiii).
61. Chambers, "John Pinkerton," p. 246.
62. Robert Heron, Esq. (pseud. John Pinkerton), *Letters of Literature* (New York: Garland Publishing, 1970; rpt. London: G. G. and J. Robinson, 1785), pp. 383–6.
63. Duncan, "Authenticity Effects," pp. 97–8, 105. On this specifically Scottish sense of "postmodernism," see also Duncan's related essay "Edinburgh: Capital of the Nineteenth Century," in James Chandler and Kevin Gilmartin, eds, *Romantic Metropolis: The Urban Scene of British Culture, 1780–1840* (Cambridge: Cambridge University Press, 2005), pp. 45–64; and Jerome McGann, "Walter Scott's Romantic Postmodernity," in *Scotland and the Borders of Romanticism*, eds Leith Davis, Ian Duncan, and Janet Sorensen (Cambridge: Cambridge University Press, 2004), pp. 113–29.
64. *Letters of Literature*, pp. 216–18.
65. Jane Austen, *Northanger Abbey*, ed. Barbara M. Benedict and Dierdre Le Faye (Cambridge: Cambridge University Press, 2006), p. 110.
66. David Hume, *A Treatise of Human Nature*, ed. L. A. Selby-Bigge. 2nd edn., rev. P. H. Nidditch (Oxford: Clarendon Press, 1983), pp. 97–8.
67. Hume, *Treatise*, p. 146.
68. Scott, "Remarks on Popular Poetry," p. 14.
69. Hume, *Treatise*, pp. 96, 146.
70. Ritson, *Scotish Song*, vol. 1, p. lxxix.
71. Scott, "Remarks on Popular Poetry," pp. 26–7.
72. David Hogg, *The Life of Allan Cunningham, with Selections from his Works and Correspondence* (Dumfries: John Anderson & Son, 1875), p. 50.
73. Ibid., p. 72.

74. Ibid., pp. 103–7.
75. See the biographical essay on Cunningham in Charles Rogers, *The Modern Scottish Minstrel* (Edinburgh: Adam & Charles Black, 1856), 6 vols; vol. 3, pp. 2–8.
76. Hogg, *Life of Cunningham*, p. 80.
77. Ibid., p. 51.
78. Ibid., p. 75; "R. H. Cromek" [Allan Cunningham], *Remains of Nithsdale and Galloway Song: With Historical and Traditional Notices Relative to the Manners and Customs of the Peasantry* (London: T. Cadell and W. Davies, 1810), pp. ii–iii.
79. Hogg, *Life of Cunningham*, pp. 87, 89.
80. Samuel Taylor Coleridge, *Collected Letters*, ed. Earl Leslie Griggs (Oxford: Clarendon Press, 1956–1971), 6 vols; vol. 1, p. 453.
81. Hume, *Treatise*, pp. 259, 261.
82. Ibid., p. 255.
83. I summarize a consensus on Hogg, redacted from studies including: Margaret Russett, *Fictions and Fakes: Forging Romantic Authenticity, 1760–1845*; Peter T. Murphy, *Poetry as an Occupation and an Art in Britain, 1760–1830* (Cambridge: Cambridge University Press, 1993), pp. 136–81; Ian Duncan, "Authenticity Effects"; and Robin W. MacLachan, "Hogg and the Art of Brand Management," *Studies in Hogg and His World* 14 (2003).
84. Quoted in Caroline McCracken-Flescher, "You Can't Go Home Again: James Hogg and the Problem of Scottish 'Post-Colonial' Return," *Studies in Hogg and His World* 8 (1997), p. 35.
85. James Hogg, *The Queen's Wake* [1813], ed. Douglas S. Mack (Edinburgh: Edinburgh University Press, 2005), p. 168, l. 197.
86. Quoted in Mack, ed., "Introduction" to *The Queen's Wake*, p. lii.
87. Ibid., p. xliii; *Eclectic Review* quoted p. xxxv.
88. James Hogg, *The Poetical Mirror*, ed. T. Earle Welby (London: The Scholartis Press, 1929), pp. 123–39; ll. 11–12, 150–2.
89. James Hogg, *The Works of the Ettrick Shepherd. Centenary Edition. With a Memoir of the Author, by the Rev. Thomas Thomson* (London: Blackie & Son, 1876).
90. Hume, *Treatise*, p. 261.

2
'A Blank Made': *Ossian*, Sincerity and the Possibilities of Forgery

Dafydd Moore

On the face of it, trying to understand James Macpherson's *Poems of Ossian* in terms to do with sincerity or authenticity would seem a perverse and potentially frustrating activity. Whatever ambitions Macpherson might have had for his poems, they have gone down in history as an archetype of the inauthentic, the charlatan, the opposite of everything or anything that might conceivably be meant by literary sincerity. It is for this reason, for example, that John Valdimir Price is 'only too happy to admit that [he] get[s] no real literary pleasure from reading the works', and why as sympathetic a reader as Joep Leerssen can claim that 'there is no way of reading *Ossian* for mere textual pleasure' in the face of the 'unavoidable genetic issue of authenticity'.[1] However, in this chapter I will try to suggest a way in which the later Romantic engagement with *Ossian* was in significant part to do with an engagement with the possibility and definition of a troubling but ineffably Romantic type of authenticity as a category beyond the conventional ones of truth and sincerity. Notions of the insincere and inauthentic will always exist in a close and at times potentially troubling proximity to those of the sincere and authentic, but I hope to go beyond drawing attention to this obvious binary and suggest something else about *Ossian's* use within Romantic imaginative sincerity. It may be unclear whether *Ossian* stimulated such a formulation or merely outlined the problems of the project, but what seems to be undeniably the case is that the poems were frequently in the picture.

It is worth noting at the outset that the status of the poems as forgeries has not been a central concern of the revisionism that Macpherson has undergone in the past 20 years. An emphasis or interest in this dimension of Macpherson's work is usually interpreted as old-fashioned, even reactionary, in the face of historicist accounts of *Ossian*, and so-called

'Four Nations' readings of eighteenth-century literature. This revisionism has reoriented the field in such a way as to make the eighteenth-century Scottish context of the poems – be that thought of as Gaelic Highland or 'Lowland' Enlightenment – of key importance, and made the role played by *Ossian* in the creation of Scottish and wider Celtic identities in the late eighteenth century a central concern.[2]

The question of forgery has not slipped down the agenda by accident: it was to a large extent actively removed. A belief that D. S. Thomson's *The Gaelic Sources of Macpherson's Ossian* of 1952 had more or less settled the matter of *Ossian*'s authenticity to any reasonable person's satisfaction has been coupled with a conviction that forgery was on the whole a way of not talking about *Ossian*, of not engaging with what was and is most significant about poems whose influence on 'the literary scene of the late eighteenth century eclipsed all others' by setting 'the literature of sentiment and sensibility on a whole new footing'.[3] Furthermore, a well-established tradition stretching from Samuel Johnson to Hugh Trevor-Roper, and in some cases beyond, of using the charge of forgery not only as a stick to beat Macpherson but Scottish culture more generally has done little to encourage interest amongst recent revisionists.[4] Thus the desire to move critical discussion away from the question of forgery has come about through a combination of the standard academic drive towards the establishment of fresh critical hunting grounds and some sort of cultural good faith. This state of affairs has not gone uncontested by those who continue to deny that there was and is anything in the emphasis on forgery beyond intellectual honesty and critical care, but this particular spat is not of present (or really any) interest.[5]

Given then Macpherson's position in the roll call of master literary hoaxers, remarkably little of recent *Ossian* criticism has engaged with the idea of forgery, and that which has done so has sought to tackle it in a way that circumvents questions of morality in order to consider the question within the context of, for example, eighteenth-century epistemology, changing notions of the literary artefact and literary creativity, and the pressures and potentials of national building (needless to say the perceived dangerous relativism of this has placed these critics too in the bad books of the guardians of Johnsonian propriety within literary critical practice). Thus Ian Haywood's *The Making of History: A Study of the Literary Forgeries of James Macpherson and Thomas Chatterton in Relation to Eighteenth-Century Ideas of History and Fiction* (Associated University Press, 1986) sidesteps questions of charlatanism in order to locate the poems within the genealogy of the historical novel.

Leith Davis and Katie Trumpener have considered the question in relation to the creation of national heritage and a number of critics have considered the '*Ossian* Wars' in terms of the politics of ancient poetry and cultural heritage.[6] David Punter has read the ambiguities and doubts surrounding the provenance of the poems as a Gothic archetype.[7] Nick Groom has considered Macpherson's place within a Romantic movement that 'produced a canon of forgers and maintained forgery as a site of inspiration' whilst also, through its own intense emphasis on originality and inspiration 'provided the ideological means of disabling their work'.[8] Most recently, Margaret Russett's examination of how 'the archaeology of the spurious clarifies the authenticating devices of the Romantic literary work' includes Macpherson as part of 'the so-called golden age of forgery', even though her primary focus is on other texts and examples.[9]

This chapter takes its cue from these studies, and particularly Groom's suggestion that the Romantic forgery 'interpret[s] the rules of representation to create a hybrid realism, both true and false' and Leerssen's characterization of the 'ambiguous ontological status' of the poems by suggesting that it is precisely this hybridity that was used by certain writers in the wake of Macpherson when they activated the idea of *Ossian* and the Ossianic.[10] At the same time it also responds to Leerssen's call for a 'slightly wider and vaguer approach to the impact of Macpherson's *Ossian*', one which considers something to be Ossianic 'not because it might or might not be possible to register similar imagery more or less verbatim in such-and-such a portion of Macpherson's work, but because of a general imaginative strategy involving the distribution of emotion, space and chosen moment.'[11] That is to say, the chapter is not, or not only, interested in nailing down exact genealogies or textual analogues (although at times they are part of the mix) but in considering the way that the idea of *Ossian* operates at key moments.

The notion of hybridity or ambiguity is useful in relation to Romantic responses to *Ossian*, not because it accurately encapsulates the mixture of the authentic and inauthentic in fact represented in the poems (as established by twentieth-century Gaelicists) but because it isolates a peculiarly ambiguous response to the poems at the time, one which accommodated both belief and disbelief in the authenticity of the poems and, perhaps more importantly, both belief and disbelief in the *importance* of that authenticity. It has long been assumed that the story of the poems' reception followed a straightforward path: popularity was decisively tied to a belief in their provenance as third-century epic, and when doubts about the latter surfaced, then that popularity suffered, a position summarized neatly by Jonathan Wordsworth's assumption that 'if *Ossian* had not been thought to be authentic, it would have had few readers then, and fewer now.'[12] With a different emphasis but in similar vein, Marjorie Levinson, in her account of the Romantic Fragment poem, claims that 'the reader who hoped to motivate [*Ossian*] on any level was obliged to commit himself to one of two cognitive (interpretive, evaluative) protocols' based upon the assumption that the poems were either 'genuinely archaic works' or 'modern imitations'.[13]

However, there is substantial evidence to suggest that eighteenth- and early nineteenth-century readers kept questions of literary merit and authenticity separate, and could choose not to commit – at least not consistently or wholeheartedly – to either of Levinson's protocols. Early reviews of the poems, and more strikingly, early (and very hostile) pastiches of the poems, discussed – and in some cases attacked – almost every aspect of the poems without openly addressing the issue of authenticity.[14] The publication in 1805 of the great debunking documents of the *Ossian* debate – Malcolm Laing's exhaustive tracking down of sources in his two-volume *Works of James Macpherson* and *The Report of the Committee of the Highland Society of Scotland Appointed to Enquire into the Nature and Authenticity of the Poems of Ossian* did nothing to dampen the *Ossian* publication industry, with more editions published in the following 30 years than in the preceding 30.[15] Furthermore Lord Byron, William Blake, William Hazlitt and Alfred Tennyson all shared Walter Scott's opinion (expressed in agreement with Anna Seward) that 'the question of authenticity ought [not] to be confounded with that of literary merit.'[16] The importance of this reception history, and the reason for its relative neglect are not the central concerns of this chapter, but it is important for the current purposes to appreciate the ambiguous status the poems had during the Romantic period and how the relationship between their reception and their authenticity was not straightforward. For some, doubtless, authenticity mattered a great deal and the stench of deception was too strong to stomach. Others seemed determined to salvage the truth of the poetry from the truth of the provenance of the poems, while for some, most famously William Hazlitt, the notion of forgery held an illicit allure in itself:

If it were indeed possible to shew that this writer was nothing, it would only be another instance of mutability, another blank made, another void left in the heart, another confirmation of that feeling which makes [Ossian] so often complain, 'Roll on, ye dark brown years, ye bring no joy on your wings to Ossian'.[17]

By ravelling up the idea of the fake into the nihilism of the poems, Hazlitt not so much negates the importance of forgery as celebrates its aesthetic congruence with *Ossian*'s world: the forged status of the text is an objective correlative for the sensibility found within it.

Thus, an understanding of *Ossian*'s reception involves a double act of historical imagination: first, to imagine a world in which *Ossian* had any perceived literary merit (an impossible enough task for many modern readers); and, secondly, to imagine this as conditioned by, but not totally in thrall to, the question of the status of the poems as genuinely ancient remains. In the rest of the chapter I want to explore one manifestation of this by considering the use of the idea of *Ossian* in specific writings by Walter Scott and William Wordsworth. The focus is necessarily narrow and I hope the conclusions not too sweeping. The aim is to suggest one way in which *Ossian* figured in the Romantic imagination, particularly in connection with ideas of authenticity and sincerity.

What Edward heard: *Waverley* and the delusion of Romance

In Chapter 22 of Walter Scott's *Waverley* (1814), Edward, falling under the spell of the beautiful Flora, meets her for an assignation in a Highland glen and hears her perform Gaelic verse. In this key moment in the novel's plot, Scott explicitly invokes the idea of *Ossian*, and it is worth considering how, and to what effect.

Scott's interest in Macpherson and *Ossian* was long-standing in work and life. He records his fascination with the poems as a child in the letter to Seward cited above. Here, while admitting that *Ossian* (and, it is worth noting, Spenser) contain 'more charms for youth than for a more advanced stage', as an adult he remains torn between disbelief in the literal provenance of the poems and admiration of their literary merits, lamenting that the lack of real authenticity 'destroys that feeling of reality which one should otherwise combine with our sentiments of admiration'.[18] This breaks into outright contradiction in his review of Laing's edition of *Ossian* and the Highland Society Report for *The Edinburgh Review*. Convinced by Laing of Macpherson's imposture, he concludes, 'let us hear no more of Macpherson' before immediately claiming that it should be a matter of national pride that 'a remote and barbarous corner of Scotland produced, in the eighteenth century, a bard, capable not only of making an enthusiastic impression on every mind susceptible of poetic beauty, but of giving a new note to poetry throughout Europe.'[19] As a critical response this is on a par with that of Thomas Gray some

40 years earlier, caught between the unlikelihood of the poems being either genuine or the work of a Highland schoolmaster, and hits the central paradox for many readers about Macpherson squarely amidships: if *Ossian* was to be thought a fake, Macpherson must be thought of as some sort of literary genius (although some, most famously Samuel Johnson of course, did not succumb to the logic of the position or the poems' strange charms). In any case, it is hardly surprising that Scott's work contains, in Fiona Robertson's usefully oxymoronic phrase, many 'studiously irreverent references' to *Ossian*.[20] For example, she notes that in *The Antiquary*, *Ossian* is a part of the portrayal of 'simple-minded patriots' such as Hector McIntyre.[21] Indeed, Scott goes so far as to associate the notional author of two of the Waverley Novels with Macpherson: the author of *Ivanhoe* is 'a second Macpherson' and that of *A Legend of Montrose* 'Secundus Macpherson'. As Robertson puts it in connection with *Ivanhoe*, this is:

> An ominous hint that the Author is not to be trusted with the material he passes off as authentic. Macpherson's is not a neutral name to conjure up in the reader's mind at the beginning of a historical novel.[22]

In Ian Haywood's words, 'however wry or ironical the connection, Scott equated himself with Macpherson' because of his importance in the creation of a crucial 'dualism' between 'scholarly authentication ... and "emulation" or invention.'[23] Thus, the ambiguous tutelary figure of Macpherson is part of the equation whereby Scott explores, or teases his reader, over questions of literary authenticity and truth-telling. The example of *Waverley* is particularly interesting in combining this with a concern over Scotland's heroic heritage.

Edward is in the Highlands, falling under the spell of Gaelic Chief Fergus MacIvor, his beautiful sister Flora, and the Jacobite cause both espouse. In a scene that represents 'a *mélange* of every crowd-pulling device known to the tourist guides of the day', Flora inducts Edward into a land of romance and heroic Gaeldom via the recital of some of her translations of the poems of the family bard Mac Murough.[24] Macpherson/*Ossian* is an unspoken presence in the scene in a number of ways, at least for a reader in 1814. First the reader is offered a picture of a Highland landscape synonymous (for its early readers at least) with *Ossian* – indeed the poems were in large measure responsible for the popular image of the Highlands at the time as a literary landscape of sublime splendour touched with melancholy. Secondly, the Gaelic poem recited is in content and provenance of a piece with *Ossian* in its gloominess. The poem opens: 'There is mist on the mountain, and night on the vale, | But more dark by far is the sleep of the sons of the Gael', and Flora sings it to a harp whose use 'had been taught to Flora by Rory Dall, one of the last harpers of the Western Highlands' (lastness and exotic extinction being a key component in Ossianic melancholy).[25] Compare the general set up of scene and mood here with this passage, the end of 'The War of Caros':

> But lead me O Malvina, to the sound of my woods, and the roar of my mountain streams. Let the chace be heard on Cona; that I may think on the days of other years. – And bring me the harp, O maid, that I may touch it when the light of my soul shall arise. – Be thou near, to learn the song; and future times shall hear of Ossian.
>
> The sons of the feeble hereafter will lift the voice on Cona; and, looking up to the rocks, say, 'Here Ossian dwelt.' They shall admire the chiefs of old, and the race that are no more: while we ride on our clouds, Malvina, on the wings of the roaring winds. Our voices shall be heard, at times, in the desert; and we shall sing on the winds of the rock.[26]

Finally Flora's descriptions of Gaelic poetry are highly reminiscent of Macpherson's strictures on the subject. She explains her removal of Waverley from the castle and to the glen:

> a Highland song would suffer still more from my imperfect translation, were I to introduce it without its own wild and appropriate accompaniments. To speak in the poetical language of my country, the seat of the Celtic muse is in the mist of a secret and solitary hill, and her voice in the murmur of the mountain stream. He who woos her must love the barren rock more than the fertile valley, and the solitude of the desert better than the festivity of the hall.[27]

Again, this identification of misty hill tops, mountain streams and the 'desert' as sites of poetic inspiration and interpretation is part of the Ossianic world view. It is as if Flora has combined such poetic evocations as seen in the quotation from 'The War of Caros' with what Macpherson says about the poems as a whole:

> It will seem strange to some, that poems admired for many centuries in one part of the kingdom should be hitherto unknown in the other ... This, in great measure, is to be imputed to those who understood both languages and never attempted a translation. They ... despaired of making the compositions of their bards agreeable to an English reader. The manner of those compositions is so different from other poems,

and the ideas so confined to the most early state of society, that it was thought they had not enough of variety to please a polished age.[28]

However, it is generally agreed that the clinching moment comes when Scott has Flora anticipate Macpherson in a comment not far from Scott's own reflection on Macpherson's legacy quoted above:

> The recitation ... of poems, recording the feats of heroes, the complaints of lovers, and the wars of contending tribes, forms the chief amusement of a winter fireside in the Highlands. Some of these are said to be very ancient, and if they are ever translated into any of the languages of civilized Europe, cannot fail to produce a deep and general sensation.[29]

Assuming for a moment that *Ossian* is what the reader thinks it is at this moment (on which, more below) Flora, literally speaking 'Sixty Years Since', is predicting what, from the vantage point of 1814, the reader knows to have been imminent in 1759: the publication of the first part of what by 1765 was *The Poems of Ossian*. But by 1814 the reader is also likely to know that *Ossian* was a fraud. Thus what Haywood has called Flora's 'cunningly self-fulfilling prophecy' is doubly tainted with the idea of imposture.[30]

This trickiness can be read as one of the ways in which Edward's flirtation with Highland Jacobitism is a naïve enthusiasm, the actions of an innocent abroad, hoodwinked by virtue of a Romantic disposition into a bogus cause as Flora 'literally enchants Waverley and lures him into the romance of Gaeldom and Jacobitism'.[31] But, in this scene, Gaelic poetry – to the extent that it is associated with readers of *Ossian* – and Jacobitism exist in a mutually reinforcing image of the fraudulent. After all, the poem Edward hears may start as what sounds like a lament for heroic Celticism, but is in fact a call to arms on behalf of Charles Edward Stuart's cause, and ends:

> Be the brand of each Cheftain like Fin's in his ire!
> May the blood through his veins flow like currents of fire!
> Burst the base foreign yoke as your sires did of yore,
> Or die like your sires, and endure it no more![32]

By being bewitched by the romance of heroic Gaeldom, Edward is being seduced into treason.

This sense of delusion is enhanced by the repeated references to romance in the scene (the insistent use of simile is worth noting here, as Scott draws attention to the gap between appearance and reality). Edward is 'like a knight of romance' travelling into 'the land of romance'; Flora and her companions appear 'like inhabitants of another region' in a 'sylvan amphitheatre';[33] the waterfall is 'romantic' as is the 'romantic wildness of the scene'.[34] Edward has seen nothing like it 'in his wildest dreams' and he approaches Flora as if she were 'a fair enchantress of Boiardo or Ariosto'.[35] This is significant not merely because knights of romance sometimes find themselves led astray or imprisoned by seemingly fair enchantresses. For most in the enlightened eighteenth century, and in particular those of a Whig persuasion, such figures and a desire to understand the world in romance terms is synonymous not only with Jacobitism (via the association with cavaliers) but also with a weak grasp on reality, with delusion and madness.[36]

As Margaret Russett has pointed out, the word delusion 'was routinely used in the eighteenth and nineteenth centuries as a synonym for "fraud"' and her emphasis on the 'various experimental and transgressive practices that cluster under the Romantic heading of romance' is a valuable way of understanding this moment, most immediately in her reminding us that, for Johnson, romance referred both to a literary genre and a speech act, that of lying.[37] Certainly, the description of Flora and her glen reveals the extent to which she has stage-managed this scene and only heightens the impression of entrapment, of a false consciousness being encouraged. In terms of style, as the examples in the previous paragraph reveal, simile is the key rhetorical device as Edward makes his way up the glen. But even the physical environment is not as it seems. His progress up the wild valley is via what appears to be a rugged path but is in fact one 'rendered easy in many places for Flora's accommodation'. Indeed, there is an air of contrivance in the apparent difficulty of his course:

> In one place a crag of huge size presented its gigantic bulk, as if to forbid the passenger's farther progress; and it was not until he approached its very base, that Waverley discerned the sudden and acute turn by which the pathway wheeled its course around this formidable obstacle.[38]

Equally, the scene of the poetic encounter, itself exactly the sort of locale in which Macpherson has Ossian holding forth, is not as natural as it seems:

> Mossy banks of turf were broken and interrupted by huge fragments of rock, and decorated with trees and shrubs, some of which had

been planted under the direction of Flora, but so cautiously, that
they added to the grace, without diminishing the romantic wildness
of the scene.[39]

And at the centre of it all is Flora herself, stage manager of and also
central figure in this tableau. She appears with her attendant 'as it were
in mid air' on the bridge;[40] later she is described (again in a simile,
the construction of which foregrounds the artifice) as 'like one of those
lovely forms which decorate the landscape of Poussin'.[41] At the climax
to the scene-setting, Scott acknowledges Flora's sense of the effect of the
scene on Waverley (and the reader must recall that the characters find
themselves here by her design):

> Flora, like every beautiful woman, was conscious of her own power,
> and pleased with its effects, which she could easily discern ... but, as
> she possessed excellent sense, she gave the romance of the scene, and
> other accidental circumstances, full weight in appreciating the feel-
> ings with which Waverley seemed obviously to be impressed.[42]

On one level this is merely Scott anatomizing the artful arrangement
of the picturesque landscape, the tamed Sublime so much in vogue at
the opening of the nineteenth century. Yet, when considered in the
context of the business of the scene and the overall plot of the novel,
the impression of carefully concealed artfulness goes beyond a matter
of aesthetic comment and into the realm of the moral, as Scott reveals
the deceptive allure of this world, and particularly the political cause
of Jacobitism with which it is associated. As Murray Pittock has put it,
'Flora's knowingness, and the deliberate quality of her scene setting
invalidates the struggle for "domestic liberty" praiseworthy in an earlier
age'.[43] The scene is sentimental, not naïve, and in this context suspect
as a consequence.

Yet having said all that, there is more to this scene than this cat-
egorical dismissal, and it would be wrong to read the scene and,
indeed, the novel, as a whole in terms of the complete undermining
of Romantic idealism. We should not forget that, after all, Scott was
responsible for the very Romantic idealism surrounding Highland
Scotland otherwise being revealed as a sham here. Ronald Paulson has
noted in his study of *Don Quixote* in Britain how 'with the '45 came
associations with lost causes and a poetics of the primitive, defeated
and mythic', a positive interpretation for the knight-errant as 'standing for outmoded chivalric ideals defeated by the more modernized

military forces of England'.[44] Certainly, Scott's own view of chivalry and romance sought to rehabilitate the order from accusations of excess, 'harebrained madness and absurdity' as a model of 'general urbanity, decency and courtesy'.[45] In connection with this scene, Pittock has noted that, however knowing the scene is, 'it still leaves, in its collocation and bardic exaltation, a delicious sense of readerly involvement in the gloaming of a world about to be lost'.[46] Indeed, in a version of what elsewhere might be thought of as Romantic irony, it is precisely *because* of that knowingness that the image is created so powerfully:

> By acknowledging the deliberateness of Flora's device ..., Scott averts attention from his own: and this passage is by no means the only one in which he offers a vision of the past whose factitiousness is concealed by a partial authorial confession to narrative device.[47]

There is no better example of this switching of attention than the 'prediction' of *Ossian* by Flora: what Haywood calls the 'cunning self-fulfilling prophecy' cannot of course really be thought of as any such thing. She cannot be guilty of insider trading via knowledge available only to her author writing 60 years later. But that is not to say that this is not what it feels like at this particular moment.

On the question of Gaelic verse, Scott knew perfectly well that what he has Flora say is true, regardless of the case of Macpherson. There was much poetry in the Highlands, much of it of considerable age, much of it connected to the cause of the Stuarts. In 1752 Alexander Macdonald (who amongst other Jacobite credentials had been laureate and Gaelic tutor to Charles Edward during 1745–1746) had even beaten Macpherson to the punch with his (entirely 'genuine') collection *The Resurrection of the Ancient Scottish Language*, and in 1758 Jerome Stone had published a Gaelic romance and English translation in *The Scots Magazine*.[48] Scott almost certainly knew both these, although it is unlikely that it was these examples rather than *Ossian*, the most famous ancient Gaelic poet, that any reader in 1814 would have had in mind after Flora's speech (notably, Macdonald had not provided any English translations in his book, which was in turn burnt as seditious, thus making it doubly inaccessible to most readers). Scott thus invokes a body of literature that does exist but whose most famous (indeed, so far as the vast majority of readers were concerned, *only*) eighteenth-century manifestation was itself of dubious provenance. The 'forger's shadow' (to use Groom's phrase) works as an image of the dangerous power of a Scottish past, but not as a wholly or unambiguously inauthentic one. *Ossian* is something to be believed and not believed, both a possibility and a blind alley, a testament to the potential richness and the potential delusion of Scottish heritage. Scott, as the commonplace has it, did not feel that Jacobitism was a grown-up option. As Andrew Hook puts it in the introduction to his edition of *Waverley*, the clear implication of Scott's anatomization of Waverley's joining the cause is that 'Scott does not seem to have been able to believe that any rational, level-headed person could have decided to become a Jacobite in 1745'.[49] Like Jacobitism, an enthusiasm for *Ossian* belongs to reckless and impressionable youth (as we saw in the letter to Seward). In the long run both are to be abandoned for the more worthy, sober and genuine pursuits of fully functioning political and poetic adulthood. But neither are they empty, unreal things. At the beginning of his walk Waverley is confronted by two streams, one of which is usually taken to represent British Unionism, the other Scottish nationalism and Jacobitism.[50] The streams are different in source and in the vista they present, but also in 'character':

> The larger was placid, and even sullen in its course, wheeling in deep eddies, or sleeping in dark blue pools; but the motions of the lesser brook were rapid and furious, issuing from between precipices, like a maniac from his confinement, all foam and uproar.[51]

There are no prizes for guessing which represents which, and the reader knows which one Waverley will chose. And while as readers we might know which one in the long run offers the wiser course of action, we are hardly upset that our young hero follows the latter.

'Ossian was 'ere': Wordsworth's counterfeit remains

William Wordsworth was far less interested in Macpherson than Scott, and his published strictures on *Ossian* in the 'Essay, Supplementary to the Preface' of the *Poems* of 1815 indicate, as we shall see, a considerable hostility to what he termed a 'Phantom ... begotten by the smug embrace of an impudent Highlander upon a cloud of tradition'.[52] William Blake, in his annotations to the 'Essay' was perhaps the first to wonder whether its author was the same man who had written Wordsworth's poems, and what J. R. Moore subsequently termed 'Wordsworth's unacknowledged debt' to Macpherson has been perhaps the major critical interest in the relationship between Macpherson and the High Romantics.[53] In the present context, I want to consider two short poems in which Wordsworth evokes and discusses the idea of *Ossian*, and what *Ossian* might stand for, in relation to the power of the imagination.

Evidence of Wordsworth's association of *Ossian* with this question of imaginative truth-telling and authenticity can be found outside of his poetry, even if it emerges rather paradoxically from his well-known dismissal of *Ossian*. That said, this is in some ways emblematic of the fraught and ironic relationship between them. In the 'Essay Supplementary to the Preface', the reasoning whereby Wordsworth thinks Macpherson a fraud has nothing to do with the inconsistencies in Macpherson's historical schema or a scepticism about the viability of oral tradition. There are some rather laboured comments about the unlikelihood of Macpherson's 'car-borne' heroes finding enough flat ground upon which to ride their chariots in the Highlands, but the most significant of Wordsworth's arguments are to do with *Ossian's* false depiction of nature:

> Having had the good fortune to be born and reared in a mountain-ous country, from my very childhood I have felt the falsehood that pervades the volumes imposed upon the world under the name of *Ossian*. From what I saw with my own eyes, I knew that the imagery was spurious. In nature everything is distinct, yet nothing defined into absolute independent singleness. In Macpherson's work, it is exactly the reverse.[54]

The obvious retort to Wordsworth would be that Macpherson was also brought up in a mountainous country and that the poems of Ossian were the product of the Highlands whenever you happen to think that production occurred historically. But this would of course miss the point of Wordsworth's attack: he knows these poems to be a fraud because they are imaginatively fraudulent, their style the inevitable result, he says in a Coleridgean moment, of 'words' being 'substituted for things'. From childhood Wordsworth did not perceive or detect the imposture, he 'felt' it.

In 'Glen Almain' (1807) Wordsworth meditates on the legendary grave of Ossian in the Highlands. The poem makes no direct reference to Macpherson, and indeed the latter's poems make no reference to Ossian's last resting place. But the question of Macpherson's Ossian hovers over the poem in a number of ways. In the first instance,

Wordsworth uses the name 'Ossian' (and not 'Oisin' or 'Oscian') because of Macpherson's version of the fian-lore (indeed, it could be argued that it is only because of Macpherson's activities that Wordsworth is aware of the Celtic bard at all, however he chooses to spell his name). More generally, the entire aesthetic frame of reference within which Wordsworth reads the Highland scene (and which is, as we shall see, vital to the conclusion of this poem) is conditioned by Macpherson's vision of the Gaeltachdt. As was suggested above in relation to Scott's highland scene, by this time *Ossian* was what Paul Baines has termed 'a literary Claude glass through which the Highlands could (almost could only) be viewed in attitudinizing aspect', and there is no better proof of this than Wordsworth's poems inspired by the Highlands.[55] To give a related example, if a reader were to ask why it is that Wordsworth assumes that the Solitary Reaper in the poem of the same name might be singing of 'old, unhappy, far-off things, | And battles long ago' (ll.19–20), the answer would be found in the influential vocabulary and frame of reference for articulating the Gaelic experience in the eighteenth century provided by *Ossian*. In terms of the Glen Almain poem, another feature more directly reminiscent of *Ossian* is its specific Highland graveside setting, since 'the representative Ossianic locale is a visited grave' in which the 'potent mixture of peace and unrest … is arrived at by permeating the secluded place with unappeased energies'. We see this at the start of book 4 of *Fingal*:

> Who comes with her songs from the mountain, like the bow of the showery Lena? It is the maid of the voice of love. The white-armed daughter of Toscar. Often hast thou heard my song, and given the tear of beauty. Dost thou come to the battles of thy people, and to hear the actions of Oscar? When shall I cease to mourn by the streams of the echoing Cona? My years have passed away in battle, and my age is darkened in sorrow.[56]

The poem is one of the body of Wordsworth's work that explores the connection between place and human sympathy, between location and imagination, and the psychological connection between culture, history, collective memory, and the imaginative reading of human history in a landscape. Thus, given the poem's interest in the relation between empirically verifiable truth and the truth of the subjective imaginative experience, it is fitting that Ossian is the figure under discussion, a figure for whom no empirical evidence exists but whose truth can only rely upon the truth of the poetic vision. The crux of the poem is that the scene matches the legend associated with it, and thus the legend is imaginatively true, even if no empirical evidence exists to corroborate it. Thus the central question 'Does then the Bard sleep here indeed | Or is it but a groundless creed' is answered through a commitment to the power of the imagination provoked by the 'lonely spot' whose stillness 'is not quiet, is not ease; | But something deeper far than these'. The way is then open for the poem to conclude that 'therefore was it rightly said | That Ossian, last of all his race! | Lies buried in this lonely place'. It is rightly said because of the way this scene recommends itself to the viewer, through the medium of Macpherson's Ossian:

> Narrow is thy dwelling now; dark the place of thine abode. With three steps I compass thy grave, O thou who wast great before! Four stones, with their heads of moss, are the only memorial of thee.[57]

This meditation on Ossian the bard is, then, one on the power of imagination and authenticity in a way that transcends historical reality or empirical evidence. It might, perhaps, be argued that this has nothing to do with Macpherson's *Ossian*, though as I have indicated this would be to misread the encoding of the Gaelic Highlands in the early nineteenth century. Nevertheless, the one poem of Wordsworth's that explicitly meditates on Macpherson accuses him of destroying the very possibility of authentic imaginative engagement celebrated in the Glen Almain poem. Yet in this poem, 'Written on a Blank Leaf of Macpherson's *Ossian*' (1827), it is possible to discern a similar emphasis on issues of authenticity, a similar dependence on a set of cultural assumptions derived from *Ossian*, and an unwillingness to jettison entirely the possibilities *Ossian* represents.

The poem opens with a famous assault on *Ossian*, attacking the notion of 'counterfeit remains' in favour of the eloquent silence of ruins and the 'majesty of honest dealing' (l.16): let 'authentic words be given, or none' (l.30) is the ringing, Johnsonian verdict on Macpherson's confection. Yet the rhetoric of forgery is something of a red herring, since Wordsworth's main objection to Macpherson's activities is, as might be anticipated from the 'Essay Supplementary to the Preface', predominantly not moral but aesthetic: 'what need then of these finished strains' (l.11), asks the poet, when fragments are so much more imaginatively suggestive and can offer far more powerful effects. Macpherson's intervention is to draw the analogy with the Glen Almain poem, the equivalent of an enterprising local inscribing 'Ossian R.I.P.' on his supposed burial cairn in an effort to provide literal-minded corroboration for the legend. Such an effort which would not only be deaf but positively counterproductive to the power of imaginatively authentic if intangible qualities of atmosphere, mood and scene.

Wordsworth was not, however, a very good reader of Macpherson, when judged by his pronouncements on (rather than adoption of) the Ossianic. *Ossian*, after all, provides one of the key moments in the creation of the sensibility of the fragment, and an important missing link in the relationship between the cult of Sentiment and Romantic poetics.[58] The experience of reading *Ossian* is that of reading a text torn between centrifugal and centripetal forces; between the fragment and the notion of the unified whole. This tension is clear in Macpherson's initial comments on the poem's provenance, usually quoted for other reasons. *Fingal* was gathered on a tour to the Highlands and with the help of 'several gentlemen':

> it was by their means I was enabled to compleat the poem. How far it comes up to the rules of the epopaea, is the province of criticism to examine. It is only my business to lay it before the reader, as I have found it.[59]

Doubtless Macpherson had his reasons for presenting a moving target here, and for blurring the distinction between 'compleat[ing]' the poem and merely laying it out 'as I have found it'. But it also is symptomatic of the war within the text between completion and fragmentation. Thus, the intrusive footnotes (many of which contain scraps of other poems) the lacunae, and the increasing habit of breaking off towards the end of the story, not to mention a narrative style closer to that of Aeschylus than Homer, provide an ever-more assertive counterpoint to the project of Augustan improvement than Macpherson might otherwise claim. Indeed, leaving aside claims for the importance of Macpherson to the inauguration of the fragment style in English poetry (his development of what Levinson calls a 'new cognitive paradigm ... essential to the aestheticisation of the poetic fragment') many accounts of the popularity of the poems stress what might later be termed the 'negative capability' of the poems, their ability through their very lack of finish to draw readers into, and into creating, their imaginary worlds.[60]

This peculiar reproaching of Macpherson by way of an aesthetic idiom for which he is in large measure responsible mirrors the odd way in which Wordsworth evokes an Ur-Ossian (what David Radcliffe has termed a 'transcendental Ossian') that is, an Ossian uncontaminated by Macpherson's 'counterfeit remains' via a classically Macphersonian vocabulary, locale and sensibility:

> Spirit of Ossian! if imbound
> In language thou may'st yet be found,
> If aught (intrusted to the pen
> Of floating on the tongues of men,
> Albeit shattered and impaired)
> Subsist thy dignity to guard,
> In concert with the memorial claim
> Of old grey stone, and high born name
> That cleaves to rock or pillared cave
> Where moans the blast, or beats the wave,
> Let Truth, stern arbitress of all,
> Interpret that Original,
> And for presumptuous wrongs atone; –
> Authentic words be given, or none! (ll.17–30)

Here, the material traces of the poet Wordsworth evokes are entirely Macphersonian ones. Wordsworth thinks the old grey stone and moaning blast are places where the residual echo of the poet might reside because this is where they reside in the counterfeit remains of Macpherson's *Ossian*:

> Let the tomb open to Ossian, for his strength has failed. The sons of the song are gone to rest; my voice remains, like a blast, that roars, lonely, on a sea-surrounded rock, after the winds are laid.[61]

The same point can be made about the final description of Ossian, where again the image of the true Ossian and his poetic activities is derived from that which Macpherson had presented to the world:

> Ye, when the orb of life had waned,
> A plenitude of love retained:
> Hence, while in you each sad regret
> By corresponding hope was met,
> Ye lingered among human kind,
> Sweet voices for the passing wind;
> Departing sunbeams, loth to stop,
> Though smiling on the last hill-top!
> Such to the tender-hearted maid

> Even ere her joys began to fade;
> Such, haply, to the rugged chief
> By fortune crushed, or tamed by grief;
> Appears, on Morven's lonely shore,
> Dim-gleaming through imperfect lore,
> The son of Fingal; (ll.65–79)

Indeed, this construal of Macpherson's poems as both corrupt copy and the only access to an assumed historical figure was a common response to *Ossian*. Many of the versifications of the poems that appeared in the 50 years after their publication not only use the word 'translation' to describe their activities, but furthermore, claim to be more accurate or faithful than Macpherson's version. But faithful to what? Macpherson's *Ossian* is treated as one version, yet it is in effect the original: there is no other common source to which to return. The appearance of the – almost entirely fraudulent – 'Gaelic' Ossian in 1807 muddies the water here to some extent, but the majority of these efforts predate the appearance of this edition.[62] The entirety of what the Anglophone reader knows about Ossian comes from Macpherson, but Macpherson's *Ossian* is considered to be either inadequate or fraudulent or, as in the case of Wordsworth, both. Thus when we see 'through' the fake Ossian we arrive at an Ossian who is, as it turns out, almost inseparable from the fake, as when the tearful maids and defeated warriors of Wordsworth's alternative are lifted entirely from Macpherson. That the 'authentic' Fian-lore (unavailable to Wordsworth of course) is nothing like this in tone or vision is beside the point and yet absolutely underlines it.[63]

There is, however, a further animating contradiction in the poem's attitude to Ossian. Wordsworth's comments on Macpherson lead to more general reflections on the endurance – or non-endurance – of poets and poetry. The works of some, such as Orpheus and Musaeus, are lost on account of Time's 'ruthless appetite' for poetry; others die young; others are 'self-betrayed' and end up 'frantic' and 'friendless, by their own sad choice'. But others, 'bards of mightier grasp' endure both during their lifetimes (through a devotion to their vocation) and in posterity. As we have seen, this vocation is conceived of in terms of sociability, connectedness, and the ability of the poet to resonate with the rest of mankind and its sorrows. However decrepit such poets become, in each is 'a plenitude of love retained'. And the trio of poets he gives as examples of this supreme state are Milton, Homer and Ossian – viewed, at the time, to be entirely conventional.

Thus Ossian provides the link between the two halves of the poem, as both a fraud – or perhaps the victim of a fraud – and as an enduring poet. Wordsworth creates what David Radcliffe has called a 'transcendental Ossian', placed 'entirely beyond the reach of time's baleful tooth'.[64] Furthermore, the second half of the poem could be seen no less than the first as an exploration of the true and the false, the genuine and the fake, authentic and forged, in terms of poetic career. The poem thus questions the nature of cultural endurance in the context of a text – the very *literal* context of it given that the lines are inscribed within a copy of the *Poems of Ossian* – which itself poses these questions with some insistence.

This chapter has examined two different evocations of the idea of Macpherson's *Ossian* within quite different sorts of Romantic writing. In both instances the question of the poems' provenance has not been ducked but incorporated into what the poems signify for later readers. In different ways Macpherson's *Ossian* offers both potential and dangerous allure, the promise of something and its negation, or perhaps a negation that does not quite banish the promise entirely. This is expressed in the figure of Scott, the collector of genuine ballad material invoking a disreputable version of his own scholarly activity, or in Wordsworth, holding on to an image of Ossian derived entirely from Macpherson through the misrepresentation he considers Macpherson's Ossian to be. And central to this promise is the question of sincerity, of commitment to a truth that is beyond the normative categories of empirically established reality. *The Poems of Ossian* would seem to offer a category for these Romantic writers that is stimulating to the imagination precisely because of the way they offer 'the balance or reconcilement of opposite or discordant qualities', and in particular something which 'blends and harmonises the natural and the artificial.'[65] Against all the odds, then, *Ossian* can emerge, through a particular Romantic alchemy, as a touchstone of literary authenticity, or belief in the possibility of such a thing.

Notes

1. John Valdimir Price, 'Ossian and the Canon in the Scottish Enlightenment' in *Ossian Revisited*, ed. Howard Gaskill, (Edinburgh: Edinburgh University Press, 1991), pp. 109–28, (p. 127); Joep Leerssen, 'Ossianic Liminality: Between Native Tradition and Preromantic Taste' in *From Gaelic to Romantic: Ossianic Translations*, eds Fiona Stafford and Howard Gaskill, (Amsterdam: Rodopi, 1998), pp. 1–16, (pp. 1, 3).

2. See Richard Sher, '"Those Scotch Impostors and their Cabal": Ossian and the Scottish Enlightenment' in *Man and Nature: Proceedings of the Canadian Society for Eighteenth-Century Studies*, eds Roger Emerson et al., (London, Ontario, 1982), pp. 55–65; Fiona Stafford, *The Sublime Savage: James Macpherson and the Poems of Ossian* (Edinburgh: Edinburgh University Press, 1988); Ken Simpson, *The Protean Scot: The Crisis of Identity in Eighteenth-Century Scottish Literature* (Aberdeen: Aberdeen University Press, 1988); *Ossian Revisited*; *From Gaelic to Romantic*; Dafydd Moore, *Enlightenment and Romance in James Macpherson's Poems of Ossian* (Aldershot: Ashgate, 2003).
3. Jerome McGann, *The Poetics of Sensibility: A Revolution in Literary Style* (Oxford: Clarendon, 1996), p. 33.
4. Johnson's famous comments can be found in his *Tour to the Western Isles of Scotland* (1774), while Trevor-Roper's can be found in his 'The Invention of Tradition: The Highland Tradition of Scotland' in *The Invention of Tradition*, eds Eric Hobsbawm and Terence Ranger, (Cambridge: Cambridge University Press, 1983).
5. See Thomas M. Curley, 'Samuel Johnson and Truth: The First Systematic Detection of Literary Deception in James Macpherson's Ossian', *The Age of Johnson*, Vol. 17 (2006) pp. 119–96; but also a response from Nick Groom, 'Samuel Johnson and Truth: A Response to Curley', pp. 197–201.
6. A recent and erudite example of this is Philip Connell's 'British Identities and the Politics of Ancient Poetry in Later Eighteenth-Century England', *The Historical Journal* **49**(1) (2006), pp. 161–92.
7. Leith Davis, *Acts of Union: Scotland and the Literary Negotiation of the British Nation 1707–1803* (Stanford: Stanford University Press, 1998), pp. 74–106; Katie Trumpener, *Bardic Nationalism: The Romantic Novel and the British Empire* (Princeton: Princeton University Press, 1997); David Punter, 'Ossian, Blake, and the Questionable Source' in *Exhibited by Candlelight: Sources and Developments in the Gothic Tradition*, eds. Valeria Tinkler-Villani et al., (Amsterdam, 1995), pp. 25–41.
8. Nick Groom, *The Forger's Shadow: How Forgery Changed the Course of Literature* (London: Picador, 2002), p.15.
9. Margaret Russett, *Fictions and Fakes: Forging Romantic Authenticity, 1760–1845* (Cambridge: Cambridge University Press, 2006), p. 4.
10. Groom, *Forger's Shadow*, p. 15; Leerssen, 'Ossianic Liminality', p. 9.
11. Leerssen, 'Ossianic Liminality', pp. 2–3.
12. James Macpherson, *James Macpherson's Fingal (1792)*, ed. and intro. Jonathan Wordsworth (Poole, 1996), unpag.
13. Marjorie Levinson, *The Romantic Fragment Poem: A Critique of a Form* (Chapel Hill: University of North Carolina Press, 1986), p. 34.
14. For these documents, and a discussion of them, see Dafydd Moore, *Ossian and Ossianism*, 4 volumes, (London: Routledge, 2004), vol. 3 (documents), vol. 1 (discussion).
15. 18 editions were published between 1765 and 1800, but 27 between 1801 and 1830. See John Dunn, 'The Influence of Macpherson's Ossian on British Romanticism' (unpublished PhD thesis, Duke University, 1965), pp. 107–8.
16. Scott to Seward, September 1806, in H. J. C. Grierson (ed.), *The Letters of Walter Scott 1787–1807* (London: Constable, 1932), p. 321. Other views along these lines are cited in Moore, 'Examining *Ossian*'s Romantic Bequest'

in *English Romanticism and the Celtic World*, eds. Alan Rawes and Gerard Carruthers, (Cambridge: Cambridge University Press, 2003), pp. 38–53.

17. William Hazlitt, 'On Poetry in General', *The Complete Works of William Hazlitt*, ed. P. P. Howes, 21 volumes (London, 1930), vol. 5, pp. 1–18 (p. 18).

18. Scott to Seward, pp. 320, 321.

19. Scott, anonymous review in *The Edinburgh Review, Or Critical Journal*, vol. 6, July 1805, pp. 429–62 (pp. 461, 462).

20. Fiona Robertson, *Legitimate Histories: Scott, Gothic and the Authorities of Fiction* (Oxford, 1994), p. 124.

21. Ibid., p. 221.

22. Ibid., p. 124.

23. Ian Haywood, *The Making of History: a Study of the Literary Forgeries of James Macpherson and Thomas Chatterton in Relation to Eighteenth-Century Ideas of History and Fiction*, (Rutherford: Farleigh Dickinson University Press, 1986) pp. 151, 162.

24. Murray G. H. Pittock, 'Scott and the British Tourist' in *English Romanticism and the Celtic World*, eds Gerard Carruthers and Alan Rawes, (Cambridge: Cambridge University Press, 2003), p. 159.

25. Walter Scott, *Waverley*, ed. Andrew Hook (Harmondsworth, 1972), p. 176. For Macpherson's role in the creation of the image of the Highlands and Celtic Titanism see Peter Womack, *Improvement and Romance: Constructing the Myth of the Highlands* (Basingstoke: Macmillan – now Palgrave Macmillan, 1992).

26. James Macpherson, *Fingal ... and Other Poems* (1761), p. 103. All quotations are from this edition, as reprinted in *Ossian and Ossianism*, vol. 3.

27. Scott, *Waverley*, p. 177.

28. Macpherson, 'A Dissertation concerning the Antiquity & c. of Ossian's Poems', in *Fingal*, pp. xiii–xiv.

29. Scott, *Waverley*, p. 173.

30. Haywood, *The Making of History*, p. 162.

31. Leerssen, 'Ossianic Liminality', p. 9.

32. Scott, *Waverley*, p. 180.

33. Ibid., p. 175.

34. Ibid., p. 176.

35. Ibid., p. 177.

36. See Ronald Paulson, *Don Quixote in England: The Aesthetics of Laughter* (Baltimore: Johns Hopkins University Press, 1998), p. 48.

37. Russett, *Fictions and Fakes*, pp. 6–7.

38. Scott, *Waverley*, p. 175.

39. Ibid., p. 176. For Ossian thus accommodated see, for example, Fragment VIII, *Ossian and Ossianism* vol. 1, p. 155.

40. Scott, *Waverley*, p. 175.

41. Ibid., p. 176.

42. Ibid., p. 177.

43. Pittock, 'Scott and the British Tourist', pp. 158–9.

44. Paulson, p. 184. For the Highland romance of defeat see Womack, *Improvement and Romance, passim*.

45. Scott, 'Essay on Chivalry' (1818) in *The Miscellenious Prose Works of Sir Walter Scott*, 3 volumes, (Edinburgh, 1847), vol. 1, pp. 525–53 (pp. 527, 544).

46. Pittock, 'Scott and the British Tourist', p. 159.

47. Ibid., p. 159.
48. See Moore, *Ossian and Ossianism*, vol. 1 for reprints of Macdonald and Stone.
49. Andrew Hook, Introduction, *Waverley*, p. 21.
50. See Pittock, 'Scott and the British Tourist', p. 157.
51. Scott, *Waverley*, pp. 174–5.
52. 'Essay, Supplementary to the Preface', *Wordsworth: Poetic Works*, ed. Thomas Hutchinson, rev. Ernest de Selincourt, (Oxford: Oxford University Press, 1936), p. 748.
53. See Blake, *The Poetry and Prose of William Blake*, ed. Geoffrey Keynes, (London, 1967), p. 822; J. R. Moore, 'Wordsworth's Unacknowledged Debt to Macpherson's Ossian', *P.M.L.A.* **40** (1925), 362–78; Fiona Stafford, '"Dangerous Success": Ossian, Wordsworth, and English Romanticism', *Ossian Reevisited*, pp. 49–72.
54. 'Essay', p. 748.
55. Paul Baines, 'Ossianic Geographies: Fingalian Figures on the Scottish Tour 1760–1830', *Scotlands* 4.1 (1997), pp. 44–61 (p. 54).
56. Womack, *Improvement and Romance*, p. 79; Macpherson, *Fingal*, p. 49.
57. Macpherson, 'The Songs of Selma', *Fingal*, p. 214.
58. Recent Macpherson criticism has made much of this. See Keymer, 'Narratives of Loss: *The Poems of Ossian* and *Tristram Shandy*', *Ossian Revisited*, pp. 79–96; Manning, 'Henry Mackenzie and Ossian: Or, The Emotional Value of Asterisks', *Ossian Revisited*, pp. 136–52; Robert Crawford, *The Modern Poet: Poetry, Academia and Knowledge since the 1750s* (Oxford: Oxford University Press, 2001); Mary-Ann Constantine and Gerald Porter, *Fragments and Meaning in Traditional Song* (Oxford: Oxford University Press/British Academy, 2003), pp. 22–30.
59. Macpherson, *Fingal*, preface, a.1.ver.
60. Levinson, *The Romantic Fragment Poem*, p. 43. For the negative capability of Ossian see, for example, Womack, *Improvement and Romance*, p. 107.
61. Macpherson, 'The Songs of Selma', *Fingal*, p. 218.
62. See John Wodrow, *Fingal: An Ancient Epic Poem: In 6 Books. By Ossian ... translated into English verse* (1769); Richard Hole *Fingal, a poem in 6 books, by Ossian. Translated from the Original Gaelic by Mr Macpherson and rendered into verse from that translation* (1772); Ewan Cameron, *The Fingal of Ossian, An Ancient Epic Poem* (1777). There were at least four other versions of *Fingal* by 1820 and many others of lesser poems.
63. For the Gaelic sources of Macpherson's Ossian see Neil Ross (ed. and trans.) *Heroic Poetry from the Book of the Dean of Lismore* (Edinburgh, 1939); Gerald Murphy, *Duanaire Finn: The Book of the Lays of Fionn*, parts 2 and 3, Irish Texts Society nos. 28 (London, 1933) and 43 (Dublin, 1953). For analysis of the differences between them see Moore, *Enlightenment and Romance*, pp. 56–60.
64. David Hall Radcliffe, 'Ossian and the Genres of Culture', *Studies in Romanticism* 31.2 (1992), pp. 213–32, (p. 230).
65. Samuel Taylor Coleridge, *Biographia Literaria* (1817), Chapter 14 in *Romanticism. An Anthology*, ed. Duncan Wu. (Blackwell, 2009) 3rd edn, p. 694.

3
Authenticity among Hacks: Thomas Chatterton's 'Memoirs of a Sad Dog' and Magazine Culture

Daniel Cook

> *'in truth he was fonder of inventing great bards, than of being one'*
>
> (Horace Walpole)

Thomas Chatterton's forged *Poems, supposed to have been written at Bristol, by Thomas Rowley, and Others, in the Fifteenth Century* (London, 1777) has dazzled critics and poets since it appeared as a 'most singular literary curiosity' seven years after his premature death.[1] In many of the periodicals, reviews, newspapers and literary clubs the 'Rowley debate' immediately ensued.[2] Although notionally concerned with the authenticity of the works, this debate played a larger and more important role in the unresolved axiological tensions in the supremacist battle between the ancients and moderns.[3] Chatterton's numerous fashionable modern works in poetry and prose by contrast were often associated with the trashy modern novel. A review of *Miscellanies in Prose and Verse; by Thomas Chatterton* (London, 1778) in the *Gentleman's Magazine* treats them as the 'loose, immoral pieces' appropriate for a writer now as 'famous' as Laurence Sterne – famous, lest it be forgotten, as the outed author of the new-old medieval forgeries.[4] For the reviewer 'Memoirs of a Sad Dog', 'which none but a *sad Dog* could write', is an appropriate self-expression of this young libertine writer as depicted in contemporary anecdotes.[5] In many uncomfortable ways this presupposes that even in the process of unifying the canon under the head of Thomas Chatterton, the Rowley poems remained charismatically ancient, segregated from Chatterton and the grubbily modern.

'Sad Dog' was published in the gossipy *Town and Country Magazine* in two parts in 1770, two months before Chatterton died and a month or so after. It was republished in the *Miscellanies* in 1778, an ink-blotted, mis-typeset edition rushed through the press to meet the sudden demand for his works.[6] It also appeared in a 1786 issue of *New Novelists* and the monumental 1803 collection, *The Works of Thomas Chatterton* edited by Joseph Cottle and Robert Southey. Is 'Sad Dog' a further prostitution of the enormous talent so extravagantly displayed in his modern-ancient Rowley project?[7]

His first biographer of sorts, Sir Herbert Croft, popularized a schematic distinction when he observed that, 'in his character, [Chatterton] painted for booksellers and bread; in Rowley's, for fame and eternity'.[8] In 1782 Vicesimus Knox writes: 'the little compositions which he wrote for the magazines, were written in a careless mood, when he relaxed his mind from his grand work ... to procure him a halfpenny roll and a draught of beer'.[9] Such assessments might remind us of Dr Johnson's pejorative definition of hack writing as 'temporary'.[10] Thomas Warton is even more explicit: 'Chatterton lavished all his powers on the counterfeit Rowley ... his Miscellanies were the *temporary* progeny of indigence [my emphasis]'.[11] The editor of Chatterton's *Miscellanies* attempts to divorce the modern works from the connotations of hack writing; Chatterton becomes 'the literary phenomenon of the times' and deserves to enter literary posterity, rising above the 'trash of monthly compilations'.[12]

Even the sole critical account of the first collection of Chatterton's modern works is primarily concerned with the *authenticity* of the pieces rather than their own literary merit.[13] Again, this long-standing interest in the authenticity of the works is tied into the assumption that the Rowley poems are *the* literary achievement in his canon, and the modern works the incidental result of having to earn a living. Such an assumption is entrenched in a Romanticized cultic faith in original genius as well as a residual Augustan denigration of the jobbing writer.[14] It relies on the essentialist belief that Chatterton was a medievalist genius led astray by the grubby profession of metropolitan writing. And so, rather than suggest that noetically Chatterton is more like an Augustan satirist or a pre-emptive Romantic, I want to trace a tension between satire and literary sentimentalism in terms of mid-century hack writing. Satire, whether we refer to the disdaining rhetoric of Pope or Swift or the self-obsession of Charles Churchill, is confronted by the sentimental mode in the mid-century, in memoirish novels and in the prose and poetry of the trashy magazine writers Chatterton mimicked.[15] With this in mind we can approach mid-century satire in a more open way, less as a moralizing agent and more the textual interplay of modish contributors.[16] This provides a new context in which to appreciate Chatterton's neglected modern works as well as his unknown hack colleagues in the magazines.

It has become commonplace since Pat Rogers's groundbreaking *Grub Street* to consider the physical locale of hack writers, and so Chatterton ought to be considered in such an environment. By then a resident of Holborn, Chatterton was attentive to the socio-political machinations of the 1760s London coffee house. He was a people-watcher, frequenting the coffee houses of merchants and stockjobbers like Tom's on Cornhill as part of 'my present profession'.[17] Far from discouraging this approach, I narrowly focus on textual more than physical attributes of hack writing. The rhetorical gestures of hack living, which interest me here, are by no means incompatible with an appreciation of its bodiliness. Chatterton references Thomas Amory's *The Life of John Buncle* in 'Sad Dog', a brusquely exaggerated depiction of hack life, in which 'Translators in pay, lay three in a bed, at the Pewter-Platter Inn in Holborn' – where Chatterton was researching and writing 'Sad Dog' and most of his works in 1770.[18]

Here, instead, I explore the materialist hermeneutics manifest in printed versions of 'Sad Dog' in terms of Chatterton's reputation and the reception of his works, in contemporary attitudes towards literature implicit in such responses, as well as his own playful relationship to the story he tells. The looseness of the plot in 'Sad Dog' affords Chatterton ample room for rumination on how to be a successful (that is, published) author in the modern marketplace. Under the guise of Harry Wildfire, Chatterton teases the timidity of patriot publishers, even the book trade in general: 'as I know the art of Curlism, pretty well, I make a tolerable hand of it', a belated reference to the controversial and inventive 'literary pirate' Edmund Curll, who had unsettled Swift and Pope so much that they printed their own, official, authorial *Miscellanies in Prose and Verse*.[19] Like many mid-century satirists, Chatterton, by contrast, embraces seedy publishing, invades contemporary fiction, pirates it, and makes it something creatively new. This new magazine-based collective of hacks began to embrace the literary marketplace rather than give up their literary integrity.

To say Chatterton pirates contemporary fiction is not to say he plagiarizes it. Often alien notions of authorship and literary property have been grafted onto Chatterton and his contemporaries, unfairly undermining their modish game-playing. Louise Kaplan observes that Chatterton's 'Maria Friendless' is a plagiarism 'nearly word-for-word' of Samuel Johnson's *Misella* (*Rambler* nos. 170, 171) yet paradoxically identifies a lack of 'faith in human nature ... the works betray restlessness combined with deep melancholy'.[20] Kaplan has read the piece as somehow osmotically autobiographical. I would read such a piece as part of

Chatterton's broader analysis of modern-day authorship. His plagiarism (or rearrangement) of Johnson here is another fashionable attempt to write to order. A better way to look at the textual and material aspect is to employ Nick Groom's distinction between forgery and plagiarism:

> The forger is an actor who constructs by collage, who utilizes surrounding sources, who ventriloquizes a position ... To plagiarise is to assert the integrity of the original artist, to affirm that fictions are grounded in individual experience.[21]

This, along with K. K. Ruthven's 'authenticity-effects', allows the complex relations between authorial authenticity, textual integrity and forgery to be drawn without diminishing the presence of the author.[22] Commonly associated with the early novel, the 'authenticity-effects' wrought by a reportage style, the affected non-literariness of the story, and long and plotless digression, reveal an indexical disturbance between fiction and autobiography, so fitting for the allonymity of the magazines. 'Sad Dog' is in many ways typical of such generic happenings and yet irreducibly true to his life story as shaped by Chatterton and his critics.

Memoirs of a Sad Dog

Like dozens of other pretended memoirs, 'moral tales' and anecdotes in the *Town and Country Magazine*, 'Sad Dog' is a story about how a well-to-do youth came to his ruin through dissipation. Ostensibly in a literary/economic exchange for 'a dinner', that is, Harry Wildfire (Chatterton) relates his own story.[23] With a legacy of £5,000 in one hand and *The Way to Save Wealth* – a genuine late-seventeenth-century guidebook – in the other, he undertakes a debauched life with his brother-in-law Sir Stentor Ranger. They fritter the inheritance on drink, extravagant food, gambling and prostitutes. At the bagnio (brothel) of Miss Fanny H—t, Jack N—tt, a successful merchant, quarrels with Harry but 'Miss Fanny thinking me a better paymaster, heroically turned him out of the parlour; telling him, for his comfort, that he should have his month another time'. Jack is turned to the Ministry by his greed and friendship with the real-life Wills Hill, Earl of Hillsbrough. Whereas Jack is invited to turtle feasts and grows fat on his political allegiances, Harry falls further into poverty, and so seeks money as a 'fortune hunter' (a seducer of women), a familiar literary figure around this time.[24] Although his private life is not beyond reproach he loyally conceals the name of the alderman husband and fellow patriot he has cuckolded. The husband unexpectedly returns and demands two thousand pounds in damages from Harry. In revenge Harry seduces the alderman's daughter Sabina, who falls in love with him and begs he prevents her professed marriage to Mr Lutestring the mercer. With barely £500 pounds left, he seeks the aid of a now very drunk Sir Stentor who offers him a position in his stables attending the racehorses. In the meantime Baron Otranto, a conjectural antiquarian, visits Sir Stentor's home on the hunt for curiosities. In 'all the splendour of an Englishman' Harry then travels to Paris and inadvertently marries a poor marquise, is forced to settle her debts and is thrown into prison. He soon returns to Sir Stentor, whose fortune he has made, but is poorly paid. After a stint as a stockjobber[25] he seeks money as a hack writer as a last resort:

> The first fruits of my pen were a political essay and a piece of poetry: the first I carried to a patriotic bookseller ... and the poetry was left with another of the same tribe ... Mr Brittannicus at first imagining the piece was not to be paid for, was lavish of his praises ... but when he was told that I expected some recompense, he assumed an air of criticism ... he did not think it good language, or sound reasoning.

This is also a personal riposte at the patriot booksellers abandoning Chatterton. Michael F. Suarez, SJ conjectures that Chatterton was about to take up a staff position on Isaac Fell's *Freeholder's Magazine* until the editor was arrested for his attacks on the Ministry.[26] Chatterton writes excitedly about his contributions to *Freeholder's* yet only two pieces appeared there. The patriot *Middlesex Journal* also printed much fewer Decimus (Chatterton) pieces in 1770 after an initial flurry.[27] Referencing the unscrupulous early-century bookseller/forger Edmund Curll, Harry Wildfire continues:

> I was not discouraged ... and as I know the art of Curlism pretty well, I make a tolerable hand of it. But, Mr Printer, the late prosecutions against the booksellers having frightened them all out of their patriotism, I am necessitated to write for the entertainment of the public, or in defence of the ministry.

Harry indicates that within his story political writing is necessarily subordinated to entertaining the fashionable reading public. Even this authorial mission statement is fabricated with the verbal threads of 1760s literary fashions. The debauched narrator is a sentimental villain 'lying and intriguing' innocent girls. Even the reader is intrigued as Harry feigns the somatic sincerity of a man of feeling: 'I blush to write the rest'.

Indeed he places himself in the company of sensationalist, neo-Curllist memoirists. 'The sentimental John Buncle should not be forgotten', Harry insists half wistfully, after ironically praising the 'tolerable work' of the chevalier John Taylor, pseudo-author of tediously long memoirs published in the early 1760s.[28] In the frame of 'Sad Dog' Taylor is no longer 'constrained' by 'truth', a quality associated here with 'classical elegance'. The relationship between literature and rhetoric is an honourable one for the ancients; for the moderns it has descended into desperate sensationalism. The modern literary world, under the strain of 'Curlism', has descended into literary indecorum with authors all indiscriminately seeking attention from the expanded numbers of leisured readers.

In 'The Art of Puffing by a Bookseller's Journeyman', Vamp (Chatterton) advises the 'Sons of Apollo' that 'The Author who invents a title well,/Will always find his cover'd Dullness sell'. This is another reference to the exploitative practices epitomized by Edmund Curll, one of Pope's most enduring Dunces. Observing that Curll's career is 'in flagrant opposition to the ideals of the Copyright Act', which 'had defined the *authentic* as the *authorised*', Ian Haywood perceptively argues that 'unauthorised printing is therefore a forgery'.[29] But more accurately, Curllist hacks (including Chatterton) short-circuit author-authentic parameters. The most familiar of Curll's staff of hacks is Richard Savage, who under the aptronymous guise of Iscariot Hackney smugly confesses 'I wrote Obscenity and Profaneness, under the Names of Pope and Swift. Sometimes I was Mr. Joseph Gay … ', lulling readers into buying a book by 'J. Gay' only to find it does not refer to the popular poet John Gay.[30] Title pages would misinform the reader, offering a complete or official collection or treatise only for the reader to discover scraps culled from other booksellers:

> Versed by Experience in the subtle Art,
> The mysteries of the Title I impart.
>
> ('The Art of Puffing')

Though written around the same time as 'Sad Dog', 'The Art of Puffing' did not appear in print until 1783; Chatterton's ostensive act of naming Curll is belated and by then appropriated into a narrowed liberalist rationale. Is this not straightforwardly an ironic endorsement, a satiric jab at modern publishing or is Curll perhaps a more appropriate bookseller than Dodsley or Walpole after all, both of whom rejected Chatterton's faux-medieval curiosities?[31] After all, with a publisher like

Curll, precisely because of his unscrupulousness, 'the Work will never die'.[32] Chatterton writes to his mother, 6 May 1770: 'No author can be poor who understands the arts of booksellers – Without this necessary knowledge, the greatest genius may starve'.[33] Confident in his genius, Chatterton felt he knew how to get ahead in the piratical world of the literary magazine.

In many ways the mid-century magazines were broadly predicated on the spurious, piratical 'Art of Curlism'.[34] The *Town and Country*, the *Lady's Magazine*, the *Sentimental Magazine* and others repeatedly reprinted variously altered pieces from each other, even from the more curiosity-minded *Gentleman's Magazine*.[35] This perambulating intertextuality short-circuits Dr Johnson's definition of such writing as 'temporary'. In fact it echoes the flagrant plagiarisms and recycling of modern and renaissance authors in the more celebrated book-print satires, such as Jonathan Swift's outlandish portrayal of hack life in *A Tale of a Tub* and Laurence Sterne's creatively derivative *Tristram Shandy*.[36] It is just that big names were not attached.

> For this each Month new Magazines are sold,
> With Dullness fill'd and transcripts of the Old.
> The *Town and Country* struck a lucky hit,
> Was novel, sentimental, full of Wit.
>
> ('The Art of Puffing')

Aside from echoes of Sterne, Swift and his coterie, Chatterton often appropriates the rhetoric of The Nonsense Club, chiefly Charles Churchill and Robert Lloyd.[37] In Lloyd's 'The Puff, a Dialogue between the Bookseller and Author', for example, we witness a world in which 'Bare Merit never will succeed'. This is how Chatterton understands the mechanics of the literary market, cannily puffing himself. Although his work appeared in many of the magazines, Chatterton discriminates between them in his suggestion that *Town and Country* was his favoured outlet. *Court and City* had featured Chatterton's 'Heccar and Gaira', 'A Song: Addressed to Miss C—am', and 'An African Song', and yet Chatterton's Vamp says it 'hobbles far behind' the *Town and Country*. Boastfulness aside, on 20 July 1769 Chatterton writes to Mr Stephens:

You may inquire if you please for the Town and Country Magazines wherein all signed D. B. and Asaphides are mine. The Pieces called

Saxon are originally and totally the product of my Muse […] As the
sd. Magazine is by far the best of its kind I shall have some Pieces in
it every Month.[38]

It has been suggested more recently that *Town and Country* had
'higher literary quality' than most mid-century magazines and perhaps
Chatterton agreed.[39] More work needs to be done on the literariness
of *Town and Country* and eighteenth-century magazines more broadly,
though the comparative success and audience of them has been well
discussed. In Walter Graham's classic account of the English periodical,
Town and Country is a 'very pretentious and successful serial'.[40] Markman
Ellis shows it 'addressed an audience composed of the rakish metropolitan society'.[41] *Town and Country* certainly made a show of being unable
to meet demand for space in their magazine. In the 'Acknowledgments
to our correspondents' at the beginning of each issue they list some
select items they could not include or did not wish to include. May
1770, for example, dismisses the works of the excluded contributors as
'incomprehensible', 'inadmissable' or 'too imperfect'. It is a public site
of literary quality control.

In the April issue of 1769, this relatively new magazine included a
letter from 'L. O.' in which he describes the social cleansing power
of Popeian satire: *'people who were not afraid of being wicked, were
ashamed of being made ridiculous'*.[42] Chatterton, like many of the
Town and Country contributors he imitates, appropriates the mechanisms of Popeian satire. The pretended authenticity of magazine
literature (and memoirish novels more broadly) effaces its origins in
the serial tradition of Addison and Steele and the rise of the modern novel.[43] The alignment of bourgeois domesticity and literary
sentimentalism imposes a leisurely game-playing on the intimate
relationship between literature and rhetoric. This partly explains the
phenomenon whereby mock memoirists have to break their own
rhetorical illusions because of an ethical duty to their naïve reader,
who may misunderstand the fine line of in-joke satire if taken to
represent societal life rather than literature. The writer of *Memoirs
of the Celebrated Miss Fanny M—* introduces a preface to the second
edition to remind readers, and her own bookseller, that the satire
was 'only founded in imagination'.[44] Chatterton, on the other hand,
exploits the fine line between fact and fiction. A central recurring
feature in *Town and Country*, the domineering Tête-à-têtes too made
great literary efficacy out of the blurred line between fact and fiction, between history writing and literature, between genuine and

pretended memoirs.[45] Chatterton's 'Harry Wildfire' is not dissimilar to Sir Harry Hairbrain, a vain gambling womaniser in 'Character of a well-known Baronet'.[46]

But Chatterton infuses his pirated text with strong allusions to his own literary background. In his *Town and Country* take on Popeian harrowing, one high-profile target to feature in a digressive aside in 'Sad Dog' is Horace Walpole, later 4th Earl of Orford, amateur antiquary and author of *The Castle of Otranto* (1764), a mock-medieval novella that many regard to be the legitimate foundation of the English Gothic novel. Walpole's name recurs throughout Chatterton's authentic and misattributed works, and throughout *Town and Country* and many of the magazines and periodicals. In Chatterton's canon Walpole appears as Horatio Otranto in 'The Polite Advertiser', Horatio Trefoil in *The Woman of Spirit*, as well as Baron Otranto in 'Sad Dog'. Even though the narratorial contexts of the plots are very different, Horatio Trefoil, like Baron Otranto, lampoons Horace Walpole as a gentleman antiquarian, as Walpole well knew.[47] He is one of the 'antiquated friends' of Latitat along with Lord Anthony Viscount Rust, Col. Tragedus, Professor Vase, and Counterfeit the Jew. Lord Rust recalls Samuel Foote's Martin Rust in *The Patron* (1764). And Samuel Foote is himself Distort, a nickname derived from Churchill's *Rosciad* (1761).[48] In 'Sad Dog' the allusions to Walpole are especially thick. Baron Otranto's obsession with a conjectural approach to antiquarianism is pirated from Walpole's *Anecdotes of Painting* (1762–1764), the work that had prompted Chatterton to send 'Ryse of Peynctenynge' and 'Historie of Peyncters' to his potential patron. Walpole has a long note beginning 'I cannot help hazarding a conjecture' and ending 'However I pretend to nothing more in all this than meer [sic] conjecture'.[49] There are also explicit references to the real Walpole's *Historic Doubts on the Life and Reign of King Richard the Third* (1768), his 'favourite hero'.

'The Polite Advertiser', following the first half of 'Sad Dog' in the *Town and Country* of July 1770, also refers to Walpole as Horatio Otranto. Regardless of whether Chatterton wrote both works, which has been seriously doubted, the editors picked up on the continual references to Walpole, inserting cross-references in round brackets and so tying the works together.[50] It is also unclear whether Chatterton wrote the outrageous Tête-à-tête in *Town and Country* for December 1769 where Otranto's 'Gothic taste for Mrs Heidelburgh' is a thin disguise for Walpole's intriguing relationship with the comic actress Kitty Clive.[51]

But he certainly did appropriate the association in 'The Advice' and one of his *Exhibitions*, without the veils:

> To keep one lover's flame alive
> Requires the genius of a Clive,
> With Walpole's mental taste.
>
> ('The Advice')[52]

Such appropriation is not uncommon among contributors. 'Allusions to the Tête-à-têtes throughout the *Town and Country Magazine* as well as within the sketches themselves, and the letters to the editors about them helped to keep this feature before the public'.[53] Chatterton understood the prominence of the Tête-à-têtes within the magazine. In 'Astrea Brokage', published in the January issue of 1770, the narrator claims to 'know all the real names of your Tête-à-têtes', as though it were a qualification for entry into magazine culture.

With this qualification in purview Chatterton brings his own interests to the magazine. In 'Sad Dog' Chatterton ridicules Walpole and the Society of Antiquaries, depicted here as a fusty and pompous club of disinterested clergymen and Latinists who believe the derivation of *kine* from *cowine* to be 'one of the most important discoveries'. And yet Chatterton was elsewhere a professed antiquarian. 'I am versed a little in antiquities', he writes to Walpole, seeking his patronage. If we follow Lionel Trilling's suggestion that eighteenth-century sincerity is defined by our recorded actions, then Chatterton is a sincere antiquary.[54] His Rowley project was erected from a vast body of antiquarian sources from Camden to Gough. Many of his creative 'antiquarian' works perform an authenticating function. 'Antiquity of Christmas Games' is a history of drama that legitimizes *Ælla*, and Chatterton's other ancient efforts, as evidence of Bristol's achievements in medieval drama ('I ... cannot think our ancestors so ignorant of dramatic excellence as the generality of modern writers would represent').[55] It also offers a ready example of Chatterton's attempts to reconcile antiquarian audiences with the fashionable new audiences of 'the sentimental': moderns 'may paint in more lively colours to the eye' but ancients 'spoke to the heart'.[56]

Playfully in 'Sad Dog', Chatterton alludes to serious antiquarian tomes (Camden, Dugdale, Leland and Weever) at the same time as pirating earlier sources from the *Town and Country*. In October 1769 'Theates Aoratus' resolves an inscription from the previous issue: 'Here reposeth Claud Coster, Tripe-seller of Impington, As doth also his

Consort Jane'.[57] In 'Sad Dog' Baron Otranto finds 'a stone which had no antiquity at all' but, determined to employ his 'speculative talents', he attempts to decipher it. Taking at face value Harry's assertion that the original inscription was 'James Hicks lieth here, with Hester his wife', we can see that Otranto has over-elaborately construed '*Hic jacet corpus Kenelmœ Sancto Legero. Requiescat, &c, &c*' from:

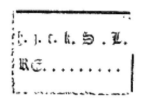

By performing the *Town and Country* solution rather than using Olaus Worm's *Lexicon Runicum*, a source visible elsewhere in Chatterton's 'Fragmentes of Anticquitie', pulp literature has trumped Enlightenment antiquarianism. This was not the *Gentleman's Magazine* after all; Chatterton knew his audience. Many of the works attributed to Chatterton that were published in the *Town and Country* are dubious, especially the Hunter of Oddities series.[58] This reveals a lot about the emphasis placed on intertextuality in the magazine and how fully Chatterton revels in its communal horizon of expectations.

As well as undermining the intellectual grounding of his own conjectural antiquarianism, Chatterton was not above lambasting his own reliance on the Ossianic sublime as a source for his Rowley project. In 'Sad Dog' Harry suddenly adopts 'the language of high-sounding Ossian' as the only suitable literary means to describe sex with the alderman's wife:

> The wild boar makes ready his armour of defence. The inhabitants of the rocks dance, and all nature joins in the song. But see! riding on the wings of the wind, the black clouds fly. The noisy thunders roar; the rapid lightnings gleam; the rainy torrents pour, and the dropping swain flies over the mountain.

Two days after asking *Town and Country* to print 'Ethelgar', moreover, Chatterton burlesques heroic language in a letter to his best friend:

> my friendship is as firm as the white Rocks when the black Waves roar around it, and the waters burst on its hoary top, when the driving wind ploughs the sable Sea, and the rising waves aspire the

clouds teeming with the rattling Hail; so much of Heroics; to speak in plain English, I am and ever will be your unalterable Friend.[59]

'Ethelgar', in sync with Chatterton's other Ossianics, has: 'Comely as the white rocks; bright as the star of the evening; tall as the oak upon the brow of the mountain; soft as the showers of dew, that fall upon the flowers of the field, Ethelgar arose, the glory of Exanceastre [Exeter]'.[60] Which is the 'authentic' Chatterton, or whether we assume the private letter to be the most logically authentic source, is beside the point. Chatterton frequently pirates the fashionable Ossianic style, although he pushes it into caricature. This self-critique makes visible the problem of locating an authentic Chatterton in his text. Against the backdrop of this intertextual magazine culture instead we can witness a young author exploiting the materials around him to create a witty and insightful literary collage of such a culture.

1778–1971

This witty engagement with the idiom of the *Town and Country* is obfuscated when 'Sad Dog' is singled out in the 1786 issue of *The New Novelists Magazine* along with his 'Maria Friendless' and 'Godred Crovan' and certainly in its narrowly libertine reorientation in the 1778 *Miscellanies*. In the *New Novelists* version Chatterton himself is 'A SAD DOG', as the label is associated with the authorship, with Harry Wildfire elided. The phrase 'sad dog' has its own literary history into which the historical Chatterton was by then appropriated. In *A Classical Dictionary of the Vulgar Tongue*, Francis Grose has:

SAD DOG, a wicked, debauched fellow, one of the ancient family of sad dogs, Swift translates it into Latin by the words, *tristis canis*.[61]

Other than by Swift, the phrase had been used early in the eighteenth century (and before) to loosely denote a vice-ridden, debauched counterculture. Tobias Smollett's *Roderick Random* (1748), a novel frequently mentioned in the *Town and Country*, has a sad-dog fortune-hunter seeking his own 'five thousand pounder':

When we had feasted sumptuously ... he began thus, 'I suppose you think me a sad dog, Mr. Random, and I do confess that appearances are against me – but ... I am to marry very soon ... a five thousand pounder ... '

A 1773 translation of Martial and Horace has a long digression on the motto 'Beware of Dogs!'[62] There is a now a 'certain kind of *Dogs* called Sad Dogs: too many of which are now running about the *Nation*'. In the new political climate 'Patriotism flys so much about' that these dogs, like Beelzebub, seek 'whom They may devour'. By the mid-century 'sad dog' had acquired specifically Wilkesite overtones.[63] The profligacy of John Wilkes and his supporters was widely discussed in the gossipy magazines and newspapers in the 1760s, especially *Town and Country*. Chatterton would have certainly been aware of the scandal caused by his infamous No. 45 issue of *The North Briton*, a Scotophobic attack on Lord Bute and the King in April 1763. Wilkes was arrested for seditious libel. Let off on a technicality he was soon arrested when an open-ended warrant unearthed the manuscript of his pornographic *Essay on Woman*. Exiled in the mid-1760s, the street soon rang to the chants of 'Wilkes and Liberty' when he re-entered politics in 1768. Wilkes was fearless of arrest – no doubt exploiting its popularizing appeal – even if the radical publishers were not. Junius, a popular and mysterious 1760s satirist much admired by Chatterton, endorsed the appropriateness of Wilkes's canny exploitation of persecution; it allowed his authentic patriotism to thrive.[64]

Chatterton was familiar with Johnson's *The False Alarm* (1770), a short polemic that dismisses the patriotism of oppositional Whigs as '*false patriotism* that pretended love of freedom, that unruly restlessness'.[65] In the Tory view patriots like Wilkes are insincere, self-interested political and social upstarts. There was an ungentlemanly, Currlite overtone to Wilkes's and the Wilkesites' exploitation of the popular press. Written by a patriot sad dog, 'which none but a sad dog could write', so the *Gentleman's Magazine* assumed, Chatterton's seemingly authentic pro-Wilkes piece becomes embroiled in this contemporary debate about the sincerity of oppositional patriots.[66] Fittingly many pro-Wilkes pieces that have been ascribed to Chatterton appear in the large Works of Doubtful Authenticity section of the modern canon.[67] In addition to this, Meyerstein introduces a Chatterton letter attacking Wilkes, in the hand of Michael Lort the antiquary. It concludes: 'Mr Wilkes now shines at the head of the patriots. He is the epitome of the faction; self-interested, treasonable and inconsiderable. That minister must be virtuous who is opposed by such pretended Patriots'.[68] As is typical of Chatterton, he even mocks his own pretensions as a boy poet and supporter of John Wilkes in terms that suggest he is far from original or sincere: 'Now infant authors, madd'ning for renown … [Rave] about Wilkes, and politics, and Bute'.[69] Much of this interplay is obfuscated in this reorientation of the piece.

Whatever Chatterton's views, 'Sad Dog' had been firmly associated with Chatterton in his libertine *Miscellanies* of 1778. David Fairer is right to suggest that with the appearance of *Miscellanies* in 1778 readers were officially acquainted with the 'libertarian and satiric Chatterton', very different to the charity schoolboy who unearthed and disturbed the found Rowley texts.[70] His name was by now associated with the new-old Rowley poems more conclusively, following the authoritative pronouncements of Thomas Warton and Thomas Tyrwhitt. With the ongoing unification of the Chatterton canon there were even attempts in the 1780s to push the faux-medieval poems into a wholly modern, Wilkesite orientation, in order to reconcile the canon, as a trajectory of this local celebration of Chatterton.[71] Characters from Chatterton's works are reconfigured as modern liberals: 'The *charitable Priest* attends,/And *patriot Goddwyn* joins the Throng'.[72] Chatterton's libertine works had been available in the *Town and Country* but pseudonymously of course. It is the *Miscellanies* that codifies him as a libertine writer, with its inauthentic frontispiece of Lord Mayor Beckford and various misattributed pro-Wilkes pieces brought together under the banner of Thomas Chatterton, modern writer, one who was not a mere hack of course.

Despite reproducing the *Miscellanies* as one volume of the three-volume 1803 edition, co-edited with Robert Southey, Joseph Cottle later dismissed the modern works as beneath Chatterton's talents, and hence dismissed their authorial authenticity. 'Sad Dog', and most of the *Miscellanies*, could not possibly be Chatterton's as they do not come close to the poetic achievements of the Rowley project:

> This opportunity is taken to do some justice to the memory of Chatterton ... A subsequent examination, however, with some fresh sources of information, has satisfied them [Southey and Cottle] that the 'Memoirs of a Sad Dog' (a low and worthless piece) ... was *not* written by him. This remark applies to several of the other pieces.[73]

More recently, in accounting for the authenticity of pieces ascribed to Chatterton in the first modern-work collection, Donald Taylor describes the Ossianic *Gorthmund* and 'the obviously autobiographical' 'Sad Dog' as 'both very easy guesses' contra Cottle.[74] Authenticity is a fraught issue in Chatterton's canon. Not only because he was a medieval forger by night and a raffish Modern by day, but because the Modern hacks were far from transient. Literature at large is a spurious enterprise in which the sincerity of the author taunts the critic and the reader. Which is the authentic Chatterton? What would that question even mean in the 1760s? There is a danger of isolating Chatterton from the environs of the magazine culture he engaged with in works like 'Sad Dog' even in the critical act of understanding him in such contexts. Canonical literary histories return on us, reminding us that in the Romantic process of individuating authors Chatterton was also different to these hacks; he is given to us as the creator of the Rowleyan curiosities when many of the wonderfully playful hacks of this generation remain undisturbed. But Johnson was right and wrong – this magazine culture was 'temporary' in that many of these writers failed to achieve Chatterton's belated status as the 'literary phenomenon of the times', rising above the 'trash of monthly compilations', and yet their intertextual piracies gave magazine culture a literary sense that has been too long ignored.[75]

Notes

1. Thomas Chatterton, *Poems, supposed to have been written by Thomas Rowley*, ed. Thomas Tyrwhitt (London, 1777), p. xii. For Chatterton's life and fame see E. H. W. Meyerstein, *A Life of Thomas Chatterton* (London, 1930), hereafter cited as *Life*. Also Linda Kelly, *The Marvellous Boy: The Life and Myth of Thomas Chatterton* (London, 1971) and *Thomas Chatterton and Romantic Culture*, ed. Nick Groom with a foreword by Peter Ackroyd (Basingstoke, 1999; repr. 2001), hereafter cited as *Romantic Culture*. Also *The Complete Works of Thomas Chatterton: A Bicentenary Edition*, ed. Donald S. Taylor and Benjamin B. Hoover. 2 vols (Oxford, 1971). Hereafter cited as *Works*.
2. For the philological orientation of early discussion in the Clubs see Pat Rogers, 'Chatterton and the Club', *Romantic Culture*, pp. 121–51. For the longer relationship between forgery and textual authority see Anthony Grafton, *Forgers and Critics: Creativity and Duplicity in Western Scholarship* (Princeton, 1990).
3. See Maria Grazia Lolla, '"Truth Sacrifising to the Muses": The Rowley Controversy and the Genesis of the Romantic Chatterton', *Romantic Culture*, pp. 151–72.
4. Similarly the *Gentleman's Magazine* attacks the *Supplement to the Miscellanies of Thomas Chatterton* (London, 1784): 'Nothing but the name of Chatterton could ever gain such trash a second reading' (November 1784), pp. 848–9. For the Sternean novel and the moderns see Thomas Keymer, *Sterne, the Moderns, and the Novel* (Oxford, 2002).
5. *Gentleman's Magazine* (September 1778), p. 424.
6. Michael Lort to Horace Walpole, 29 July 1778, *Horace Walpole's Correspondence*, eds W. S. Lewis et al. (New Haven, 1937–83) Vol. 16, p. 177.
7. For the complex relationship between spurious forgery and legitimate literature see Nick Groom, *The Forger's Shadow: How Forgery Changed the Course of Literature* (London, 2002) and 'Thomas Chatterton Was A Forger', *The Yearbook of English Studies* **28** (1998), pp. 278–91. Also see Nick Groom and Charlie Blake, 'Introduction', *Narratives of Forgery*, ed. Nick Groom, *Angelaki* 1:2 (winter 03/04).

8. Herbert Croft, *Love and Madness* (London, 1780), p. 234.
9. Vicesimus Knox, 'On the Poems attributed to Rowley', *Essays, Moral and Literary* (London, 1782), p. 249.
10. Samuel Johnson, *Dictionary of the English Language* (London, 1755).
11. Thomas Warton, *An Enquiry into the Authenticity of the Poems attributed to Thomas Rowley* (London, 1782), p. 90.
12. Thomas Chatterton, *Miscellanies*, pp. ix–xxiii.
13. Donald S. Taylor, 'The Authenticity of Chatterton's *Miscellanies in Prose and Verse*', *The Papers of The Bibliographical Society of America*, **55** (1961), pp. 289–96. Although see Claude Rawson, 'Unparodying and Forgery: The Augustan Chatterton', *Romantic Culture*, pp. 15–32 for a superb account of impersonation and forgery in the modern and Rowleyan works.
14. Michael F. Suarez, SJ, '"This Necessary Knowledge": Thomas Chatterton and the Ways of the London Book Trade', *Romantic Culture*, pp. 96–113 (p. 111). Donald Taylor challenges a distinction between Chatterton's careers as the Rowleyan dreamer and modern hack in 'Chatterton: The Problem of Rowley Chronology and Its Implications', *Philological Quarterly*, **46** (1967), pp. 268–76.
15. Claude Rawson, *Satire and Sentiment 1660–1830: Stress Points in the English Augustan Tradition* (New Haven and London, 1994). Thomas Lockwood, *Post-Augustan Satire: Charles Churchill and Satirical Poetry, 1750–1800* (Seattle and London, 1979).
16. Pat Rogers, *Grub Street* (London, 1972) and *Hacks and Dunces* (London, 1980), Jeremy Treglown ed. *Grub Street and the Ivory Tower* (Oxford, 1998), Philip Pinkus, *Grub Street Stripped Bare* (London, 1968), Nigel Cross, *The Common Writer: Life in Nineteenth-Century Grub Street* (Cambridge, 1985) and Brean Hammond, *Professional Imaginative Writing in England, 1670–1740* (Oxford, 1997).
17. Bryant Lillywhite, *London Coffee Houses* (London, 1963), pp. 151–5, 581–5. Thomas Chatterton to Mary Newton, 30 May 1770 *Works*, Vol. I, pp. 587–89.
18. Pinkus, *Grub Street* p. 71.
19. Chatterton, *Miscellanies*, p. 207. Alexander Pope and Jonathan Swift, *Miscellanies in Prose and Verse: The First Volume* (London, 1727): 'Having both of us been extreamly [sic] ill treated by some Booksellers, (especially one *Edmund Curll*,) it was our Opinion that the best Method we could take for justifying ourselves, would be to publish whatever loose Papers in Prose and Verse, we have formerly written', pp. 3–4. 'Literary pirate' is Pinkus's phrase, p. 52.
20. Louise J. Kaplan, *The Family Romance of the Imposter-Poet Thomas Chatterton* (Berkeley and Los Angeles, 1987; repr. 1989), p. 178. See *Works* II: 1100–2 for a verbal comparison of Chatterton and Johnson. I am arguing that Chatterton's changes are extensive in terms of rearrangement and context if not verbally.
21. Nick Groom, 'Forgery or Plagiarism? Unravelling Chatterton's Rowley', *Narratives of Forgery*, ed. Nick Groom, *Angelaki* **1**:2 (winter 03/04), p. 43.
22. K. K. Ruthven, *Faking Literature* (Cambridge, 2001), pp. 146–71.
23. See *Life*, pp. 416–9.
24. For example, John Oakman, *The Life and Adventures of Benjamin Brass, an Irish Fortune-Hunter* (London, 1765) and Edward Kimber, *The Life and Adventures of Joe Thompson* (London, 1750).

25. Stockjobber: 'a low wretch who gets money by buying and selling shares in the funds', Samuel Johnson, *Dictionary.*
26. Suarez, 'This Necessary Knowledge,' p. 99.
27. Ibid., p. 98.
28. [John Taylor], *The History of the Travels and Adventures of the Chevalier John Taylor, Opthalmiator* (London, 1761–62). *Works* is a wonderful resource for references such as this, although sometimes Taylor provides erroneous dates or follows later editions.
29. Ian Haywood, *Faking It: Art and the Politics of Forgery* (Sussex, 1987), p. 34. For copyright issues see Mark Rose, 'The Author in Court: *Pope v. Curll* (1741)', *The Construction of Authorship: Textual Appropriation in Law and Literature*, eds Martha Woodmansee and Peter Jaszi (Durham and London, 1994), pp. 211–31.
30. [Richard Savage], *An Author to be Lett* (London, 1729), partly quoted in *Faking It*, p. 34. An aptronym is a name that aptly describes the person. It is an authentic name, as it were. For Curll's rumoured mistreatment of his hacks see Ralph Strauss, *The Unspeakable Curll* (London, 1927). Also Samuel Johnson, *Life of Savage* (London, 1744)
31. For the interchange of 'the "authentic" authority' of Walpole and Chatterton as forger see Marlon B. Ross, 'Authority and Authenticity: Scribbling Authors and the Genius of Print in Eighteenth-Century England', *The Construction of Authorship*, p. 253. For Chatterton's appeals to James Dodsley and Horace Walpole see *Life*, *passim*, and Suarez, 'This Necessary Knowledge', pp. 100–2.
32. Thomas Amory's *The Life of John Buncle* has an oft-cited description of Curll. Amongst other things he is a 'debauchee'.
33. Chatterton, *Works*, Vol. I, p. 561.
34. For 'plagiaristic practices' see Robert D. Mayo, *The English Novel in the Magazines 1740–1815* (London, 1962), pp. 225–8.
35. Edward W. R. Pitcher, *An Anatomy of Reprintings and Plagiarisms: Finding Keys to Editorial Practices and Magazine History, 1730–1820* (New York, 2000), pp. 89–103.
36. Thomas Keymer, *Sterne, the Moderns, and the Novel* (Oxford, 2002) , op. cit., 153ff.
37. Ibid., pp. 158–65 and Lance Bertelsen, *The Nonsense Club: Literature and Popular Culture, 1749–1764* (Oxford, 1986).
38. *Works*, Vol. I, pp. 338–9.
39. Pitcher, p. 20. Eleanor Jane Drake Mitchell, 'The Tête-à-Têtes and Other Biography in the *Town and Country Magazine*, 1769–1796' (unpublished doctoral thesis, University of Maryland, 1967). Mitchell says *Town and Country* had 'superior literary offerings'. Robert D. Mayo calls *Town and Country* 'townish' as opposed to 'genteel' (such as *Lady's Magazine*), *English Novel*, p. 188.
40. Walter Graham, *English Literary Periodicals* (New York, 1930); *British Literary Magazines: The Augustan Age and the Age of Johnson, 1698–1788*, ed. Alvin Sullivan (Connecticut and London, 1983), pp. 327–30.
41. Markman Ellis, *The Politics of Sensibility: Race, Gender and Commerce in the Sentimental Novel* (Cambridge University Press, 1996), p. 39.
42. *Town and Country* (April 1769), pp. 174–5.
43. Melvin R. Watson, *Magazine Serials and the Essay Tradition, 1746–1820* (Baton Rouge, 1956), pp. 3, 13–14, 50 and *passim*.
44. *Memoirs of the Celebrated Miss Fanny M---*, 2nd edn (London, 1759), pp. i–vi.

45. See Chung Nan Lee, 'A Study of the *Town and Country Magazine*' (unpublished doctoral thesis, New York University, 1963). Whereas Lee suggests the column is scandal-mongering on the whole, Eleanor Mitchell suggests they are 'remarkably accurate', 'Tête-à-Têtes' p. 3.
46. *Town and Country* (April 1769), pp. 183–4.
47. Walpole, *Horace Walpole's Correspondence*, Vol. 2, pp. 107–10 and Vol. 16, p. 347. In his copy of *Miscellanies* Walpole writes his own initials in the margin against 'the redoubted baron Otranto': 'Mr H. W. author of the *Castle of Otranto*'. Also see *Life*, pp. 272, 416–18.
48. Chatterton, *Works*, Vol. II, p. 1111.
49. *Life*, p. 254n.
50. 'The Polite Advertiser' appeared in *Town and Country* the same month as the first half of 'Sad Dog' did, July 1770. It is catalogued under 'Works of Doubtful Authenticity' in *Works*.
51. See R. W. Ketton-Cremer, *Horace Walpole: A Biography* (London, 1964), p. 265.
52. 'The Advice', *Town and Country* (Supplement 1769). Also *Exhibitions* in *Middlesex Journal* (26 May 1770).
53. Mitchell, 'Tête-à-Têtes' p. 7.
54. Lionel Trilling, *Sincerity and Authenticity* (London, 1972).
55. Possibly written as early as October 1768 (see *Works*, Vol. II, p. 1014), printed in *Town and Country* (December 1769), p. 623. *Miscellanies*, p. 133.
56. *Miscellanies*, p. 130.
57. *Town and Country* (October 1769), p. 550 and (September 1769), p. 464. *Life*, p. 272.
58. See *Works, passim*.
59. Chatterton to John Baker, 6 March 1769, *Works* Vol. I, p. 256. For the parody of Ossian in 'Sad Dog' see Donald S. Taylor, *Thomas Chatterton's, Art*, pp. 273–4.
60. Chatterton, *Miscellanies*, p. 6. Because of the scholarly effort required, 'Chatterton's Ossianics were for him neither joke nor hackwork' (*Thomas Chatterton's Art*, p. 282). This seems too causal and unnecessarily clear-cut to me.
61. Francis Grose, *A Classical Dictionary of the Vulgar Tongue* (London, 1785). Grose's dictionary was frequently pirated. For example, James Caulfield's *Blackguardiana: or, a dictionary of rogues, bawds, pimps, whores, pickpockets, shoplifters* (London, 1793).
62. 'To Charles Vere, Esq', *Epigrams of Martial, &c. with mottos from Horace, &c. translated, imitated, adapted, and addrest to the nobility, clergy, and gentry. With notes*, ed. Rev. Mr. [William] Scott (London, 1773), pp. 246–50.
63. Thomas Bridges refers to the 'dirty joking' of baboon-like Wilkesites in his update of Homer, *A Burlesque Translation of Homer. In Two Volumes*, 4th edn (London, 1797), Vol. I, p. 95. For a discussion of Curlism and libertinism in the *Pamela* controversy see James Grantham Turner, 'Novel Panic: Picture and Performance in the Reception of Richardson's *Pamela*', *Representations*, No. 48 (Autumn 1994), pp. 70–96 (p. 81).
64. Junius to Lord Grafton, *The Letters of Junius* (London, 1770). His letters were frequently printed in the magazines throughout the 1760s and this is not the first collection. The patriot *Middlesex Journal* printed seven of Chatterton's eight Decimus letters in 1770. Modelled on Junius they often addressed Grafton.

65. See Michael Meehan, *Liberty and Poetics in Eighteenth-Century England* (London, 1986), pp. 124–31. See also Gösta Langenfelt, 'Patriotism and Scoundrels', *Neophilogus*, **17**:1 (1932), pp. 32–41.
66. Hans Robert Jauss, 'Literary History as a Challenge to Literary Theory', *Toward an Aesthetic of Reception*, trans. Timothy Bahti with an introduction by Paul de Man (Minneapolis, 1982).
67. *Works*, Vol. II, pp. 688–767.
68. *Life*, p. 369.
69. 'February', *Town and Country* (February 1770), ll.13–32.
70. David Fairer, 'Chatterton's Poetic Afterlife, 1770–1794: A Context for Coleridge's *Monody*', *Romantic Culture*, pp. 228–52 (p. 250, n. 18).
71. See Robert W. Jones, '"We Proclaim our Darling Son": The Politics of Chatterton's Memory during the War for America', *The Review of English Studies* (2002), pp. 373–95.
72. Richard Jenkins, *The Ode, Songs, Chorusses, &c. for the concert in commemoration of Chatterton, the celebrated British poet* (London, 1784).
73. Joseph Cottle, *Early Recollections* (London, 1837), II: 293n. Meyerstein assumes Cottle is inventing his 'fresh sources', *Life*, 416n.
74. Taylor, 'The Authenticity of Chatterton's *Miscellanies in Prose and Verse*', pp. 289–96.
75. Chatterton, *Miscellanies*, pp. ix–xxiii.

Part II
Acts of Sincerity

4
The Scandal of Sincerity: Wordsworth, Byron, Landon

Angela Esterhammer

'Sincerity', as a critical concept, did not do very well in the twentieth century. The New Critics, in particular, were unimpressed with an interpretative criterion that seemed to emphasize authorial intention; to them, 'Is the poet sincere?' was 'always an impertinent and illegitimate question'.[1] In philosophical terms, too, sincerity has been displaced and overshadowed since Heidegger and Sartre by the notion of authenticity, which can be applied to objects, works of art or human subjects, in the context of ontology, epistemology or aesthetics. Although elusive, authenticity has proved an effective and adaptable notion for what we recognize, in the mode of nostalgia or desire, as a free and truthful relation to the world.

Compared with the diffuse concept of authenticity, sincerity has somewhat more specific criteria and a longer, if chequered, history. In its modern usage, 'sincerity' can only be applied to human beings and human action, and it always involves a relation between inward disposition and outward expression. From the Latin *sincēr-us* 'clean, pure, sound', it was originally applied to physical substances such as wine or bodily fluids to mean 'pure' or 'unmixed'. Taking on a figurative meaning in religious literature during the seventeenth century, this notion of purity came to be applied to the soul and to a person's disposition; a 'sincere' Christian, in the terms of the *Oxford English Dictionary*, is 'not falsified or perverted in any way', but, rather, 'characterized by the absence of all dissimulation or pretence'. With this idea of dissimulation, two very important notions become attached to sincerity: that of correspondence between (inner) reality and (outward) appearance, and that of *not pretending* or *not acting*. Nowadays, the adjective 'sincere' can no longer be applied to water or urine, but only to human forms of expression: a sincere promise, a sincere apology, sincere appreciation, or 'sincerely' at the close of a letter, implying (at least by convention) a correspondence between what the letter-writer actually feels and what he or she has written. The notion of a 'sincere intention' is somewhat more internalized, but even here the criterion of sincerity is only meaningful when the inward intention can be tested against the resulting visible behaviour. One can refer to a person as 'sincere', but this is an applied sense of the word used when the person's disposition, as manifested in behaviour, is usually or always seen to correspond with his or her verbal self-expression. At the beginning of his insightful book *Sincerity and Authenticity*, Lionel Trilling defines sincerity as 'a congruence between avowal and actual feeling'.[2] The relevance of sincerity to verbal expression and the public sphere is also reflected by its prominence in the Anglo-American speech-act theory of J. L. Austin and, even more, John Searle. With the notion of *Wahrhaftigkeit* (veracity), it turns up again in another influential theory of verbal utterance, the universal pragmatics of Jürgen Habermas.

Intention, then, must be visible and readable in some external manner – through speech, behaviour, gesture or facial expression – in order for the standard of sincerity to come into play. To put it somewhat more polemically, intention must be *performed* – and, as soon as it is, it enters the realm of the socially determined codes and conventions by which speech-acts, gestures and expressions are interpreted by others. Trilling makes the interesting observation that 'sincerity' entered the English language during the first third of the sixteenth century, which is also the epoch of 'the sudden efflorescence of the theatre'.[3] This paradoxical conjunction between sincerity and theatricality famously recurs with reference to Romanticism in Matthew Arnold's 1881 preface to the *Poetry of Byron*. Echoing Swinburne, Arnold identifies 'the splendid and imperishable excellence of sincerity and strength' as the crucial attribute of Byron's poetry – while, in the same breath, critiquing the 'affectations and silliness' of 'the theatrical Byron'.[4] Once again, sincerity and theatricality appear oddly conjoined. By definition, sincerity is anti-performative – 'not feigned or pretended', in the words of the *OED* – yet an awareness of sincerity seems to arise amidst heightened theatricality. Hence the scandal of sincerity: it is inimical to performativity; however, it must be read in or on the body, and through the semiotic systems by which body language gets interpreted, and in that sense it is coextensive with performance.

I take the term 'scandal' from Shoshana Felman, whose 1980 book *Le Scandale du corps parlant* was recently reissued in English translation, this time under its original title: *The Scandal of the Speaking Body* (it had previously been published as *The Literary Speech Act*). In this study of speech-acts in philosophy and literature, Felman shows that:

> The [human] act, an enigmatic and problematic production of the *speaking body*, destroys from its inception the metaphysical dichotomy between the domain of the 'mental' and the domain of the 'physical', breaks down the opposition between body and spirit, between matter and language.[5]

The body, as the inalienably organic and material component of action, ensures that acts (including speech-acts) are never pure representations of spiritual or mental intention. As Judith Butler explains in her Afterword to Felman's book, 'the body signifies what is unintentional, what is *not* admitted into the domain of "intention"' – that is, 'primary longings, the unconscious and its aims'.[6] In order to be expressed in speech or action, intention must open itself up to the unconscious or the non-intentional, just as the anti-performative mode of sincerity must open itself up to performance.

If Felman shows that the components of interior intention and verbal expression are incompatible but inseparable, the concept of sincerity brings still another component into play that is at odds with both of the first two. This is the realm of semiotic codes and conventions by which we evaluate the physical or verbal expressions of others. A word, like a gesture or a look, only has meaning within a societal context, in relation to other signs and to other occasions on which the same signs have been used. By definition, sincerity demands an exact correspondence between state of mind and expression; yet the only available forms of expression demand to be interpreted according to public codes that belong to a different semiotic system than private mental states.

The concept of sincerity, then, involves three distinct registers: interior states of mind and emotions; speech and body language; and the social codes used to interpret language. Identifying these three levels brings into clearer focus the connotations that 'sincerity' has taken on in recent studies of Romantic literature. In *The Romantic Ideology* (1983) and other works, including his extensive studies of Byron, Jerome McGann resurrects sincerity in the form of a trope, or as what he calls the '*conventions* of sincerity' that characterize Romantic poetry. '[T]he fact that ... the famous "true voice of feeling" is an artful construction' in Romanticism, writes McGann, 'remains widely unappreciated'.[7] Similarly, in the context of a reading of Byron, Ian Dennis discusses sincerity as 'one move in the game', and two recent books analyse sincerity in nineteenth-century literature as a prevailing construct or a far-reaching convention.[8] In *Sincerity's Shadow* (Harvard University Press, 2004), Deborah Forbes redefines sincerity as a self-consciously constructed dimension of British Romantic and twentieth-century American lyric poetry, while Pam Morris, in her *Imagining Inclusive Society in Nineteenth-Century Novels: The Code of Sincerity in the Public Sphere* (2004), treats sincerity as a public, performative code based on a false assumption of shared inner feeling. Reading political and non-fictional writers of the 1840s such as Carlyle and Gladstone, Morris examines the way leadership in the public sphere was constructed as a 'public interpellative code', relying on an already existing post-Romantic 'assumption of common human interiority'.[9]

These recent readings of Romantic sincerity as a convention or code form a small second wave of 'sincerity studies', following on a brief but distinct resurgence of interest in the concept of sincerity in philosophy and literary criticism during the 1960s and 1970s, after it had fallen completely out of favour at the height of the mid-twentieth-century New Critical era. The decade of renewed interest beginning around 1963 resulted in a number of important publications on the philosophical definition of sincerity, and its relevance for literature and aesthetics, by writers including Donald Davie, Patricia Meyer Spacks, Herbert Read, Stuart Hampshire and Lionel Trilling.[10] As far as Romantic studies are concerned, this was the era that identified Romanticism, and the poetry of Wordsworth in particular, as the inauguration of a new ideal of sincerity that has influenced poetic practice ever since. 'In the transformation of poetry throughout the eighteenth century', writes David Perkins at the beginning of *Wordsworth and the Poetry of Sincerity* (1964), 'nothing is more remarkable than the emergence of sincerity as a major poetic value, and, indeed, as something required of all artists. One can hardly overstress the novelty of this demand.'[11] A decade later, Leon Guilhamet's *The Sincere Ideal* traced the growth of sincerity as a literary value through the eighteenth century, culminating with Wordsworth as the first poet to take sincerity for granted and theorize it in his Preface to *Lyrical Ballads*, which Guilhamet calls 'a revolutionary presentation of the first elaborate theory of sincerity'.[12]

This two-phase return of the criterion of sincerity into literary criticism, then, records the major changes of perspective that have taken place in Romantic studies over the past generation. The first wave of 'sincerity studies' in the 1960s and 1970s focused on Wordsworth and recognized him, against an eighteenth-century background, as the first poet to cultivate sincerity as a poetic value. A recent, second wave, which is much more likely to adopt Byron as its model, interprets sincerity as a code or convention, thereby historicizing Romanticism as a movement defined by its materialistically determined construction of its own values. In turning now to three Romantic literary treatments of sincerity – Wordsworth on epitaph and elegy, and Byron's and Landon's critiques of Regency society – I would like to revisit this apparent contrast. Although these three reflections on sincerity appear at first to be poles apart, my contention is that they actually form a continuum: that Byron and Landon develop a paradoxical notion of *performative sincerity* that is at least latent in Wordsworth. In doing so, moreover, Byron and Landon shape the context in which the later Wordsworth enters the early Victorian public sphere. In this reading, both the 'essential' and the 'constructed' sincerity that critics have associated with Wordsworth and Byron, respectively, form part of a more deliberate and sustained Romantic analysis of sincerity that probes the limits of expressibility and interpretability.

Wordsworth's revolution in poetic form in the Preface to *Lyrical Ballads*, although not explicitly under the rubric of sincerity, evokes this concept through his promotion of 'the spontaneous overflow of powerful feelings' and the notion of poetry as lived experience. His 'Essays upon Epitaphs' explicitly invoke sincerity, and effect a transition from the religious connotations of the word to new, literary-critical ones by undertaking literary interpretations of the epitaphs inscribed on gravestones, a form of writing in which serious and spiritual purpose is paramount. In the second of the three essays, which was written around 1810 but not published during his lifetime, Wordsworth seeks a 'criterion of sincerity' by which epitaphs could be tested for correspondence with the 'primary sensations' from which mourning should spring, so as to determine 'that the Author [of an epitaph] was a sincere mourner'.[13] The stylistic criteria he identifies are, according to David Perkins' summary, 'a colloquial diction, an informal syntax, a natural or psychologically probable movement of thought', and 'strong passion'.[14] But it is not clear how any of these criteria manages to bridge the gap between the lines engraved on a tombstone and the writer's state of mind. While diction and syntax are features of the written text (and not of the writer), 'strong passion' can only be a state evoked in the reader by the text, or attributed to the writer on the basis of the text, not a quality of the text itself. The 'Essays on Epitaphs' already point towards the scandal of sincerity, by defining sincerity as the correspondence between the external signs on the gravestone and the writer's inner feeling, while eliding the fact that the only evidence for the writer's feeling *is* the external signs or words.

Notwithstanding this paradox, Wordsworth goes on to develop his primary criterion for sincerity in epitaphs, namely, the absence of performance or affectation:

> For, when a Man is treating an interesting subject, or one which he ought not to treat at all unless he be interested, no faults have such a killing power as those which prove that he is not in earnest, that he is acting a part, has leisure for affectation, and feels that without it he could do nothing. This is one of the most odious of faults; because it shocks the moral sense: and is worse in a sepulchral inscription, precisely in the same degree as that mode of composition calls for sincerity more urgently than any other. And indeed, where the internal evidence proves that the Writer was moved, in other words where this charm of sincerity lurks in the language of a Tombstone and secretly pervades it, there are no errors in style or manner for which it will not be, in some degree, a recompence; but without habits of reflection a test of this inward simplicity cannot be come at: and, as I have said, I am now writing with a hope to assist the well-disposed to attain it.[15]

The key distinction here is between 'sincerity' and 'acting a part'. Wordsworth proposes to guide the reader in learning the 'habits of reflection', and the habits of reading, that will allow him to discern the text's 'internal evidence' for the writer's sincerity. Leaving aside the oddity of Wordsworth's diction here, as he calls sincerity (surely a quality that demands plainness and transparency) a 'charm' that 'secretly' 'lurks' in language, it is worth noting that the examples of epitaphs he goes on to analyse are by no means unambiguous. Extravagant language and hyperbolic imagery, the features that most attract Wordsworth's attention in the epitaphs he considers, sometimes signal falsity and insincerity, but in other cases they signal the mental strain the writer is under, or his inability to express his vital feelings – in other words, the same internal features of the text may just as well be signs of *sincerity*. A more consistent criterion than diction and imagery, it turns out, is *spontaneity*. The kind of epitaph Wordsworth finds most praiseworthy is a 'simple effusion of the moment';[16] he gives the example of a stanza on the death of Charles I, spontaneously inscribed by a noble soldier with the point of his sword. 'Errors in style or manner', by contrast, are unimportant as long as the crucial criteria of simplicity and spontaneity can be discerned.

Wordsworth's 1835 poem entitled 'Extempore Effusion upon the Death of James Hogg' provides a relevant example of his own writing on the subject of death, and of the criterion of spontaneity in particular. I will return shortly to the poem's title, only noting for now its echo of the 'simple *effusion* of the moment' that Wordsworth praises in his second essay on epitaphs. Wordsworth mentions the spontaneous composition of his elegy in the notes he dictated to Isabella Fenwick in 1843, which were eventually published together with the poem. Noting that 'these verses were written extempore' in November 1835, immediately after reading in the newspaper of the death of his fellow poet, James Hogg, Wordsworth underlines the purpose of the title 'Extempore Effusion': to intensify, even to guarantee, the emotional authenticity of the poem by presenting it as an immediate, unpremeditated response to news of a death.[17]

The poem's presentation as a spontaneous utterance, however, contrasts with its formal symmetries and reflective tone. Even if stimulated by an intensely present shock, the 'Extempore Effusion' begins in a recollective mode: not with the present impetus for emotion, but with the memory of an early encounter with James Hogg. It continues in a reflective past tense, drawing its emotional power from contrasts between the past (the memories of friends) and the present (the perception of their absence). The mood of the poem is solitary and subjective, focusing on the emotive relationship between the 'I' and a series of remembered figures: James Hogg (the 'Ettrick Shepherd'), Walter Scott, Coleridge, Charles Lamb, George Crabbe and Felicia Hemans.

In its patterns of imagery and structures of reflection, this elegy seems much more redolent of 'long and deep thought' than of 'the spontaneous overflow of powerful feelings'. The recollections of perished poets do not just form a random catalogue, but show a progression from simple reminiscence towards reflective philosophy. There is a carefully developed metaphor of journeying, whereby the poet's literal walk through the valley of Yarrow, evoked in the opening stanza, prefigures the metaphorical journey through life to death in stanza 6:

> Like clouds that rake the mountain-summits,
> Or waves that own no curbing hand,
> How fast has brother followed brother,
> From sunshine to the sunless land![18]

The sunshine/sunless contrast joins up with a series of images characterizing death as sleep, darkness, cold, and freezing. Thus the poets' lives, subtly but repeatedly sketched in terms of seasonal progression with expressions like 'golden leaves', 'rolling year', 'ripe fruit' and 'summer faded', are also portrayed as journeys towards a wintry death. The symmetrical catalogue of poets builds up to the second-last stanza, which was added by Wordsworth after the first publication of the poem. The mild syntactic and metrical disruption at the beginning of this stanza ('Mourn rather ...'), marking the difference of Hemans as the one female poet in the list, and the one who died unseasonably young, only emphasizes the regular rhythm of the remaining stanzas, with their interlaced feminine endings and masculine rhymes. With the recollection of the Ettrick Shepherd, James Hogg, in the final stanza, the elegy returns to its starting point to emphasize the present moment of grief:

> No more of old romantic sorrows,
> For slaughtered Youth or love-lorn Maid!
> With sharper grief is Yarrow smitten,
> And Ettrick mourns with her their Poet dead.[19]

Whether or not there is something paradoxical in the poem's combination of spontaneous composition and reflective thought, the 'Extempore Effusion' does seem to fulfil admirably Wordsworth's own 'criterion of sincerity' as set out in the 'Essays upon Epitaphs'. Yet Wordsworth's essays, which remained for the most part unpublished, did not form the context for the reception of this poem in the 1830s; rather, it would have encountered a readership much more imbued with Byronic reflections on sincerity, as will be discussed below. In this context, the 'Effusion' inevitably reveals conventional, even performative aspects, thanks to its title, its publication venues, and the contextualizing notes with which it was eventually published. Wordsworth's niece Elizabeth Hutchinson reports that Wordsworth originally composed the poem under the more elegiac title 'The Graves of the Poets', which also directly associates it with the 'Essays upon Epitaphs'. Yet it was always published under the loaded title 'Extempore Effusion'. By the 1830s, 'effusion' was an almost technical term for an improvised poem; it was the standard translation of the Italian term *improvvisazione* before forms of the word 'improvisation' entered the English language from Romance languages. 'Effusion', with these associations, would have been familiar from the English version of Madame de Staël's wildly popular novel *Corinne*, about a female poet who improvises her songs in public, and from travel accounts that reported on the 'effusions' of performers in Mediterranean countries who made a show of spontaneously extemporizing verses. Indeed, the countless 'effusions', 'extempore effusions', and 'impromptus' published in periodicals and literary magazines, as well as the use of the term by Letitia Elizabeth Landon in her influential poem *The Improvisatrice*, would likely have associated the 'extempore effusion' primarily with female poets, or more precisely with the public forms of women's poetry. Regardless of the intensity of Wordsworth's personal feeling, the very criterion of sincerity that he evokes – that is, spontaneity – at the same time imbues his poem with the performative, and possibly also oral and feminized, connotations of the nineteenth-century extempore effusion.

Equally inevitable is the elegy's status as both an intensely private and an intensely public discourse – a tension that fascinates Wordsworth himself in his consideration of epitaphs. Composed in solitude, the 'Extempore Effusion' is immediately sent to the most public of venues, the newspaper, specifically to the editor of the *Newcastle Journal* in which Wordsworth first read of Hogg's death, and where the 'Effusion' was printed on December 5, 1835. A week later, on December 12, it appeared again in the periodical *The Athenaeum*. In 1837, Wordsworth included it in his *Poetical Works* with modest revisions and with the added stanza on Felicia Hemans, and in the posthumous edition of Wordsworth's collected poems in 1857, it appeared together with the Fenwick notes in which Wordsworth described the circumstances of its spontaneous composition. Ernest de Selincourt's twentieth-century edition of the *Poetical Works* adds further context from the reminiscences of Wordsworth's niece:

> Miss Hutchinson said that once when she was staying at the Wordsworths' the poet was much affected by reading in the newspaper the death of Hogg, the Ettrick Shepherd. Half an hour afterwards he came into the room where the ladies were sitting and asked Miss Hutchinson to write down some lines which he had just composed.[20]

While testifying to the spontaneous and solitary nature of the poem's composition, these supplementary notes create an interesting dramatic context for the effusion. We are asked to imagine Wordsworth, overcome with sorrow and inspiration on reading the death notice, entering the room with a newly composed poem, as a kind of mini-drama illustrating the criterion of spontaneity and supplementing any features of it to be found in the text itself.

Published in 1835, Wordsworth's 'Extempore Effusion' offered itself to be read in a context already coloured by Byron's reflections on sincerity in the later cantos of *Don Juan*, which appeared 11 years earlier in 1824. Byron's epic seems to celebrate performativity while satirizing sincerity, but it may also reveal something of what sincerity is all about. Certainly the word 'sincerity' occurs in a wide variety of contexts throughout *Don Juan*. Sometimes it is used of characters who seem genuinely and essentially sincere, such as the Greek maiden Haidee in canto 2, or Aurora Raby, the 'sincere, austere' Catholic girl who stands out in the Regency society of the final cantos as the one character seemingly untouched by corruption or affectation (15.46).[21] At other times, though, the narrator applies the term 'sincere' to himself and his poem, in order to present himself as impartial and unmercenary, willing to 'expatiate freely' on the shortcomings of society rather than court popularity or gain (9.26). But the narrator's claim to sincerity becomes progressively more hyperbolic, especially in the final cantos, which are set in Regency England and where the term 'sincerity' recurs rather obsessively. The narrator now characterizes himself as 'too sincere a poet' in exposing his readers as '*not* a moral people' (11.87). In the last completed canto, declaring that his muse is 'beyond all contradiction/The most sincere that ever dealt in fiction' (16.2), he crosses the line into a parody of sincerity by explicitly locating it in what is fictional, imaginary or even downright false.

The epitome of sincerity, and of Byron's parody of sincerity in *Don Juan*, is the clever society hostess Lady Adeline Amundeville, whom Juan encounters in cantos 13 to 16 of the poem. Lady Adeline is literally a performer – indeed, she is an extemporizing performer who deserves to be recognized as an English 'Improvisatrice', a fitting fictional counterpart to Letitia Elizabeth Landon, who adopted that role in London society during the 1820s and whose long poem, *The Improvisatrice*, appeared the same year as these cantos of *Don Juan*. When performing as an amateur musician, Lady Adeline conveys a naturalness which is in fact self-conscious, singing 'as 'twere *without* display,/Yet *with* display in fact' (16.42). The narrator famously sums up her emotional responses and social relations with the word 'mobility', linking this term at once with the height of sincerity:

> So well she acted, all and every part
> By turns – with that vivacious versatility,
> Which many people take for want of heart.
> They err – 'tis merely what is called *mobility*,
> A thing of temperament and not of art,
> Though seeming so, from its supposed facility;
> And false – though true; for surely they're *sincerest*,
> Who are strongly acted on by what is *nearest*. (16.97; italics added)

The telling rhyme of 'sincerest' with 'nearest' in these last two lines brings back the criterion of immediacy, now in a spatial rather than a temporal form, but it also threatens to undermine sincerity. Even if the most immediate emotional responses *are* likely to be the sincerest ones, they may also be, as this stanza hints, fickle and capricious.

The fascination of 'mobility', as Jerome McGann has pointed out, lies in its complex function as both a psychological attribute and an aspect of the structure of social relations. For McGann, the stanza quoted above 'shows that the psychological attribute and the social formation call out to each other, that they are, indeed, symbiotic and inter-dependent'.[22] Yet McGann's reading quickly reaches an unanswerable paradox: does mobility arise out of sincerity, or is it a product of insincere role-playing or artifice? Rather than a 'symbiotic' relationship between private psychology and public sociability, Byron's characterization of Lady Adeline suggests that *there is no necessary connection between these two registers*. Whether or not Lady Adeline intends her charming behaviour to correspond with her own emotional responses – an issue that the poem leaves open, implying at most that the correspondence between feeling and expression may vary from moment to moment – her subjective emotion inevitably becomes something else when translated into acceptable public expression. Byron's prose annotation on the word 'mobility' further inserts it into a network of differences between native and foreign, present and past:

> In French, 'mobilité'. I am not sure that mobility is English, but it is expressive of a quality which rather belongs to other climates, though it is sometimes seen to a great extent in our own. It may be defined as an excessive susceptibility of immediate impressions – at the same time without *losing* the past; and is, though sometimes apparently useful to the possessor, a most painful and unhappy attribute.[23]

Explicitly marked as foreign, '*mobilité*' alienates its possessors – who include Lady Adeline, Don Juan, and certainly Byron himself – from English society. Byron's own affect attaches to mobility in the phrase 'a most painful and unhappy attribute', but what his poem conveys, above all, is that emotional mobility needs to be *embodied* in order to be socially meaningful, since internal states are not directly accessible to others except through the medium of the body. The resonant rhyme of 'sincerity' with 'verity' underlines the extent to which Adeline uses facial expression to communicate her emotional state:

> Some praised her beauty; others her great grace;
> The warmth of her politeness, whose *sincerity*
> Was obvious in each feature of her face,
> Whose traits were radiant with the rays of *verity*. (16.102; italics added)

If Lady Adeline's sincerity is achieved through her facial features, Don Juan conveys the same effect with the tone of his voice: 'Sincere he was – at least you could not doubt it,/In listening merely to his voice's tone' (15.13).

In the Regency world described by Byron, the performance of sincerity can be highly effective; Lady Adeline is universally regarded as beautiful, accomplished, noble and sympathetic. She exemplifies a definition of sincerity as the subject's immediate emotional response to 'what is nearest', a response that can only be communicated at skin level – in 'each feature of her face', or in 'his voice's tone'. Spontaneity again plays a part here as an indication of genuine affect. But Byron's characterization also reveals discomfort at the idea that emotion, if so mobile, might be *merely* skin deep. The troubling uncertainty of a mobility expressed in the body is the question of how, or whether, it corresponds to an internal psychological state. This uncertainty is expressed in a fleeting observation of Juan's:

> Juan, when he cast a glance
> On Adeline while playing her grand role,
> Which she went through as though it were a dance,
> (Betraying only now and then her soul
> By a look scarce perceptibly askance
> Of weariness or scorn) began to feel
> Some doubt how much of Adeline was *real* (16.96)

Byron's analysis of sincerity as a performance reveals the aporia within sincerity itself. It requires an exact correspondence between two things that are incommensurate: private emotion and an externalized semiotic system, whether it be the lineaments of the face, the pitch of the voice or the order of language. While satirizing sincerity, Byron also exposes a scandal that sincerity can never avoid: although the *concept* of sincerity promises congruence between state of mind and expression, actual *instances* of sincerity expose an intrinsic incongruence among cognitive, physical, verbal and social processes.

Wordsworth, then, theorizes sincerity as guaranteed by spontaneity, but as antithetical to performance, yet his 'Extempore Effusion' cannot quite keep spontaneity and performance apart. For Byron, sincerity is both spontaneous and performed; it manifests as an immediate, embodied response to stimuli, a response that is read by others through a semiotics of looks, gestures, and tone of voice, as well as words. This paradoxical notion of sincerity as a *socially accessible and physically engaged performance of interior emotion* is, I would argue, paradigmatic for late-Romantic poetry, and a study of this quality complements recent work on the theatricality of Regency society such as Judith Pascoe's *Romantic Theatricality* (1997) or Penny Gay's *Jane Austen and the Theatre* (2002).[24]

An acute awareness of the scandal of sincerity also characterizes the poetry of Letitia Landon, whose poetic voice combines profound echoes of Byronic and (what is less often recognized) Wordsworthian sensibility. Like Wordsworth, Landon expresses an intense discomfort with the theatrical nature of interpersonal behaviour; she strongly implies, as Wordsworth put it, that 'acting a part' is fatal to sincerity. Writing about her contemporary, Felicia Hemans, Landon contrasts sincere poetic expression to its opposite, the *insincerity* of nineteenth-century public life:

> I believe that no poet ever made his readers feel unless he had himself felt. The many touching poems which most memories keep as favourites originated in some strong personal sensation ... No indication of its existence would probably be shown in ordinary life ... [W]e scarcely know the extraordinary system of dissimulation carried on in our present state of society.[25]

This 'extraordinary system of dissimulation' is delineated over and over in Landon's poetry, but nowhere more explicitly than in 'Lines of Life'. In the first half of this 27-stanza poem, the poet condemns herself for collaborating, albeit under constraint, with the code of falsity that rules social life:

> Well, read my cheek, and watch my eye, –
> Too strictly school'd are they,
> One secret of my soul to show,
> One hidden thought betray.

> I never knew the time my heart
> Look'd freely from my brow;
> It once was check'd by timidness,
> 'Tis taught by caution now.
> I live among the cold, the false,
> And I must seem like them;
> And such I am, for I am false
> As those I most condemn.
> I teach my lip its sweetest smile,
> My tongue its softest tone;
> I borrow others' likeness, till
> Almost I lose my own.
> I pass through flattery's gilded sieve,
> Whatever I would say;
> In social life, all, like the blind,
> Must learn to feel their way.[26]

Among the many compelling aspects of these stanzas is a performative condition acutely described as the identity of seeming and being, of *Schein* and *Sein*. Adopting the appearance of the 'false' among whom one lives, even if it is done for the sake of self-protection, is equivalent to *really being* false. Similarly, adopting the 'likeness' of others leads to becoming like others; it brings about an effacement, or a forgetting, of one's own likeness. One might expect, here, that dissimulation brings about the loss of one's own *self*; but the diction suggests, rather more potently, that the speaker's own 'likeness' or image is all of herself there ever is to lose.

'Lines of Life' begins with a deceptively casual injunction to the reader: 'Well, read my cheek, and watch my eye.' The image of 'reading' the face, which is ubiquitous in Landon's poetry, has a special relevance here with the revelation that the face's text will never allow an accurate interpretation of the heart, since the signs of cheek and eye refer outward to other (false) faces, not inward towards meaning or feeling. Reading faces is a literal and fundamental aspect of Landon's poetic practice, since a substantial amount of her poetry was commissioned to accompany visual images, usually portraits, in the annual albums and gift-books of the late 1820s and 1830s. The 'lines of life' are both the lineaments of the face (whether a real face or a printed reproduction) and the lines of the poem; language, facial expression and social convention are here aligned with one another, all of them antithetical to sincerity. Yet the latter part of Landon's poem reveals a hope that spirit and feeling might, after all, be transmitted across time through her 'lines':

> My first, my last, my only wish,
> Say will my charmed chords
> Wake to the morning light of fame,
> And breathe again my words?
> Will the young maiden, when her tears
> Alone in moonlight shine –
> Tears for the absent and the loved –
> Murmur some song of mine?
> Will the pale youth by his dim lamp,
> Himself a dying flame,
> From many an antique scroll beside,
> Choose that which bears my name?
> Let music make less terrible
> The silence of the dead;
> I care not, so my spirit last
> Long after life has fled.[27]

The lyric ends with the projected image of the lines being murmured or read by young, sympathetic readers beyond the poet's death, with the possibility that the words of the poem might 'breathe again' in the envisioned bodies of the 'young maiden' or the 'pale youth' of the future.

Landon's characteristic themes, many of them reflected in 'Lines of Life', reappear in different guises throughout her poetry. A longer poem from the same 1829 volume, 'A History of the Lyre', contains specific verbal resonances with 'Lines of Life', while its overall genre and subject have affinities with the poems of Wordsworth and Byron discussed above. Functioning as an elegy, of sorts, spoken by a male narrator for the dead poetess Eulalia, the poem characterizes Eulalia as a fashionable, witty, talented *improvisatrice*, in a manner reminiscent of Byron's Lady Adeline Amundeville. Though ultimately a more serious and sympathetic character than Lady Adeline, Eulalia, too, is distinguished by her emotional mobility: the narrator sees her robed in bright colours at the centre of a social circle, 'wholly changed' from one evening to the next, and he observes her transition from lightning wit to 'sunniest smiles' to a 'wayward' mood to 'melancholy song'.[28] Eulalia's long, self-reflective speech, which makes up the centrepiece of the poem and the majority of its lines, is triggered by the narrator's observation that, as with Byron's Adeline, this mobile exterior conceals a spiritual emptiness. His reproach, with which she concurs, is that her art and social intercourse are all 'vanity'. Eulalia could as well be the speaker of 'Lines of Life'; she, too, laments that 'My days are past/Among the cold, the careless, and the false'[29] and admits that 'half life's misery' is caused by the insincerity of appearances:

> I can judge
> Of others but by outward show, and that
> Is falser than the actor's studied part.
> We dress our words and looks in borrow'd robes:
> The mind is as the face – for who goes forth
> In public walks without a veil at least?[30]

Eulalia recognizes that, whether sincere or insincere, the mental states of others are unknowable except by the indirect evidence of appearance, language, and other external or publicly shared conventions. Her figural language connects this insight with her own role as a performer ('the actor's studied part') and as a woman (one who wears a veil in public). Eulalia's hyper-consciousness of the dissociation between external signs and inward feeling is expressed above all in the term 'borrow'd': not only are words and looks analogous to removable coverings, like articles of clothing, but they are not even the clothes that one owns or habitually wears. '*Borrow'd* robes' connote words and looks that are consciously imitated, chosen for the occasion, looks that will be put off again to be worn by others, that circulate according to convention for use when one chooses to speak 'as' this or that persona. The phrase 'borrow'd robes' is also an echo of Shakespeare's *Macbeth*, and in that context 'robes' are a metaphor for titles, or forms of language ('why do you dress me/In borrowed robes?' Macbeth asks, when he is addressed with a title he does not yet hold [I.iii.112–13]). Landon's 'Lines of Life', as discussed above, echo this passage with the phrase 'I *borrow* others' likeness, till/Almost I lose my own.' Both these contexts redouble the sense of concealment or insincerity: not only superficial robes, but *borrowed* superficial robes; not only the likeness of others, but beneath it nothing more than the *likeness* of oneself.

In 'A History of the Lyre', Eulalia reflects on her own career as a female poet, analysing how she was drawn into performative social relations that facilitate superficial interaction, yet preclude real understanding of others. Rueful retrospectives on the poet's career, which also occur in other poems of Landon's such as 'Erinna', tend to feature frequent echoes of Wordsworth, especially 'Tintern Abbey' and the Immortality

Ode – and, as in Wordsworth, sincerity functions here as an ideal with which to contrast its opposite, affectation or 'acting a part'. Yet if theatricality is ubiquitous in Landon's late-Romantic society, and in the milieus where she places her female poets and performers, there is also an omnipresent wish that affect might be transmitted to future readers through the lines of the poem: 'I believe that no poet ever made his readers feel unless he had himself felt', as Landon writes in the essay on Hemans quoted above. Her poems perpetually hold out the hope that sincere feeling might not only be imputed to her poetry, but that it might be imparted to others through poetry, if only after the poet's death.

If sincerity must always come to terms with the social semiotics of bodily and verbal expression, Landon hints, ironically, that it might return unexpectedly at the point where theatricality is most heightened – by way of the spontaneity, unpredictability, and uniqueness of a performance on stage. A contemporary quotes Landon as saying that a career on the stage might have given her access to such an experience:

> I would give all the reputation I have gained, or am ever likely to gain, by writing books, for one great triumph on the stage. The praise of critics or friends may be more or less sincere; but the spontaneous thunder of applause of a mixed multitude of utter strangers, uninfluenced by any feelings but those excited at the moment, is an acknowledgement of gratification surpassing, in my opinion, any other description of approbation.[31]

Landon's admission that she would rather be a successful actress than a writer, if only for the sake of one stellar performance, leads to yet another definition of sincerity. It is not the sincerity of the poet or speaker that is in question here, but that of the audience. Spontaneity guarantees the objectivity and purity of the audience's response; it forestalls contamination by second thoughts or ulterior motives. In this case, sincerity does not just collaborate with performativity; instead, it manifests itself only under the conditions of explicit theatrical performance. By setting sincerity into the context of performance, later Romantic writers mirror the conflicting demands of Regency society for transparency and for theatricality. Their embodied version of sincerity, which is always on the verge of succumbing to parody or excess, reveals the aporia within sincerity itself: its need to be immediate and mediated at the same time; its impossible desire for a correspondence between the incommensurate systems of internal states and public representations.

Notes

1. Donald Davie, 'On Sincerity: From Wordsworth to Ginsberg', *Encounter* 31.4 (1968): 62.
2. Lionel Trilling, *Sincerity and Authenticity* (Oxford University Press, 1972), p. 2.
3. Ibid., p. 10.
4. Matthew Arnold, 'Byron', *Essays in Criticism, Second Series*, ed. S. R. Littlewood (London: Macmillan – now Palgrave Macmillan, 1966), p. 114.
5. Shoshana Felman, *The Scandal of the Speaking Body: Don Juan with J. L. Austin, or Seduction in Two Languages*, trans. Catherine Porter (Stanford University Press, 2003), p. 65.
6. Ibid, p. 114.
7. Jerome J. McGann, *The Poetics of Sensibility: A Revolution in Literary Style* (Oxford: Clarendon Press, 1996), p. 96.
8. Ian Dennis, '*Cain*: Lord Byron's Sincerity', *Studies in Romanticism* 41 (2002): 655.
9. Pam Morris, *Imagining Inclusive Society in Nineteenth-Century Novels: The Code of Sincerity in the Public Sphere* (Johns Hopkins University Press, 2004), p. 15.
10. A partial but illustrative list would be: Henri Peyre, *Literature and Sincerity* (Yale University Press, 1963); David Perkins, *Wordsworth and the Poetry of Sincerity* (Harvard University Press, 1964); Donald Davie, 'Sincerity and Poetry' (delivered as a Hopwood Lecture in 1965, and republished as 'On Sincerity: From Wordsworth to Ginsberg' in *Encounter* 31.4 [1968]: 61–6); Patricia M. Spacks, 'In Search of Sincerity', *College English* 29 (1968): 591–62; Herbert Read, 'The Cult of Sincerity', *Hudson Review* 21 (1968): 53–74; Stuart Hampshire, 'Sincerity and Single-Mindedness', *Freedom of Mind and Other Essays*, (Oxford University Press, 1972), pp. 232–50; Leon Guilhamet, *The Sincere Ideal* (McGill-Queens University Press, 1974); A. D. M. Walker, 'The Ideal of Sincerity', *Mind* 87 (1978): 481–97.
11. Perkins, *Wordsworth*, p. 1.
12. Guilhamet, *The Sincere Ideal*, p. 283.
13. William Wordsworth, *The Prose Works of William Wordsworth*, eds W. J. B. Owen and Jane Worthington Smyser, vol. 2 (Oxford: Clarendon Press, 1974), pp. 70, 66.
14. Perkins, *Wordsworth*, p. 41.
15. Wordsworth, *Prose*, vol. 2, p. 70.
16. Ibid., p. 72.
17. William Wordsworth, *The Poetical Works of William Wordsworth*, eds E. de Selincourt and Helen Darbishire, vol. 4 (Oxford: Clarendon Press, 1940–9), p. 459.
18. Ibid., p. 277.
19. Ibid., p. 278.
20. Ibid., p. 462.
21. Quotations from *Don Juan* are cited from volume 5 of George Gordon, Lord Byron, *Don Juan*, vol. 5 of *The Complete Poetical Works*, ed. Jerome J. McGann (Oxford: Clarendon Press, 1986); quotations of poetry are referenced in parentheses by canto and stanza number, and quotations from the notes by page number.

22. Jerome J. McGann, *Byron and Romanticism*, ed. James Soderholm (Cambridge University Press, 2002), pp. 39–40.
23. Byron, *Don Juan*, p. 769.
24. Judith Pascoe, *Romantic Theatricality: Gender, Poetry, and Spectatorship* (Cornell University Press, 1997); Penny Gay, *Jane Austen and the Theatre* (Cambridge University Press, 2002).
25. Letitia Elizabeth Landon, *Selected Writings*, eds Jerome McGann and Daniel Riess (Peterborough, ON: Broadview, 1997), p. 175.
26. Landon, *Selected Writings*, p. 111.
27. Ibid., p. 114.
28. Ibid., pp. 117–18.
29. Ibid., p. 122.
30. Ibid., p. 121.
31. Quoted in Glennis Stephenson, *Letitia Landon: The Woman behind L.E.L.* (Manchester University Press, 1995), pp. 107–8.

5
Making Sense of Sincerity in *The Prelude*

Tim Milnes

The idea of 'sense' undergoes a radical transformation in significance and normative power during the Romantic period. Fundamental to this transformation is a pronounced linguistic turn in eighteenth-century thought. David Hume, John Horne Tooke, Edmund Burke and Jeremy Bentham realised that the meaning of a word cannot be explicated purely in terms of ideas or sensations: reference, in other words, is underdetermined by 'sense'. This crisis in the referential economy of empiricism in turn provokes a range of responses: scepticism about language (Hume); a shift from ideas to words as the primary units of cognition (Tooke); the identification of language as a site of aesthetic indeterminacy figured in the sublime (Burke); and a change in the basic units of meaning from words to statements, clarified by pragmatic contextual definition, or 'paraphrasis' (Bentham). I will return to the difference between the Burkean and Benthamite strategies later. The general upshot of this linguistic turn was the perceived inadequacy of the 'language of sense', a perception that feeds Wordsworth's vacillation between the veridical immediacy of sense-experience and the numinous aura of imagination – between a natural 'sense' and a supernatural 'sense *of*'.

Closely associated with the reconstruction of 'sense' is a revaluation of the idea of 'sincerity'. By the time that Wordsworth begins work on *The Prelude*, the term's new sense of 'truthfulness' has eclipsed older connections with 'purity'. Increasingly, sincerity is applied to persons, attitudes, intentions and expressions, rather than to wine, gold or spirit. One reason for this is the rise of epistemological dualism: first, in the form of empiricism's postulation of a correspondence between ideas and objects of sense; later, in Kant's notion of a transcendental correspondence between the noumenal ideas of reason and the phenomenal objects of experience. Consequently, sincerity is increasingly thought of in epistemological, rather than ontological terms, as Aquinas's idea of the pure soul is eclipsed by Rousseau's notion of the truthful individual whose defining feature is not the possession of a certain quality of substance, but the attainment of *correspondence* between intention and expression.[1]

However, just as the correspondence theory of truth culminates in the 'intellectual intuition' of German Idealism (the ideal convergence of thought and object), so the correspondence theory of truthfulness provokes the idea of a deeper harmony of thought and behaviour: the ideal of authenticity. Thus, according to Rousseau, the more authentic (real, true) the person, the more sincere (truthful, honest) the voice, to the point where a character is so authentic (such as Wordsworth's Michael), that the question of sincerity no longer arises. The relations between sincerity and authenticity have been explored by Lionel Trilling, and, more recently, Bernard Williams.[2] In this chapter, however, I want to look at how a transformed language of *sense* relates to an emerging discourse of *sincerity*. The reason I concentrate on these two terms in particular is because of the way in which the problems that connect them converge on one question: how do we *make sense*?

David Perkins notes that the emergence of sincerity as a premium literary value in the late eighteenth century introduces a new anxiety among authors regarding communication: language comes to be seen as inadequate, saying less (or more) than is sincerely *meant*.[3] This anxiety is in turn linked to a crisis in the language of sense: words whose ideas are underdetermined by sensation, and utterances that do not correspond to a foundation of sense-data, undermine the communication of truth. This problem applies to self-knowledge as much as interpersonal knowledge: the sensory poverty of linguistic concepts used in communication does not disappear when the same concepts are deployed in self-analysis (Coleridge's efforts aside, Kant's proposal that only a transcendental method could obviate these problems is not seriously pursued in Britain until later in the nineteenth century). In turn, still deeper doubts are sown over the possibility of *truthfully* communicating one's own thoughts; in short, the correspondence model of truth and truthfulness makes the task of *making sense* to other human beings, and to oneself, appear impossible.

Viewed from certain perspectives in modern commentary and theory, this impasse betrays the extent to which 'sense' and 'sincerity' are implicated in a metaphysics of subjectivity that tends to hypostatize 'truth' as *origin* and 'meaning' as *presence*. As a result, some argue that the Enlightenment and Romantic discourse of 'thought' and 'communication' inevitably unravels around its own *aporia* and/or displacement of history. Thus, Frances Ferguson has argued that Wordsworth's metaphors of sincere communication betray their self-undermining dependence upon the material and social otherness – the 'counter-spirit' – of language. Similarly (albeit from within a different critical tradition), Alan Liu reads Wordsworth's vague, imaginative 'sense of' natural phenomena as revealing, through its very denial of history, the determining absence of history.[4]

I argue, however, that such readings misrepresent the nature of the relationship between 'sense' and 'sincerity' in Wordsworth. This misunderstanding is the product of a familiar but problematic undercurrent in counter-Enlightenment thinking, which, in attempting to view thought and communication from the standpoint of an incommensurable 'otherness' (such as language or history), fosters an intense suspicion of truth and interpretation. In the second section of this chapter, following Jürgen Habermas, I argue that replacing such suspicion with a 'holistic' view of interpretation reveals a new and entirely different dimension to Wordsworth's writing, one rooted in the Romantic counterdiscourse of communicative rationality. In the third part of the chapter, I offer a reading of the 'Blind Beggar' episode in *The Prelude*, and suggest that the poem's engagement with a contemporary discourse of intersubjectivity reveals a 'sense' of 'sincerity' in Wordsworth far removed from the familiar Enlightenment topoi of origins and essences typically foregrounded (and debunked) by modern commentary.

I

Etymology hints at the importance to Wordsworth's poetry of the relationship between 'sense' and 'sincerity', insofar as both are closely connected to notions of truth and meaning. Sincerity – both in its modern sense of 'honesty' and its older sense of 'purity' – is linked to ideas of truth and truthfulness, while the term also plays a vital background role in the pragmatics of communication. 'Sense' is a complex term, whose appearance in the previous sentence already indicates its semantic importance. However, it also has a cognitive function. In addition to denoting the signification of a term or phrase, 'sense' can signify both a *faculty* of perception (such as 'common' sense) and an *actual* perception or feeling, including, in the words of the *Oxford English Dictionary*, 'a more or less vague perception or impression *of*' a truth or meaning.[5]

As an example of this latter, 'vague' sense, the *OED* cites Wordsworth's 'sense sublime', in 'Tintern Abbey', 'Of something far more deeply interfused.' As William Empson observes, while this intuitive use of the term gained wider currency in the late eighteenth century, Wordsworth endeavours to 'interfuse' the semantic 'sense' of language with the new, numinously cognitive 'sense *of*' truth. This strategy, which underpins the 1805 *Prelude*'s 'dim and undetermined sense/Of unknown modes of being' (1.418–420), soon throws up problems. Does 'sense *of*' connote an unmediated perceptual access to truth, or a purely imagined meaning? How do we *make* sense of the world and of others when we are unclear about what sense the word 'sense' has? The 'language of sense', the language of empiricism and associative materialism, seems ill-equipped to validate Wordsworth's visionary fusion of truth and meaning. As a result, Empson argues, *The Prelude* simply *jumps* from the language of sensation to the language of imagination. In the 'Simplon Pass' episode, this jump is sudden, unexplained, and disorientating:

> Nature is a ghastly threat in this fine description; he might well as in his childhood, have clasped a tree to see if it was real. But what all this is *like* ... is 'workings of one mind' (presumably God's or Nature's, so it is not merely *like*),
>
> > Characters of the great Apocalypse,
> > The types and symbols of Eternity,
> > Of first, and last, and midst, and without end. [6.570–72]
>
> The actual horror and the eventual exultation are quite blankly identified by this form of grammar.[6]

As the 'light of sense/Goes out' (6.534–35), the critic observes, the *natural* senses are dimmed at the very moment that the poet's *vision* is extended 'out' into the world. Empson, however, complains that in this blank, apocalyptic identification of sense and imagination, 'what is jumped over is "good sense"; when Wordsworth has got his singing robes on he will not allow any mediating process to have occurred'.[7]

For Empson, the issue at stake is one of style: while Wordsworth does not have a *theory* of sense, he is willing to profit from the epistemological ambiguity of a complex word. The payoff in *The Prelude*, Empson claims, is a blurring of the boundaries between the factual and the imaginary, enabling 'Sensation and Imagination [to] interlock'.[8] From a phenomenological point of view, however, the relationship between the two faculties looks more like sublation. On Geoffrey Hartman's reading, Wordsworth remains ambivalent about both sense and the visionary because of the dialectical cast of his consciousness. Far from jumping into imagination, the poet's 'shrinking from visionary subjects' betrays a fear of falling into a senseless (meaningless and incomprehensible) apocalypse of imagination. Contrary to Empson's diagnosis, then, the *Prelude*'s *via naturaliter negativa* reveals a universe in which *everything* is mediated: as Hartman puts it, the paradox of Wordsworth's poetry lies in its attempt to describe the 'difficult process whereby the soul, having overcome itself through nature, must now overcome nature through nature'.[9] In seeking to transcend the language of sense, imagination merely attests to the fact that it *cannot make sense* of itself in the absence of sense-experience.

For some commentators, however, the ambiguous category of 'sense' in Wordsworth is determined by networks of difference that are material and contingent, rather than ideal and dialectical. To the extent that a poem such as *The Prelude* promotes the idea that 'sense', or meaning, resides in a shadowy dialectic between a 'natural' faculty of sense and a 'supernatural' power of imagination, it betrays its own inability to get on terms with reality, to submit to what Alan Liu calls the 'sense of history'. Liu's influential account is based on two key premises: meaning is essentially historical, and history has no essence. Like Frederic Jameson and Louis Althusser, Liu sees history as the absent cause that determines how arbitrary structures of discourse come to be determined as truth and ordered knowledge. The 'sense' or meaning of a text lies in what is *not* given immediately; it lies in what is repressed, displaced, or denied by sense and sensation. From this perspective, Wordsworth's 'natural' sense-experience is the denial of history, averting an apocalyptic encounter between the self and the incommensurable otherness, the sheer contingency, of history, 'when the sense of history and imagination thus became one, and nature, the mediating figure, is no more'.[10]

Liu's approach reflects a broader suspicion in modern criticism and commentary of epistemological and hermeneutical categories descended from the Enlightenment. This suspicion intensifies around concepts such as 'sense' and 'sincerity' because of their ostensibly privileged connections with meaning and truth. Wordsworth's 'sense of' nature, at once semantic and cognitive, is cast as an idealistic obfuscation, an attempt to escape the epistemology of the 'language of sense', the latter bankrupted by its failure to render the promissory notes of language into the basic stuff of raw experience. The demise of 'sense', however, has a further sting in the tail for the poet. Disconnected from its empirical truth-conditions, expression becomes fraught with uncertainty; how can one express oneself when self-reflection is severed from the 'sense' of self? This problem appears as more than just a practical difficulty. It is no longer clear what it *means* to express something truth-fully because it is no longer clear what 'meaning' means. Once sense, the correspondence between words, concepts and sensations, falls to pieces, what remains of sincerity, the correspondence between words and intentions?

For Liu, these questions cannot be answered until the Enlightenment superstructure of subjectivity is fully dismantled, and with it the notions of meaning as an essential 'presence' in language and truth as the 'origin' of meaning. Only then can 'sense' and 'sincerity' be his-toricized and translated into the *rhetoric* of understanding and truthful-ness. Accordingly, sincerity reappears in modern historicist readings of Romantic literature as the performance of an 'ideal' in which, according to Jerome McGann's analysis, there are 'two related problems, the one a contradiction, the other an illusion'. The 'contradiction', McGann finds, is 'concealed in the Romantic idea(l) of self-integrity', which – because subjectivity is 'an existential and not a logical (or dialectical) process' – cannot avoid the transformations wrought by representation; the 'illusion', meanwhile, is one of 'spontaneity and artlessness' pre-sented by the artful rhetoric of Romantic poets such as Wordsworth.[11]

II

Postmodern historicism, then, traduces Romantic sincerity by implicat-ing it in discredited models of meaning and truth rooted in the notion of a 'centred' self. This account usually relies upon a background narra-tive according to which the sensory, punctual self of the Enlightenment transcends itself through Romantic irony, only to become the property of dialectic in Hegel and Marx, and, later, metaphor in Nietzsche. Some, however, have questioned this story of the self. Jürgen Habermas, most notably, argues that it overlooks a 'counterdiscourse' of decentred, communicative rationality in the eighteenth and nineteenth centu-ries.[12] This counterdiscourse, Habermas claims, underwrites a form of self-critique that patrols the boundaries between the constitutive yet pragmatic and communicative rationality of the 'lifeworld', and a pre-supposed and regulative 'system' of reflective thought and truth.[13]

William Godwin registers such boundaries when he claims in *Political Justice* that 'Truth may be considered by us, either abstractedly, as it relates to certain general and unchangeable principles, or practically, as it relates to the daily incidents and ordinary commerce of human life.'[14] Generally, Godwin adheres to an empirical, positivist conception of truth, treating it as the immutable foundation of discourse. Elsewhere in

Political Justice, however, he remarks that 'if there be such a thing as truth, it must infallibly be struck out by the collision of mind with mind'.[15] Contained in the phrase 'struck out' is the suggestion that, rather than a foundation, truth is something *sustained by* communication between minds in the 'ordinary commerce of human life'. On this model, the self, reason, truth and meaning are not transcendent logoi, but what Habermas would term intersubjective norms, placeholders for ideals of an absolute convergence of beliefs in everyday communication.

Habermas's account of the counterdiscourse of communicative rationality in Enlightenment and Romantic thought suggests that critics such as Liu and McGann have been too eager to seize upon the aesthetic pathway as the hypostasized antithesis or 'negation' of an intolerable historical contingency. Instead, he suggests, what we frequently find in Romantic writing are the 'body-centred experiences of a decentred subjectivity that function as the placeholders for the other of reason'.[16] This approach has further implications for how we view the transformation of the language of 'sense' in Wordsworth, whereby correspondence with empirical realities is eschewed in favour of an epistemologically ambiguous 'sense *of*' the relationship between truth and meaning. From Habermas's perspective, what is questionable in the historicist approach is the assumption that an enhanced 'sense of' the interpenetration of truth and meaning in poems such as 'Tintern Abbey' and *The Prelude* necessarily betokens a form of political obfuscation, a purely negative historical consciousness.

One example, particularly relevant in the present context, of how misleading this assumption can be is John Barrell's discussion of natural description in 'Tintern Abbey'. Barrell argues that in the late eighteenth century the language of sense fell foul of a 'class distinction'.[17] Increasingly persuaded that many words acquire meaning not via sensation, but through use and context, theorists such as Burke pressed referential indeterminacy into the service of (bourgeois, male) aesthetic pleasure. Consequently, Barrell claims, abstract words like 'honour' and 'beauty' came to be seen as 'fiduciary symbols' whose irreducibility to humble sense-experience 'invited the polite male to experience a peculiar satisfaction in contemplating the vast gap which separated him from ... the uneducated rustic and the impressionable female'.[18]

Barrell's analysis of the language of sense brings us back to a distinction I drew at the beginning of this chapter between 'aesthetic' or Burkean and 'pragmatic' or Benthamite theories of meaning. Both Burke and Bentham understand that, on the empirical model, 'meaning' is fatally underdetermined by 'truth', and that the 'sense' of words is not sustained by the correspondence between the concepts they signify and the sensations or impressions those concepts represent. Crucially, however, each writer responds to this predicament in different ways. Burke sublimes the failure of correspondence into the kind of ineffable aesthetic sense-experience that is deconstructed/historicized by Barrell. Bentham, however, turns the tables on empiricism by reconfiguring the concept of 'truth' itself as merely 'the coin of necessity' in communication.[19] In his later work, Bentham came to see abstractions like 'truth', 'idea' and 'sense', as 'fictitious entities, those necessary products of the imagination, without which, unreal as they are, *discourse* could not, scarcely even could *thought*, be carried on'.[20]

Barrell disregards this counterdiscourse of communicative rationality in the Romantic period because he is intent upon exposing how truth, conceived as an origin or foundation, inevitably collapses under the weight of its own concealed absences. And yet, while Burke responds to the failure of 'correspondence' by hypostatizing truth and meaning in the inaccessible domain of the sublime, Bentham treats the indeterminacy of truth as a feature of its status as the figural precondition of communication. Like John Horne Tooke, Bentham comes to see truth not as an origin (what Tooke lampoons as the idea that truth lies 'at the bottom of a well'), but as a background condition for interpretive acts within a community.[21] People need a concept of truth in order to make sense of themselves and each other, Bentham maintains, but the idea itself only emerges once individuals begin to communicate. As Tooke puts it: 'TRUTH supposes mankind: *for whom* and *by whom* alone the word is formed, and *to whom* only it is applicable. If no man, no TRUTH.'[22]

This strategy brings us back, once again, to sincerity. Like Burke, Bentham places trust at the heart of the business of acquiring and communicating beliefs. In Bentham, however, this trust relates not to the 'connotative aura' of 'fiduciary symbols', but to the *truthfulness* of other human beings. By replacing a model of reason constructed around subjectivity or consciousness with one based on communication, Bentham translates the problem of making sense to others and (equally importantly) to oneself into a question of how one participates in the language games of a community. As a result, while the sense of an utterance is inextricably bound up with its truth, 'truth' is not conceived empirically, but holistically, as one of the vectors necessary for thought and social interaction. In the practical sphere of everyday communication, then, our 'sense of' truth (and meaning) depends greatly upon the truthfulness, the sincerity, of others.

To the suspicious, this claim might appear to substitute one dubious 'origin' (truth) with another (truthfulness). After all, critics have long made hay with how the gulf between an original 'intention' and its material signification embarrasses Wordsworth's treatment of sincerity. Perkins, for instance, notes that, while in his *Essay on Epitaphs* Wordsworth resists any distinction between the sincerity of a poem and its truth ('meaning by "truth" a harmony with ultimate realities') in his practical demonstrations of epitaphic sincerity the poet is confined 'to naming probable signs, what people will usually accept as indications of sincerity'.[23] As I have argued, however, the idea of a correspondence or 'harmony with ultimate realities' was not the only concept of truth circulating in this period. Just as Bentham and others saw that the notion of semantic correspondence produces a hypostatized ideal of meaning or 'sense', so others came to feel that attempting to explain 'sincerity' in terms of a correspondence between intentional states and expressive behaviour only made the notion more mysterious and paradoxical. Raising the stakes in this debate, moreover, was the emergence of a new, more exigent conception of the correspondence between self and language: what Bernard Williams calls the 'ambiguous invention' of personal authenticity.

For Williams, the invention of the modern idea of authenticity is 'ambiguous' because underlying it are 'two different conceptions of the self and of self-understanding, which imply different ideas of sincerity and its relation to society'.[24] The first of these is the notion of authenticity as self-transparent originality, an idea Williams attributes to Rousseau. Rousseau's conception of authenticity in his *Confessions* presupposes the existence of 'a real character, an underlying set of constant motives', in which the true self can be said to consist.[25] In this scheme, sincerity enjoys a privileged place among the virtues; the obligation it enjoins demands that language corresponds to the intentional states of a fully self-aware individual. The problem with this conception, however, is that the more the self is probed, the less transparent it appears. Indeed, Williams notes that later, in the *Reveries*, Rousseau himself comes to suspect that 'one may be in the dark about what one most wants or most deeply needs'.[26] As a result, the problem of apperception continues to worry at the idea of personal authenticity, producing the transcendental irony of the Romantics, the search for an 'intellectual intuition' of self, and ultimately, as Trilling indicates, Hegel's architecture of dialectical consciousness, the 'truth' of which, at one stage, 'consists in its being *not* true to itself'.[27]

Williams, however, identifies a second Enlightenment discourse of sincerity, associated with Denis Diderot, which offers an alternative to talk of correspondence and self-coincidence. In *Rameau's Nephew*, Williams claims, Diderot creates a character that, while undeniably authentic on Rousseau's terms (he has clarity about his own intentions) and sincere (he is 'unguardedly spontaneous'), is neither virtuous nor admirable.[28] Though perfectly consistent, Rameau's nephew lacks what Williams calls steadiness of mind. Indeed, he changes his position so often that it is not even clear that he possesses beliefs rather than just 'propositional moods'.[29] For Williams, Diderot's honest flatterer indicates that our beliefs and sense of self are not determined internally, but within a *social* space of reasons and other persons. Communicating with other human beings is thus a precondition of having a clear awareness of oneself as a thinking being: as Williams argues, 'we need each other in order to be anybody'.[30]

The figure of Rameau's nephew, Williams concludes, implies conceptions of sincerity and authenticity far removed from those advocated by Rousseau. Following Diderot's lead, Williams uncouples sincerity from the discourse of consciousness and origins, and moves towards a view of sincerity as the *precondition*, rather than the *expression* of a stable self. Like Godwin, he conceives sincerity or truthfulness as an epistemic virtue, a value that forms part of the network of background conditions necessary for communication, identity, and a shared sense of truth. In *Political Justice*, Godwin highlights this background when he argues that insincerity is blameworthy insofar as it 'destroys that confidence on the part of my hearers, which ought to be inseparable from virtue'.[31] Similarly, Williams emphasizes the connection between truthfulness and confidence or *trust* in the assumptions and the sincerity of other people. We depend for our sense of self upon our interpretations of the truthfulness of others. In this way, 'I become my interpretation of their interpretation of what I have sincerely declared to them.' Thus, through everyday mutual interpretation, 'where the presence of other people is vital, sincerity helps to construct or create truth'.[32]

Thanks to Habermas and Williams, then, we can now answer a question raised earlier: what becomes of sincerity, the correspondence between words and intentions, once sense, the correspondence between words, concepts and sensations, falls to pieces? What remains, for Diderot, Godwin, Bentham and other writers whose work forms the 'counterdiscourse' of reason within Enlightenment and Romantic thought, is the *precondition* of sincerity: the trustfulness without which communication with others and, consequently, coherent thought would be impossible. In the pragmatics of interpretation, sincerity is what makes us make sense.

III

One way of describing this counterdiscourse of communicative rationality in Enlightenment and Romantic thought is as the replacement of constitutive objectivity by regulative intersubjectivity. Thus, truth and meaning cease to be viewed as determined by the correspondence between a centred subjectivity and an external world and are seen instead as governed by pragmatic preconditions for mutual understanding between persons whose subjectivity depends upon the possibility of interpreting, and being interpreted by, others. I make sense to myself, in other words, only on the condition that I make sense to others. Making sense to others, in turn, involves engaging with what Bentham calls the logical 'fictions' that act as the preconditions for communication, foremost among which is truth, which in practical terms means presupposing that most people speak and write truthfully most of the time.

How might an awareness of this decentred discourse of the self affect our reading of *The Prelude*, a poem considered so self-*centred* by its author that he balked at publishing it during his lifetime? First, it enables us to discard the postmodern rubric of hypostatized otherness (difference, history and so on), which is the reflex of Romantic idealism.[33] This is not to deny the poem's investment, buoyed up by the inflatus of imagination, in the transcendental stock categories of 'self', 'mind' and 'meaning', but rather to allow that different understandings of such categories may also be signalled by the text. For Wordsworth, the experience of a 'decentred' subjectivity emerges as a 'sense *of*' truth, meaning not a vague gesture towards a transcendent truth that passes all understanding, but an acknowledgement of the indeterminate, porous relationship between truth and interpretation, subjective (ap)perception and intersubjective norms.

It is this relationship that Wordsworth explores in the 'Blind Beggar' episode of Book 7. This celebrated passage recounts the poet's encounter in London with a man who 'Stood propped against a wall, upon his chest/Wearing a written paper, to explain/The story of the man, and who he was' (7.613–5). In the image of the beggar, the poet experiences an epiphany, finding in the label a 'type/Or emblem' of all we can know:

> Both of ourselves and of the universe,
> And on the shape of this unmoving man,

His fixèd face and sightless eyes, I looked,
As if admonished from another world.

(7.621–3)

In an influential reading of this passage, Frances Ferguson argues that the intrusion of intentionless language (the 'written paper') into the relationship between the poet and beggar unsettles the ideal exchange between mind and world that the poem aims to commemorate, exposing the otherness and materiality upon which the poem's construction of consciousness and its own acts of communication depend. What the poet takes to be his *own*, subjective world is, like that of the beggar, already inscribed or 'written down' for him: it is, in other words, always determined by language and the intervention of others. As Ferguson puts it:

> the label is 'an apt type' of the limits of human knowledge of the self and of the universe precisely because it is an external form pleading for meaning from the reader ... The self cannot know itself, because it is ineluctably not really a self but rather a composite of selves intertwined through a chain of the affections and continually reaching out in an appeal to additional selves.[34]

Ferguson's identification of the poem's awareness of its own dependence for meaning upon the 'pleading' external form of language, and upon 'an unfathomably extensive chain of affections' for knowledge, distantly echoes Perkins's observation that Wordsworth's theory of epitaphs relies upon 'probable signs' as indications of sincerity. For Ferguson, however, such manoeuvres are 'epitaphic' on a deeper level, revealing that it is only through the hidden workings of otherness that we can 'imagine the possibility of meaning in the face of all evidence to the contrary'.[35]

Ferguson's analysis certainly highlights the peculiar rhetoric of Book 7, in which the negative energy of urban London propels a narrative ascent towards Book 13 and the visionary summit of Snowdon. From this perspective, it is tempting to read the 'Blind Beggar' spot in time as a rupture in the logic of transcendence, a point where the pressure of denied alterity is exposed as the blindness enabling poetic insight. According to this reading, a fully material otherness (of language, people, history) can be seen ultimately to determine the 'shape of this unmoving man' through which Wordsworth accesses a chastising vision. In this way, the poetic subject foregoes the materiality and contingency of London's 'vulgar forms' (8.695) in order to be 'admonished from another world'.

Such an interpretation assumes, however, that *The Prelude* consistently figures human understanding and communication as forms of transcendence, whereby the (underdetermined) language of *sense* is trumped by the (overdetermined) *sense of* otherworldly truth and meaning. There is evidence in *The Prelude*, however, of a discourse in which the poet's swerve away from empirical language is driven by an altogether more earthly, relational understanding of the world, others and himself. In order to see this, we must read the 'Blind Beggar' passage in the context of Book 7's general concern with social alienation. In his early days in the metropolis, the poet is struck by 'how men lived/Even next-door neighbours, as we say, yet still/Strangers' (117–20). Once he is caught up in 'the Babel din,/The endless stream of men and moving things' (157–8), however, the young Wordsworth experiences urban anonymity at first hand:

> How often in the overflowing streets
> Have I gone forwards with the crowd, and said
> Unto myself, 'The face of every one
> That passes by me is a mystery.'
> Thus have I looked, nor ceased to look, oppressed
> By thoughts of what, and whither, when and how,
> Until the shapes before my eyes became
> A second-sight procession, such as glides
> Over still mountains, or appears in dreams,
> And all the ballast of familiar life –
> The present, and the past, hope, fear, all stays,
> All laws of acting, thinking, speaking man –
> Went from me, neither knowing me, nor known.
>
> (7.595–607)

For some critics, these lines merely betray Wordsworth's social conservatism, a 'parochial paternalism' that hankers after rural familiarity and 'the good old days when everybody knew each other and their place'.[36] Far more provoking, however, is the poem's treatment of how the social disconnectedness of London life affects the relationship that people have with language. Book 7 is notable for the way it describes the increasing dislocation of words from the communicative acts that form the basis of relationships. Thus, the shop-fronts of houses are described as made up 'like a title-page/With letters huge inscribed from top to toe' (176–7), while a demobbed sailor, also reduced to begging, is depicted lying 'beside a range/Of written characters, with chalk inscribed/Upon the smooth flat stones' (215–23). As in the case of the blind beggar, these instances of language remain untranscribed by the poet, portrayed starkly as a set of marks disconnected from the practicalities of communication.

On one hand, it might seem reasonable to agree with Ferguson that such episodes underscore the power of language as 'counterspirit' to the self in *The Prelude*, preparing the reader for the unsettling insight of the 'Blind Beggar' scene, and the revelation that language, which is the mediator, not the instrument of knowledge, works blindly. However, this would be to ignore the way in which the poem adumbrates a view of the 'self' based upon the pragmatics of mutual understanding. Significantly, it is only once 'all the ballast of familiar life' has gone from the poet – the recognition and acknowledgement of others, the practices and 'laws of acting, thinking, speaking man' – that he loses his sense of self. The poet is lost to himself, in other words, insofar as he feels that he is 'beyond/The reach of common indications' (608–9): without the deictic gestures of others, and without the ability to be 'known', he is incapable of 'knowing'.

In this way, Book 7 of *The Prelude* opens a gateway to an understanding of the self as open, plural and socially embedded. Without the acknowledgement and genuine recognition of others, the only 'sense' of self that remains is the 'shape' of a 'fixèd face and sightless eyes'. The blinding vision of the beggar reveals to the young poet the interdependence of self and other, looking and being looked at, knowing and being known. In order to think, we need to communicate with others, using, among other things, gestures, sounds and writing. Indeed, the problem with language that emerges from these passages is not that it is all-determining, but rather that, outside human interaction, language, conceived as a system of formal conventions, determines nothing. For Wordsworth, communication consists in the practical activity of understanding the actions of others within a shared lifeworld. Outside human relationships and the practical business of getting on with mutual understanding, language is merely 'a range/Of written characters.'

This is a conception of meaning quite at odds with the language of sense. Rooted in a discourse of communicative rationality underpinning a model of subjectivity not hypostasized in 'origins' or in a privileged, centred consciousness, but ineluctably social and relational, it bypasses the sublimation of reference that Barrell claims to identify in 'Tintern

Abbey'. Indeed, the 'Blind Beggar' passage implies that our 'blindness' to the workings of language, the impossibility of meaning what we say, will only be conceived as threatening if a nostalgia for the language of sense leaves us yearning for the impossible correspondence of word and experience. Eschewing such nostalgia, Book 7 of *The Prelude* acknowledges that in order to make sense of ourselves, we blindly depend on others to interpret us. Abstracted from the social scene, the young Wordsworth discovers that intersubjective norms, not sensation, form the preconditions of discourse. Finally, we rely for our 'sense of' self upon communication and 'all the ballast of familiar life': recognition, the acknowledgement of others and trust.

With trust, the bond deemed by Godwin essential for the communication of truth, we return once again to the matter of sincerity. Read in its proper context, the 'Blind Beggar' episode demonstrates that Wordsworth's conception of sincerity is not always invested in an originative, expressive model of consciousness; indeed, it frequently engages with the social practices that *presuppose* sincerity. For these practices, trust is essential. And yet, trust is the very quality Wordsworth finds lacking in the streets of London. This is why, when the dislocated poet, 'oppressed/By thoughts of what, and whither, when and how', imagines, and is 'admonished' from, another world, the blindness with which one embarks on mutual interpretation is figured not as the pragmatic condition of communicative reciprocity, but merely as the alienating condition of having another's written words stand in for one's own. Without the trust implicit in sincerity, communication, indeed, thought, begins to break down. As Perkins notes, much of the appeal of Wordsworth's poetry of sincerity lies in the trust it generates. 'The sincerity of another man', he observes, 'increases our own'.[37] What Perkins misses and Wordsworth recognizes, however, is how, by creating trust in mutual interpretation and thereby enabling individuals to make sense of themselves and others, sincerity can help to create truth.

Notes

1. The conception of sincerity as truthfulness has been challenged by Stuart Hampshire, who argues that since the predicate 'sincere' can be applied to states of mind as well as utterances, the discrepancy between 'what I am disposed to say about myself and what I am disposed to do' remains a gap within thought, not between thought and expression. Hampshire offers an alternative, Spinozan conception of sincerity as 'undividedness or singleness of mind', which he believes obviates the Romantic idea that self-consciousness is the enemy of sincerity ('Sincerity and Single-Mindedness', *Freedom of Mind*

[Oxford University Press, 1972], pp. 244–5). This account is in turn contested by A. D. M. Walker on the grounds that it attributes sincerity to the person who single-mindedly sets out to deceive others. Rejecting both the 'truthful' and 'single-minded' theories of sincerity, Walker offers an analysis based upon the term's etymological roots in 'purity' ('The Ideal of Sincerity', *Mind* 87 [1978]: 489).

2. See Lionel Trilling, *Sincerity and Authenticity: The Charles Eliot Norton Lectures, 1969–1970* (1971, Oxford University Press, 1974) and Bernard Williams, *Truth and Truthfulness: An Essay in Genealogy* (Princeton University Press, 2002).
3. See David Perkins, *Wordsworth and the Poetry of Sincerity* (Harvard University Press, 1964), p. 2.
4. See Frances Ferguson, *Wordsworth: Language as Counter-Spirit* (Yale University Press, 1977) and Alan Liu, *Wordsworth: The Sense of History* (Chicago University Press, 1989).
5. 'Sense, *n.*', *The Oxford English Dictionary*, 2nd edn, CD-ROM (Oxford University Press, 1992).
6. William Empson, *The Structure of Complex Words* (Chatto & Windus, 1951), pp. 302–3.
7. Ibid., p. 304.
8. Ibid., p. 299.
9. Geoffrey Hartman, *Wordsworth's Poetry 1787–1814* (1964, Yale University Press, 1971), p. 221.
10. Liu, *Wordsworth*, p. 31.
11. Jerome McGann, 'Private Poetry, Public Deception', *Byron and Romanticism*, ed. James Soderholm (Cambridge University Press, 2002), pp. 115–17.
12. Jürgen Habermas, *The Philosophical Discourse of Modernity: Twelve Lectures*, trans. Frederick Lawrence (1985, Cambridge, MA: The MIT Press, 1987), p. 295.
13. Jürgen Habermas, *The Theory of Communicative Action*, trans. Thomas McCarthy, vol. 1 (1981, Boston: Beacon Press, 1984), p. 82.
14. William Godwin, *An Inquiry Concerning Political Justice, and its Influence on General Virtue and Happiness*, vol. 1 (London, 1793), p. 211.
15. Ibid., vol. 1, p. 21.
16. Habermas, *Philosophical Discourse*, p. 306.
17. John Barrell, *Poetry, Language and Politics* (Manchester University Press, 1988), p. 136.
18. Ibid., pp. 163, 165.
19. Jeremy Bentham, 'A Fragment on Ontology', *The Works of Jeremy Bentham*, ed. John Bowring, vol. 8 (Edinburgh, 1838–43), p. 199.
20. Jeremy Bentham, 'Essay on Logic', *Works*, vol. 8, p. 219.
21. John Horne Tooke, *Epea Pteroenta, or the Diversions of Purley*, ed. Richard Taylor, rev. edn, vol. 1 (London, 1829), p. 10.
22. Tooke, *Diversions*, vol. 2, pp. 402–3.
23. Perkins, *Wordsworth*, pp. 39, 41.
24. Williams, *Truth*, p. 173.
25. Ibid., p. 178.
26. Ibid., p. 182.
27. Trilling, *Sincerity*, p. 44.
28. Williams, *Truth*, p. 189.

29. Ibid., p. 191.
30. Ibid., p. 200.
31. Godwin, *Inquiry*, vol. 1, p. 256.
32. Williams, *Truth*, pp. 203–4.
33. As Habermas argues in *Knowledge and Human Interests*, trans. Jeremy J. Shapiro (Heinemann, 1972), much modern criticism and commentary remains captivated by Hegel's audacious decision to turn epistemological doubt back upon epistemology itself, thereby subordinating communicative reason to 'abstract negation' (9). One enduring consequence of Hegel's failure is that postmodern suspicion remains locked into an unhappy form of critical chiasmus. Lacking cognitive traction, and yet fixated, largely thanks to Nietzsche, on locating a point of radical exteriority *within* the discourse of reason, this kind of commentary can do little more than enact the hypostatized, incommensurable 'other' of reason through inverted gestures of cognition. Postmodern topoi such as rhetoric, difference and power emerge on this picture as shadowy doubles of the 'presence' and 'origin' they seek to overcome.
34. Ferguson, *Wordsworth*, pp. 144–5.
35. Ibid., p. 154.
36. Roger Sales, *English Literature in History 1780–1830: Pastoral and Politics* (Hutchinson & Co., 1983), pp. 65–6.
37. Perkins, *Wordsworth*, p. 269.

6
Too Good to be True? Hannah More, Authenticity, Sincerity and Evangelical Abolitionism

Kerry Sinanan

Much has been written recently about the roles of sentiment and sensibility in the abolitionist movement of the 1780s and of anti-slavery in Romantic literature.[1] Related to these is another category, that of 'sincerity' which, as outlined in the introduction to this volume, poses many challenges for critics who no longer believe in holistic selfhood and for whom the essentialist categories of 'good' and 'evil' are problematic. In the context of slavery and abolition in the Romantic period such problems, arguably, become even more complex as the urgency of retaining ethical parameters is felt. In this chapter I want to explore the ways in which understanding more about the historical specificities of both sincerity *and* authenticity is crucial for how we inflect our critical analyses, especially when we consider the abolitionists whose literary outpourings coincided with the high watermark of Romanticism. Hannah More is an individual whose sincerity about social reform and abolitionism remains fodder for academic debate because of her Evangelical motivations. Despite Ann Stott's revisionist biography, which goes a long way to rebalance the field of criticism against the 'many scholars who show an almost personal dislike of More', for current critics, More's abolitionism, intertwined with Evangelical fervour, remains unpalatable.[2] In *Subject to Others* (1992), Moira Ferguson eloquently argued that More's abolitionism was complicit with 'preserving rigid social hierarchies' because the Evangelical promise of salvation rendered revolution in this world unnecessary: ultimately, More's 'Evangelical pro-conversion propaganda cannot mask its counter-revolutionary impact'.[3] Ferguson's language, here, clearly suggests that there is an insincerity, a 'masking' of true purpose, in More's Evangelical abolitionism. The prevalence of this view has been countered by Stott who argues, 'her remarkable achievements and her multiple contradictions mean that Hannah

More will always elude precise terminology, easy labels, and glib sim-
plifications'.[4] Perhaps even more stridently, Anne K. Mellor describes
More as a powerful agent of social reform, arguing that 'More's writings
consolidated and disseminated a revolution, not in the overt structure
of public government, but, equally important, in the very culture and
mores of the English nation'.[5] Mellor's account refuses to allow More
to remain ignored by social historians and defiantly lays the ground for
further defences of 'the most influential woman living in England in
the Romantic era'.[6] In this chapter, I want to continue this response to
More's contradictions and complexities by attempting to describe the
parameters of her Evangelicalism as a moral source and her sincerity in
attempting to draw on that source.

If, as Mellor and Stott demonstrate, More's faith was fundamental
to her belief in the need for social reform, then we need to take full
account of her Evangelical abolitionism. By drawing on the work of
Charles Taylor I want to argue that More's Evangelicalism constitutes an
ethics of authenticity, as defined by him, and that her desire to do good
can be read as sincere, rather than as a strategic wielding of reactionary,
Christian ideology. In this way I discuss More's authenticity, in Taylor's
terms, as something 'born at the end of the eighteenth century' that
begins with the assumption 'that human beings are endowed with a
moral sense', thereby locating the sources of that morality 'within'.[7] In
The Ethics of Authenticity Taylor argues that it is this relocation of moral
sources that leads to the emergence of a culture of authenticity in the
Romantic period. Whereas, before, the sources of 'God' or the 'Idea of
the Good' were external moral sources, 'now the source we have to
connect with is deep in us. This is part of the massive subjective turn of
modern culture, a new form of inwardness, in which we come to think
of ourselves as beings with inner depths'.[8] For the Evangelical, the self-
reflection and self-scrutiny that are part and parcel of this faith-based
way of life, are a means to access God within. As Taylor notes, 'this
idea that the source is within doesn't exclude our being related to God,
or the Ideas; it can be considered our proper way to them'. Throughout
this essay, I shall, therefore, discuss More's *sincerity* in accessing her
Evangelical faith as a moral source and argue that this way of life
constitutes an ethics of authenticity as defined by Taylor.

The Evangelical tradition from its early modern origins had always
put an emphasis on internal scrutiny when the confessional diary enabled a practical emphasis 'on the internal spiritual welfare of the soul,
and on the importance of self-examination'.[9] As Taylor proposes, the
Puritan tradition thus merged with the secular version of the individual

as a moral being by the end of the eighteenth century. And abolitionism went hand-in hand with the Evangelical revival: 'the anti-slavery crusade originated in part in a revival movement initiated by William Wilberforce and the Clapham Sect, that was an attempt to revivify Evangelical Christianity in the face of the growing infidelity of the educated classes.'[10] Hannah More's own beliefs were forged within the moment of the Evangelical revival through her friendships with figures such as William Wilberforce and John Newton. The Evangelical precept of self-scrutiny involves a continual critique of self and of one's motives and thus I will discuss More's own self-interrogations as acts of sincerity.

This discussion may be viewed as an intervention into the much wider critique over the sources of the abolitionist impulse in the Romantic era which essentially questions how sincere the abolitionists were about their anti-slavery propositions. Famously, in his seminal *Capitalism and Slavery* (1944) Eric Williams argued that abolition was not a sincerely humane revolution on Britain's part, but a combination of economic necessity and structural change in the run up to the industrial revolution. 'The abolitionists were not radicals', Williams announced and what humanitarian impulses that there were, were tempered by 'the unprofitableness of the West Indian monopoly'.[11] In contrast, David Brion Davis has famously argued in his study, *The Problem of Slavery in Western Culture* (1966) that, while the men of the late eighteenth century cannot be considered to be 'more virtuous' than their ancestors, nevertheless, 'The emergence of an international antislavery opinion represented a momentous turning point in the evolution of man's moral perception, and thus in man's image of himself'.[12] For Davis, this realization that man was indeed endowed with moral sense, was core to the success of abolition.[13]

It is in the context of these wider debates that I situate my reappraisal of More's Evangelical abolitionism. As Clare MacDonald Shaw notes, it is crucial to take note of the ways in which she is at once 'politically counter-revolutionary and morally radical' without attempting to erase this political complexity.[14] I would argue that these contradictions need to be viewed, not as evidence of hypocrisy which limits abolitionism with the interests of the ruling class, but as part of a historically specific, cultural shift when the anti-slavery movement of the Romantic period, as Taylor argues, blended 'theistic and secular moral sources'. As he notes, 'The roots in Puritanism account for that peculiar amalgam of radicalism, social reform, and moral rigourism which was typical of the English-speaking movements'.[15]

In what follows I shall first argue that More's Evangelical Christianity can be regarded as a moral source as defined by Taylor and note More's sincere attempts to correspond with this source. Such an argument is, I feel, a necessary antidote to the general dismissal of More's religion as reactionary by a secular, liberal academy that often struggles to take full account of ethics founded on religious beliefs. In the second section I will describe, more fully, More's sincerity as forged in her core relationship with the reformed slave trader and leader of the Evangelical revival, John Newton. While Newton was one of her advisers, he has a particularly interesting relationship to the abolitionist movement due to his own role as a slave trader and their letters to each other offer insights into how they viewed their own anti-slavery interventions. In the third section I shall discuss current views of More's abolitionism. Clare Midgley's synopsis is typical: 'Hannah More believed in the spiritual equality of men and women, black and white, but was convinced that social order could only be maintained by retaining hierarchical social relations'.[16] Such views, I argue, collapse the reforming potential of slave conversion and dismiss More's own belief in Christianity as a radical force. In the final section I turn to More's only novel, *Coelebs in Search of a Wife* (1808) to discuss it in the light of Lionel Trilling's account of sincerity in his seminal *Sincerity and Authenticity* (1972). Trilling focuses on *Mansfield Park* (1814), which Austen based on More's *Coelebs*, as a site of conservative sensibility. I highlight the ways in which the vision of Evangelical sincerity, outlined in More's novel, is, by comparison, much more radical and promising of social reform. Despite the allusion to abolition in its title, which invokes the ameliorative Mansfield Decision of 1778, Austen's novel is ambivalent about the reforming potential of Fanny's sincerity. In contrast, More's much less exciting novel outlines a rigorous programme of social reform based on Evangelical precepts, sincerely carried through.

Evangelical Christianity as a source of abolitionism

More made two famous poetic contributions to British abolitionism, 'Slavery, A Poem' (1788) and 'The Sorrows of Yamba; or The Negro Women's Lamentation' (1795), published as part of her *Cheap Repository Tracts*. Although both poems were highly influential in the anti-slavery cause they have been regarded with suspicion by current critics who read in them a dual agenda, utilizing abolition to forward anti-Jacobin sentiments. Thus, in her discussion of 'Slavery', Ferguson reads the slave Quashi who commits suicide rather than murder his abusive master, as 'an idealized member of the laboring class in the eyes of middle-class conservatives who dreaded class insurrection'.[17] And Marcus Wood argues that, for Hannah More, 'the only good freed slave was a Christian freed slave'.[18] In such readings, More's abolition is ultimately replaced with other forms of mastery and social control. Alan Richardson's reassessment of 'The Sorrows of Yamba', specifies the changes that More made to the poem that was originally submitted to her by the more radical writer, Eaglesfield Smith. Richardson argues that the published poem combines the antithetical discourses of both authors thus registering the 'tensions and contradictions' of the political spectrum of British anti-slavery. In his meticulous discussion of this poem, which was to become highly influential as a literary model, Richardson notes how 'More's revision catches early in its rise a nascent, more conservative, more militantly religious sensibility that would eventually be labeled "Victorian".'[19] In such ways, More's abolitionism has been read as limiting freedom and 're-colonising' slaves with an Anglocentric, Christian ideology.

Yet it is, ultimately, too simplistic to cite More's Evangelical faith as the source of conservatism in her abolitionist writings. As Tim Fulford and Peter J. Kitson outline, 'men and women, Romantic and Evangelical opposed slavery in different ways, but both reinstate some of its informing assumptions within their opposition'.[20] Following this argument, the rearticulation of power is a potential dynamic of abolitionist discourse in the hands of the enfranchised writing on behalf of the disenfranchised, regardless of political affiliations to the right or left. What we need to take account of, then, is the sincerity of the abolitionist's intention to do good, to end the slave trade and to ameliorate suffering, all of which were common goals of abolitionists across the political spectrum. In *Slavery and the Romantic Imagination*, Debbie Lee argues that, in reading slavery in Romantic literature, we must note how 'the creative act differs from the imperial act, how imagination is distinguished from colonization'.[21] Her references to More's anti-slavery poems note the tropes and images that she draws upon in common with more radical Romantic authors to suggest that the Romantic imagination itself is inevitably changed and extended by the fact of slavery. Taking Lee's argument as a starting point it is, therefore, possible to read More's representations of slaves, especially Quashi and Yamba, as acts of 'empathy' that are sincere attempts 'to write creatively about the complex and glaringly unequal relationships between Africans and Britons'.[22]

In 'Slavery', these unequal relations are certainly perceivable as More justifies her desire to sing Quashi's praises by lamenting Africa's lack of civilization:

> For thou wast born where never gentle Muse
> On Valour's grave the flow'r's of genius strews;
> And thou wast born where no recording page
> Plucks the fair deed from Time's devouring rage. (ll. 85–8)

Yet, notwithstanding the presumption of her own cultural superiority, the poet is pushed to imagine the other's suffering in an act of empathy which, ultimately, expresses equality born out of common feeling:

> Whene'er to Afric's shores I turn my eyes,
> Horrors of deepest, deadliest guilt arise;
> I see, by more than Fancy's mirror shewn,
> The burning village, and the blazing town:
> See the dire victim torn from social life,
> The shrieking babe, the agonizing wife!
> She, wretch forlorn! is dragg'd by hostile hands,
> To distant tyrants sold, in distant lands!
> Transmitted miseries, and successive chains,
> The sole sad heritage her child obtains!
> Ev'n this last wretched boon their foes deny,
> To weep together, or together die.
> By felon hands, by one relentless stroke,
> See the fond links of feeling nature broke!
> The fibres twisting round a parent's heart,
> Torn from their grasp, and bleeding as they part. (ll. 95–110)

In this extract More's speaker imagines a scene of pillage and rapine in which she feels morally implicated and uses highly emotive sentimental language to move the reader also to imagine such horrors. 'I see', notes the speaker's feeling of personal responsibility and guilt is acknowledged. Here, the imaginative focus on the harrowing effects of slavery on families, leads to a powerful empathetic moment in which feelings are elicited that may be potentially reformative. But the ultimate outrage for More is the spiritual robbery that slavery involves; 'MAN' is 'the traffic', but 'SOULS the merchandize!' (ll. 146). It is her Evangelical zeal which enables her ultimate denunciation of slavers as she addresses the imagined slaves: 'They are *not* Christians who infest thy shore' (ll. 188).

What I would emphasize, here, then, is that ethical dimensions of More's Evangelicalism underlie her critique of slavery and need not be regarded as merely politically suspicious. It was the very force of religious conviction that gave abolition its power. In terms of anti-slavery, Evangelicalism encouraged the feeling individual to empathize with their enslaved brothers and sisters and so promote their liberty. Roger Anstey argues that 'there were three core Evangelical concepts that reveal the movement's affinity with abolitionism: the concept of redemption involving a transformation from darkness to light, the belief in God's protection and actual liberation of his chosen people, and the law of love, which prohibited those who were once "enslaved" from perpetrating the same offence against others'.[23]

In *Sources of the Self*, Taylor also insists upon the value of Christianity as a moral source that was vital to the success and force of the transatlantic abolitionist movement:

> The driving force of both the British anti-slavery movement and American abolitionism was religious. It is difficult indeed to imagine these movements attaining the same intensity of commitment, the same indomitable purpose, or the same willingness to sacrifice in the English-speaking societies of that time outside of this religious mode.[24]

Crucially, Taylor argues, it was the Christian element that defied the proto-racist assertions of the polygenists and 'it was believers who felt called upon to defend passionately the unity of the human race'.[25] More's 'Slavery' urges precisely this point, as she argues that darker skin cannot exclude slaves from God's grace:

> Does then th'immortal principle within
> Change with the casual colour of a skin?
> Does matter govern spirit? or is mind
> Degraded by the form to which 'tis join'd?
> No: they have heads to think, and hearts to feel,
> And souls to act, with firm, tho' erring, zeal;
> For they have keen affections, kind desires,
> Love strong as death, and active patriot fires;
> All the rude energy, the fervid flame,
> Of high-soul'd passion, and ingenuous shame:
> Strong, but luxuriant virtues boldly shoot
> From the wild vigour of a savage root. (ll. 63–74)

While it is undeniable that More's representation of Africans, here, is imbued with the sense that they may be improved by Christianity, I feel it is an anachronistic misreading, transporting back our more secular distrust of such zeal, to read this as a conservative mode of extending slavery through conversion. Writing out of Christianity as a moral source, More's ultimate objects of liberation are the slaves' souls. As Patricia Demers notes, in 'Slavery' Christian conversion is a 'necessary corollary' to freedom, not a limiting contingency.[26]

Not only, then, is More's faith a moral source that she pursues in her attempts to live authentically, but, perhaps most importantly, she repeatedly articulates her sincerity about accessing this source. This sincerity about her own morality is crucial if we are to take full account of More's seriousness about abolitionism. As she wrote in a letter to a friend in 1787:

> the great object I have so much at heart, [is] the project to abolish the slave trade in Africa. This most important cause has very much occupied my thoughts this summer … It is to be brought before parliament in the Spring. Above one hundred members have promised their votes. My dear friend, be sure to canvas every body who has a heart. It is a subject too ample for a letter, and I shall have a great deal to say to you on it when we meet. To my feelings, it is the most interesting subject which was ever discussed in the annals of humanity.[27]

This extract shows, then, not just the situation of More within the very core of the Evangelical, abolitionist lobby, but the vital importance to her of anti-slavery as a sincerely held, personal concern.

Sincerity is a facet of individual morality that More articulates in many of her writings. In 1788, an important year for the first wave of abolitionist activity, she anonymously published her moral essay 'Thoughts on the Importance of the Manners of the Great to General Society' (1788) in which she recommended those of the *Belle Monde* who professed to hold Christian values dear to be wary of the influence of the world and of fickle society in distracting them from their religious duties. She warns there will come a time when, not the world, but God, 'will make strict inquisition into *sincerity* of heart and uprightness of intention' (my emphasis).[28] More's language here is precise: it is not merely the outward show of duty or goodness, but the purity of motivation that matters. While in her later *Cheap*

Repository Tracts More urged the poor to be dutiful, in 'Thoughts' she first 'castigated the gentry for neglect of their paternalistic role'.[29] The upper classes have duties too. Interestingly, More lied about her authorship of this piece to protect her reputation from imputations of female impropriety after daring to accost her powerful peers in such a manner. But, as she explained to her friend Elizabeth Montagu of the Bluestockings, 'I am so afraid that strangers will think me good! And there is a degree of hypocrisy in appearing so much better than one is.'[30] In this instance, paradoxically, More's lie helps her maintain the sincerity of her message and is born out of her awareness that her moral code is something to strive for. Truth could result in hypocrisy. She is not at all complacent about herself as a model of goodness and this sincerity about the honesty of her own intentions is something that we cannot dismiss with ease.

Prioritizing More's sincerity about her moral source, draws our attention to the back-to-front way in which More's agenda has been read, namely as using 'print [as] a powerful tool with which to maintain social order through evangelism.'[31] Claudia Thomas Kairoff's common reading of More, here, is inaccurately formulated: what I am arguing, is that More does not utilize religion cynically in order to prevent social change, but that she sincerely prioritizes the reform of conversion over revolution because of her belief in Christianity as a moral source of authenticity. However much we may wish to dispute the political tendencies of More's aims, we also need to grapple with her sincere attempts to minimize suffering which she, as an Evangelical, regarded as an inevitable part of life in an imperfect world. As Taylor warns, the danger of persistent scepticism about moral sources is that we are left without an answer to the question of what will constitute our own, current, moral sources: 'In some cases the answer will be quite unarticulated, because of the reluctance of the unbelieving Enlightenment to face the issue of moral sources'.[32]

More's good works are well known: after a spell of London celebrity in which she consorted with the Bluestockings, was Garrick's protégé and mixed with the contemporary intelligentsia, she retired into rural life in Somerset, embraced Evangelicalism and, with her sisters, established many schools around Bristol and its outlying impoverished villages. Between 1795 and 1798 she was responsible for the prolific *Cheap Repository Tracts* (written as a corrective to the 'pernicious trash' of the Minerva Press)[33] which gave instruction to the poor, recommending piety in the face of poverty, as well as writing vigorously in the abolitionist cause. Writing, publishing and educating all constitute the pragmatic elements of More's Evangelical faith. As she wrote in a letter to her friend Mrs Kennicott:

> We have often agreed that 'To mend the world's a vast design', and I am now convinced of the truth of this, by the difficulties attending the half dozen parishes we have undertaken. It is grievous to reflect, that while we are sending our own missionaries to our distant colonies, our own villages are perishing for lack of instructions ... yet I could not be comfortable till something was attempted (p. 213).

What is noteworthy, here, is that More regards the poor in her own country as worthy of the same attention as colonized 'others'. Her belief is that all people, regardless of class, should be enabled to read and therefore to pursue a proper Christian life. Not only were slaves often denied this right, but, as she recognized, so too were the poor in Britain. Her views express the emphasis on pragmatics: 'I had rather *work* for God than *meditate* on him'.[34] And she repeatedly articulates that she believes in the sincerity of her own actions: 'it would be false humility not to say that the whole drift and tendency has been right to the very best of my power'.[35]

Hannah More, John Newton and Evangelical sincerity

It was primarily More's acquaintance with the reformed slave trader, John Newton, that facilitated her religious development. Newton's *Cardiphonia, or the Utterance of the Heart, in the course of a Real Correspondence* (1780) expressed, in epistolary form, the centrality of his role as a key spiritual director of individuals in the Evangelical revival. This volume made an enormous impact on More and, tracing her relationship with Newton, we can see that More's abolitionism was inseparable from her Evangelical faith and desire to do good in the wider social sphere.[36] More and Newton began their acquaintance in 1787 while her popular sentimental drama, *Percy*, was playing in Covent Garden. In a letter to her sister she notes, 'To-day (Tuesday) I have been into the city to hear good Mr. Newton preach; and afterwards went and sat an hour with him, and came home with two pockets full of sermons'.[37] From this point on, she and Newton were correspondents and her reading of *Cardiphonia* marked her transition from the 'world' to religious spirituality.

Perhaps More has been castigated for being an insincere abolitionist because Newton himself remains a controversial figure. Newton is probably known to most as the author of the hymn 'Amazing Grace', and his peculiar story – a slave trader who became an abolitionist – has attracted the attention of historians and literary critics of the period. The vacillations of his life incline current postcolonial critics to view his abolitionist credentials with scepticism, not least because he undertook slave trading after himself working as a slave. In his autobiography, Newton claims that, as a young man, he was traded by his ship's captain for unruly behaviour into the hands of a planter on the Guinea Coast. After a period of being enslaved himself, he persuaded his employers to allow him to progress to be manager of a slave factory and was brought back to England by an associate of his father in 1748. It was during a sea storm, when many of his fellow travellers perished, that Newton felt he received grace and wrote the words to the famous hymn: he had been saved in both senses. This conversion was to be the subject of his famous spiritual autobiography *Authentic Narrative* (1764). As D. Bruce Hindmarsh notes, the *Narrative* was seminal in forming the new 'Evangelical ethos' and was published ten times in Britain and eight times in North America before the end of the century.[38]

The coincidence of Newton's later Evangelical development and of his movement to a strong abolitionist perspective was enhanced by his relationship with the poet William Cowper, who was stridently anti-slavery, and with William Wilberforce who had come to Newton for spiritual direction in 1785. As Cowper wrote in his poem 'Table Talk', dedicated to Newton:

> Stop, while ye may, suspend your mad career;
> O learn from our example and our fate,
> Learn wisdom and repentance ere too late. (ll. 435–7)

In 1788 Newton had learned repentance and supplied information based on his first-hand experience of being a slave ship's captain to the House of Commons in the run-up to the passing of the bill and wrote his abolitionist argument in the pamphlet, 'Thoughts on the African Slave Trade'. Newton referred to this himself as a 'public confession'.[39] 'Perhaps what I have said of myself may be applicable to the nation at large. The slave trade was always unjustifiable; but inattention and interest prevented, for a time, the evils from being perceived.'[40] The light of grace enables his abolitionism and Newton can be regarded as embodying the revolution that Britain itself underwent, moving from considering the slave trade eligible to arguing for its cessation.

Such vacillations are received with scorn by some critics: in his recent study Marcus Wood insists it is vital to return to Newton as 'one of the most terrifying personalities of the second half of the eighteenth century'[41] asserting, '[a]s the voice of John Newton comes through his unadulterated texts surely this requires us to protect its ghastly authenticity'.[42] I read this as Wood's insistence that Newton's 'terrifying' nature, exemplified in his role as a slave captain, cannot be watered down, or revised by his conversion or later anti-slavery activities. Wood wants Newton's role as a slave trader to be the static version of Newton's selfhood that defines him. Yet this view clearly does not deal with the fact that Newton does repent and does seek, through his Evangelical faith, to live a more authentic life. In this sense, authenticity is not about a holistic, stable selfhood but, as Taylor defines it, about a search to live more fully the life that is truest to oneself by pursuing a moral ideal: 'What do I mean by a moral ideal? I mean a picture of what a better or higher mode of life would be, where "better" and "higher" are defined not in terms of what we happen to desire or need, but offer a standard of what we ought to desire'.[43] Taylor's language here shows that reform of the self is necessary to pursue what one 'ought' to want. I read Newton's revolution and unease with his own actions as a powerful *disruption* of the principles that enabled slavery and his move to access a better moral source. This is not merely theoretical disruption: as a member of the Clapham Sect, Newton was one of the founding members of the Abolition Society in 1788 and was certainly one of its most influential figures. It is, perhaps, more useful to read his writings as signs of a contested, internally fraught culture in which slavery was a huge problem.[44]

Crucially, Evangelicalism prioritizes within the rational, Protestant individual the necessity of feeling. In *Cardiphonia* Newton highlights the importance of feeling: 'I think I may lay claim to a little of that pleasing, painful thing, sensibility. I need not boast of it, for it has too often been my snare, my sin and my punishment. Yet I would be thankful for a spice of it ... Where there is this sensibility in the natural temper, it will give a tincture or cast to our religious experience'[45]. Yet, as we can see, Newton's language is cautious. Ultimately, the self, through thoughts, feelings and imagination, may pose a block to accessing God as moral source; 'I daily groan under a desultory ungovernable imagination, and a palpable darkness of understanding, which greatly impede me in my attempts to contemplate the truths of God.'[46] As we can see, then, in the Evangelical mode, self is not to be trusted and this interrogation of self leads to sincere critique which is at odds with Romanticism's more general validation of punctual, unmediated selfhood.

It is this awareness in the Evangelical that feeling simultaneously poses a potential 'snare', and is a vital part of religious experience, that leads to continual self-scrutiny and so the commitment to sincerity. More had written her own examination of feeling in the poem 'Sensibility: A Poetical Epistle to the Hon. Mrs Boscawen' (1782). In this she highlights that empathy is only possible between sincere poets and readers: 'And those whose gen'rous souls each tear wou'd keep/From others' eyes, are born themselves to weep.' (ll. 73–4). Yet More warns of self-deception: 'And while Discretion all our views should guide,/ Beware, lest secret aims and ends she hide' (ll. 191–2). And prudence can make one 'unjust' (ll. 195). Even in this secular poem, then, we see the need for self-scrutiny allied to a sincere search for a moral source. Feeling can be a guide to enacting the golden rule of treating others as you would yourself, but vigilance about one's motivations needs to be maintained.

This awareness of the difference between true and false feeling had long been a subject of More's: in 1778, in 'On the Danger of Sentimental or Romantic Connexions', she warns young women against sentimentalism: which has 'infested letters and tainted morals' ... 'Sentiment is the varnish of virtue, to conceal the deformity of vice'.[47] Here, sentiment is dangerous as it is an external projection of a false feeling that in turn affects actions. The concern is not so much that actions are not representative of the true self, but that the self will be tricked by her own sentiment into believing that the source of the actions is pure when it may not be. The Evangelical is always interrogative of the link between source, feeling and action. This qualification, then, explains why More is able to praise true sensibility, which she calls enthusiasm:

> And enthusiasm is so far from being disagreeable, that a portion of it is perhaps necessary in an engaging woman. But it must be the enthusiasm of the heart, not of the sense. It must be the enthusiasm which grows up from a feeling mind, and is cherished by a virtuous education; not that which is compounded of irregular passions, and artificially refined by books of unnatural fiction and unnatural adventure'.[48]

Despite being accused by clergy who resented her interventions in their parishes to educate the poor, of being an enthusiast, More's enthusiasm is emphatically to do with sincerity and is not in the Methodist mode.

More herself declaimed extreme religious views in her letters while noting that the reform of religion was vital: 'I do not vindicate enthusiasm; I dread it. But can the possibility that a few should become enthusiasts be justly pleaded as an argument for giving them all up to actual vice and barbarism?'[49]

In their search for sincerity, More and Newton's didacticism was accompanied by subjecting themselves to rigorous scrutiny. As Newton wrote to More of his own dilemmas:

> Though the Lord has in mercy opened my eyes, I cannot see without lights, and this light is not in myself. I depend upon an agent which I cannot command, but which I can, and do, too often grieve. In proportion as this influence is suspended or diminished, I revert again to my original self … To this it is owing that I am such a riddle to myself, such a medley of inconsistencies and contradictions'[50]

Self may not be trusted but there is a sincere attempt to be sincere and it is the source, not the self, that is the moral guide. More, similarly, confesses to him her difficulty in accessing the authenticity that may flow from her moral source:

> I am certainly happier here than in the agitation of the world, but I do not find that I am one bit better; with full *leisure* to rectify my heart and affections; the disposition unluckily does not come. I have the mortification to find that petty and (as they are called) innocent employments, can detain my heart from heaven as much as tumultuous pleasures. If to the pure all things are pure, the reverse must also be true when I contrive to make so harmless an employment as the cultivation of flowers stand in the room of a vice, by the entire portion of time I give up to it, and the entire dominion it has over my mind … I pass my life in intending to get the better of this, but life is passing away, and the reform never begins.[51]

If we accept that More's Evangelical faith is a moral source then we can read her interactions with Newton and others, regarding her abolitionism and evolving faith, as acts of sincerity, articulating the desire to live an authentic life that flows from a moral source. This articulation is vital for Taylor:

> Moral sources empower. To come closer to them, to have a clearer view of them, to come to grasp what they involve, is for those who

recognize them to be moved to love and respect them, and through this love/respect to be better enabled to live up to them And articulation can bring them closer.[52]

For Taylor, articulating our sense of our moral source is necessary but, crucially, does not enable an uninterrupted access to that source: the articulation is an act engaged in due to a sincere desire to bring us closer to our sources and is the means by which their 'power' and 'force' are released.[53] In his reply to her concerns, Newton offers comfort to More, not by telling her that she is a better person than she thinks, but by assuring her that she must not expect her inauthentic self to be her guide:

> The disorder we complain of is *internal*, and in allusion to our Lord's words upon another occasion, I may say, it is not that which surrounds us, it is not anything in our outward situation ... that can prevent or even retard our advances in religion; we are defiled and impeded by that which is within.[54]

The only corrective for the Evangelical to the erring self is to access God, who More herself crucially describes as 'the source of all spiritual light, life, comfort and influence'.[55] What Newton and More's writings show us is that, in the Evangelical model, the self is immune to the Romantic elision of sincerity and authenticity discussed in the introduction to this volume. Rather, sincerity is the necessary attitude of the individual who wishes to live authentically as a result of accessing a moral source.

More's controversial abolitionism

More's and Newton's letters to each other, then, increasingly take on the character and quality of the spiritual diary in which each confesses to the other their progression in faith, with Newton as the teacher and guide. In his letters to More, Newton openly scrutinizes his own abolitionist effort. Having published his tract 'Thoughts', Newton in fact registers in his letters to More that it is not, in fact, quite the full confession it might have been. The very language distances himself from the acts he would have undertaken as slave captain: 'I have seen them sentenced to unmerciful whippings ... I have seen them agonizing for hours, I believe for days together, under the torture of the thumbscrews.'[56] His own agency is rewritten in this tone of sincere reporting as he removes himself from his role as sentencer and torturer. In this way, Newton registers the unease that is apparent throughout his writings in a critique of the trade: an explicit critique of self remains suppressed. Yet a letter to More shows that he is aware of this suppression:

> My account of the slave trade has the merit of being true ... Some of my friends wish I had said more, but I think I have said enough. They who, (admitting that my testimony is worthy of credit), would hardly be persuaded by a folio filled with particular details of misery and oppression. What may be done just now, I know not, but I think this infamous traffic cannot last long, at least this is my hope.'[57]

So, we can see here that, for Newton, it is important that his account be credited and he himself regards it as sincere while he acknowledges its limits.

In her letters to her sister, More also confesses that her own abolitionist literary effort 'Slavery, a Poem 1788', is not the ideal contribution:

> I grieve I did not set about it sooner; as it must now be done in such a hurry as no poem should ever be written in ... but good or bad, if it does not come out at the particular moment when the discussion comes on in parliament, it will not be worth a straw ... I would on no account bring out so slight and so hasty a thing on any less pressing occasion, but here time is every thing.[58]

This anti-slavery literary effort, then, for More, is a practical act that she hopes will have a perceivable impact. Such a pragmatic approach was, as Stott argues, part of her religious life, fulfilling 'the imperative of Evangelical religion that laid such stress on the life of active goodness'.[59] In both cases, More and Newton are focused on the practical applications of their various contributions: they acknowledge them not to be ideal, or ultimately representative of the self writing them, but to be sincere in their purpose.

Reading More's practical assessment of her own input to abolitionist activity at this time offers an alternative view of the sources underpinning it to the one propounded in accounts of More that construct her as a hired polemicist for powerful Anti-Jacobin abolitionists. As I have noted, Ferguson articulates the ways in which More's anti-slavery is read as a sinister perpetuation of inequality. Since 'Slavery' was to become a literary model for much abolitionist propaganda, what is says 'about "the slave" becomes, for an indoctrinated British public, what the slave is – a non-sovereign, passive, alien individual in need of European allies'.[60]

More's other famous anti-slavery poem, 'The Sorrows of Yamba', has similarly led to accusations that the author is complicit with the ultimate subordination of slaves. Alan Richardson argues that More's right-wing Christianity is manifest in her rewriting of Eaglesfield Smith's poem 'The Sorrows of Yamba'. More's rewriting controversially inserts a conversion scene in which Yamba, contemplating suicide as she mourns for her home and family, meets a 'missionary man'. He gives her the Bible and converts her to Christianity. Yamba claims:

> Now I'll bless my cruel capture,
> (Hence I've known a Saviour's name)
> Till my grief has turned to rapture,
> And I half forget the blame. (ll. 125–8)

More's rewriting, Richardson argues, is 'infantilizing and reactionary' and tends to shift the poem from being a radical critique of British hypocrisy to an 'Anglocentric' advocacy of Christianity, colonization and domination.[61] In a similar vein, Marcus Wood argues that Yamba, the slave, 'in becoming simultaneously emancipated and Christianized ... swaps one master for another ... the sinister links between Evangelical missionary fervour and British imperial ambition' are manifest.[62] For Richardson and for Wood, the obfuscation of the horrors of slavery with conversion is unforgivable and the sincerity of More's abolitionism is eroded by her religious motivations which they read as, ultimately, imperialistic.

Yet, such criticism is in danger of misreading religion as reactionary, and conversion as oppressive, by wresting a Christian ethics from its eighteenth-century context and placing it within the secular liberalism of the current academy. Julia Saunders similarly warns against misreading More's morals in the light of our own, arguing that 'The main obstacles to a progressive reading of Hannah More's tracts are our own dominant cultural assumptions, which tend to be secular, liberal and – until very recently – masculine.'[63] Even if we do not share her religious convictions, we do need to take account of the fact that More sincerely regarded the saving grace of Evangelical Christianity as the epitome of liberty. The conversion of slaves as represented by Yamba, becomes a radical proposition since all men are equally God's people within an Evangelical view. Yamba's very words, blessing her cruel capture, can, indeed, be read, not as an Anglicization and domesticization of a potentially revolutionary other, but as a direct echo of the former slave Phillis Wheatley's words in her famous poem 'On Being Brought from Africa to America' (1773):

> 'Twas mercy brought me from my pagan land
> Taught my benighted soul to understand
> That there's a God, that there's a Saviour too:
> Once I redemption neither sought nor knew,
> Some view our sable race with scornful eye,
> 'Their colour is a diabolic die'.
> Remember Christians; Negroes, black as Cain,
> May be refin'd, and join th'angelic train.

Wheatley's slyly complex poem captures perfectly the paradox of Christian salvation for the enslaved who must, if they believe in their own conversion, be thankful for their 'cruel capture'. Her astounding first line, which implicitly replaces the word 'slavery' with 'mercy' in an almost imperceptible sleight of hand, condenses the logic of Evangelical Christianity for the slave who finds that the very culture which was barbarous enough to take away liberty, is also enlightened enough to offer eternal salvation. This need not be read as a glib dismissal of slavery's horrors, but, rather, as a sincere awareness of the miraculous reversal of fortunes which a journey through to the other side of slavery can promise. It is in this way that we can read Yamba's words, included in the poem by More; as an ironic awareness of the force of Christianity to revolutionize the slave's spiritual life.

Lionel Trilling, sincerity and More

It is in her only novel, *Coelebs in Search of a Wife*, (1808) that More fully expresses the type of social revolution, initiated by Evangelical reform, that she believes will change the world. Change is desirable but not through bloody revolution. Despite More's immense popularity in her own time, she has been largely ignored as a literary figure and Mellor notes the numerous dismissals by critics of More's novel in her own time and today.[64] Perhaps her prose may be regarded as not very good for reasons that are inescapable but these very reasons are interesting for what they might have to say about More's striving for sincerity in her life and writings. I want, now, to conclude by considering More in the context of Lionel Trilling's seminal work, *Sincerity and Authenticity* (1972). While I may have shown that More is as true as she is good, she is not regarded as 'good' in a literary sense. What I want to note, then, is that because good literary writing (whatever we may mean by such a value judgement) is incompatible with Evangelical sincerity, we can read her novel as prioritizing moral goodness over literary merit. Having read More's poem 'Slavery', and her 'Thoughts on the manners of the great', Newton writes to her, noting that she is sacrificing the praise of literary achievement in attempting social reform: 'You could easily write what would procure you more general applause. But it is a singular privilege to have a *consecrated* pen, and to be able and willing to devote our talents to the cause of God and religion'.[65]

As I have mentioned, More herself felt that her poem on slavery was not very good but she did not let literary vanity get in the way of what she believed to be a necessary intervention. Yet the slightly sub-standard quality of the poem may not simply be due to the fact that it was written in haste, but also to the subject matter of slavery itself. In his letters, William Cowper described the difficulty of writing about the subject in a literary manner: 'The more I have consider'd it the more I have convinced myself that it is not a promising theme for verse. General censure on the iniquity of the practise will avail nothing, the world has been overwhelm'd with such remarks already, and to particularise all the horrors of it were an employment for the mind both of the poet and his readers of which they would necessarily soon grow weary'.[66] Interestingly, we hear in this the echoes of Newton's reticence about his own abolitionist tract: credibility in this matter lies in understatement. Despite having urged her to write in the cause of religion, Newton remained suspicious of the merits of More's Evangelical novel: 'I hoped your just censure of novels would have extended to the proscription of the whole race, without mercy and without exception'.[67] Not only was slavery a tricky topic from which to produce literature, but religious piety itself is antipathetic to the literary endeavour.

Perhaps anti-slavery poems by Cowper, More and many others go some way to proving Oscar Wilde's maxim that 'all bad poetry springs from genuine feeling'. Trilling glosses Wilde's position as a claim that trying to unite experience and expression does not always result in 'truth'.[68] More and Newton are certainly not wearing the Nietzschean masks that, for Wilde, enable truth: they are not 'ironic', they are sincere and morally earnest.[69] *Coelebs in Search of a Wife* has been noted for its influence on the much more interesting and intriguing *Mansfield Park*. Jane Austen was well aware of More's work, both practical and literary, and went to visit her one day but, in fact, the two never met. While *Mansfield Park* did not receive a single review for its first edition,

Coelebs spawned a host from all quarters, was read widely and had run to 12 editions within a year.

In this novel, which is essentially an extended conduct book, Charles goes from family to family trying to find his perfect wife whose ideal model is no less than Milton's Eve. He is the perfect Evangelical Christian and most of his encounters are scenes in which his principles and opinions on morals and manners may be explored through visiting various households. The novel is related to *The Spectator* and, as Jane Nardin points out, fulfils Johnson's criteria, outlined in the *Rambler*, in exhibiting exemplary moral practice and in expunging wit from its observations while striving to maintain a realism that does not stretch credibility too far.[70] This ideal world is certainly found in *Coelebs*, thereby making the novel a dull read, devoid of layered literary sophistication unlike its much more ambivalent and multi-layered successor *Mansfield Park*.

In particular, the novel is a model for female behaviour and Lucilla, the progenitor of Fanny, is the perfect female:

> Lucilla Stanley is rather perfectly elegant than perfectly beautiful ... Her conversation, like her countenance, is compounded of liveliness, sensibility and delicacy. She does not say things to be quoted, but the effect of her conversation is, that it leaves an impression of pleasure on the mind, and a love of goodness on the heart. She enlivens without dazzling, and entertains without overpowering. Contented to please, she has no ambition to shine. There is nothing like effort in her expression, or vanity in her manner.[71]

Suddenly we yearn for the wildly inappropriate Mary Crawford with her puns on rears and vices: but, of course, it is Mary's wit that marks her as insincere and, ultimately, corrupt. Mr Stanley, Lucilla's father, is another ideal Evangelical Christian in the novel and outlines the centrality of sincerity for good works: 'God, who expects not perfection, expects sincerity. Though complete, unmixed goodness is not to be attained in this imperfect state, yet the earnest desire after it is the only sure criterion of the sincerity we profess'.[72] This expresses perfectly that, for the Evangelical, it is the sincere striving for goodness that matters, and he does not expect, in a Romantic way, the external self always to be synonymous with the moral source. Hence we find Lucilla echoing More's words exactly: 'I am often afraid of appearing better than I am, and of pretending to feel in my heart what perhaps I only approve in my judgement'.[73] This is the model of Evangelical sincerity at the heart of the novel.

We note, then, that More deliberately expunges from her writing, any pretensions to literary merit, prioritizing, instead, an instructive morality which fulfilled the prevailing tastes of the age. For Trilling, in contrast, *Mansfield Park* contains a more sinister, solid core of sincerity at its heart. Trilling argues that the novel projects, through Fanny, a version of Hegel's 'honest soul' articulated in *Phenomenology of Spirit* (1807). This exists:

> in a wholly harmonious relation to the external power of society, to the point of being identified with it ... Hegel calls this 'the heroism of dumb service'. This entire and inarticulate accord of the individual consciousness with the external power of society is said to have the attribute of 'nobility'.[74]

But, as Trilling argues, in the end; 'The honest soul is rejected by Hegel because it is defined and limited by its "noble" relation to the external power of society, to the ethos which that power implies.'[75] The astounding thing for Trilling is that Austen's novel refutes Hegel's judgement and proposes a non-dialectical version of the self that is obediently sincere: 'Seven years after the publication of the *Phenomenology* this novel tells us in effect that Hegel is quite wrong in the method of judgement he propounds and exemplifies.'[76] Through the character of Fanny Price, nobility, *Mansfield Park* tells us, 'lies through duty acknowledged and discharged, through a selfhood whose entelechy is bound up with the conditions of its present existence'.[77] The novel challenges us with its 'restrictive moralism, its partisanship with duty and dullness, its crass respectability'.[78] What I want to end by arguing, then, is that, if we accept Trilling's argument about the ultra-conservative mode of sincerity that Fanny embodies, then, notwithstanding literary merit, the mode of Evangelical sincerity in *Coelebs* is much more radical, for Lucilla, despite her Christian piety, is not a version of Hegel's noble soul because her submission is founded on Evangelical precepts. While Lucilla may well be a progenitor for Austen's version of the noble soul, More's insistence on duty is not the insistence on authenticity as achievable through synonymity with social pressures: she proposes, instead, duty as a strategic means to engage with an imperfectible world (in the Evangelical sense) but this very submission will allow the expression of a sincere self that feels for others. Evangelical sympathy, therefore, will lead to reform. It is this sincere sympathy, based on a moral source, that More articulates in her abolitionist writings. Despite current critics' protests about More's politics, her anti-slavery poetry was highly effective in the propaganda war that was to be won eventually against the interests of planters.

In contrast, Fanny's transformative powers are arguably extremely limited: while Sir Thomas Bertram and Henry Crawford may wish to regard her as an agent of moral reform, ultimately she changes no one and nothing. Even as a putative abolitionist, her question to Sir Thomas about the slave trade is welcomed with a deafening silence. Her feelings and sympathies remain subservient to the power structures around her and we are told that Sir Thomas Bertram's trip to Antigua has restored his plantations' profitability. Her manner is not an example to anyone and, in the end, Edmund turns to her as to a sister who will be a companion for the rest of his life. Fanny's sincerity, then, for Trilling, is compliance and the means by which to perpetuate the status quo. Now Trilling does read a radical version of *authenticity* in *Mansfield Park*, in the figure of Lady Bertram. In *Beyond Culture* Trilling argues that the 'biological fact' of the self will 'sooner or later' 'judge the culture and resist and revise it'.[79] As Peter Rawlings puts it, for Trilling, the 'stubborn matter' of Lady Bertram, who refuses to move, to respond or to act in any way, is the embodiment of that biological self that remains beyond culture.[80] Her inertia and indolence are 'vigorously resistant'. Despite some moments of physical inertia, when she is tired, ultimately, Fanny does her duty which Trilling reads as her acquiescence to the Hegelian noble soul.

Clearly Evangelical duty is very different to the obedient duty of the noble soul and the Evangelical's entelechy, or essence is fundamentally at odds with the world as it is: this is a very different kind of submission to Fanny's obedience. In *Coelebs*, the biological self is a *feeling*, benevolent self, guided by the sensibility of the golden rule. This transformative power, then, comes from the sincerity of Evangelical feeling: the Belfield family, more secular in their view and quite suspicious of Evangelicalism, are, by degrees, improved and transformed by the active examples of the Stanley family. Charitable duty is an active, pragmatic expression of ideals: Mrs Barlow, in the novel, is the wife of a clergyman who 'gets her hands dirty' in the parish: her striving to act out of a moral source is *active*, in contrast to Lady Bertram's immobility. 'She is as attentive to the bodies as her husband is to the souls of his people'.[81] The Evangelical paradox is that, though the world is not perfectible, the fulfilment of Christian duties will ultimately transform the external.

In conclusion, More presents a dialectical view of self that must sincerely interrogate the sources of the self, but that must actively participate in the world as it is now. This, as I have tried to show, is living authentically, according to Taylor's philosophy: it is, as he describes it, an attempt to unify the 'heart' with an 'intense practical concern'.[82] As More herself says in one of her letters, 'Sensibility appears to me neither good nor evil in itself, but in its application'.[83] That very 'application', if engaged in with sincerity, may be transformative. This is the type of active sympathy that can transform the world.

Notes

1. See, for example, Brycchan Carey, *British Abolitionism and the Rhetoric of Sensibility: Writing, Sentiment and Slavery, 1760–1807* (Basingstoke: Palgrave Macmillan, 2005); Deirdre Coleman, *Romantic Colonization and British Anti-Slavery* (Cambridge: Cambridge University Press, 2005); Markman Ellis, *The Politics of Sensibility: Race, Gender and Commerce in the Sentimental Novel* (Cambridge: Cambridge University Press, 1996); Debbie Lee, *Slavery and the Romantic Imagination* (Philadelphia: University of Pennsylvania Press, 2002); Helen Thomas, *Romanticism and Slave Narratives: Transatlantic Testimonies* (Cambridge: Cambridge University Press, 2000); Marcus Wood, *Slavery, Empathy and Pornography* (Oxford: Oxford University Press, 2002).
2. Ann Stott, *Hannah More, the First Victorian,* (Oxford: Oxford University Press, 2004) pp. ix–x.
3. Moira Ferguson, *Subject to Others: British Women Writers and Colonial Slavery, 1670–1834* (London: Routledge, 1992) pp. 214–7.
4. Stott, *Hannah More,* p. xi.
5. Anne K. Mellor, *Mothers of the Nation: Women's Political Writing in England, 1780–1830* (Bloomington: Indiana University Press, 2000) p. 14.
6. Ibid., p. 14.
7. Charles Taylor, *The Ethics of Authenticity,* (Cambridge: Harvard University Press, 1991) pp. 25–6.
8. Ibid., p. 26.
9. See *The Evangelical Conversion Narrative: Spiritual Autobiography in Early Modern England.* D. Bruce Hindmarsh (Oxford: Oxford University Press, 2005), p. 42.
10. Charles Taylor, *Sources of the Self: The Making of Modern Identity* (Cambridge: Cambridge University Press, 1989) p. 399.
11. Eric Willliams, *Capitalism and Slavery* (Chapel Hill: The University of North Carolina Press, 1944) pp. 181–8. See, especially the chapter entitled, 'The "Saints" and Slavery'.
12. David Brion Davis, *The Problem of Slavery in Western Culture* (Ithaca: Cornell University Press, 1966) pp. 41–3.
13. For a more recent intervention into this debate see, Christopher Leslie Brown, *Moral Capital: Foundations of British Abolitionism* (Chapel Hill: The University of North Carolina Press, 2006).
14. Clare MacDonald Shaw, ed. *Tales for the Common People and Cheap Repository Tracts* (Nottingham: Trent Editions, 2002) p. vii.
15. Taylor, *Sources of the Self,* p. 399.

16. Clare Midgley, *Women Against Slavery, the British Campaigns 1780–1870*. (New York: Routledge, 1992) p. 200.
17. Ferguson, *Subject to Others*, p. 152.
18. Wood, *Slavery Empathy and Pornography*, pp. 226–7.
19. Alan Richardson, '"The Sorrows of Yamba," by Eaglesfield Smith and Hannah More: Authorship, Ideology, and the Fractures of Antislavery Discourse', in *Romanticism on the Net* (Issue 28 November 2002) [11 August 2009]. <http://users.ox.ac.uk/~scat0385/more.html>
20. Tim Fulford and Peter J. Kitson, eds. *Romanticism and Colonialism: Writing and Empire, 1780–1830* (Cambridge: CUP, 1998), p. 11.
21. Lee, *Slavery and the Romantic Imagination*, p. 3.
22. Ibid., p. 3.
23. Roger Anstey, *The Atlantic Slave Trade and British Abolition, 1760–1810* (London: Macmillan, 1975), p. 157.
24. Taylor, *Sources of the Self*, p. 400.
25. Ibid., p. 400.
26. Patricia Demers, *The World of Hannah More* (Lexington: University Press of Kentucky, 1996) p. 60.
27. Hannah More to Mrs Carter n.d., 1787, in William Roberts ed. *Memoirs of the Life and Correspondence of Mrs Hannah More*, vol. 2, (London: R. B. Seeley and W. Burnside, 1834) pp. 70–1.
28. Hannah More 'Thoughts on the Importance of the Manners of the Great to General Society', 4th edn, (Dublin, 1788) p. 9.
29. David W. Bebbington, *Evangelicalism in Modern Britain: A History from the 1730s to the 1980s* (London: Routledge, 1989) p. 69.
30. More, *Memoirs*, vol. 2, pp. 136–7.
31. Claudia Thomas Kairoff, 'Eighteenth-century women poets and readers', *The Cambridge Companion to Eighteenth-Century Poetry*, ed. John Sitter (Cambridge: CUP, 2001) pp. 173–4.
32. Taylor, *Sources of the Self*, p. 399.
33. More, *Memoirs*, vol. 2, p. 429.
34. More, *Memoirs*, vol. 3, p. 62.
35. Ibid., p. 136.
36. John Newton, *Cardiphonia or the utterance of the Heart, in the course of Real Correspondence* (London, 1786).
37. More, *Memoirs*, vol. 2, p. 54.
38. Hindmarsh, pp. 15–16.
39. Newton, 'Thoughts', p. 98.
40. Ibid., p. 100.
41. Wood, *Slavery*, p. 23.
42. Ibid., p. 64.
43. Taylor, *Ethics of Authenticity*, p. 16.
44. I of course invoke David Brion Davis, *The Problem of Slavery in Western Culture* (New York: Oxford University Press, 1966).
45. Newton, *Cardiphonia*, vol. 2, p. 23.
46. Newton, *Cardiphonia*, vol. 1, p. 15.
47. Hannah More, 'On the Danger of Sentimental or Romantic Connexions' (1778), *Essays on Various Subjects, Principally Designed for Young Ladies*, 5th edn, (London: T. Cadell, 1791) p. 78.

48. More, *Memoirs*, vol. 4, pp. 295–307.
49. More, *Memoirs* vol. 3, p. 138.
50. More, *Memoirs*, vol. 2, p. 185.
51. Ibid., p. 88.
52. Taylor, *Sources of the Self*, p. 96.
53. See Taylor, *Sources of the Self*, p. 96 passim.
54. More, *Memoirs* vol. 2, p. 91.
55. Ibid., p. 92.
56. John Newton, 'Thoughts on the African Slave Trade', in *The Journal of a Slave Trader*, eds. Bernard Martin and Martin Spurrell (London: Epworth Press, 1962) p. 104.
57. More, *Memoirs*, vol. 2, p. 85.
58. Ibid., pp. 97–9.
59. Stott, *The First Victorian*, p. 119.
60. Ferguson, *Subject to Others*, p. 147.
61. Richardson, 'The Sorrows of Yamba' <http://users.ox.ac.uk/~scat0385/more.html>
62. Marcus Wood, *The Poetry of Slavery: An Anglo-American Anthology* 1764–1865 (Oxford: Oxford University Press, 2003), p. 100.
63. Julia Saunders, 'Putting the Reader Right: Reassessing Hannah More's Cheap Repository Tracts', in *Romanticism On the Net* 16 (November 1999) [11 August 2009]. <http://users.ox.ac.uk/~scat0385/more.html>
64. See Mellor, *Mothers of the Nation*, pp. 17–18.
65. More, *Memoirs*, vol. 2, pp. 54–5.
66. William Cowper, *The Letters and Prose Writings of William Cowper*, ed. James King (Oxford: Oxford University Press, 1988), vol. 3, p. 72.
67. More, *Memoirs*, vol. 3, p. 77.
68. Trilling, *Sincerity and Authenticity*, p. 119.
69. Ibid., p. 120.
70. See Jane Nardin, 'Jane Austen, Hannah More and the Novel of Education' in *Persuasions*, 1998, vol. 20, pp. 15–20.
71. Hannah More, *Coelebs in Search of a Wife*, ed. Mary Waldron (Bristol: Thoemmes Press, 1995), p. 64.
72. More, *Coelebs*, p. 116.
73. Ibid., p. 145.
74. Trilling, *Sincerity and Authenticity*, p. 35.
75. Ibid., p. 42.
76. Ibid., p. 77.
77. Ibid., p. 78.
78. Ibid., p. 79.
79. Cited in, Peter Rawlings, *American Theorists of the Novel: Henry James, Lionel Trilling, Wayne C. Booth.* (London and New York: Routledge, 2006), p. 46.
80. Rawlings, *American Theorists*, p. 49.
81. More, *Coelebs*, p. 70.
82. Taylor, *Sources of the Self*, p. 399.
83. More, *Memoirs*, vol. 2, p. 202.

7
Sincerity's Repetition: Carlyle, Tennyson and Other Repetitive Victorians

Jane Wright

'Have I involved you in double postage by this loquacity?', Thomas Carlyle worries in a letter to Ralph Waldo Emerson of 1835; 'I did not intend it when I began; but today my confusion of head is very great and words must be multiplied with only a given quantity of meaning.'[1] Commenting on some of the rhetorical strategies evident in Carlyle's lectures, *On Heroes, Hero-Worship, and the Heroic in History* (delivered 1840, published 1841), this chapter explains how sincerity is fundamental to the sage's verbose inarticulacy. Via Carlyle's professed admiration for Tennyson's *Poems* (1842), it then discusses other Victorians whose writing highlights important literary relations between repetition and sincerity, though in ways that can seem to place sincerity and repetitive language at odds with one another. Finally, it argues that such apparent opposition offers a means by which to appreciate the ineluctable relationship between methods of writing and sincerity – a relationship exposed as a matter of trust and exchange, and one which reaches an especial intensity in the work of a number of important Victorian writers.

Three meanings of 'Sincerity's Repetition' emerge: the first applies the phrase to Carlyle's repetition of the word 'sincerity' itself (and how this in turn affects the sense of what sincerity is or means in his work); the second takes the phrase in its extended form ('sincerity is repetition') and considers style or 'accent' as a species of repetition which constitutes a form of literary sincerity in its own right; finally, the third sense, which grows out of this discussion of style, considers (via the possessive case) the kind of further repetition within the reader for which such literary sincerity may be responsible – a repetition, that is, of the kinds of struggle with, and necessary faith in, language that the author has discovered. The discomfort of this exchange (the author's discomfort about possibly being misunderstood, and the reader's in trying to understand) is the discomfort of learning to trust: of learning to be 'involved' in the expense of 'words multiplied', and to accept the 'given quantity of meaning' that they offer.

When a person feels or believes something, he or she may simply have to state it and, unable to explain it in a satisfactory manner, state it again and again if he or she wishes to be heard. Carlyle understood this all too well. Later in 1835 he wrote to Emerson:

> What you say about the vast *imperfection* of all modes of utterance is most true indeed. Let a man speak and sing, and do, and sputter and gesticulate as he may, – the meaning of him is most ineffectually shown forth, poor fellow; rather *indicated* as if by straggling symbols, than *spoken* or visually expressed! Poor fellow! So the great rule is, That he *have* a good manful meaning, and then that he take what 'mode of utterance' is honestly the readiest for him.[2]

Carlyle (never famed for taciturnity) was acutely conscious of the way he spent his words, and of the inadequacies of words and speech. In his lectures 'On Heroes, Hero-Worship, and the Heroic', frequently the harder Carlyle wishes to emphasize a point the fewer different words he uses to define it, but the longer he holds the idea in the minds of his audience. The result is repetition in one or more of its rhetorical forms. Such repetitiveness has been seen by some critics (suspicious of rhetoric) as obfuscatory, particularly when it comes to his uses of the word 'sincerity' itself, a term which he never explicitly defines; but the repetitiveness goes hand-in-hand with Carlyle's desire for clarity, and it is a direct result of his anxieties about the effectiveness of language and getting his point across. He is concerned that sincerity and utterance are at odds with one another, and he manifests this concern in language that increasingly seems to aggravate that opposition. For this reason it becomes crucial to attend to the details of his language, because the difficulties and emphases it performs become themselves a description of sincerity as Carlyle understands it, and they render any more explicit definition of sincerity both insufficient and beside the point.

In his correspondence with Carlyle, Emerson soon made critical enquiries regarding what he called the 'form' and 'diction' of Carlyle's work. Emerson (later so heavily influenced by Carlyle) was not entirely happy with the ironic style of *Sartor Resartus* (1833–4) nor the apparent extravagance of Carlyle's prose, and he urged that 'At least in some of your prefaces you should give us the theory of your rhetoric.

I comprehend not why you should lavish in that spend-thrift style of yours celestial truths'.[3] Charles Eliot Norton footnotes that on receiving this letter from Emerson, Carlyle recorded in his diary that it was 'sincere, not baseless, of most exaggerated estimation'.[4] And here Carlyle's application of 'sincere' is a microcosm of his own understanding and uses of the term elsewhere. It is linked, without any sense of difficulty or question, with exaggeration; the term is divided from, but also connected to, the acknowledgement of exaggerated feeling by the affirmative statement 'not baseless'. The words 'not baseless' apply backwards and forwards both to Emerson's sincerity and to his exaggerated estimation, so that, syntactically, being 'sincere' is not just an alternative to 'baseless[ness]' but becomes a form of base in itself, from which exaggeration can be accepted and appreciated. Exaggeration will express truth, even if not always comfortably. This is the principle upon which Carlyle's lectures and many subsequent literary strains of sincerity in the nineteenth century would best be read.

A cultural sage who exerted an extensive influence on later nineteenth century writers, Carlyle has been accused of contributing significantly to the downfall of sincerity as a useful (indeed, meaningful) critical term. Lionel Trilling wrote little about Carlyle in *Sincerity and Authenticity* (1972) – an omission which, even given Trilling's obvious debts to Matthew Arnold, seems odd considering the amount Carlyle had to say on the subject; and eight years earlier (in 1964) Patricia Ball considered that by his many uses of the term Carlyle merely 'throws an aura round sincerity ... [and] makes of it a mystique'.[5] One might suspect that Ball would have agreed with Theodor Adorno that certain cultural terms can develop a mere 'aura' of value and cease to have clear meaning; 'sincerity', in this case, becomes no more than a counter, passing for a value that remains obscure, or which masks a lack of, and potential immunity to, precisely that value and force that it claims to attest.[6] But while Ball spotted a problem with Carlyle's style, she did not address it in such terms, and so did not interrogate the possibilities and hopes of 'sincerity' as Carlyle repeated it. Given the nature of the dangers to sincerity that Carlyle perceives (that adequate language for being sincere, if there ever was such a thing, has been broken down by this point in the nineteenth century) it seems inevitable that he should be seen to succumb to those dangers: language itself is the difficulty. But there is a significant difference between prompting a decline in the validity of sincerity as an important literary term, and making, as Carlyle did (in the words of Wordsworth's 'Note' to 'The Thorn' (1800)), 'consciousness of the inadequateness of our own powers and the deficiencies of language' fully correspond to his method of speaking and writing.

Wordsworth writes that:

> every man must know that an attempt is rarely made to communicate impassioned feelings without something of an accompanying consciousness of the inadequateness of our own powers, or the deficiencies of language. During such efforts there will be a craving in the mind, and as long as it is unsatisfied the Speaker will cling to the same words, or words of the same character. There are also various other reasons why repetitions and apparent tautology are frequently beauties of the highest kind. Among the chief of these reasons is the interest which the mind attaches to words, not only as symbols of the passion, but as *things*, active and efficient, which are of themselves part of the passion.[7]

Eric Griffiths rightly notes of this passage that Wordsworth:

> moves between two conceptions of language, conceptions which, were we to treat them as elements of a unified theory, would not only be diverse but contradictory. At first, he speaks as if states of consciousness and their linguistic expression were identifiable apart from each other, so that a speaker might spot a mismatch between them, but in repetition of his second type words are 'not only ... symbols of the passion, but ... *things*, active and efficient, which are of themselves part of the passion'. In these terms, the feeling of 'mismatch' or let-down is harder to explain.[8]

The point is, of course, that the *feeling* of mismatch between language and consciousness doesn't always mean that there *is* a mismatch; it may mean, for instance, that the writer's own feeling of disjunction, of word-transcending passion, or of faith has found a just expressive form. If words can be '*things*', that is, (as even Wordsworth's use of italicization hints) the 'feeling of "mismatch"' may be harder to explain but precisely the affective proof that language and feeling (or belief or state of consciousness) are 'part of' one another after all. Samuel Beckett's 'Try again. Fail again. Fail better' was one characteristically repetitive way of expressing this kind of fundamental feature of our relationship with language and art.[9]

In his response to Emerson's letter quoted above, Carlyle attempts to account for his style. He does not offer a 'theory of [his] rhetoric', but instead acknowledges rhetoric to be part of the problem faced by sincere expression, especially in the nineteenth century. He writes:

> With regard to style and so forth, what you call your 'saucy' objections are not only most intelligible to me, but welcome and instructive. You say well that I take up that attitude because I have no known public, am alone under the heavens, speaking to friendly or unfriendly space; add only, that I will not defend such attitude, that I call it questionable, tentative, and only the best that I, in these mad times, could conveniently hit upon. For you are to know, my view is that now at last we have lived to see all manner of Poetics and Rhetorics and Sermonics, and one may say generally all manner of *Pulpits* for addressing mankind from, as good as broken and abolished: alas yes! if you have any earnest meaning which demands to be not only listened to, but believed and done, you cannot (at least I cannot) utter it *there*, but the sound sticks in my throat, as when a solemnity were *felt* to have become a mummery; and so one leaves the pasteboard coulisses, and three unities and Blair's Lectures, quite behind; and feels only that there is *nothing sacred*, then, but the *Speech of Man* to believing Men! ... is it not pitiable? ... Pity us therefore; and with your just shake of the head join a sympathetic, even a hopeful smile. Since I saw you I have been trying, and still trying, other methods, and shall surely get nearer the truth as I honestly strive for it. Meanwhile, I know no method of much consequence except that of *believing*, and being *sincere*: from Homer and the Bible down to the poorest Burns's Song, I find no other Art that promises to be perennial.[10]

Carlyle acceded to the potential problems of his own ironic and rhetorical striking of attitudes ('I will not defend such attitude'), which themselves threaten to turn something real ('a solemnity') into inarticulacy or impersonation ('a mummery'). In 'these mad times', however, although Carlyle's manner (or mannered way) of speaking was self-confessedly 'questionable, tentative', it was still the 'best' that he felt he could achieve. What it required, beyond his own continued struggle, was 'believing Men' to recognize and understand it. Carlyle explained to Emerson what most twentieth-century commentators on nineteenth-century sincerity overlook: that what appeared to be merely rhetorical attitudinizing was inseparable, 'in these mad times', from the importance Carlyle placed *on* sincerity. In order to continue being sincere one had to attitudinize all the more.[11] Note, too, that '*believing*' and 'being

sincere' constitute a 'method' and that that method is an 'Art that promises to be perennial'. The concern is not with whether sincerity can be
achieved or not, but with the difficulties of the 'method' it is.[12] This
method – *'believing'* and 'being *sincere'* – is still available to Carlyle, he
writes, even though 'all *manner* of Poetics and Rhetorics and Sermonics'
have been fractured (emphasis added). Authenticating language (in
both senses of that phrase) seems to have become more difficult – the
contexts for it lost. And as the modes of address are 'broken', so is the
voice, which, having an 'earnest meaning' to impart, cannot '(at least
I cannot) utter it *there*, but the sound sticks in my throat'. The continued attempt to be sincere did not prevent sounds sticking in Carlyle's
throat, however, but meant that the word 'sincerity' itself became one
of those sounds.

In the Heroes lectures, Carlyle does not explain what he means by
'sincerity' because it is, first, an *archai*, or first principle, of heroism;[13]
secondly, it is his mode of utterance, and so one and the same as the
characteristic features of his style: his struggling, repetitive, emphatic,
prose; and, thirdly, because he believes that such explanation is at odds
with sincerity (as I discuss further below).[14] The contexts of Carlyle's
uses of the word associate sincerity with 'consciousness ... of sin',
'divine mystery', 'direct insight' or seeing 'beyond the shows of things';
for the Poet, with the capacity for 'musical thought' (which is always
deep thought), 'sympathy', *'effort'*, and *'suffering'*; while, for the Man of
Letters, it is connate with inspiration, 'originality', and 'genius'.[15] These
are not supposedly clearly laid out Wordsworthian criteria for a creative
theory of sincerity (such as those in the 'Preface' to *Lyrical Ballads* or
the 'Essays on Epitaphs'), but, use by use, Carlyle builds a set of associations around 'sincerity' which leaves the term itself to denote a kind
of felt presence for which these other terms and phrases collectively
gather force. Far from Ball's complaint that sincerity is a word used
easily and coercively by Carlyle – 'the word repeated, intoned, invested
with power simply by rhetorical sleight of hand'[16] – Carlyle is crucially
explicit about his own vagueness. For Ball, 'it is the unfortunate price
of [Carlyle's] stylistic power that he gives the illusion that the word
['sincerity'] may stand alone'.[17] But, on the contrary, given in outline
and no more, Carlyle states openly that 'sincerity' in the end denotes
'the heroic quality we have no good name for'.[18] Our own discomforted
sense of the unformulated (or, perhaps worse, unadmitted) definitions
that he works with, which may leave us feeling suspicious about his
own sincerity as well as his uses of 'sincerity', is itself an important
aspect of the kinds of relationships he asks us to be attentive to. The

same discomfort alerts us to how he asks us to acknowledge the complexity of the relationships between urgency and reserve, the emphatic and the unspoken, our profound faith in the power of words and our knowing reticence about their effectiveness.[19]

Carlyle associated sincerity with originality, for instance, not because he held originality to be a mysterious or necessarily rare quality, but because he held it to be descriptive of the value and the process of arriving at individual belief. Originality is linked with sincerity because a true belief (a belief formed in good faith) on Carlyle's terms must involve a commitment of faith which is self-constituting. In 'The Hero as a Man of Letters', he explains:

> The merit of *originality* is not novelty; it is sincerity. The believing man is the original man; whatsoever he believes, believes it for himself, not for another. Every son of Adam can become a sincere man, an original man, in this sense; no mortal is doomed to be an insincere man.[20]

The syllogistic nature of this passage (a syllogism itself a form of argumentation linked both to sound reasoning and to trickery) lends logicality to Carlyle's assertions, but offers only a vague description of sincerity (though a description nevertheless). Originality is linked with sincerity; believing is linked with originality; *ergo* (we are told): sincerity is linked with believing. This is not thoroughgoing reasoning – not, at least, in the fully explanatory sense. And yet when we are told that sincerity, not novelty, is the merit of originality and is evident in a person who believes for her- or himself, we are told so in prose, the self-contained movements of which make it a model of what it describes. For Carlyle is not saying anything new to his audience, but is asserting again his own belief that sincerity is of the utmost importance. The anxiety that lingers in such a repetitive voice that we might not believe him, or, worse, might not believe that he believes, seems to console itself with the sense that repetition may be not just a return to, but a re-enactment of, a first utterance or originating moment. But it also thereby becomes not a performance but a *form* of the commitment of belief that it identifies as valuable. The passage, partly by whittling down the number of different words it uses, partly by repeated and echoed sentence structures, and partly by being a now-characteristic reiteration of belief, seeks not just to console itself but to reassure the listener of its trustworthiness.

Carlyle found his 1840 lecturing a trying business and felt that his audience often misunderstood him. His insistence on the foundational

nature of sincerity to heroism was an attempt to reclaim a resistant
and resistless ground for speech of the kind I discussed above, but a
representative section from 'The Hero as Prophet' further exemplifies a
kind of rhetorical strategy that occurs throughout the lectures. Carlyle
asserts that:

> No Mirabeau, Napoleon, Burns, Cromwell, no man adequate to do
> anything, but is first of all in right earnest about it; what I call a
> sincere man. I should say *sincerity*, a deep, great, genuine sincerity, is
> the first characteristic of all men in any way heroic. Not the sincerity
> that calls itself sincere; ah no, that is a very poor matter indeed; –
> a shallow braggart conscious sincerity; oftenest self-conceit mainly.
> The Great Man's sincerity is of the kind he cannot speak of, is not
> conscious of: nay, I suppose, he is conscious rather of *in*sincerity; for
> what man can walk accurately by the law of truth for one day? No,
> the Great Man does not boast himself sincere, far from that; perhaps
> does not ask himself if he is so: I would say rather, his sincerity does
> not depend on himself; he cannot help being sincere![21]

The passage claims that no man is adequate to do anything unless
'first of all' being what Carlyle calls 'a sincere man'. The next sentence
repeats this point, adding a series of intensifiers to 'sincerity', first
in italics, or an emphatic tone, and then adjectivally: 'deep', 'great',
'genuine'. The audience is told what sort of 'sincerity' this is 'not' – not
a sincerity 'that calls itself sincere'; the man 'in right earnest' is made
adequate 'to do', not to talk about his sincerity. Carlyle then suggests
what kind of consciousness sincerity does involve: a consciousness of
its opposite, 'of *in*sincerity'. And finally, after repeating these points in
a different form ('No, the Great Man does not boast himself sincere ...
perhaps does not ask himself if he is so'), he asserts that the sincere
man 'cannot help being sincere'. The sincere man, this passage tells us,
is sincere. That is, after a series of clauses intensifying or specifying sincerity, the initial assertion has not been much advanced, but restated,
and the concept of sincerity (if we call it a concept for a moment) is not
defined but *re*fined. (The sense that there may be anything as unified
as a 'concept of sincerity', however, becomes a clumsiness here.) In rhetorical terms this passage is an instance of *commoratio* or refinement by
repetition, an argumentative figure through which one (as Sister Miriam
Joseph relates) 'seeks to win an argument by continually coming back
to one's strongest point'.[22] But none of this is to say that Carlyle fails
to tell us what he means by sincerity. In the process of providing this

seemingly tautological account, the audience *has* been told that a man must be sincere before he is adequate to 'do' anything, and that the sincere man 'cannot help being sincere'. In other words, a sincere man seems (according to Carlyle) to possess a forcefulness based upon a kind of helplessness, and this after all was one dimension of his own concern, but also hope, regarding the misrepresentations of his own language. Carlyle, that is, describes here what he felt his own language was already doing – making a consciousness of inadequateness work to the advantage of force, and force of feeling. He is, on his own terms, doing sincerity with words; and in demonstrating that he has made himself adequate to 'do' this, he simultaneously and without direct comment, *demonstrates* the sincerity he implicitly describes. Again, there is no theory of sincerity here – of what sincerity otherwise might mean – and certainly nothing like Wordsworth's ideal of a perceptible 'tranquillity' of composition.[23] Instead there is a voice straining, awkward, dangerously close to self-contradiction, and at times truculent; but which is itself a *form* of literary sincerity in which possible theorization and the method of expression have become inextricable (in which words have become '*things*'). Sincerity is evolving, and it is doing so precisely through the complexity of the relationship that Carlyle emphasizes between sincerity and verbose, struggling, or formally heightened language.

Amid a continued suspicion of rhetoric in the later twentieth century, such an important but involved mode of sincerity seemed to slip out of literary criticism. George Eliot, in 1855, saw the danger of this for later readers of Carlyle's work; but she also astutely pointed out that already 'Much twaddling criticism has been spent on Carlyle's style' and conceded that:

> Unquestionably there are some genuine minds, not at all given to twaddle, to whom his style is antipathetic ... But instinctive repulsion apart, surely there is no one who can read and relish Carlyle without feeling that they could no more wish him to have written in another style than they could wish gothic architecture not to be gothic, or Raffaelle not to be Raffaellesque.[24]

One danger for sincerity is precisely that it may be unconvincing, misunderstood (a fact which gives the edge to Gilbert's quip in Oscar Wilde's 'The Critic as Artist': 'I live in terror of not being misunderstood').[25] But Carlyle is a writer for whom, Eliot adds, 'perhaps, his greatest power lies in concrete presentation'.[26] And here is a further aspect of the literary relationship between sincerity and repetition

which Carlyle's example magnifies for the nineteenth century: an ener-
getic reconnection of nature or self with literary style. Carlyle (as I have
explained) associated sincerity with responsiveness to, and the creation
of, presence. Of the heroic man and his belief, he writes that '[w]ith
bursting earnestness, with a fierce savage sincerity, half-articulating, not
able to articulate, he strives to speak it, *bodies it forth* in that Heaven or
that Hell' (my italics).[27] Style and form can be literary versions of such
presence or bodying forth.

In the 1980s, a renewed critical interest in rhetoric went some way to
enhancing a positive focus on Carlyle's style (though it had nothing to
say about either his sincerity or views on sincerity).[28] So when, in her
book of 2004, Pam Morris discusses 'a performative code of sincerity' in
the nineteenth century and suggests that 'Carlyle exerted an enormous
influence [on Victorian writers], not only by his passionate advocacy
of sincerity in *On Heroes and Hero-Worship*, but also by his own distinctive and foregrounded style of sincerity in speaking and writing', one
might be led to hope that a 'foregrounded style of sincerity' by now
carries positive implications of the importance of attending to linguistic
and literary forms. But there is still a remarkably awkward relationship
between sincerity and style in Morris's book.[29] First, Morris's notion of a
'code' of sincerity isn't entirely helpful (neat though it is for the purpose
of one view of social interactions), because although 'code' may mean
simply 'a collection of rules' (*OED*), for Morris it retains a restrictive
suspicion: a code is also a system of rules deployed specifically to enable
secrecy, convenience, or deception. The suspicion that Morris's book
harbours is that we can only attend to sincerity in literature either as
a kind of thematic preoccupation (a feature of content) or as a style of
writing (or behaving) apparently formulated to insinuate a political
or social perspective (not so much a feature of literary form as a feature of
an even less graspable thing: ideology). Morris's 'code of sincerity',
she acknowledges, is 'ideological'; it is a 'sincerity [... which has a]
manipulative or insinuating force as an interpellative code proffering
an invitation to community'.[30] However, the details of this so-called
code are never just literary details, and it seems that as such Morris still
finds a need to acknowledge that in Victorian literature there remains
'"genuine" sincerity, as opposed to duplicitous sincerity' – a phrase in
which sincerity is still getting lost and 'genuine', in its scare quotes, is
suspect.[31]

In any case, having noted Carlyle's 'style of sincerity', it is not Morris's
concern either to say what that style is or how it is that we might accept
it (as it has not always been accepted) as specifically 'of sincerity'.[32]

Good critical attention to form never went away, of course, but nevertheless, in recent years in the field of later nineteenth century studies, critics have renewed close attention to literary form as necessary to a proper and historicized understanding of Victorian literature. The lessons of such attention point to a reinvigoration of interest in sincerity (even though the term itself often remains elusive), but they also demand a refreshed sense of how or what, in literary forms, sincerity is conceived to be. Literary criticism itself, then, returns to old subjects and repeats established principles, not only because new information or newly developed concepts may have reshaped critical thinking and now demand a new discussion, but sometimes simply because those subjects and principles matter, and because a drive for newness – vital and creative in itself – can sometimes otherwise threaten to obscure them.

In light of the difficulties of how the sincere man may 'bod[y] ... forth' his sincerity, then, I want in the last part of this chapter briefly to consider some instances of other Victorian writers for whom repetition lies at the heart of the difficult relation between sincerity and style. John Ruskin, Alfred Tennyson, Charles Dickens, Matthew Arnold, G. H. Lewes, Gerard Manley Hopkins, Christina Rossetti, and Coventry Patmore are some of those Victorian writers who either demonstrate or protest that the unavoidable inconsistencies of human behaviour and linguistic self-expression may be both attested and compensated by repetition. Tennyson, like Carlyle, finds in repetition a consoling verbal ability to linger between utterance and the unutterable; but the force of his repetitiveness is often different, and makes clear another literary relation of repetition and sincerity. From early in life, Tennyson linked repetition with his sense of identity. Recorded in the *Memoir* is his well-known account of a state of mind that he could create – 'a state of transcendent wonder' – by repeating his own name to himself. Following the repetition:

> all at once, as it were out of the intensity of the consciousness of individuality, the individuality itself seemed to dissolve and fade away into boundless being, and this not a confused state, but the clearest of the clearest, the surest of the surest, the weirdest of the weirdest, utterly beyond words, where death was an almost laughable impossibility, the loss of personality (if so it were) seeming no extinction but the only true life.[33]

At once compelling and potentially nulling, the repetitions in this passage become incantatory themselves ('clearest ... clearest ... surest ...

surest ... weirdest ... weirdest'), both drawing us into understanding the experience and threatening momentarily to dissipate the sense of the passage into dreamy echoing. Repetition cuts along this line; it may amount to accrual, confirmation, assurance, or threaten to become hollow, stagnant, self-undermining.

As another of Carlyle's heroes, the Poet was primarily defined by sincerity, to which Carlyle connected the idea of accent. 'Accent', he writes:

> is a kind of chanting; all men have accent of their own, – though they only notice that of others. Observe too how all passionate language does of itself become musical, – with a finer music than that of mere accent ... The Poet is he who thinks in that manner ... it is a man's sincerity and depth of vision that makes him a Poet.[34]

The poet's art is founded upon patterns of repetition, and Tennyson is well known for being an especially repetitive poet and also for seeming to 'chant' his poems.[35] Griffiths has (invoking Proust) called the 'characteristic "accent"' of Christina Rossetti's poetry the 'verbal stubbornesses [that] hang on in her voice', which 'may or may not be deliberated but which [are] integral to the work and to the person we find there'.[36] Finding a person 'there', in poems, nicely opens up the question of sincerity without defining or confining it either to strictly biographical concerns or to questions of intention or form. Without the Proustean nuances of 'accent', however, one might also invoke, not only Carlyle (as in the passage on the Poet I quote above), but Matthew Arnold, who in 1888 considered that the 'accent of sincerity' in a poet's work gives a sense of 'the man speaking to us with his real voice'.[37] Itself intangible, an 'accent' provides the repeated lilts and hints of emphasis that tell you where a person comes from, and, colloquially speaking, where he or she is coming from. Sincerity in poetry might also be thought of as the pattern of such repetitive emphases or features of style – the manner or method by which one repeatedly has brought to one's attention what matters.[38] Something similar to the notion of 'characteristic "accent"', or an 'accent of sincerity', was also expressed by Gerard Manley Hopkins (who was influenced, like Rossetti, by the value of repetition in Tractarian poetics). Hopkins used the term 'Parnassian' to describe the characteristic nature of individual poets' language, and it is a kind of language that is, in another sense, based on repetition because it develops out of the poet's repeated activity of seeing and expressing the world in his or her unique way.[39]

Repetition, however, has been as much of a difficulty for Tennyson and his readers as for Carlyle in his thumpingly repetitive prose. Tennyson, too, has been criticized for repetitiveness that risks emptying words of meaning. His style, as Walt Whitman noted of a characteristically repetitive example, can come close at times to hollowing out his words and luxuriating only in their sounds and in the purely formal qualities of verse; 'To me', Whitman wrote, 'Tennyson shows more than any poet I know (perhaps has been a warning to me) how much there is in finest verbalism. There is a latent charm in mere words, cunning collocutions, and in the voice ringing in them … – as in the line "And hollow, hollow, hollow all delight".'[40] 'Charm' and 'ringing' here pick out the role of repetition in constituting Whitman's sense of 'finest verbalism', even before that role is implicit again in his chosen example. But that there is charm is compelling. And 'cunning collocutions' suggest that there is real insight to be had from the exchanges such words incite.

Contrasting some particular repetitions of Wordsworth's with Tennyson's, Seamus Perry draws attention to Tennyson's view that Wordsworth erred in allowing the word 'again' to recur 'four times in the first fourteen lines' of *Tintern Abbey*. Alongside Tennyson's own obvious proclivity for repetition, Perry notes an unpublished song, written for *The Princess*, in which Tennyson repeats precisely the same word ('again') and so, Perry writes, 'exploit[s] such underlining self-reference far beyond the well-spaced recurrence of the word in Wordsworth's lines'.[41] Tennyson may have felt pleased, Perry suggests, by the fact that by not publishing this verse he had 'resisted a temptation publicly to indulge in such repetitive satisfactions himself'. Whatever the case was, however, Tennyson appears to come out worse in such a comparison and to show a hypocritical sensitivity to a quality also manifested in his own work. But there is an obvious difference between Wordsworth's repetition here and Tennyson's, and that is obviousness. The repetitive lines of Tennyson's unpublished song are:

> Then we brought him home again,
> Peace and order come again,
> The river sought his bound again,
> The child was lost and found again,[42]

The 'satisfactions' Perry refers to are those resulting from the simple pleasure of repetition; though, if such repetition might be considered erroneous, they are satisfactions in another sense insofar as they 'place on the record' and give clear 'proof' of their presence (*OED*). They are satisfactions, that is, of an almost religious kind: disclosed, overt, self-confessing. Unlike Wordsworth's repetitions, Tennyson's (which frequently work with smaller units of sound as much as with whole words) are often brought to the surface in this way, made obvious by their closer proximity to one another or exposure at points of stress or line-endings. By comparison, Wordsworth's repeated words seem submerged and risk the disingenuousness of (formally) hiding something, even though they in fact remain (in Perry's words) 'discreetly fine' correspondents to the returning and dwelling of the subject of Wordsworth's poem. Wordsworth, as Perry suggests, was not at all as explicitly repetitive as some of his literary inheritors. Nevertheless, the literary force of sincerity (of the communication of feeling and the way it might be recognized by readers) in the later nineteenth century develops to a considerable degree through the literary associations with repetition that it acquires when the values of repetitiveness are newly and variously foregrounded by early-nineteenth-century writers such as Wordsworth, Coleridge and Carlyle. Sincerity, in this sense, is something that gets built into the style and subject-matter of works of literature by the repeated demands that they make on readers, and by the recognition (expressed by Wordsworth in the 'Note' to 'The Thorn' and reiterated subsequently) that those repetitions are of value. To this extent, the obviousness of Tennyson's repetitiveness (if repetitions are to be resisted as, to use Perry's apt term, 'temptation') is also a 'payment duly made' for the indulgence, and so carries yet another sense of 'satisfaction' (*OED*); there is honesty invested in obviousness.

In 1890, Coventry Patmore wrote of the Poet that:

> He must have won your credit and confidence in his words, by proofs of habitual veracity and sincerity, before you can so receive the words which come from his heart that they will move your own.[43]

Patmore explains neither exactly what veracity and sincerity are, nor, directly, how it is possible to judge that a poet has been veracious and sincere; and yet, we are told that such a judgement (inspiring, with a hinted sense of investment, our 'credit and confidence') will be concerned with 'proofs' of the 'habitual' nature of those qualities. It is, once more, a mode or method, and not an explicit or particular kind of content, that is important. Habits, of course, can be dangerous things. The repetitions that define them may be either deadening (as Coleridge worried and some of Beckett's characters cry out) or, as in this case, positively affirmative. Repetition, Patmore suggests, is important to sincerity; it endorses a writer's sincerity by helping to make it evident, and, because evidence ('proof' – especially when repeatedly presented) is convincing, it increases the likelihood that words will have their further repetitive, affective impact and (re)create a feeling in the audience or reader. Sincerity, in this respect, both develops and develops out of repetition. Patmore might have felt this particularly, having just repeated, in a quotation above his own assertive words, Wordsworth's lines from 'The Poet's Epitaph': 'You must love him ere to you/He will seem worthy of your love'. Like Carlyle for his declamatory prose, Tennyson for his luxuriously echoing sounds, Arnold for his dramatic and reiterative criticism, Patmore's Poet must be accepted on his own terms before the value of those terms can begin to be appreciated.

The joy of accepting another's terms, however, is partly that those terms thereby become one's own, even if only a little and incompletely. I want to end, therefore, with a couple of brief points about perceptions of such acceptance and its relation to repetition and sincerity for the writers in question. This is the last sense I give to the phrase 'sincerity's repetition' – its prompting of a kind of repetition within the reader. The feeling for repetition is evident not only in both Carlyle's and Tennyson's work but also at the start of their friendship in Carlyle's first praise of the *Poems* of 1842. Shortly after the publication, he writes to Tennyson:

> Dear Tennyson,
> Wherever this find you, may it find you well, may it come as a friendly greeting to you. I have just been reading your Poems; I have read certain of them over again, and mean to read them over and over till they become my poems: this fact, with the inferences that lie in it, is of such emphasis in *me*, I cannot keep it to myself, but must needs acquaint you too with it.[44]

Carlyle's repeated reading of the poems ('some of them over again') swells an intention for further repeated reading ('over and over'), and endorses what he means as well as what he means to do. Such repeated reading, he suggests, will somehow join him with the poems and personalize them: make them 'my poems'. Emphasis, such as that which Carlyle notes in order to exert the force of his feeling on this subject, may itself be considered a species of repetition. The word '*me*' (whether italicized on the page or spoken emphatically) is both 'me, the person I wish to identify to you' and 'me plus the emphasis that tells you that it is me who is special or specific to, or is feeling emotionally charged about, this statement: a sort of "me *plus* me"'. Both Carlyle's repeated reading and his emphasis are important, he suggests, because they concern his self. Repeated reading here, then, is a creative, even a self-constituting act (it results in 'my poems'). In expressing this feeling about reading, Carlyle incorporates repetitive forms into his language of self-expression, both in emphasizing how emphatic his feeling is ('such emphasis in *me*'), and in his wish for Tennyson to register that emphasis ('must needs acquaint you too with it'). That 'I cannot keep it to myself', finally draws out the repetition latent in the desire and act of transmitting 'this fact' to another's mind: I cannot keep it to myself, but must seek to (re)produce awareness of it in you. It would muddle the case, here, to think of sincerity as merely the linguistic performance of an ideal rather than as a background condition to the expression, for which Carlyle must find an adequate form; but any sense of that background, nevertheless, is established and supported by Carlyle's repetitive practice and repetitive expression, which (precisely by being repetitive) seems to signal a prerequisite coherence and invite trust in their truthfulness.

As a final point, then, it is worth noting that, beyond private exchanges such as this one, and in the wider context of literary communication, the dogmatism which became associated with sincerity in later nineteenth-century writing (when sincerity itself had become linked to repetition and emphasis) can be accepted (and was by some Victorians) to be the very sign that sincerity is present.[45] The apparent circularity of such logic is outweighed, these writers deemed, by the moral benefits of sincerity (as a kind of expressive recurrence but also the act of recognition and acceptance of that recurrence) and the liberating implications these could have for individuals. 'Dogmatic truth', writes Coventry Patmore, 'is the key and the soul of man is the lock; the proof of the key is in its opening of the lock; and, if it does that, all other evidence of its authenticity is superfluous ... it is only by "doing the commandments" that we can "know of the doctrine," a sincere and businesslike mind will at least consider the experiment of that moral perfection to which such wonderful things are promised worth trying'.[46] Patmore's distinctly Catholic perspective yet echoes Carlyle's faith that knowing comes chiefly from doing. The sincere mind may be 'businesslike' – suggesting order – but those who attempt to articulate what they learn will only speak in fragmented but emphatic utterances: 'interjections, doxologies, parables, and aphorisms, which have no connecting unity but that of a common heat and light.'[47] Patmore's sincere person submits to a structure which makes it difficult to speak understandably; but sincerity is still readable in the material shape or method of that speaking, and the reader's willingness or ability to recognize this reproduces such submission in her- or himself: it is sincerity in turn.

John Ruskin, noting the accusations of dogmatism laid against anyone who makes emphatic pronouncements on the truths and laws of art, remarks that there are many 'stages of knowledge' that cannot (or should not) be dogmatically stated. However, consciously defending himself from critics' accusations of dogmatism, he goes on to explain that 'it will be found, by any candid reader, either of what I have before written, or of this book [*Modern Painters* III (1846)], that, in many cases, I am *not* dogmatic. The phrase, "I think so," or, "it seems to me," will be met with continually; and I pray the reader to believe that I use such expression always in seriousness, never as a matter of form'.[48] Here the positive aspects of 'form' (to which Ruskin was so alive) meet the negative associations it has developed in its centrality to aestheticism and a potentially hollow, politically dubious social or artistic focus. The apparently foot-shooting quality of Ruskin's emphatic *'not'*, however, (in a way similar to Carlyle's repetitiveness) is proof of its own assertion; not because it is aptly ironic or self-defeating, but because such emphasis is an immediate demonstration of Ruskin's assured feeling that allegations of dogmatism are far less of a concern than is announcing the informed critic's right to authoritative assertions. Ruskin's faith in his assertive method – and so the consequent onus on readers to attend to that method, understand it, and not demand another – is instantly asserted again, and to this extent demands assent. Assenting readers will be 'candid' because, by echoing the writer's struggle, they not only agree to take him on his own terms, they also prove themselves able to experience and accept the difficulties that are integral to the relationship between language and forceful feeling. Ruskin balances his weighty assertion with the phrases that he now explains he uses 'continually' (repeatedly) elsewhere – phrases that become retrospectively implicit in that *'not'*. His repeated use of these phrases, in turn, is one reason that the reader should 'believe' what Ruskin now asserts. The fact that the phrases express subjective qualification ('I think so', 'it seems to me') compounds the importance of lifting emphasis off absolute statement in the interest of, paradoxically, emphasizing how absolutely one feels or believes. It is important to sincerity, in other words, that it is ready to self-undermine as sometimes the best 'method' by which nevertheless to self-assert and even to assert absolutely. That *'not'* is emblematic of one aspect of the difficulties Victorian writers so often demonstrate when attempting to say something that matters. 'Sincerity, I think,' writes Carlyle, 'is better than grace',[49] and he means by 'grace' simultaneously pleasingness of manner and the gift of good favour – a gift for which he, like many of his contemporaries, relies upon the careful and repeated attention of 'candid' readers.

Notes

1. Thomas Carlyle, 'To Ralph Waldo Emerson', 3 February 1835, *The Correspondence of Thomas Carlyle and Ralph Waldo Emerson, 1834–1872*, ed. Charles Eliot Norton, vol. 1 (London: Chatto & Windus, 1883), p. 46. Hereafter cited as *CCE*.
2. Thomas Carlyle, 'To Ralph Waldo Emerson', 29 August 1845, *CCE*, vol. 2, p. 96.
3. Ralph Waldo Emerson, 'To Thomas Carlyle', 14 May 1835, *CCE*, vol. 1, p. 14.
4. *CCE*, vol. 1, p. 21n.
5. Lionel Trilling, *Sincerity and Authenticity* (Oxford University Press, 1972). Patricia Ball, 'Sincerity: The Rise and Fall of a Critical Term', *Modern Language Review*, 59.1 (1964): 3.
6. Theodor Adorno, *The Jargon of Authenticity*, trans. Knut Tarnowski and Frederic Will (London: Routledge, 2003).
7. William Wordsworth, *Wordsworth: Poetry & Prose*, ed. W. M. Merchant (London: Rupert Hart-Davis, 1967), p. 236. Hereafter cited as *WP*.
8. Eric Griffiths, 'The Disappointment of Christina G. Rossetti', *Essays in Criticism*, 47.2 (1997): 110.
9. Samuel Beckett, *Worstward Ho* (London: John Calder, 1983), p. 7.
10. Thomas Carlyle, 'To Ralph Waldo Emerson', 12 August 1834, *CCE*, vol. 1 pp. 22–4.
11. Trilling recognized the performative element of sincerity and set it in opposition to what he saw as the more comprehensive interiority of authenticity. For a discussion of evolving associations between theatricality and sincerity during the Victorian period, see Lynn Voskuil, *Acting Naturally: Victorian Theatricality and Authenticity* (University of Virginia Press, 2004).
12. Deborah Forbes, *Sincerity's Shadow: Self-Consciousness in British Romantic and Mid-Twentieth-Century American Poetry* (Harvard University Press, 2004).
13. See Wayne C. Anderson, '"Perpetual Affirmations, Unexplained": Coleridge, Carlyle, and Emerson', *Quarterly Journal of Speech*, 71 (1985): 40.
14. See Ball, 'Sincerity,' pp. 3–4.
15. Thomas Carlyle, *The Complete Works of Thomas Carlyle*, vol. 5 (London: Chapman and Hall, 1899), pp. 83–4, 91–3, 155. Hereafter *CWC*.
16. Ball, 'Sincerity,' p. 3.
17. Ibid., p. 4.
18. *CWC*, vol. 5, p. 155.
19. Carlyle's silence on the subject of his own expressive problems and processes is nicely illuminated by J. Hillis Miller, '"Hieroglyphical Truth" in *Sartor Resartus*: Carlyle and the Language of Parable', *Victorian Perspectives: Six Essays*, eds. John Chubbe and Jerome Meckier (University of Delaware Press, 1989), in which Miller argues that Carlyle's performative use of language 'discounts

itself in its acts of being proffered' (p. 7). See also Christina Persak, 'Rhetoric in Praise of Silence: The Ideology of Carlyle's Paradox', in *Rhetoric Society Quarterly*, 21.1 (Winter 1991): 38–52.

20. *CWC*, vol. 5, pp. 125–6.

21. Ibid., p. 45.

22. Miriam Joseph, *Shakespeare's Use of the Arts of Language* (Columbia University Press, 1947), p. 220.

23. 'Preface' to *Lyrical Ballads*, 1800, *WP*, p. 230.

24. George Eliot, 'Carlyle,' *George Eliot: Selected Essays, Poems and Other Writings*, eds. A. S. Byatt and Nicholas Warren (London: Penguin, 1990), pp. 344–5.

25. Oscar Wilde, 'The Critic as Artist, Part I', *Oscar Wilde: The Soul of Man Under Socialism and Selected Critical Prose*, ed. Linda Dowling (London: Penguin, 2001), p. 222.

26. Eliot, 'Carlyle', p. 345.

27. *CWC*, vol. 5, p. 47.

28. See Wayne C. Anderson, 'The Rhetoric of Silence in the Discourse of Coleridge and Carlyle', *South Atlantic Review*, 49.1 (1984): 72–90, and 'Perpetual Affirmations, Unexplained: The Rhetoric of Reiteration in Coleridge, Carlyle, and Emerson', *Quarterly Journal of Speech* 71: 37–51. Anderson followed the lead of John Holloway, *The Victorian Sage: Studies in Argument* (London: Macmillan, 1953).

29. Pam Morris, *Imagining Inclusive Society in Nineteenth-Century Novels: The Code of Sincerity in the Public Sphere* (Johns Hopkins University Press, 2004), p. 44. See James Richardson, *Vanishing Lives: Style and Self in Tennyson, D. G. Rossetti, Swinburne, and Yeats* (University Press of Virginia, 1988).

30. Morris, *Imagining*, p. 226.

31. Ibid., p. 226.

32. An illuminating debate on the subject of Carlyle's sincerity follows the publication of D. R. M. Wilkinson's 'Carlyle, Arnold, and Literary Justice', *PMLA*, 86.2 (March 1971): 225–35. See Rodger L. Tarr, 'Carlyle, Tennyson, and "Sincere" Literary Justice', and 'Mr. Wilkinson replies', *PMLA*, 88.1 (January 1973): 136–8. Neither Wilkinson nor Tarr chooses to explore very far what 'sincerity' might mean or be, but they respond in opposed ways to the same kind of feature in Carlyle's prose: Wilkinson finds 'insincerity' in Carlyle's seeming 'unawareness of his own tone and manner' and his lack of 'self-questioning', and to prove these cites a repetitive passage from 'The Hero as Prophet', which I discuss shortly (pp. 230–1); Tarr finds Carlyle sincere because, he 'anticipates and answers' charges of insincerity (in *Past and Present*), and because he 'restates', 'reinforces', and 'emphasize[s]' the things he writes (p. 136), although he doesn't hint *why* such emphasis indicates sincerity.

33. Recounted by Hallam Tennyson, *Alfred Lord Tennyson: A Memoir by His Son*, vol. 1 (London: Macmillan – now Palgrave Macmillan, 1897), p. 320.

34. *CWC*, vol. 5, p. 90.

35. See, for example, discussions by Martin Dodsworth, 'Patterns of Morbidity: Repetition in Tennyson's Poetry', in *The Major Victorian Poets: Reconsiderations*, ed. Isobel Armstrong (London: Routledge & Kegan Paul, 1969), pp. 7–34; Dwight A. Culler, *The Poetry of Tennyson* (Yale University Press, 1977), pp. 1–13; and Seamus Perry, 'Two Voices: Tennyson and Wordsworth', *Tennyson Research Bulletin*, 8.1 (2002): 11–27.

36. Griffiths, 'Disappointment,' p. 108.
37. Matthew Arnold, 'The Study of Poetry', *The Complete Prose Works of Matthew Arnold*, ed. R. H. Super, vol. 9 (University of Michigan Press, 1960–77), p. 183.
38. Walter Pater writes of the author in this regard that 'with his peculiar sense of the world ever in view, in search of an instrument for the adequate expression of that, he begets a vocabulary faithful to the colouring of his own spirit, and in the strictest sense original': 'Style', *Appreciations* (London: Macmillan – now Palgrave Macmillan, 1890), p. 11.
39. Gerard Manley Hopkins, 10 September 1864, *Further Letters of Gerard Manley Hopkins*, ed. Claude Colleer Abbott, 2nd edn. (Oxford University Press, 1956), pp. 216–17.
40. See *Tennyson: The Critical Heritage*, ed. John D. Jump (London: Routledge & Kegan Paul, 1967), pp. 349–50.
41. Perry, 'Two Voices', pp. 18–19.
42. Alfred Tennyson, *The Poems of Tennyson*, ed. Christopher Ricks, vol. 2 (Longman, 1987), p. 299.
43. Coventry Patmore, 'Poetical Integrity', *Principle in Art* (London: George Bell, 1890), pp. 56–61.
44. The letter is quoted in Hallam Tennyson, *Memoir*, vol. 1, 213–14. As Carlyle frequently emphasizes words, and as this is often part of his rhetorical strategy, all emphases in quotations are original unless stated otherwise.
45. Touching the question of dogmatism, for instance, Donald Davie wrote in 1966 that 'a poem is valuable according as the poet has control of it; now we must learn to call that control "sincerity". For after all, what is the alternative? Are we to collect gossip about his private life? Are we to believe the poet sincere because he tells us so? Or because he shouts at us? Or (worst of all) because he writes a dishevelled poetry, because the poem and the experience behind the poem are so manifestly out of his control?' ('Sincerity and Poetry', *Michigan Quarterly Review*, 5.1 (1966): 7). In so doing, Davie expressed a critical perspective that was recurrent during the mid-twentieth century, and one which implicitly parodies and dismisses earlier (Romantic and Victorian) possible forms of sincerity and ways of expressing it ('because he tells us so? ... because he shouts at us?').
46. Coventry Patmore, 'People of a Stammering Tongue', *Religio Poetæ* (London: George Bell, 1893), pp. 47–8.
47. Patmore, 'People', p. 49.
48. John Ruskin, 'Author's Preface', *Modern Painters* III, *The Works of John Ruskin*, eds. E. T. Cook and Alexander Wedderburn, vol. 5 (London: G. Allen, Longmans, Green & Co., 1903–12), p. 5.
49. *CWC*, vol. 5, p. 30.

Part III
Marketing the Genuine

8
By Its Own Hand: Periodicals and the Paradox of Romantic Authenticity

Sara Lodge

The early nineteenth century saw growing public interest in the value of authenticity. The much-publicized Roxburgh sale (1812) of an antiquarian book collection, including a 1471 edition of Boccaccio's *Decameron*, then believed to be unique, for the unprecedented sum of £2,260, drew attention both to the riches represented by early and 'original' texts and to the pursuit of such texts as a gentlemanly sport. The sale led to the formation of the Roxburghe Club of bibliophiles, who took turns to present the society with a transcription or facsimile of some rare or unpublished work in their possession. The fashion for keeping personal albums of signatures and for literary annuals and pocketbooks, which was at its height during the 1820s and 1830s, similarly signals a newly widespread preoccupation amongst the middle classes with autograph, textual rarities and private collection. In 1826, Joseph Niepce produced the first permanent photograph, recording the landscape from his window with unprecedented fidelity. Niepce had studied lithography, a craze which had been sweeping France since 1815, and it was his pursuit of methods of reproducing engravings that led to his experiments with light-sensitive varnish. In all these instances it is notable that the pursuit of authenticity and the pursuit of new forms of reproducibility are inseparable. The increasing ubiquity and diversity of printed products and the lengthening commercial chains that separate the producer from the buyer stimulate increased desire for articles that pre-date modern production or embody a more direct, and hence plausibly more accurate or meaningful, form of contact between the text held by the reader and the original agent and moment of creation. Yet, with inevitable irony, the increasing ubiquity and diversity of printed products is also fed by this desire, developing new subjects, products and technologies that attempt to incorporate and replicate the signs of that evanescent contact.

The periodical is the essential vector in the traffic in authenticity in the 1820s and 1830s. Periodical literature, which burgeoned after the Napoleonic wars was, as contemporaries noted, the primary literary vehicle of the era.[1] On the one hand, the presence of verifiable data, local allusion, the speed of transmission and familiar contributors present apparent markers of authenticity. Readers were frequently invited to submit contributions, suggesting the possibility of a still more direct and spontaneous relationship between author and audience. On the other hand, magazines such as the *London Magazine* and *Blackwood's Edinburgh Magazine* foreground aspects of their rhetoricity and textual unreliability. Most articles appeared without attribution or under a pseudonym; many represented multiple voices, including overt and covert editorial intervention; the deliberate weave of texts also produced implicit dialogues between articles whose nuances were often only available within a coterie of contributors.[2] Self-consciously meta-textual, these magazines invite readers to participate in their own play: to relish wondering which writer(s) lie(s) behind a particular pseudonym, which contributions are claiming an identity to which they have no title, and which views are expressed ironically. Indeed, they explore an emergent consciousness of the inescapability of persona and both vaunt the pleasure of subjective self-revelation and implicitly caution that all autography is innately fictive and constructed by and for an audience.

This chapter looks at two examples of early-nineteenth-century periodical writing that trade on the quest for authenticity in this period while simultaneously exposing the paradoxes inherent in its pursuit. Charles Lamb's Elia essays in the *London Magazine* (1820–1825) both invite and rebuff the desire for what Walter Benjamin calls the 'aura' of the authentic, the unique presence of a work of art at a particular place and moment, which gives it a cult value.[3] Their local detail, seasonal particularity and personal tone all convey a genuineness that inspires affection. Yet the essays are a multi-layered tissue of irony, 'Elia' an overt fiction. How should we read Elia's self-consciously contradictory idiom? I shall argue here that Lamb's art deliberately undermines the patriarchal quest for origins as a source of authenticity and authority. Lamb plays with the Romantic appetite for prior artefact and confessional anecdote while suggesting the limitations of an essentialist conception of literary value and of single selfhood. Where meaning is always deferred and role-play inevitable, value is not located in the imponderable 'authentic' subject or object but is produced between writer and reader through the mutual act of self-production and self-recognition.

The literary annuals of the 1820s and 1830s undercut the rising market for Romantic authenticity in a different way. Economic products of the new fascination with 'original' text, celebrity artefacts and self-writing, the annuals offer their readership affordable opportunities to collect and to practise autograph. However, their sharp commercial tactics and promiscuous print culture suffuse their advertised ideology of authenticity and sincerity with unintended ironies that tend towards self-deconstruction. In both cases, as Margaret Russett observes '[m]agazine production *dialectically* negates book-market discourses of authenticity'.[4] The textual cult of Romantic authenticity authors its own demise, betrayed by its own hand. Yet the outcome is far from negative. In pointing to the reader as co-author of an ostentatiously fabricated text, early-nineteenth-century periodicals initiate an increasingly democratic era of writing and social self-determination.

*

Charles Lamb's first essay for the *London Magazine*, written in the person of 'Elia', was 'Recollections of the South Sea House', published in August 1820. It begins:

> Reader, in thy passage from the Bank – where thou hast been receiving thy half-yearly dividends (supposing thou art a lean annuitant like myself) – to the Flower Pot, to secure a place for Dalston, or Shacklewell, or some other thy suburban retreat northerly, – didst thou never observe a melancholy-looking, handsome, brick and stone edifice, to the left – where Threadneedle-street abuts upon Bishopsgate? I dare say thou hast often admired its magnificent portals ever gaping wide, and disclosing to view a grave court, with cloisters, and pillars, with few or no traces of goers-in or comers-out – a desolation something like Balclutha's.[5]

Elia's opening is conversational. He buttonholes the reader and identifies a passage through the streets of London that they have likely shared, a momentary view of a building, the South Sea House, that both 'gapes wide' to public scrutiny and is mysteriously uncommunicative. In the essay, Elia offers us a tour of this normally private building, though he describes the House as it was when he knew it, 'forty years ago'.[6] In its depiction of an actual location and historic premises the essay deploys markers of authenticity that readers could recognize and corroborate. An essay by 'Vitruvius' in the April 1820 *London Magazine* had similarly discussed 'The Bag-Piper in Tottenham Court Road', a statue that had become a London landmark.[7] Elia's assumption as to the reader's similar condition (dependent upon the income from a small investment) and residence (suburban) create the conditions for immediate familiarity ('thou' not 'you'). When he then apparently unlocks the doors of memory and invites us into the interior of the building that has before excluded access, he conjures, for the House and for himself, what Walter Benjamin calls the 'authenticity of a thing ... the essence of all that is transmissible from its beginning, ranging from its substantive duration to its testimony to the history which it has experienced'.[8] The South Sea House is, Elia observes, like Herculaneum. It is a collection of artefacts preserved because buried. Elia describes the 'long worm-eaten tables', 'massy silver inkstands long since dry', and the 'great dead tomes ... with their old fantastic flourishes, and decorative rubric interlacings', which date from the early eighteenth century.[9] He then depicts the eccentric clerks, themselves curious artefacts, who worked at the House during his time there in the late eighteenth century. Like Oxford in the vacation or the Inner Temple, the South Sea House is one of Lamb's many 'museums': spaces dedicated to arcana that evoke the private life of the mind itself. The layering of strata – of dust, of successive periods of use, of types of document associated with the House – creates a convincing impression of the building's historic actuality and prolonged decline; this confers upon Elia, too, a certain credibility, a sense of his place within a history of meticulous record. Some readers may even have recognized the names of the clerks in the House, which, registers show, were accurate.[10]

Like Benjamin, Lamb evokes the special, threatened aura of the relation between the pre-industrial object and its viewer. The 'costly vellum covers', immense size, and 'formal superfluity of ciphers' in the old account books are lovingly detailed; Henry Man's (a clerk's) 'two forgotten volumes' of jokes 'rescued' by Elia from a stall in Barbican, briefly resurrect their author, 'terse, fresh, epigrammatic, as alive'.[11] The humour and pathos of 'Recollections of the South Sea House' are rooted in a sense of shared loss, briefly recuperated. Since the authentic is a state that is inherently prior, the assertion of loss serves in the essay as an authenticating device. Although the essay is part of a modern, mass-printed periodical, it allies itself with more antiquated forms of writing whose value is largely commemorative, ritualistic. The alternative value of Elia's textual tender is underwritten by the modest social and commercial status at which he hints. Elia is seemingly a clerk, or ex-clerk, who haunts old libraries and second-hand book dealers; he is imbued with the pre-industrial aura of the manuscripts and 'dead tomes' he depicts: inextricably obsolescent and authentic.

Yet, 'Recollections of the South Sea House', like all of the Elia essays, is also a blatantly rhetorical exercise that advertises and revels in its unreliability. 'Elia', which Gerald Monsman calls Lamb's 'ironym'[12] is obviously (perhaps too obviously) an anagram of 'a lie'. Famously, at the end of the essay, Elia proclaims: 'already I have fooled the reader to the top of his bent ... Reader, what if I have been playing with thee all this while – peradventure the very *names*, which I have summoned up before thee are fantastic insubstantial like Henry Pimpernel, and old John Naps of Greece: –'.[13] The use of quotation is itself equivocal. Henry Pimpernel and old John Naps of Greece are figments from *The Taming of the Shrew*. When Christopher Sly, the drunken tailor, is duped into believing that he is a lord who has just awoken from a 15-year coma, his attendants claim that, in his sleep he called out for Pimpernel and Naps, 'which never were nor no man ever saw'.[14] Since, however, this quotation is from a play within a play, and moreover one where the speaker aims to mislead Sly, we cannot know whether these names relate to 'real' persons or not. Elia calls attention to the text's infinite capacity for double bluff, to the ultimate impossibility of determining its authenticity.

The South Sea House itself stands in the essay as a metaphor for the opacity of the text. We are invited to peruse it: Elia seems to offer us disclosure where there has previously been mystery. But the House still stands at two removes from its would-be readers. Its name and defunct purpose date from the 1710s; Elia's recollections date from 'forty years ago'. Of the House as it is, the essay tells us nothing. The context of the South Sea scheme, that 'tremendous HOAX' where fortunes were staked and lost investing in a company that, other than converting national debt, proved to have little meaning or value, likewise evokes the fragile and fictive nature of the structures – words, accounts, '*things* (as they call them in the city)'[15] – on which large-scale credit is built. The South Sea House proved to be a bubble; the essay of that title may be one too. 'Recollections of the South Sea House', then, establishes a dynamic that will be crucial to Lamb's success as the star author of the *London Magazine*. It forges an intimate relationship with the reader based on shared sites of experience, a familiar tone, and an evocation of the personal qualities of reading and writing that gathers value from its association with a lost authenticity. On the other hand, it participates in teasing rhetorical play common to other contributors in the *London Magazine*, that persistently casts doubt on the topoi of authorship, authenticity and identity. The magazine is a peculiarly fruitful space in which to perform this double act because its ensemble of articles and contributors, constantly interpreting each other, both provides a corroborative framework supporting the 'reality' of its observations and emphasizes the floating nature of signification, its reliance upon context and upon reception. Thus, various articles appeared in the *London* lauding 'ingenuous Elia'[16] and claiming him as their 'friend', but another hinted that Elia's phrase about fears 'just now expressed, or *affected*' gave a 'clue to his design' – that he was not always in earnest, and that he might be 'the very Janus who hast always delighted in antithetical presentments,'[17] that is, Janus Weathercock, one of three personae in fact inhabited by another contributor, Thomas Griffiths Wainewright.

The form of the periodical encourages ongoing inter- and intra-textual conversation about literary authority and authenticity. In the November 1821 *London Magazine*, 'A Letter from Elia' appeared in 'The Lion's Head', an introductory space reserved for correspondence between the editor(s) and correspondents, some of whom were fictitious. Elia uses the opportunity to tease various correspondents who think they have detected inconsistencies in his 'autobiography'. Is he of Italian extraction? Is he from Calne? Or was he really born in the Inner Temple? Elia in reply states that, like Bacchus, he can be born in more than one place.[18] Elia's self-identification with Bacchus, who was born twice, once of a female (Semele) and once of a male (Zeus) and traditionally contains equivocally masculine and feminine, civilizing and anarchic powers, is suggestive. Elia's delight in claiming this god-like polyvalency echoes that of Janus Weathercock (Wainewright), who, as the editor jokingly complained in a footnote is: 'sometimes … *we* and sometimes *I*; giving thereby to suspect that he intends to throw ridicule on *us*'.[19] Traditional hierarchies are gently eroded here: the editor, like the king, is normally plural, but Janus and Elia co-opt this right. Readers, too, could weigh in to discussion about the status of the work before them, such as Thomas De Quincey's equivocal response, in the December 1821 'Lion's Head', to James Montgomery, who had asked whether the 'Confessions of an English Opium Eater' were 'real or imaginary'.[20] The result is a periodical that is both unusually concerned with questions of authenticity and exposes the precariousness of the trope. 'Elia' is self-confessedly twice-born, a creation of the magazine and its readers and independent of their terms. If 'the author' is not located in a single, 'original' source, the patriarchal and lineal basis of 'authenticity' is creatively undermined.

The conceptual and practical debate about authenticity conducted in early-nineteenth-century periodicals was not wholly benign. Notoriously, the *London Magazine*'s first editor, John Scott, died in 1821 after a duel with a representative of the editors of *Blackwood's Edinburgh Magazine*.[21] He had challenged *Blackwood's* over its use of pseudonyms to conceal those responsible for potentially libellous attacks and for the two-faced political gamesmanship the editorial mask permitted. With tragicomic irony, Scott, an upholsterer's son, died defending an aristocratic convention regarding the identity of name and honour that his social superiors were too cavalier to take seriously. However, for Charles Lamb and other lower-class or white-collar contributors to magazines such as the *London*, the fiction of identity explored through the periodical was liberating and empowering. As Alan Vardy has shown, John Clare, the agricultural labourer and poet introduced to *London Magazine* readers as 'the Northamptonshire Peasant' broke into some of the literary circles of which he coveted membership through posing in print as 'Percy Green' (a pseudonym that gestures towards Shelley) and 'Frederic Roberts', then exposing his successful charade.[22] Fictionalizing his self proved the means to literary self-actualization. John Hamilton Reynolds, who went by the aristocratic pseudonym 'Edward Herbert' in the *London*, humorously blurred the literary and class boundaries between Byron, Scott, Wordsworth and *London* contributors such as Lamb and Clare by imaging them all as crooks charged with various crimes at 'The Literary Police Office, Bow-Street'. Wordsworth, 'a pedlar by trade, that hawks about shoe-laces and philosophy' is accused of passing himself off as his grandmother,[23] while 'Sir Walter Scott, alias THE GREAT UNKNOWN, alias BILL BEACON, alias CUNNING WALTER' is implicated in 'a sort of *novel* fraud ... of a very extensive nature'.[24] Reynolds, with this neat conceit, emphasizes the shared imposture involved in all literary work and the commercial ends it serves. Elia, in 'On Witches and Other Night-fears' compares his dreams with those of Coleridge in 'Kubla Khan' and De Quincey in 'Confessions of an English Opium Eater'; Lamb features imaginatively as a *'leading god'* in a marine procession only to land the essay with a pedestrian bump back to safe and inglorious 'reality' at the foot of Lambeth Palace.[25] In all these instances, the periodical's play around the authentic is a form of homage to high Romantic forebears that turns into spoof: the *London*'s writers not only assert their own freedom from the constraints of undistinguished genealogy through the ostentatious use of persona, they also critique inherited patrician models of literary selfhood.

Elia's essays transform the meaning of dependency into disquisitions on the dependency of meaning. In them, authentication remains forever imminent, subject to re-vision. In 'Recollections of the South Sea House', Elia remarks the 'charts' on the walls, 'which subsequent discoveries have antiquated'. These maps are validated as historical artefacts by their datedness, but as maps (as purported representations of correspondence between sign and referent) they are invalid, their meaning has changed in ways that their makers could not anticipate. Elia explores more fully the ways in which meaning changes with time and place, in ways beyond the author's control, in his essay 'Distant Correspondents' (March 1822). The essay is written in the form of a letter to an old friend, 'B. F. Esq., at Sydney, New South Wales'. Elia discusses the problems that attend writing letters that will be received ten months thereafter: news that was true at the time of writing may no longer be true at the time of reading, while fibs may have become actualities: 'Not only does truth, in these long intervals, un-essence herself, but (what is harder) one cannot venture a crude fiction for the fear that it may ripen into a truth upon the voyage'.[26] The text is here presented as organic, living: it contains its own capacity for change, growth, dissolution. Meaning is therefore necessarily deferred and Elia identifies that what is true for the letter to Australia is, though on a smaller scale, true of all communication. In a sense, we are all, always distant correspondents. Once again the form of the essay is intimate: it makes us, by proxy, into the old friend in New South Wales Elia addresses. It validates itself through confession, memory and self-conscious analysis of its own form, while simultaneously making us aware of the necessarily compromised status of its own discourse; this isn't the letter it purports to be, nor is any letter. The reader is made unusually conscious of the uncertain journey between transmission and reception inherent in communication and of his or her vital role as addressee in producing meaning.

Indeed, Elia's essays insist upon the reader as co-participant in a performative interaction where s/he agrees to suspend disbelief. This claim has social implications, as is evident in 'A Complaint of the Decay of Beggars in the Metropolis' (June 1822), an essay in which Elia laments the decline in the number of beggars on London streets. The subject was topical. The Society for the Suppression of Mendicity, founded in 1818, was dedicated to tackling the upsurge in street begging accompanying the end of the Napoleonic wars, and aimed to force the homeless and destitute to leave the streets and repair to the workhouse, an ambition realized in the Vagrancy Act of 1824. Elia's response to the widespread fear of fraudulent beggars is both characteristic and novel. He argues that it doesn't matter whether the beggars are authentic or not:

> Reader, do not be frightened at the hard words, imposition, imposture – *give, and ask no questions* ... Shut not thy purse-strings always against painted distress. Act a charity sometimes. When a poor creature (outwardly and visibly such) comes before thee, do not stay to enquire whether the 'seven small children,' in whose name he implores thy assistance, have a veritable existence ... It is good to believe him ... When they come with their counterfeit looks, and mumping tones, think them players. You pay your money to see a comedian feign these things, which, concerning these poor people, thou canst not certainly tell whether they are feigned or not.[27]

In comparing beggars with actors, who are rightly paid for performing a role, Elia re-frames a debate whose central premise had been beggars' negative socio-economic impact. 'Much good could be sucked from these beggars', he insists. The reader gains from the beggar as 'an emblem' of man free from defining social ties and obligations, and from the empathetic process of almsgiving (it is 'good', in various senses, to believe the beggar). The transaction is suggestively close to that between writer and reader. The fact that both parties may be role-playing is immaterial. Since authenticity is indeterminable, it becomes a shared construct whose worth lies in the use-value it generates rather than the exchange-value it represents.

Elia's essays were, in the early twentieth century, routinely dubbed 'artificial' and 'inconsequential': their distrust of 'importance' is read as a failure of intellectual and moral seriousness, the 'fake personality' as an exploitative device designed to milk the sympathies of the uneducated and sentimental reader.[28] A more modern form of discomfort is expressed in Mark Parker's analysis of the politically conservative ends to which, he argues, the *London*'s editor, John Scott, turned Elia: 'Recollections of the South Sea House', in his view, is an evasive piece that displaces attention from a political landscape of riot and reform toward quiescence and nostalgia.[29] Such criticisms, however, fail to plumb the pleasures of the essays, which are not weakly consolatory or compromising. On the contrary, what strikes some critics as inauthentic – the openly studied nature of the Elian persona, or the 'displacement' of the actual by memory or daydream – is better seen as a reflection on the chimerical nature of the quest for authenticity, with the pursuit of origins it implies. Elia emphasizes the role of reception in creating literary value; in this model, the reader's choice to accept the play of the text and respond to it is more crucial than the imponderable identity of the author or the work. This insight carries over to the domain of social class and authority. The teasing, transparent figure of Elia empowers Lamb and his readers. Imitative Elian essays swiftly appeared in the *London*, taking on his character as Lamb takes on that of others. As Margaret Russett has remarked, 'the fantasmatic equivalence between producers and consumers articulated in the premise that "thou art a lean annuitant like myself" begets new writers whose essences preserve the stamp of their simulacral originals'.[30] Elia is also able to write his own eulogy, pre-empting command of his legacy: he is reported dead and Phil-Elia (another also-Lamb) mourns his loss. Elia confers the freedom of literary ghosting: to be and not be, to be multiply fathered and to father oneself. In doing so, he disrupts patriarchal authority at its textual roots. Lamb's shadow-play challenges precisely because of the provoking absence it offers to the potential detractor. It needs to be seen in the context of the early-nineteenth-century periodical to appreciate fully its participation in a dialogue about the paradoxical nature of literary authenticity in which the medium is perpetually engaged.

*

The literary annuals of the 1820s and 1830s are rarely discussed and such historical and modern critical notice as they have received has often been scathing. Yet they are of considerable interest. Like the monthly magazines whose contributors they often shared, these periodicals respond to the premium placed on literary authenticity, while simultaneously exposing the contradictions inherent in the trope.

Rudolf Ackermann is generally credited as having initiated the craze for literary annuals with his *Forget Me Not*, first published in 1823. Drawing on the German fashion for literary albums, the *Forget Me Not* offered a miscellany of prose, poetry and engravings, attractively produced in a dainty duodecimo format. Designed to catch the growing Christmas market – the *Forget Me Not* was subtitled 'A Christmas and New Year's Present' – the annual was a genteel yet affordable gift. Imitators swiftly followed, picking up key elements of the *Forget Me Not*'s marketable aesthetic: the selection of original pieces from well-known authors; the feminine attractions of the volume's size, decoration and subjects; and the emphasis on memory, in which the annual becomes a link binding the gift-giver, the recipient, and the cultural producers and artefacts it contains.

Authenticity and sincerity were, from the first, key values in the annuals. The names they chose – the *Forget Me Not*, *Friendship's Offering*, the *Keepsake*, the *Pledge of Friendship* – implied that the annual constituted an expression of sincere feeling that could become a unique personal token of regard, its particular meaning conveyed in the dedication page on which the donor was invited to inscribe his or her name with that of the donee. Annuals likewise pursued original contributions and Romantic reliques, setting great store by items, such as previously unpublished work by Byron, Keats and Shelley or an engraving of a family portrait of Sir Walter Scott in peasant garb, that offered unique access to hitherto private literary materials. For example, *Friendship's Offering* for 1826 printed some unpublished verses by Byron 'extracted by Washington Irving from the album of Captain Medwin' and others from a notebook belonging to Lady Caroline Lamb.[31] Living contributors frequently also conveyed the sense that their work in the annual had originated in a private context of unpaid literary exchange. James Montgomery published in *The Literary Souvenir* for 1825 'A Poet's Benediction. Transmitted to a Young Lady in a distant county, who had desired a "few lines" in the Author's own handwriting'.[32] Such elements blurred the boundaries between the commercial annual and the personal album, also popular at this time, in which a woman (usually) would collect samples of her friends' writing, which also served as a bouquet of tributes to her own popularity and the cultural life of her circle. The annuals liked to reproduce 'handwriting' where they could. The *Forget Me Not* for 1827, offered 'a fac-simile … as accurately it could be copied' of 'the inscription, or rather incision' of 'Byron 1816' carved by the poet into a pillar in the dungeon of the prison at Chillon.[33] The *Amulet* for 1828 printed facsimile 'autographs of those involved in the Gunpowder Plot and against the Spanish Armada'.[34] *The Literary Souvenir* published an essay 'On Autographs', claiming that 'of all the performances of man, nothing bears so exclusively the stamp of the individual as his handwriting'; it followed up its assertions by printing several series of autographs of living writers, including 'C. Lamb', 'James Hogg', 'Wm Wordsworth', 'L. E. Landon', and 'A. Opie'.[35] The annuals' preoccupation with the authentic hand was part of a metonymic association with the female body reinforced by their small size, graphic attractions and feminine bindings. That association was routinely used by writers in the annuals to emphasize their yearly appearance as a natural phenomenon, like the flowering of annual plants.

The annuals were enormously successful. In their heyday, individual titles could sell as many as 15,000 copies a year. Their popularity, however, was short-lived. One plausible explanation for their rapid rise and decline in public favour is that they are self-deconstructing artefacts: their totemization of authenticity is undermined from within. Vitally, the annuals' voiced devotion to spontaneous and 'natural' expression was undercut by their flagrantly commercial tactics and production values. Annual editors became notorious for the lengths to which they would go to obtain samples of original writing from famous authors. Private letters were copied and published without remuneration. There was a gold rush on dead celebrity artefacts. Annual verses such as 'The Poet' depict poetry as a private act in a natural landscape,[36] but the annuals' showy emphasis on material charms and their ruthless commissioning tactics gave the lie to the view of writing they promulgated. The annuals' engravings of women, as William Thackeray argued, were equally double-edged: marketed as maidenly models to teenage girls, yet also bought and extracted as pouting pin-ups by middle-aged men.[37] Indeed the tension between authenticity ('innocence') and commercial reproduction ('knowingness') in the annuals is played out via competing images of the female. Authors including Wordsworth and Coleridge found themselves in an awkward embrace with annuals that, on the one hand, offered them substantial amounts of money and raised their public profiles but, on the other, in valuing their contributions chiefly as celebrity writings, exposed the uneasy relationship between contemporary commercial demand for autograph (authentic hand) and imagery of emotional availability (authentic heart) associated with a cultural gift economy and a circle of genuinely intimate readers.[38]

Although annuals offer homage to Romantic figures and tropes, the effect of presenting this within a feminized, market-driven, composite text is often to create intended or unintended irony and riposte. Peter Manning has observed that Wordsworth's and Shelley's pieces in the annuals were sometimes juxtaposed with works whose tone and content were antithetical and potentially compromising.[39] The annuals offered in various senses an opportunity to own, join and succeed the Romantics. Thackeray shrewdly observed that both Letitia Landon and Lady Blessington, editors of competing annuals, had written postscripts to Byron's 'Selim and Zuleika'. Thomas Hood, previously a sub-editor and contributor at the *London Magazine*, edited an annual, the *Gem* for 1829, in which an unpublished sonnet by Keats, which had been part of an intimate gift exchange, was followed by comic verses on the same theme. The annual contained work by Charles Lamb, but also an irreverent sketch by Hood posing as Lamb: games played at the monthly periodical here inflect the annual, producing tension within its paradigm of purity. Pursuing authentic remains could also lead to inadvertently comic effects, as in the *Forget Me Not* for 1830, which announced that it contained:

> the first attempt of the late Lord Byron's that is known to be extant; and we consider this piece as being the more curious, inasmuch as it displays no dawning of that genius which soon afterwards burst forth with such overpowering splendour ... We regret much that the diminutive size of our pages prevented us from indulging the reader with a fac-simile of the autograph of the youthful lover, certified by the lady to whom it was addressed, and now in the possession of Miss Cursham, of Sutton, Nottinghamshire, to whom we are indebted for the communication.[40]

The annuals' reproduction of autograph neatly questions the value of authenticity in the very process of asserting it. W. B. Clarke, author of 'Visit to Chillon' in the *Forget Me Not* for 1827 was forced to admit that the epigraph 'BYRON 1816' carved into the dungeon pillar and accurately reproduced in facsimile form, at an angle on the page, is perhaps not, 'as many imagine it not to be, genuine'.[41] The article 'On Autographs' in *The Literary Souvenir* for 1825 quotes Isaac D'Israeli and Johann Kaspar Lavater in arguing that autograph is a unique record of selfhood which, like a form of phrenology by proxy, can be read to determine the gender, nationality and character of the writer. Yet, the reproduction of the autographs of famous authors in series in *The Literary Souvenir*'s pages tends to disprove the theory it expounds: it is very difficult to detect any consistent distinctions between male and female signatures (is 'C. Lamb' Charles or Caroline?), or between those of British and non-British writers, or indeed between authors of different social classes. The value of 'autograph' as unique inscription is further undermined by advertisements at the end of *The Literary Souvenir* for 1827, which reveal that the publishers are also offering separately for sale 'facsimiles of the handwriting of Scott, Lamb, Byron, Hogg, Coleridge, Southey, Wordsworth etc.' The mass-produced periodical looks back towards handwriting for its pre-industrial 'aura' of intimacy, accuracy and personal meaning but, utilizing the technology of reproduction in the service of promoting uniqueness, it draws attention to the ironic effects of its own homage. 'Autograph', meaning 'a sample signature', is a coinage of the first decade of the nineteenth century.[42] As Tamara Plakins Thornton has shown, the idea that there is a relation between handwriting and the individual writer is a relatively modern notion, which first emerges securely in the eighteenth century in contradistinction to print, 'defined as character-istically impersonal and disassociated from the author'.[43] Autograph is prized at precisely the moment when modern developments – the growing availability and anonymity of print, an increasingly literate populace, urbanization and social mobility – suggest that neither writer nor text can be securely identified. The annuals' use of autograph popularizes ideas of unique selfhood and the personal affect conveyed in handwriting. However, it simultaneously exposes the co-dependence of those ideas on a print culture that negates them.

The literary annuals of the 1820s, then, like Charles Lamb's Elia essays in the *London Magazine*, illustrate the central role of the early nineteenth-century periodical in simultaneously constructing and deconstructing the value of Romantic authenticity. In their pages, the totemization of loss becomes a casualty of its own success. The annuals were long a subject of critical disdain: read as vulgar and commercial-ized responses to a 'purer' Romantic legacy. But, as we have seen, their self-ironizing character is, in many respects merely a reflection of para-doxes inherent in the mass transmission of authenticity as a cultural good. For some the annuals offered new pleasures: women were more widely represented in their pages than elsewhere in the contemporary periodical market, and the annual, in implicitly inviting each purchaser and owner of an annual to add their name to its roster of illustrious autographs, broke down barriers between the categories of author and audience, and between private and public writing. In overtly including the reader as self-made subject in their pages, the annuals inaugurate a post-Romantic era of literary and social self-invention.

Notes

1. See for example John Wilson, 'Monologue or Soliloquy on the Annuals', *Blackwood's Magazine* 26 (1829): 950, which exclaims: 'Look at our litera-ture now, and it is all periodical together. A thousand daily, thrice-a-week, twice-a-week, weekly newspapers, a hundred monthlies, fifty quarterlies, and twenty-five annuals!'
2. For a groundbreaking discussion of these phenomena in early-nineteenth-century periodicals see Mark Parker, *Literary Magazines and British Romanticism* (Cambridge University Press, 2000).
3. Walter Benjamin, 'The Work of Art in the Age of Mechanical Reproduction', *Illuminations*, trans. Harry Zohn (London: Fontana, 1992), p. 215.
4. Margaret Russett, *De Quincey's Romanticism: Canonical Minority and the Forms of Transmission* (Cambridge University Press, 1997), p. 118. Russett partially quotes here Susan Stewart, *Crimes of Writing: Problems in the Containment of Representation* (Oxford University Press, 1991), p. 22.

5. Charles Lamb ('ELIA'), 'Recollections of the South Sea House', *London Magazine* 2 (1820): 142. As Elia supplies in a footnote to his essay, the reference to passing by the desolate walls of Balclutha is from the poetry of Ossian – 'discovered' by James Macpherson – another hint, perhaps, that Lamb is participating in a literary tradition of mingling recollection and hoax.
6. In fact it was not 40, but around 28 years since Charles Lamb had worked in the South Sea House. See David Chandler, 'Charles Lamb and the South Sea House', *Notes and Queries* 51 (2004): 139.
7. 'Vitruvius', 'The Bag-piper, in Tottenham Court Road', *London Magazine* 1 (1820): 389–90.
8. Benjamin, *Illuminations*, p. 215. Benjamin's rueful yet ludic persona as an essayist seems to draw on Elia's, especially in pieces such as 'Unpacking my Library'.
9. Lamb, 'Recollections,' p. 143.
10. Chandler, 'Charles Lamb and the South Sea House,' p. 140.
11. Lamb, 'Recollections', p. 145.
12. Gerald Monsman, *Charles Lamb as the London Magazine's 'Elia'* (Lampeter: Mellen, 2003), p. 1.
13. Lamb, 'Recollections', p. 146.
14. William Shakespeare, *The Taming of the Shrew*, Act I, Scene II. Elia's other quotation here is also equivocal. It is Hamlet who is 'fooled to the top of his bent', but he says this while 'feigning' madness and appears to mean not that he is tired of being deluded, but tired of being treated as if he were deluded.
15. Lamb, 'Recollections', p. 144.
16. C. A. Elton ('Olen'), 'Epistle to Elia', *London Magazine* 4 (1821): 139.
17. Horace Smith ('H'), 'Death – Posthumous Memorials – Children', *London Magazine* 3 (1821): 250.
18. Charles Lamb ('ELIA'), 'Elia to His Correspondents', *London Magazine* 4 (1821): 465–6.
19. John Scott, footnote to 'Janus's Jumble', *London Magazine* 1 (1820): 628.
20. Thomas De Quincey ['X.Y.Z'], Letter to the Editor in 'The Lion's Head', *London Magazine* 4 (1821): 584–6.
21. For discussions of the duel see Peter Murphy, 'Impersonation and Authorship in Romantic Britain', *English Literary History* 59 (1992): 625–49; Parker, *Literary Magazines*, p. 27; and Margaret Russett, *Fictions and Fakes: Forging Romantic Authenticity, 1760–1845* (Cambridge University Press, 2006), p. 176.
22. Alan Vardy, *John Clare: Politics and Poetry* (Basingstoke: Palgrave, 2003), pp. 118–23. See also Russett, *Fictions and Fakes*, Chapter 6 on 'Clare Byron'.
23. John Hamilton Reynolds, ('Edward Herbert'), 'The Literary Police Office, Bow-Street', *London Magazine* 7 (1823): 157–8.
24. Ibid., p. 160.
25. Charles Lamb ('ELIA'), 'On Witches, and Other Night-fears', *London Magazine* 4 (1821): 387.
26. Ibid., 'Distant Correspondents', *London Magazine* 5 (1822): 282.
27. Ibid., 'A Complaint of the Decay of Beggars in the Metropolis', *London Magazine* 5 (1822): 536.
28. See Augustine Birrell, *Obiter Dicta*, Second Series (London: Elliot Stock, 1887), p. 225: 'If it be really seriously urged against Lamb as an author that he is fantastical and artistically artificial, it must be owned he is so … ['In Praise

of Chimney Sweepers' has] not what can be called a natural sentence in it from beginning to end. Many people have not the patience for this sort of thing; they like to laugh and move on. Other people again like an essay to be about something really important, and to conduct them to conclusions they deem worth carrying away.' Denys Thompson, in 'Our Debt to Lamb', *Determinations: Critical Essays* ed. F. R. Leavis (London: Chatto and Windus, 1934), complains of Lamb's triviality, whimsy, fake personality and pernicious literary influence.

29. Parker, *Literary Magazines*, p. 44.
30. Russett, *De Quincey's Romanticism*, p. 124.
31. Byron, 'Stanzas to her who Best can Understand Them', *Friendship's Offering* (London: Lupton Relfe, 1826), pp. 102–5; Byron, 'To Lady Caroline Lamb', pp. 230–2.
32. James Montgomery, 'A Poet's Benediction … ', *The Literary Souvenir* (London: Hurst, Robinson, 1825), p. 198.
33. W. B. Clarke, 'Visit to Chillon, On the Lake of Geneva. (Extracted from an unpublished Manuscript)', *Forget Me Not* (London: Ackermann, 1827), p. 306.
34. 'Autographs of the Principal Conspirators concerned in The Gunpowder Plot' and 'Autographs of the Principal Officers Employed against the Spanish Armada', *The Amulet; or Christian and Literary Remembrancer* (London: Baynes, 1828), pp. 419–21.
35. 'On Autographs', *The Literary Souvenir* (London: Hurst, Robinson, 1825), p. 384.
36. Frederic Shoberl Junior, 'The Poet', *Forget Me Not* (London: Ackermann, 1830), p. 342.
37. William Thackeray, 'A Word on the Annuals', *Fraser's Magazine* 16 (1837): 758.
38. For a fuller account of the annuals, gender and Romantic writing see Sara Lodge, 'Romantic Reliquaries: Memory and Irony in the Literary Annuals', *Romanticism* 10 (2004): 23–40.
39. Peter J. Manning, 'Wordsworth in the Keepsake, 1829', *Literature in the Marketplace: Nineteenth-century British Publishing and Reading Practices*, eds. John O. Jordan and Robert L. Patten (Cambridge University Press, 1995), p. 55.
40. Frederic Shoberl, *Forget Me Not* (London: Ackermann, 1830), pp. iv–v.
41. W. B. Clarke, 'Visit to Chillon,' p. 306.
42. OED gives Isaac D'Israeli's *Curiosities of Literature* (1807–1817) as the first text to use 'autograph' meaning 'a person's own signature'. D'Israeli's article 'Autographs', repr. in *Curiosities of Literature*, vol. 3 (London: Moxon, 1849), p. 180, articulates the same anxieties as the annuals in a different form, insisting that nature prompts each individual to have distinct writing, but complaining that 'regulated as the pen is now too often by a mechanical process, which the present race of writing-masters seem to have contrived for their own convenience, a whole school exhibits a similar hand-writing; the pupils are forced in their automatic motions, as if acted on by the pressure of a steam-engine'.
43 Tamara Plakins Thornton, *Handwriting in America: A Cultural History* (Yale University Press, 1996), p. xiii.

9
Acts of Insincerity? Thomas Spence and Radical Print Culture in the 1790s

John Halliwell

This chapter investigates the role of radical print culture in challenging the authenticity of key symbols, forms and modes in political discourse in the 1790s. I will examine the work of Thomas Spence and in particular his radical periodical *Pig's Meat* which was published from 1793 to 1795, and argue that through a complex strategy of excerption, adaption, appropriation, imitation and satire, Spence sought to contest not only the authenticity of the most potent tropes in political discourse, but also the way in which authenticity was assigned in the political sphere. However, I will begin by offering a brief theoretical appraisal of the notion of authenticity in relation to political discourse and radical print culture. I use the word 'authenticity' with close attention to its etymological links to 'authority'. The first OED entry under 'authentic' reads, 'Of authority, authoritative (*properly* as possessing original or inherent authority, but also as duly authorized); entitled to obedience or respect.' My consideration of authenticity is concerned less with questions of originality or genuineness than with contests over the way in which certain symbols, forms and modes came to be possessed with authority in political discourse. In other words, authenticity can be defined as a status whereby meaning is determined by the exertion of political authority. I will examine the way in which developments within radical print culture in the 1790s changed the way in which political authority was exerted, thereby changing the way in which the status of authenticity was assigned within the political sphere. James Epstein describes how:

> Under the influence of the French Revolution and the subsequent wars with France, key terms in England's political vocabulary were

called into question, destabilised, or transvalued: words such as 'the people', 'sovereign', and 'patriot' were newly inflected.[1]

I will suggest that this destabilization was experienced as a contest over the way in which the authenticity of such terms, as well as that of a variety of forms and modes from popular anthems and satiric motifs to legal discourse, came to be authorized within political discourse.

My notion of political discourse is based on Jürgen Habermas's groundbreaking text, *The Structural Transformation of the Public Sphere* (1962) in which Habermas established the public sphere as the social space between the private sphere and the state in which the middle class organized itself as a public over the course of the eighteenth century. It was in that space that 'political discourse' was created, in the opening out of matters of state to rational-critical debate in arenas like the coffee-house and the newspaper press. As a result of that opening out of issues of state the authenticity of key political terms became increasingly contested, in that their precise meaning was no longer assigned by the state but negotiated between the state and the bourgeois public sphere.

However, my particular focus on radical print culture in the 1790s necessitates a re-evaluation of the Habermasian paradigm, which originally failed to include the plebeian classes that were excluded from the bourgeois public sphere and thus from political discourse, but which nevertheless had begun to establish an alternative public sphere through the creation of a network of societies and associations linked through the medium of print. From the outset, Habermas announced that his own investigation 'leaves aside the plebeian public sphere as a variant that in a sense was suppressed in the historical process.'[2] This elision of the plebeian public sphere has since been countered by a number of revisionist strategies which have sought to pluralize the concept of the public sphere, creating a series of alternative or counter-public spheres. For example, Terry Eagleton observes that:

[w]hat is emerging in the England of the late-eighteenth and early-nineteenth centuries ... is already nothing less than a 'counter-public sphere.' In the Corresponding Societies, the radical press, Owenism, Cobbett's *Political Register* and Paine's *Rights of Man*, feminism and the dissenting churches, a whole oppositional network of journals, clubs, pamphlets, debates and institutions invades the dominant concensus, threatening to fragment it from within.[3]

Eagleton's outline of a radical 'oppositional network' is one of a number of reformulations of theories of the public sphere which have since led Habermas to revise his original formulations, declaring:

> The plebeian public sphere is, in a manner of speaking, a bourgeois public sphere whose social preconditions have been rendered null. The exclusion of the culturally and politically mobilized lower strata entails a pluralization of the public sphere in the very process of its emergence. Next to, and interlocked with, the hegemonic public sphere, a plebeian one assumed shape.[4]

According to Habermas, the development of the plebeian public sphere in the eighteenth century was a symptom of the mechanism of exclusion necessary for the formation of the 'hegemonic' or bourgeois public sphere. As Habermas explains, these alternative public spheres 'were denied equal active participation in the formation of political opinion and will'[5]: in other words, they were excluded from the political process by their inability to contest the authenticity of the key symbols, forms and modes of political discourse. In the context of the 1790s, the outpouring of loyalist propaganda that sought to suppress the developing plebeian public sphere of radical culture is an exemplar of such a mechanism of exclusion, in that it aimed to consolidate the exclusion of the plebeian classes from political discourse, and in doing so to negate the challenge posed by radical print culture to the specific political rendering of key terms in political discourse.

Loyalist propaganda operated on the basis of an inseparable link between political order and linguistic order – the ability to control the way in which key terms in political discourse could be deployed was essential to the maintenance of political authority. As James Epstein explains, 'the authority to give accent or meaning to such signs [within political discourse] is an essential part of the exercise of political power. Struggles to enforce or destabilize such meanings often define the contested terrain of politics.'[6] Through loyalist propaganda, the state sought to protect the authenticity of key terms in political discourse, but as Epstein continues, 'radicals were able to employ symbolic gestures in ways that served not only to reinforce but also to alter or subvert meanings apparent within written or verbal discourse'.[7] The challenge posed by radical print culture to the authenticity of the key terms in political discourse was experienced both as a challenge to linguistic order and as an assertion of political power.

My discussion of the role of Thomas Spence in this radical challenge is based on his innovative deployment of a range of rhetorical strategies, which would later inspire radical activists and publishers ranging from his contemporary Daniel Isaac Eaton to William Hone and Thomas J. Wooler. Spence himself was born in Newcastle in 1750, his father Jeremiah having moved to Newcastle from Aberdeen in 1739. He was denied a formal education but educated himself sufficiently to become a clerk and then a schoolmaster. His early intellectual development was influenced by the Reverend James Murray, a member of the Presbyterian Church of Scotland who had graduated from Edinburgh University in 1760 before moving to Newcastle in 1764. Murray's presence in Newcastle forged a major link between the Scottish Enlightenment and indigenous Newcastle culture. His best known work, the series of *Sermons to Asses, Ministers of State, Doctors of Divinity and Lords Spiritual* (1771–1780), scathingly satirized evangelicalism, the government and the state of society and was later reprinted by William Hone in 1817–1819. Murray's own experiences as an editor, pamphleteer and satirist profoundly influenced the course of Spence's career, whilst his religious and political beliefs, from millenarianism to his arguments for political liberty on an economic basis, provided a basis for Spence's own radicalism.

Spence remained in Newcastle until the early 1790s, publishing countless pamphlets and broadsides, as well as working on a phonetic alphabet and dictionary in order to correct what he described as the 'defective pronunciation' of the lower classes. However, after the death of Murray in 1782, and an unhappy marriage, Spence became increasingly isolated in Newcastle society. In 1792, he moved to London and quickly became involved in a variety of radical activities, becoming an influential member of the London Corresponding Society, allowing the militant Lambeth Loyal Association to practise drills in his premises and extending his publishing activities to include his periodical *Pig's Meat; or Lessons for the Swinish Multitude*. Spence's periodical, which was published from 1793 to 1795, combined the functions of a political reader, satirical broadsheet and literary magazine, and its price of a penny located it firmly with the 'counter-public sphere' of plebeian culture. Spence's aim, as he phrased it in the journal's frontispiece, was:

To promote among the Labouring Part of Mankind proper Ideas of their Situation, of their importance, and of their Rights.
AND TO CONVINCE THEM

That their forlorn Condition has not been entirely over-looked and forgotten, nor their just cause unpleaded, neither by their Maker, nor by the best and most enlightened of Men in all Ages. (I, i, 1; August 1793)[8]

To achieve such ends, Spence printed extracts from a huge variety of classic literary and political texts by authors ranging from Oliver Cromwell to Joseph Priestley.

The very title of the periodical, *Pig's Meat; Lessons for the Swinish Multitude*, in its reworking of the characterization of the masses as 'the Swinish Multitude' by Edmund Burke (a point considered in greater detail below) locates Spence at the heart of the radical riposte to the loyalist reaction to the French Revolution. At the same time however, Spence, as Malcolm Chase puts it: 'avowedly espouses the "good old cause", giving extracts from Cromwell, Harrington, Sydney, and a *Modest Plea for an Equal Commonwealth* (1659), by William Sprigge, a follower of Harrington'.[9] The most frequently quoted work of those figures was James Harrington's *The Commonwealth of Oceana* (1656). Harrington was of profound influence in the development of Spence's thought, and was central to the development of his notions of the natural rights and the natural equality of all men, his belief in the power of reason, and the idea of progress. By reprinting extracts from figures such as Harrington and Cromwell, Spence makes a powerful connection between his own political beliefs and the arguments behind the pursuit of a republican Commonwealth in the seventeenth century. He also locates himself in the eighteenth-century intellectual, dissenting tradition through his inclusion of extracts from George Lyttelton's *Letters from a Persian in England to his Friend at Ispahan* (1735) and John Locke's *An Essay Concerning The True Original Extent And End Of Civil Government* (1690). Finally, Spence's selections reveal an acute awareness of contemporary politics, through the excerption of passages from Joseph Priestley's *An Essay on the First Principles of Government* (1771), Richard Price's *Observation on the Nature of Civil Liberty* (1776) and Joel Barlow's *Advice to the Privileged Orders* (1792) as well as translations of Volney's *Ruins of Empire* (1787) and the French Constitution of 1793.[10]

Spence was strongly motivated to make expensive and inaccessible political writings available in the digestible form of a penny weekly in order to educate his plebeian audience in the language of political discourse. For example, Volney's *Ruins of Empire*, a work that was extremely influential on English radicalism, is a republican fantasy in which the people subdue their oppressors not through physical force, but through rational argument.[11] Spence was one of the earliest popularizers of the work, and by providing extracts from that text in *Pig's Meat*, Spence sought to extend the boundaries of political discourse to include the plebeian classes.[12] However, his calling as an educator also ran parallel to a desire to establish not only his own political ideas, but also the path of the radical movement in line with a political tradition which reached back from thinkers such as Priestley and Price, through Berkeley and Locke, to Harrington. As Anne Janowitz puts it:

> *Pig's Meat*, sets a precedent for organising and inventing a cultural tradition, laying claim to texts from the past, and juxtaposing them in such a way as to generate new meanings which fasten these texts to the social and political claims being made by the unenfranchised and labouring poor.[13]

In doing so, Spence lays claim to a cultural and political tradition stretching back to Oliver Cromwell. That cultural tradition was also extended to include the establishment of a literary lineage through the inclusion of excerpts attributed to writers from Goldsmith, Swift and Fielding to Milton and Spenser.[14] Spence works to extract such figures from one position in culture, and shape them into a radical tradition by situating them alongside, for example, excerpts from Price's *Observations on the Nature of Civil Liberty* (1776) or the first English translation of the *Marseillaise* (I, vi, 67–8; September, 1793). The result is that the covert political content of works such as Goldsmith's *The Deserted Village* (1770) is made overtly political in order to establish a politically radical precedent for the endeavours of the radical movement of the 1790s.

That strategy of tracing the philosophical, ideological and cultural precedents for contemporary radicalism and manipulating them in such a way as to make their political inclinations overt operated in tandem with more explicitly satirical endeavours. What was at stake in this complex strategy of excerption, as in the deployment of a variety of satiric forms, was the ability of marginalized radicals like Spence, and more importantly his readers, to contest the authenticity of the language, modes and forms of political discourse. The inclusion of such a variety of texts in *Pig's Meat* sought to educate its readers in the language of political discourse at the same time as overtly satiric texts sought to undermine loyalist control over political discourse. One of the chief means by which that control was asserted, and protected, was through the dissemination of loyalist propaganda. Consequently, in order to subvert loyalist control of political discourse, Spence deployed a range of satirical devices to undermine loyalist propaganda, including parodies of the most popular loyalist hymns and anthems.

In an early edition of *Pig's Meat*, Spence prints a parody of 'God Save the King' entitled 'The Jubilee Hymn':

> **Tune, "God Save the King,"**
> HARK! how the trumpet's sound
> Proclaims the land around
> The Jubilee!
> Tells all the poor oppress'd
> No more they shall be cess'd
> Nor landlords more molest
> Their property. (I, iv, 42; August/September, 1793)

'God Save the King' was first publicly sung at the Theatre Royal, Drury Lane in September 1745, on the occasion of the defeat of the army of King George II by the 'Young Pretender' to the British Throne, Prince Charles Edward Stuart, at Prestonpans, near Edinburgh. The words and tune of the song have not been definitively attributed since different versions of the song had been in circulation for well over half a century, mainly amongst supporters of the exiled Stuart dynasty. Its emergence as a loyalist anthem owed much to the political and military context, in which its words offered, according to Linda Colley, 'what their protestant culture had taught them to demand: yet another assurance that – although surrounded by enemies – they were in God's particular care.'[15] In the context of the 1790s, as the spectre of war against revolutionary France loomed, the patriotic sentiments of the song had a particular currency as a loyalist anthem.

However, in Spence's parody what was largely an anthem of patriotism is parodied to promote the Levitican idea of the jubilee. The law of the jubilee, as it is written in Leviticus, calls for social renewal under the principles of justice, communal ownership, liberty and the rights of labour. For the radical movement in the 1790s, the idea of the jubilee, as part of a radical vocabulary associated with millenarianism, might be equated with the advent of liberty and equality. For Spence, however (for whom the jubilee clarified his call for the restoration of society to its natural state in his land plan), the jubilee became synonymous with his notion of revolution. Malcolm Chase's essay, 'From Millennium to Anniversary: the Concept of Jubilee in Late Eighteenth-Century and Nineteenth-Century Thought,' charts the history of the word 'jubilee' from its radical application in the 1790s through to its use in the Chartist movement in the 1840s against the backdrop of the loyalist reclamation of the role of the jubilee in political discourse through the 'Jubilee' of George III in 1809. As Chase puts it, 'Effectively the idea of jubilee had become contested territory, appositely illustrated in the Spencean's use of the tune "God save the King" for their "Jubilee Hymn"'.[16] In using the word 'Jubilee' as a synonym for revolution within the framework of a parody of 'God Save the King', Spence redirects the potency of that anthem as a rallying call for loyalists during the political turmoil of the 1790s into a rallying call for the people to rise against their oppressors. In this instance Spence uses the template of a loyalist anthem to produce a radical anthem. The Jubilee Hymn was the most frequently published of Spence's works, and it survived into the 1840s, appearing in Chartist literature as a means of celebrating the Chartist land plan.

Spence was also to make use of the satiric possibilities of parody in his recasting of another popular loyalist anthem, 'Rule Britannia', in 'The Progress of Liberty':

> **THE PROGRESS OF LIBERTY Tune "Britannia rule the Waves"**
> Hark! hark! on yonder distant shore,
> The noisy din of war I hear;
> The sword's unsheath'd – the cannons roar,
> And Gallia's sons in arms appear.
> 'Tis France, 'tis France, the people cry,
> Fighting for sacred Liberty.
> Though num'rous armies her invade,
> Of warlike slaves a barbarous host;
> Of despots crown'd, a grand crusade,
> To crush her Liberty they boast,
> But France like England will be free,
> Or bravely die for Liberty. (I, xxiv, 280–1; November, 1793)

'Rule Britannia' itself was written by the poet James Thomson and put to music in 1740 by Thomas Augustine Arne. By the 1790s it had become, like 'God Save the King' an unofficial national anthem, and an anthem used to garner support for the Pitt administration and its campaign against revolutionary France. At the same time, 'Rule Britannia', like 'God Save the King', was a popular source of parody. Both of these anthems had been parodied in the American Press in the 1760s and 1770s, appropriated from their origins in British patriotism to serve the cause of rebellion against the British government. For example, a parody of 'Rule Britannia' entitled 'A New Liberty Song' was published in the *Boston Gazette* on 16 May, 1769.[17] That appropriation of 'Rule Britannia' was continued by the British radical movement in the 1790s, as the forms, modes and anthems of governmental authority were adapted to serve the radical cause.

This particular parody of 'Rule Britannia' offers a triumphant celebration of French liberty as akin to British liberty. Thus, the opposition established in loyalist propaganda between the vices of French liberty and the virtues of its English counterpart is undermined. The notion of English Liberty had its origins in events such as the signing of the Magna Carta in 1215 and the Glorious Revolution of 1688, which guaranteed the constitution as the preserver of liberty. However, radical attempts to claim this notion of 'Liberty' were countered by the loyalist strategy of misrepresenting and distorting the language of radical political discourse. In loyalist propaganda 'Liberty' had been equated with anarchy, famine and injustice, but in 'The Progress of Liberty' it is celebrated as a triumph against despotism. In the original version of 'Britannia Rule the Waves' the resistance to despotism is celebrated as a singularly British triumph:

> Thee haughty tyrants ne'er shall tame:
> All their attempts to bend thee down,
> Will but arouse thy generous flame;
> But work their woe, and thy renown.[18]

However, in 'The Progress of Liberty' the praise for defeating the forces of despotism is instead lavished on the French. The effect is to subvert the form and the language of Thompson's original song in celebration of the achievements of the French Revolution at the same time as revalorizing the notion of 'Liberty' as a vital component of the language of radical political discourse.[19]

The effect of parodying the hymns and anthems of loyalist propaganda to serve the radical cause was complicated by the publication in *Pig's Meat* of the first English translation of the *Marseillaise*. That publication was of course saturated with political significance in its rallying call to overthrow the tyrannies of government, and undoubtedly such controversial material supported the loyalist denigration of the radical movement under the label of 'Jacobinism'. However, at stake in the inclusion of the *Marseillaise* was a contest around the fraught notion of authenticity in political discourse, since in translation, the *Marseillaise* was revealed to be deploying much of the same patriotic language that had consistently been deployed in British loyalist hymns and anthems.

The Marseilles March, or Hymn
Ye sons of France! awake to glory,
Hark! Hark! what myriads bid you rise!
Your children, wives, and grandsires hoary,
Behold their tears, and hear their cries.
Shall hateful tyrants, mischief breeding,
With hireling hosts a ruffian band,
Affright and desolate the land
While peace and liberty lie bleeding!
To arms, to arms, ye brave,
Th' avenging sword unsheathe;
March on, march on, all hearts resolv'd
On victory or death.
(I, vi, 67–8; September, 1793)

Here the patriotic invective against 'hateful tyrants' is joined with an emotive call to arms to protect the children and wives of France against the 'ruffian band' of foreign invaders. The hymn deploys much the same language as, for example, 'Rule Britannia', in which British patriotic zeal is aimed at deposing 'haughty tyrants' and encouraging military resistance to foreign arms:

Still more majestic shalt thou rise,
More dreadful from each foreign stroke;
As the loud blast that tears the skies
Serves but to root thy native oak.[20]

Thus, beyond the obviously politicized act of publishing the *Marseillaise* in a radical periodical, Spence reveals that the language of loyalist propaganda, like the language of political discourse, can be contested: it can be used to glamorize the French Revolution just as effectively as it can be deployed to propagate a conservative political agenda. More specifically, Spence published this translation to present the French Revolution in a positive light. Thus the language of loyalist propaganda, language that is typically employed to denounce the violence and anarchism of 'Jacobinism' is redirected to denounce the 'hateful tyrants' of the Pitt administration.

This effect of subverting the language of loyalist propaganda, and of extending the boundaries of political discourse is here achieved through the medium of translation. The very act of translation is itself a form of imitation that reconstitutes an original text, or source material.

The imitative nature of translation is exposed in Lauren G. Leighton's suggestion that:

> A translation is a version, rendering, adaptation, imitation, paraphrase, parody, transposition, transformation, reformulation, performance, dialogue, dialectic, synthesis, interpretation and reinterpretation, exegesis, and of course traduction.[21]

However, in Spence's translation what is being imitated or adapted is not just the patriotic triumphalism of the *Marseillaise*, but also the language of British loyalist anthems. Leighton asserts that translators can operate across a spectrum of intention, 'at one end of the spectrum, translators are guided by the text, at the other they translate with their readership in mind.'[22] Spence offers his translation with his readership very much in mind, deliberately using translation in order to contest the language of loyalist propaganda.

One of the most influential motifs deployed within loyalist propaganda remained the characterization of the lower classes as swine, a characterization that stemmed from Edmund Burke's portrayal of the masses as 'The Swinish Multitude.'[23] Clearly, the title of Spence's journal, *One Pennyworth of Pig's Meat; or, Lessons for the Swinish Multitude* operates in reaction to Burke's phrase, appropriating the swine motif as a means of venerating radical print culture. That appropriation is further developed in two poems entitled 'Burke's Address to the "Swinish Multitude"'. Both poems use the swine motif to replicate Burke's portrayal of the plebeian classes as passive, ignorant and submissive:

> Ye vile SWINISH HERD, in the Sty of Taxation,
> What would ye be after? – disturbing the Nation?
> Give over your grunting – Be off – To your Sty!
> Nor dare to look out, if a KING passes by:
> Get ye down! down! down! – Keep ye down! [...]
> What know ye of Commons, of KINGS, or of LORDS,
> But what the dim *Light* of TAXATION affords?
> Be contented with – and no more of your Rout:
> Or a new *Proclamation* shall muzzle your Snout! [...]
> To conclude: Then no more about MAN and his Rights.
> TOM PAINE, and a Rabble of *Liberty Wights*:
> That you are but "SWINE", if ye ever forget,
> We'll throw you alive to the HORRIBLE PIT! (I, xxi, 250–1;
> December, 1793)

In this example, the description of 'grunting' gives a sense of inarticulacy, whilst the mention of 'Sty' implies the moral and social deprivation of a class forced to live in hovels. Even the ballad form becomes a means of ironically imposing deference, as the 'Derry Down' refrain is transposed to 'Get ye down'. Spence thus offers the poem as an exaggerated version of Burkean conservatism in order to demonstrate how the lower classes are excluded from political discourse through passivity whilst parodying the condescension of Burke's position.

In the second of the poems entitled 'Burke's Address to the "Swinish Multitude"', the poem is prefaced by a quotation from Burke:

> 'Here is the constitution, which we have made for you and for your posterity for ever. We buckle it on your back, for you are beasts of burden, you must not dare to touch it,' Burke

> Ye Swinish Multitude who prate,
> What know ye 'bout the matter?
> Mysterious are the ways of state,
> Of which you should not chatter. [...]
> CHORUS
> Then hence ye Swine nor make a rout,
> Forbearance but relaxes;
> We'll clap the muzzle on your snout,
> Go work and pay your taxes.
> (*Pig's Meat*, II, iv, 39; January, 1794)

The poem offers an exaggerated imitation of one of the key themes of loyalist propaganda, the insistence that the masses lacked the intellectual capacities to comprehend the complexities of politics. Clearly, the intention of the poem is to expose how loyalist propaganda aims to encourage ignorance in its plebeian audience. However, the inclusion of the quotation from Burke adds another dimension to the poem, since that quotation was made famous by Thomas Erskine in his defence of Thomas Paine during his trial on 18 December, 1792. Erskine demanded of the court:

> Look now at the address of Mr. Burke. Here is your constitution, which we have made for you and for your posterity for ever. We buckle it on your back, for you are beasts of burden, you must not dare to touch it – you have entered into a compact which is indissoluble. Are such doctrines a legitimate way of endearing the

constitution to the people? And I mention all this to shew you what the book of Mr. Paine is; for Paine's book is an answer to those doctrines of Mr. Burke – doctrines more injurous than any that could ever be asserted by republicans and levellers.[24]

Erskine's defence of Paine was an impassioned argument in support of the freedom of the press – his speech was widely published in radical circles and was serialized in *Pig's Meat* itself.[25] The poem's reference to Erskine thus makes a tacit appeal for the freedom of the radical press, thereby advocating an extension of the boundaries of political discourse whilst presenting Burkean conservatism as the complete exclusion of the plebeian classes from participation in political discourse. In both poems the swine metaphor is deployed in order to demonstrate how conservative propaganda aims to construct a social hierarchy based on the passivity and subordination of the plebeian classes. In doing so, those poems reveal the strategies behind the loyalist control of political discourse and threaten to subvert that control.

However, for all of Spence's experimentation with the swine metaphor, it is only outside of the constraints of his own publication that 'swine' becomes a term of empowerment rather than an ironic imitation of the subservience imposed by loyalist propaganda. In September 1793 Spence wrote under the pseudonym 'Brother Grunter' in a letter to Daniel Isaac Eaton's radical periodical, *Politics for the People*:

> SIR,
> As a Member of the Swinish Herd, I beg Leave to thank you for your diligence and attention, in supplying us with good wholesome Food; on which I hope we shall long continue to feast ourselves, in spite of those who would wish to ring our Noses, in order to prevent us from grubbing after Truth, or to starve us to death in the "Stye of Taxation". But knowing that we are a very voracious species of Animals, I was fearful lest the provisions should be devoured faster than ever your unremitting endeavours might be able to supply it; I have therefore taken the liberty to send you a few morsels from a store of "*Hog's Meat*" on which I have lately made a repast, and very agreeable to the Swinish Palate of
> Yours, &c.
> Brother Grunter[26]

That Spence is the author of this letter is evident from the reference to *Pig's Meat* under the synonym of '*Hog's Meat*' and the inclusion of the phrase 'Stye of Taxation', which would appear in Spence's poem 'Burke's Address to the Swinish Multitude' in *Pig's Meat* just a few weeks after it appears here (I, xxi, 250–1; December, 1793). Moreover, the offer to provide 'a few morsels', or extracts for publication, seems to have come from Spence, since Eaton published an extract from Lyttelton's *Letters from a Persian in England to his Friend at Ispahan* of 1735 (a text that features frequently in *Pig's Meat*) immediately after this letter.

Spence seems to revel in the satiric possibilities offered by the swine motif, using it not only to attack government repression ('in spite of those who would wish to ring our Noses'), but as a means of celebrating the circulation of radical literature and offering material for publication ('a few morsels ... very agreeable to the Swinish Palate'). The appropriation of the swine motif as a means of exposing the way in which loyalist propaganda operated and, perhaps more significantly, as a means of empowering the radical movement and its achievements, represents a powerful satiric gesture in which the linguistic constraints imposed by loyalist propaganda are cast off. The symbols forms and modes of loyalist propaganda were a key site of Spence's attempt to contest the state control of political discourse. An equally potent site of political power based on strict linguistic hierarchy, however, was legal discourse.

A number of critics have written at length on the procedures of the law courts, and on radical attempts to subvert legal discourse.[27] The acquittal of Thomas Hone in 1819 on three counts of blasphemy remains perhaps the most celebrated example of a successful radical engagement with legal discourse. Hone's achievement was to subvert the way in which legal discourse silenced or privileged voices through a strict hierarchy of speakers. In the courtroom, the pragmatics of speech were deeply embedded within structured relations of unequal authority, relations which Spence attempted to subvert in a biting satire of legal procedure entitled 'Examples of Safe Printing':

EXAMPLES OF SAFE PRINTING

To prevent misrepresentation in these prosecuting times, it seems necessary to publish every thing relating to Tyranny and Oppression, though only among brutes, in the most guarded manner.

The following are meant as Specimens: –
That tyger, or that other salvage wight
Is so exceeding furious and fell,
As WRONG,

> [*Not meaning our most gracious sovereign Lord the King, or*
> *the Government of this country*]
> when it hath arm'd himself with might;
> Not fit 'mong men that do with reason mell,
> But 'mong wild beasts and salvage woods to dwell;
>   Where still the stronger
>   [*not meaning the great men of this country*]
>   doth the weak devour,
> And they that most in boldness doe excel,
> And draded most, and feared by their powre.
>   (*Pig's Meat*, II, i, 14; January, 1794)

Here, the ploy of inserting square bracketed denials of seditious intent represents more than a satirical swipe at the libel laws since it derives from the trial of Daniel Isaac Eaton for publishing John Thelwall's 'Chaunticlere' allegory. During the trial on 24 February, 1794, the prosecuting attorney was forced to repeat over and over again that the game cock which is decapitated in Thelwall's allegory was 'our lord the king'. The parenthetic denials in 'Examples of Safe Printing' thus draw attention to an episode in which the strict linguistic conventions of legal discourse worked against the interests of state and in favour of the radical cause. In parodying what was an embarrassing spectacle for the prosecution and for the government, Spence demonstrates how the relations of unequal authority which govern legal discourse can be subverted.

It is also worth noting that Spence attributes the poem to 'E. Spencer'. This forged attribution is of course an obvious pun on Spence's name, but more revealingly it demonstrates the typical radical ploy of creating historical distance from the referents of the poem through false attribution, at the same time as claiming the cultural authority of Spenser for his radical cause. This symbolic gesture of invoking the cultural authority of literary figures is repeated when Spence reprints the following stanza and attributes it to Milton:

> Sole KING of NATIONS! Rise, assert thy sway,
> Thou jealous GOD! Thy potent arm display,
> Tumble the *blood-built* thrones of despots down,
> Let dust and darkness be the tyrants crown.
> (II, xvii, 204; April, 1794)

In fact, the verse is taken from a poem entitled 'The Rights of God', by the radical publisher and activist Richard 'Citizen' Lee, which was published in *Songs from the Rock* the following year.[28] However, the attribution to Milton performs the symbolic gesture of claiming Milton's cultural authority whilst simultaneously seeking to avoid prosecution through pseudonymity. That pursuit of cultural authority is evident across the complex strategy of excerption which makes up the bulk of the contents of *Pig's Meat*. It was not, however, within *Pig's Meat* that the avoidance (by radicals) of prosecution through pseudonymity was at its most creative and subversive. Instead it was in the pages of Daniel Isaac Eaton's *Politics for the People* when Spence, writing as 'Brother Grunter', joined with an array of swinish contributors including 'Pigibus', 'A young Boar', 'A Ci-devant Pig' and 'Spare Rib'. In doing so, Spence entered into a community of radical writers through the appropriation of one of the most potent motifs in loyalist propaganda – the swine motif.

Across *Pig's Meat* the challenge to linguistic order evident in the appropriation of the swine motif was repeated in radical anthems, satiric ballads and irreverent parodies of legal procedure. It was also extended to include all kinds of literary forms, from poems, hymns and anthems to handbills and showmen's notices. Skits such as the notorious Pittachio squibs and satiric poems in couplets ridiculed the most influential figures of state, from the Prime Minister William Pitt, and the Home Secretary Henry Dundas, to Edmund Burke.[29] Through irreverence and insincerity, Spence sought to subvert the authority of the leading figures of state, as well as to undermine the traditional symbols and modes through which the state communicated its authority. One of the effects of Spence's deployment of this range of discursive strategies, from excerption, adaption and appropriation to imitation and satire had been to challenge the authenticity of key modes, symbols and forms through which the state communicated its authority. Spence succeeded in opening out the closed language of political discourse to a wider audience: in doing so Spence may have reshaped authenticity as a status authorized not by the authority of the state, but by the authority of the plebeian public sphere, a political force created in part by the development of radical periodicals like Eaton's *Politics for the People* and Spence's *Pig's Meat*.

Notes

1. James Epstein, *Radical Expression: Political Language, Ritual, and Symbol in England, 1790–1850* (Oxford University Press, 1994), p. 7.
2. Jürgen Habermas, *The Structural Transformation of the Public Sphere: An Inquiry into a Category of Bourgeois Society*, trans. Thomas Burger (Cambridge: Polity Press, 1989), p. xviii.

3. Terry Eagleton, *The Function of Criticism, from the Spectator to Post-Structuralism* (London: Verso, 1984), p. 36.
4. Jürgen Habermas, 'Further Reflections on the Public Sphere', trans. P. Burger, *Habermas and the Public Sphere*, ed. Craig Calhoun (Cambridge, MA: MIT Press, 1992), p. 426.
5. Ibid., p. 428.
6. Epstein, *Radical Expression*, p. 71.
7. Ibid., p. 71.
8. All references to Spence's *Pig's Meat* are incorporated in the text by volume, issue and page numbers with approximate date.
9. Malcolm Chase, *The People's Farm: English Radical Agrarianism 1750–1840*, (Oxford University Press, 1988), p. 61.
10. Cromwell, 'Speech at the Dissolution of the Long Parliament' (I, ix, 100; October, 1793); Harrington, extracts from *Oceana* (I, vii, 79–81; September/October, 1793 and vols. I–III *passim*); Sydney, 'Character of an Evil Magistrate' (II, ii, 16–19; January, 1794); Sprigge, *Modest Plea* (I, iv, 44–9; August/September, 1793 and I, vii, 74–8; September/October, 1793); Lyttelton, 'From the Persian Letters' (I, vii, 78–9; September/October 1794 and vol. II *passim*); Locke, 'On Civil Government' (I, iv, 42; August/September, 1793 and vols. I–III passim); Priestley, 'On the Absurdity of Unalterable Establishments' (I, ix, 92–5; October, 1793); Price, 'On Civil Liberty, and the Principles of Government' (I, xviii, 205; December, 1793); Barlow, extracts from *Advice to the Privileged Orders* (I, v; September, 1793 and vols I–III *passim*); Volney, 'Translation of an extract from a late publication entitled *Les Ruines*' (I, vi, 69–73; September, 1793); 'The French Constitution of August 1793' (I, xv, 176; September, 1793).
11. Volney's *Ruins* was hugely popular in both Britain and the United States, where, according to Michael Durey, it was the bestselling French work of the 1790s. See Michael Durey, 'Review of *The French Enlightenment in America: Essays on the Times of the Founding Fathers* by Paul Merrill Spurlin', *The William and Mary Quarterly*, 44 (1987): 824–5.
12. For more on Spence's excerpts from Volney's *Ruins* see Ian Haywood, *The Revolution in Popular Literature: Print, Politics and the People, 1790–1860* (Cambridge University Press, 2004), pp. 31–2.
13. Anne Janowitz, *Lyric and Labour in the Romantic Tradition* (Cambridge University Press, 1998), p. 76.
14. Goldsmith, 'A Lamentation for the Oppressed' (I, iii, 33–5; August/September, 1793); Swift, 'An Unpleasant Lesson for the Pig's Betters' (I, viii, 86–7; September/October 1793); Fielding; 'On Kings', (II, xviii, 201–2; April, 1794); Spenser, 'Examples of Safe Printing' (II, ii, 14; January, 1794). The extracts attributed to Milton and Spenser are both forgeries, a point considered in greater detail below.
15. Linda Colley, *Britons: Forging the Nation* (Yale University Press, 1993), p. 44.
16. Malcolm Chase, 'From Millennium to Anniversary: The Concept of Jubilee in Late Eighteenth-Century and Nineteenth-Century Thought', *Past and Present*, 110 (1990): 143.
17. Arthur M. Schlesinger, 'A Note on Songs as Patriot Propaganda 1765–1776,' *The William and Mary Quarterly*, 11 (1954): 83.
18. James Thomson, 'Rule Britannia,' *The Poetical Works of James Thomson* (London, 1866), p. 266.

19. For another parody of 'Rule Britannia' in *Pig's Meat* see 'A Song' (II, vi, 67; February, 1794).
20. Thomson, p. 265.
21. Lauren G. Leighton, 'Translation as a Derived Art', *Proceedings of the American Philosophical Society*, 134.4 (1990): 446.
22. Ibid., p. 451.
23. Edmund Burke, *Reflections on the Revolution in France*, ed. Conor Cruise O'Brien (Harmondsworth: Penguin, 1985), p. 173.
24. *The Trial of Thomas Paine; for Writing and Publishing a Seditious Pamphlet. Entitled the Rights of Man Tried at the Court of King'-Bench* [sic], *Guild-Hall, London, on Tuesday, December 18th, 1792 ... with his Defence by the Hon. Thomas Erskine* (London, 1792), p. 31.
25. See for example Spence (I, xv, 168–75; December 1793).
26. Daniel Isaac Eaton, ed., *Politics for the People: or, a Salmagundy for Swine* (London, 1793–1795), vol. I, part 1, number i, (21 September, 1793). *Politics for the People* was based on the format pioneered by Spence in *Pig's Meat*.
27. See for example: Marcus Wood, *Radical Satire and Print Culture* (Oxford: Clarendon Press, 1994), pp. 96–154; Olivia Smith, *The Politics of Language, 1791–1819* (Oxford University Press, 1984), pp. 154–201.
28. Richard Lee, 'The Rights of God', *Songs from the Rock, to Hail the Approaching Day, Sacred to Truth, Liberty and Peace* (London, 1795), p. 17.
29. For more on the Pittachio squibs see John Barrell, ed., *Exhibitions Extraordinary!! Radical Broadsides of the Mid-1790s* (Nottingham: Trent Editions, 2001).

Part IV
The Case of Austen

10
Austen, Sincerity and the Standard

Alex J. Dick

In *Sincerity and Authenticity*, Lionel Trilling defined 'the sentiment of being' as 'the criterion by which Jane Austen judges the quality of the selves she brings into her purview. Whoever in her novels wins her regard – her compassionate or comic indulgence is another thing – possesses in a high degree the sentiment of being, with all that this implies of self-sufficiency, self-definition, and sincerity.'[1] Trilling was adapting an obsolete definition of sincerity, 'freedom from falsification, adulteration, or alloy; purity, correctness' as opposed to 'honesty, straightforwardness,' or 'genuineness.'[2] He then offered a material corollary for his usage: 'the sufficiency and decorum of fortunate domestic arrangements'; Austen never 'questions the "ideal" of the "noble" life which is appropriate to the great and beautiful houses with the ever-remembered names – Northanger Abbey, Donwell Abbey, Pemberley, Hartfield, Kellynch Hall, Norland Park, Mansfield Park. In them 'existence is sweet and dear' at least if one is rightly disposed; they hold nothing less than the meaning of life for those who are fitted to seek it and cherish it when it is found. With what the great houses represent the heroines of the novels are, or become, wholly in accord.'[3]

Few critics would concur that life is 'sweet and dear' at Northanger (where the heroine accuses her host of murdering his wife), Kellynch (whose bankrupt owner rents to an Admiral), Norland (whose residents are evicted by their half-brother), or Mansfield (built on the proceeds of the slave-driven sugar trade). Austen's novels broach subjects like class, slavery, and debt in ways that query even the rigors of political economy. When and whenever Austen touched on a point of political controversy she was not only exposing its conditions but also foregrounding its varied parameters. Austen knew the world was at base a mess, rife with conflict and oppression. And it is thanks to her, and writers like her, that we continue to know and understand these conflicts. The genius of free indirect discourse is that it enables the narrator to judge without doing so *sincerely*. What is more, determining what this standard might be has proved very difficult. Feminist critics have argued that Austen's narrative standard constitutes an insidious but radical form of gender critique: the voicelessness of women in the increasingly domestic and patriarchal society of the early nineteenth century is given in Austen not only a consciousness but a free-thinking, dialectical sense of its own precariousness.[4] At a more material level, Clifford Siskin has argued that the 'Austen enigma' is best understood as a by-product of the profession, *novelist,* that Austen chose to pursue after abandoning her early attempts at critical journalism and satire, a *generic* disposition he calls 'novelism.'[5] Accepting these arguments requires that we regard the novel as distinct from the other forms and disciplines such that novelistic form can be thought of as a standard of value in itself. Yet Siskin and other historians of Romantic-era print culture also show that as late as 1820 the fields of 'writing' that included fiction, political economy, science, politics, journalism, and criticism often operated in tandem with each other to produce their increasingly divergent aims and ideologies.[6]

Yet, these interpretations also suggest a correlation in Austen between the 'sentiment of being' and that most troublingly insincere of entities: money. It happens that Austen's career coincides exactly with a critical and erratic period in monetary history. Money was everywhere in the eighteenth century but what form it might take, what values it might hold, who could redeem or use it, and how it might be protected were open questions on which commentators, writers, and ordinary people had a wide variety of opinions. A particularly intense and important moment in these debates was occasioned by the British government's decision in 1797 to suspend cash payments at the Bank of England, a decision that prevented citizens from redeeming their notes in coin and that was not reversed until 1821. During this debate, in 1816, the British Parliament introduced the first-ever official gold standard, which was an effort to regulate the value of money by improving the technology of coin production and fixing the relative values of various metal and paper exchange media.[7] The fact that the lifting of the cash suspension followed the introduction of the gold standard by five years indicates how difficult translating monetary theory into practice was. Nonetheless, the gold standard was a victory for economists and politicians who had been arguing that the financial system could only operate if it had a uniform and permanent referent, even if, as they all understood, this referent – gold – was only a symbol of the confidence in permanence and uniformity that the monetary system required. My argument is that Austen's peculiarly ironic sincerity constitutes an alternative standard to gold that inheres in writing, the medium of banknotes, political controversy, and fiction alike. I refer to this standard as *embarrassment*, defined in the eighteenth century as an inability to pay debt, but understood by sociologists since the 1950s as the register of potential disruptions that also produce social cohesion.[8] Embarrassment is a peculiarly modern form of sincerity by which everything that is wrong can be acknowledged without jeopardizing the integrity of a social system. Through the debate over the standard, embarrassment became a way for people to appreciate or even feel the fundamental insincerity of commerce without causing that system to falter. In a nutshell, embarrassment was the peculiar responsibility of literature.

Confidence

Austen was familiar with the vicissitudes of debt and credit, but how attuned she was to the controversies surrounding finance is an open question.[9] We can be reasonably sure that, like most people, Austen was aware of the difficulties attending the variety of available money forms. Coins were issued by the Royal Mint, under the auspices of the government. Over the course of the eighteenth century minting technology steadily improved, yet the production of small coins which required very little precious metal was a recurrent problem. They were clipped, melted, and forged and there were complex legal arrangements for deterring these practices, including capital punishment.[10] Meanwhile, the importation of paper money, banking, and financial accounting into England, although it significantly enhanced the wealth and reputation of currency traders and merchants, also caused a good deal of legal and political consternation that accounts in large part for the development in the late seventeenth century of financial journalism and other forms of business writing.[11] The Bank of England was nothing like a modern central bank, but its 'special relationship' with the government did have significant legal and economic ramifications. Laws protecting the Bank of England ensured that no crediting agency could have more than six partners. As a result there were small banks in every town and village, some of which were, for short times, very successful, and many wealthy concerns in London. But small banks were also by law not allowed to hold cash reserves of their own and relied on their own credit with metropolitan companies or the Bank of England.[12] Each bank issued its own notes. These were poorly printed and easy to forge. Forging banknotes became a capital crime in 1742, but the laws prohibiting it were not routinely enforced until the suspension of cash payments made the protection of small notes and coins an even more pressing concern.

Does this mean that there was *no* standard of value before 1816? No: it means that the standard is not the same thing as a universal concept or unchanging truth. The standard of value is what Pierre Bourdieu calls a *habitus,* a 'feel for the game' a 'sense of place' or a 'life-style,' the beliefs which in turn constitute us as subjects in the world.[13] A habitus is primarily local in orientation. But in groups or via social institutions, like the law or the state, habitus formations come into contact with those of others and either meld or conflict until a disposition for that group is constituted, although Bourdieu is clear that 'the group only exists durably as such, that is to say, as something transcending the set of its members, in so far as each of its members is so disposed as to exist through and for the group or, more accurately, in conformity with the principles which underpin its existence.'[14] These principles are the norms or 'standards' that as active individuals we accept or reject depending on the *habitus* that we bring to the field but which, in our relationship to that field, also constitute its inherent dynamics.

The *habitus* of eighteenth-century Britain was 'confidence.' Confidence was the respect and admiration that individuals were expected to feel for the rigidly hierarchical social system into which they were born. Yet the institutions that sustained this *habitus* at the local level, including feudalism, religious conformity, and aristocratic privilege were reproduced across communities, thanks to a common language and increases in literacy. Confidence thus became an imaginary measure of the relative worth of those people, objects, and places that it served to evaluate across the nation. It was represented monumentally around the country in the form of military statues and flags or 'standards' or in the triangular peaks on neo-classical country houses or the domes on St. Paul's and the Royal Exchange. It was also manifested in the idealized personalities of 'great men' who seemed to tower over others in their sense of judgment or virtue, or who displayed a pastoral regard for the community. This local confidence was also under significant ideological pressure. Imperial expansion and its attendant institutions such as the East India Company and the Atlantic Slave Trade resisted the top-down model of value favored by the localized, landed aristocracy. The global or 'oceanic' (as opposed to land) standard was 'underwritten' by 'speculative' institutions of exchange, credit, and insurance, institutions that were not governed by networks of local authority but rather by abstract relations of addition and subtraction, supply and demand, profit and loss. It operated through flows and equivalences rather than relations and obligations; it was horizontal rather than vertical. This supremely mathematical rationality resulted in the 'decoupling of public personhood from those inherited and landed forms of property which tie individuals to a fixed, traditional community of obligations' and 'the invention of an abstract, anonymous mode of personhood invested not in the inalienable claims of the locale but in the well-being of an anonymous collective.'[15] The competition between these two standards might be said to mark the transition from one form of sincerity to another, from correctness to genuineness. In one scheme, landowners are always right. In the other, the numbers don't lie.

Remarkably, the standard did not shift from land to ocean. Isolated from centers of power in order to pursue profit, but faced at home with accusations of fraud, inhumanity, and violence, the representatives of oceanic exchange had to justify themselves through less rationalistic means. East India agents and West Indian slave-traders refashioned the vertical standard into systems of merit and racial difference, purchased country houses, and built impressive markets. The nouveau riche did not want a revolution: they wanted to be part of a system that already existed. This is why, even when it celebrates sentimentalism, skepticism, or industry, most eighteenth-century literature *also* champions the vertical order of rank and privilege.[16] In Hume's 'On the Standard of Taste,' the highly skeptical realization that there are no standards is resolved with great men's opinions.[17] In Burney's novels, the vicissitudes of city life are made palatable by the natural order of the country estate.[18] In Burke's *Reflections*, respect for hierarchical institutions sublimely adumbrates the revolutionary power of liberty.[19] Appeals to manly strength and monumental verticality are not instances of conservative nostalgia. Neither Hume nor Burney nor Burke could even be called a Tory in the old-fashioned sense; their politics were Whig, their sense of the dignity of individual liberty and the inherent goodness of market capitalism was progressive.

Pride and Prejudice shows how confidence persisted into the 1790s.[20] The Bennets represent the village gentry, subordinate to the aristocracy (Lady Catherine de Burgh) and the church (Mr. Collins), prospering through the ready availability of credit, and participating in and with a broad field of national and cosmopolitan institutions: the city, the law, the army.[21] Marilyn Butler is right to see in Darcy, his large country estate, his extensive library, his proud ancestral picture gallery, and the respect he earns from tenants and professionals alike, the image of the Burkean gentleman, justified in the pressure he exerts against the global forces of speculation by his local leadership.[22] Darcy's assurance that he can correct the damage done to the Bennet family's reputation by Lydia's elopement is a further projection of this confidence. Lydia, who is named for the country where money was invented, and Wickham, the son of Darcy's father's steward, not an independent gentleman and a minor military officer, represent the luxuriance of global finance.[23] Lydia's elopement represents the hold that the new economy of credit and speculation had over the gentry. But it also allows Austen to put ideological counter-pressure on the new forces of speculation and equality via the old notion of confidence.

Crisis

In contrast to *Pride and Prejudice*, the later novels were composed at a time when the system of confidence faced its most significant crisis. In 1797, facing a possible French invasion and having to pay British troops abroad in coin, the British Parliament compelled the Bank of England to refuse all attempts to exchange paper notes for specie. The suspension was supposed to last six weeks; it went on for 24 years. In the meantime, economists, journalists, poets, and novelists debated theories of money and value in the temporary, crisis-based financial system that to many was as inefficient as it was fraudulent. Hundreds of pamphlets, newspaper columns and journal articles were published.[24] That the crisis of value entailed a clash of different ideas about what constituted the standard is especially apparent in *Mansfield Park*. Mary Crawford's urbanity is continuously juxtaposed to the rural customs of the country estate.[25] The novel is set in the shadow of the global economy: Portsmouth is suggested by the narrator to be a city made up entirely of standards – the times of sailings, viewings, dockings, meals, reviews – reminiscent of numerical rationality and juxtaposed to the 'noise,' 'smells,' and general 'agitation' of the Price's house, which are then compared by Fanny to the 'elegance or harmony' of Mansfield.[26]

Austen probably understood the implications of these debates even if she was not conversant in their technicalities. Her brother was a successful banker until he went bankrupt in 1815, an event that some have suggested inspired *Persuasion* and *Sanditon*. But the best evidence of how Austen understood the debate about the standard is her reading. With regular access to the circulating library at Chawton, Austen was undeniably as aware of the proliferation of didactic works dealing with the subjects of financial stress and moral value as she was of the latest Gothic fictions and scandalous biographies – a mixture that I think is important for the way Austen responded to questions of moral and economic standards.[27] One writer in whom Austen took a special interest was Hannah More. More was an advocate of 'Christian capitalism'; she believed that the advent of capital was profoundly beneficial to the progress of society. Capitalism required a standard that men and women living far apart could respect. Christian capitalism stressed financial acumen but also open charity: only the constant distribution of real wealth between strangers would maintain the confidence of the capitalist system. Women had a special role in this system: the embodiment of divine grace and moral self-consciousness at the domestic 'heart' of the British Empire.[28] More outlined these principles in several didactic works; the most popular was *Coelebs in Search of a Wife*, which celebrated the morality and charity of the intended wife Lucilla Stanley. But the novel clearly belongs to an era of financial insecurity. In an early chapter Coeleb visits London and meets a host of young ladies of fortune who exemplify selfishness, ignorance, and debt. Coeleb is taken by his London hosts, Sir John and Lady Belfield (whose name conjures the beauty of land) with another friend Lady Melbury ('bad town') to visit the house of a poor family. The daughter of the family, named Fanny, makes flower arrangements, which Lady Melbury promises to buy. When they arrive at the house, Lady Melbury reveals that she already owes the poor girl £700 and offers to take more flowers on credit. Coelebs is outraged: 'I was particularly struck with the discrepancy of characters, all of which are yet included under the broad comprehensive appellation of *Christians* ... Not one who derided or even neglected its forms; and who in her own class would not have passed for religious. Yet how little of them adorned the profession she adopted! ... How superficial, or inconsistent, or mistaken, or hollow, or hypocritical, or self-deceiving, was that of all the others!' From these reflections, the novel produces its own standard of value: 'if we compare the copy with the model, the Christian with the Christianity, how little can we trace the resemblance! In what particular did their lives imitate the life of Him *who pleased not himself, who did the will of his father; who went about doing good?* How irreconcilable is their faith with the principles which He taught!'[29] What is important is not simply that felt Christianity is more genuine or honest than professed religion: rather, a sense of Christian truth measures the relative worth of the debts and speculations that both propel and endanger middle-class life.

The shift from the 'bright and sparkling' repartee of *Pride and Prejudice* to the reflective tone of *Mansfield Park* points to More's influence, though that influence is never unquestioning.[30] Fanny is certainly sincere in a way that recalls More's ideal of sincere faith, though rarely didactically so. When Henry Crawford blithely tells her that her 'judgment' is his 'rule of right,' she replies 'no! – do not say so. We have all a better guide in ourselves, if we would attend to it, than any other person can be' (*MP* 478). Edmund and Henry Crawford debate the problem of absenteeism, a concept that applied both to Anglican ministers who did not live in their parishes and to landlords who did not live on their estates, and which suggests that Austen knew the work of More's friend William Wilberforce, whose 1798 work *Practical View of the Prevailing System of Professed Christians* recommending that parsons participate actively and directly in the lives of their parishioners, was reprinted in 1811.[31] But we know from her letters that Austen was never especially satisfied with evangelicalism as a value system.[32] The opening chapter features lengthy conversations between Sir Thomas Bertram and his sister-in-law Mrs. Norris on the worldly and other-worldly benefits of the charitable plan of adopting Fanny Price, but the diction parrots the didactic speechifying of More's *Coelebs*. The episode at Sotherton chapel compares several manners of religious conviction. Austen could hardly be said to have embraced the cynical latitudinarianism of Mary Crawford: 'The obligation of attendance, the formality, the restraint, the length of time – altogether it is a formidable thing, and what nobody likes' (*MP* 101–2). Edmund concedes with Mary that church services are too long, but nevertheless contends that 'the influence of the place and of example may often rouse better feelings than are begun with' (102). Yet Edmund's charitable compromise is undermined by Julia's irreligious suggestion that since all are present, Maria and Mr. Rushworth should simply marry right there and then. The implication is that religious conviction has been replaced by other kinds of feeling – private, self-interested, even self-serving – though in a complex way those feelings themselves are inherent in the Anglicanism of Austen's day.[33]

Another scene in which Austen queries the evangelical standard of sincerity is the theatricals episode. Not really about the dangers of performing a play, the scene illustrates the dangers of 'flow,' both moral and economic. The aristocratic enthusiast Mr. Yates, whom Tom Bertram meets at the *coastal* resort town of Weymouth, is described as a kind of con man, full of fashionable 'schemes' and 'a love of the theatre so general, an itch for acting so strong ... that he could hardly out-talk the interest of his hearers ... it was all bewitching, and there were few who did not wish to have been a party concerned or would have hesitated to try their skill' (86). By refusing to *act* Fanny is refusing to *participate* in a venture that Austen links to the same oceanic ineffability that she had formerly linked to Lydia and Wickham. By acting, Fanny would have to enter into an exchange network that she has been resisting all along, but which Mrs. Norris, for one, would like her to engage with: 'I am quite ashamed of you, Fanny, to make such a difficulty of obliging your cousins in a trifle of this sort' (*MP* 172). To be obligated in this way would enmesh her in the expanding network of enthusiasms, improvements and speculations – language that Austen uses to connect the theatrical 'scheme' to financial activity – that she abhors on moral grounds. Of course, even before she agrees to 'act' Fanny participates in the preparations for the rehearsals, mending the curtains and assisting the other players with their lines. But this is a further indication of Fanny's moral rather than familial authority. Once Sir Thomas returns, Fanny does not have to act: her moral authority has been usurped by that of the confident father. It makes sense to interpret the conflict between Fanny and Sir Thomas as a realization of the tension between the old standard of vertical power and the evangelical standard of moral duty.

But Sir Thomas, a West Indian plantation owner, also embodies the ideological pressures of the oceanic economy that Darcy had contained. This complication adds an important twist to Austen's investment in evangelical standards. Austen might well have felt some uneasiness about More's friend and fellow abolitionist, Thomas Clarkson, whose *History of the Progress and Accomplishment of the Abolition of the Slave Trade*, Austen read sometime after its publication in 1808.[34] Clarkson documented the decision of the abolitionists *not* to pursue the cause of emancipation outright for fear of alienating the commercial interest or potentially supportive politicians who, following the loss of the American colonies, otherwise felt that the complete liberation of the West Indian slave populations would threaten British interests.[35] Like More and other writers of 'grateful negro' stories and poems, Clarkson believed that the end of the slave trade would make plantation owners take better care of their slaves and give the slaves themselves some cause to respect those owners and hope for future emancipation. Austen's interest in the vicissitudes of the imperial economy is further suggested by her perusal of two other authors: Claudius Buchanan and Sir Charles Pasley. These works share a concern with social and moral order in an era of changing commercial fortunes and imperial expansion.[36] In his *Essay on the Military Policy and Institutions of the British*

Empire, Pasley urged that the best way for Britain to retain her economic power was to create a permanent standing army akin to that of ancient Rome.[37] Buchanan, whose fame as the leader of the movement for the evangelical reform of both the East India Company and the subcontinent itself culminated in the publication of his *Christian Researches in Asia* similarly presumed against the prevailing Orientalist view that the economic success of the Empire could be assured only through its complete Anglicization.[38] What is most remarkable about these texts – a feature they share with More and Clarkson – is their confidence, both in the sheer bravado of their rhetoric and the global comprehensiveness of their ambitions.

It is hard to imagine someone of Austen's ironic temperament agreeing with these brazenly imperialistic proposals for securing British economic security. Austen probably saw, and to an extent respected, these writers' attempts to revive a local, hierarchical standard of confidence on an international footing. She doubtless would have remarked their utter sincerity. More, Buchanan, Clarkson, and Pasley were all, in their own ways, advocating the adoption of fixed codes of truth, honesty, and above all confidence that, applied by individuals, would produce absolute harmony within the international market. However, the complications surrounding Fanny's evangelical character, as well as those around Sir Thomas's failures of 'principle,' not to mention Austen's general *fictionalizing* of the conflict between these standards highlight Austen's reservations about the confidence she had endorsed in her earlier novels.

Indeed, we might suggest that the 'noise' of *Mansfield Park* – debate without resolution at Sotherton, Mansfield, and Portsmouth – converts into narrative form the spread of 'sincere' opinion, the crisis of value, of which her own earlier (though published at the peak of the controversy) 'Tory' novels were a part. If, however, there can be no 'true' position about what is best for the Empire, how might the 'sentiment of being' be maintained? In what exactly do we believe?

Embarrassment

The solution to the crisis was supposed to have been the gold standard adopted in 1816.[39] Based in part on the teachings of Enlightenment economists, notably Adam Smith, as adapted by commentators in the *Edinburgh Review* and elsewhere, the theory of the gold standard was simply that by lowering and fixing the price of gold against silver, the demand for gold in England would rise, allowing token silver coins and paper notes to circulate at their rate close to their low nominal value. But the gold standard was also a tool for preserving confidence in light of the need for diverse exchange media.[40] As noted explicitly by David Ricardo in the third, 1819 edition of his *Principles of Political Economy and Taxation,* the purpose of the gold standard was to avoid the embarrassment of not knowing what the standard is.[41] But even those who championed the gold standard appreciated that its power was symbolic. The gold standard was introduced through an act of *legislation*: it is an abstraction. In order for that abstract measure to operate as a standard it has to incur a general trust that it can do so. And the gold standard did not incur that trust – not completely. The price of gold continued to rise and fall in the market and this made many people very uneasy. There were bank failures and market crashes throughout the century. The leveling effect promised by the rationalistic economics of Ricardo and Bentham did *not* turn English culture away from either its ancient hierarchies or immoral luxuries. The gold standard did not solve the crisis of value: it intensified it.

The real solution to the crisis of value was the cultivation of a new disposition, embarrassment, the honest realization of the damage capitalism could do, or in the understanding that it could not do nearly as much as it promised, consoled by the recognition that there is very little that one individual *can* do in the face of capitalism's power.[42] Instead of being frustrated that a seemingly sincere confidence leads only to conflict and anxiety, embarrassment ameliorates *that* frustration with the self-conscious and pleasurable feeling of the aesthetic. This is, in fact, precisely the way Austen countered her own mixed feelings about Buchanan and Pasley. Remarking in a letter that she had initially 'protested against' Pasley's *Essay*, she nevertheless found it 'delightful written and highly entertaining. I am as much in love with the author as ever I was with Clarkson or Buchanan.'[43] This is usually taken to confirm Austen's agreement with the content of these books: but, as with More, she is more invested in the way the books are written than she is in what is said or recommended therein.[44] This investment in *writing* signals a crucial shift about where the standard of value comes from: not in the confidence that More, Clarkson, Buchanan, or Pasley offer but rather the circulation of paper and the imagination of values. In putting her faith in the 'delight' and 'entertainment' of these texts, Austen adopted a profoundly ambiguous position with regard to the imperial economy. She obviated its reliance on the limitless spread of the very medium, paper, that it also in its political economy seeks to control or, in some cases, abandon.[45] And she deliberately found that insincerity delightful.

In short, cultivating embarrassment became the work of literature – and it is hard to think of a novel more concerned with embarrassment than *Mansfield Park*. 'I blush for you Tom,' says Sir Thomas, though his declaration of embarrassment here refutes the genuineness that a physical affect like blushing is supposed to embody (*MP* 26). What I want to stress is the way Austen realizes embarrassment in *Mansfield Park* as an aesthetic, even literary disposition, one that is cultivated in works of writing *about* value other than evangelical tracts and imperialist pamphlets and one that is as much about pleasure as it is about confusion or insecurity. The literary disposition of the Bertram household is illustrated by Fanny's fondness for Sir Thomas's accounts of his West Indian adventure: 'I love to hear my uncle talk of the West Indies' she says to Edmund not long after Sir Thomas's return ... I could listen to him for an hour together. It entertains me more than many other things have done – but then' she adds, 'I am unlike other people I dare say' (*MP* 230). This is a critical distinction. Fanny admits here that she is *not* mortified by the fact that their family comforts are products of slave labour. Others in the family clearly are reluctant to know about this – or more likely just indifferent, as Fanny herself senses: 'there was such a dead silence! And while my cousins were sitting by without speaking a word, or seeming at all interested in the subject, I did not like – I thought it would appear as if I wanted to set myself off at their expense, by shewing a curiosity and pleasure in his information which he must wish his own daughters to feel' (*MP* 231). What Fanny wants to subdue here is her excitement: she is embarrassed by her own reaction and not the fact of slavery itself.

Within *Mansfield Park* is an unwritten book of confident self-justification – like Clarkson's, Pasley's, or Buchanan's – 'Sir Thomas Bertram's Adventures in Antigua'. Treating Sir Thomas's talk as narrative equates it to the salacious ('scandalous,' Mary Crawford calls it) Burney-esque 'novel,' set of course in London, about Maria Rushworth's wild and hopeless affair with Henry Crawford, which is itself the sequel to (or second part of) Tom Bertram's illness (incurred by gambling and loose living), and Mary Crawford's attempt to win back Edmund's good graces. Occupying four of the last five chapters of *Mansfield Park*, much of this story is relayed to Fanny by other people in the form of letters and one long interview between Fanny and Edmund. Austen intertwines the accounts Fanny receives of Tom's illness and Maria's indiscretions with the diction of metropolitan scandal *and* of financial controversy: Tom's illness is 'alarming,' 'distressing,' 'grieved,' 'evil' (*MP* 494–5). The affair is finally confirmed by Fanny's father who reads about it in a London tabloid. These stories of illness and scandal are a source of profound embarrassment: 'the influence of London [was] very much at war with all respectable attachments;' (*MP* 501) when Mr. Price reports the incident to her she exclaims, 'it cannot be true – it must mean some other people' (*MP* 509). But the realization that Maria's scandal *is* true produces in Fanny a new kind of response:

> She spoke with the instinctive wish of delaying shame, she spoke with a resolution which sprung from despair, for she spoke which what she did not, could not believe herself. It had been the shock of conviction as she read. The truth rushed on her; and how she could have spoken at all, how she could even have breathed – was afterwards matter of wonder to herself ... The horror of a mind like Fanny's, as it received the conviction of such guilt, and began to take in some part of the misery that must ensue, can hardly be described. At first it was a sort of stupefaction; but every moment was quickening her perception of the horrible evil. She could not doubt, she dared not indulge a hope of the paragraph being false. (*MP* 509–10)

Austen's style encompasses the journalistic language employed by Lady Bertram and Mary Crawford and this heightens the confusion Fanny feels between her sense of shame and her understanding of truth. But Fanny must 'delay' her shame and speak so that her moral conscience does not disrupt the social order. The affair is not Fanny's fault, and yet she feels keenly its disruptive effects. Mary also betrays a palpable sense of embarrassment: 'She was astonished, exceedingly astonished – more than astonished. I saw her change countenance. She turned extremely red. I imagined I saw a mixture of many feelings – a great though short struggle – half a wish of yielding to truth half a sense of shame – but habit, habit carried it. She would have laughed if she could' (*MP* 531). Edmund experiences a similar shock even when, after the fact, he relates his encounter with Mary to Fanny, who feels embarrassed for him: 'Edmund was so much affected, that Fanny, watching him with silent, but most tender concern, was almost sorry that the subject had been entered on at all' (*MP* 529) – though not altogether regretful that a truth has been exposed. But these reactions are not meant to be treated as one and the same: they register, in fact, very different kinds of standards. With her recourse to 'habit,' Mary Crawford recalls the studied confidence of Burney and Hume. Edmund and Fanny are, by contrast, embarrassingly sincere: 'The heart must be open and everything told' (*MP* 524).

Speaking the embarrassing truth does not entail a fixed standard. It allows the standards that fill the market of ideas to speak for themselves – without resolution and without assurance. As such it is a more than suitable, even more than useful standard for a culture that, as Britain had become in the nineteenth century, utterly commercialized even as it largely retained its old aristocratic structures of vertical power and local confidence. But Austen's fiction also shows us that, in the wake of the crisis of value and the introduction of the gold standard – victories for a different kind of leveling, bourgeois confidence – this archaic social structure had to represent itself in a new, more self-conscious manner. 'Let other pens dwell on guilt and misery' Austen's narrator declares in the last chapter, 'I quit such odious subjects as soon as I can, impatient to restore to everybody, not greatly in fault themselves, to tolerable comfort, and to have done with all the rest' (*MP* 553). In expressing her own embarrassment at the end of her novel – no one is at fault, there is no guilt, everyone just has to go on tolerably well – Austen is articulating a new kind of sincerity not only for realist fiction but also for modern consciousness.

Notes

1. Lionel Trilling, *Sincerity and Authenticity* (London: Oxford University Press, 1974), p. 73.
2. Definitions are from the *Oxford English Dictionary* online edition.
3. Trilling, *Sincerity and Authenticity*, pp. 73–4.
4. N. Armstrong, *Desire and Domestic Fiction: A Political History of the Novel* (Oxford University Press, 1987), pp. 134–60 and *How Novels Think: The Limits of Individualism from 1719–1900* (Columbia University Press, 2005), pp. 43–7; D. S. Lynch, *The Economy of Character: Novels, Market Culture, and the Business of Inner Meaning* (University of Chicago Press, 1998), especially Chapter 5, 'Jane Austen and the Social Machine'; C. Gallagher, *Nobody's Story: The Vanishing Acts of Women Writers in the Marketplace 1670–1820* (University of California Press, 1995); M. Poovey, *The Proper Lady and the Woman Writer: Ideology as Style in the Works of Mary Wollstonecraft, Mary Shelley, and Jane Austen* (University of Chicago Press, 1985).
5. C. Siskin, *The Work of Writing: Literature and Social Change in Britain 1700–1830* (Johns Hopkins University Press, 1998), pp. 198–203.
6. See F. Moretti, *Graphs, Maps, and Trees: Abstract Models for a Literary History* (New York: Verso, 2005), pp. 18–20, and P. Garside, J. Raven, and R. Schowerling, eds. *The English Novel 1770–1829: A Bibliographic Survey and Prose Fiction Published in the British Isles* (Oxford University Press, 2000). See also W. St. Clair, *The Reading Nation in the Romantic Period* (Cambridge University Press, 2004).
7. See A. Redish, 'The Evolution of the Gold Standard in England,' *Journal of Economic History* 50 (1990): 789–805, and G. Seglin, 'Steam, Hot Air, and Small Change: Matthew Boulton and the Reform of Britain's Coinage,' *Economic History Review* 56 (2003): 478–509.

8. See especially E. Goffman, 'Embarrassment and Social Organization,' *American Journal of Sociology* 62 (1956): 246–71, and *The Presentation of Self in Everyday Life* (Doubleday, 1959). For a useful summary of Goffman's position in light of more recent developments in the sociology of affect, see M. Schudson, 'Embarrassment and Erving Goffman's Idea of Human Nature,' *Theory and Society* 13 (1984): 633–48.

9. See E. Copeland, *Women Writing About Money* (Cambridge University Press, 1995), pp. 89–116, and 'The Austens and the Elliots: A Consumer's Guide to *Persuasion*' in *Jane Austen's Business: Her World and Her Profession*, eds. Juliet McMaster and Bruce Stovel (St. Martin's Press, 1996), pp. 136–53. See also R. Miles, '"A Fall in Bread": Speculation and the Real in *Emma*,' *Novel: A Forum on Fiction* 37 (2003): 66–85.

10. R. McGowan, 'From Pillory to Gallows: The Punishment of Forgery in the Age of the Financial Revolution,' *Past and Present* 165 (1999): 107–40; C. Wennerlind, 'The Death Penalty as Monetary Policy: The Practice and Punishment of Monetary Crime, 1690–1830,' *History of Political Economy* 36 (2004): 131–61.

11. J. Brewer, 'Commercialisation and Politics,' in M. McKendrick, et al., *The Birth of a Consumer Society: The Commercialization of 18th Century England* (Hutchinson, 1983), p. 217; W. Parsons, *The Power of the Financial Press: Journalism and Economic Opinion in Britain and America* (Rutgers University Press, 1989), pp. 11–20; M. Rowlinson, '"The Scotch Hate Gold": British Identity and Paper Money' in *Nation-States and Money: The Past, Present, and Future of National Currencies*, eds. Emily Gilbert and Eric Helleiner (Routledge, 1999), pp. 47–67.

12. For the history of banking and its relation to culture and nationalism see H. V. Bowen, 'The Bank of England During the Long Eighteenth Century, 1694–1826,' *The Bank of England: Money, Power, and Influence* 1694–1994, eds. Richard Roberts and David Kynaston (Clarendon Press, 1995), pp. 3–20; Robert Elgie and Helen Thompson, *The Politics of Central Banks* (Routledge, 1998), Chapter 3; E. Helleiner, *The Making of National Money: Territorial Currencies in Historical Perspective* (Ithica: Cornell University Press, 2003), pp. 19–59.

13. Bourdieu defines habitus as 'a system of *dispositions*, that is, of permanent manners of being, seeing, acting and thinking, or a system of *long-lasting* (rather than permanent) schemes or schemata or structures of perception, conception, and action' (*Habitus: A Sense of Place*, eds. J. Hillier and E. Rooksby, 2nd edn. [Ashgate, 2005], p. 43). See also *Distinction: A Social Critique of the Judgement of Taste*, trans. R. Nice (Harvard University Press, 1984), pp. 170–3, and *Outline of a Theory of Practice*, trans. R. Nice (Cambridge University Press, 1977), pp. 72–86.

14. P. Bourdieu, *Homo Academicus*, trans. Peter Collier (Stanford University Press, 1988), p. 56.

15. I. Baucom, *Specters of the Atlantic: Finance Capital, Slavery, and the Philosophy of History* (Duke University Press, 2005), p. 56.

16. N. Hudson 'Social Rank, "The Rise of the Novel" and Whig Histories of Eighteenth-Century Fiction,' *Eighteenth-Century Fiction* 17.4 (July 2005): 564–98.

17. See David Hume, 'Of the Standard of Taste,' *Essays Moral, Political, and Literary*, ed. E. F. Miller, (Liberty, 1985), p. 243: 'Though men of delicate taste are rare,

they are easily to be distinguished in society, by the soundness of their under-standing and the superiority of their faculties above the rest of mankind.'

18. See J. Thompson, *Models of Value: Eighteenth-Century Political Economy and the Novel* (Duke University Press, 1996); M. J. Burgess, 'Courting Ruin: The Economic Romances of Frances Burney,' *Novel: A Forum on Fiction* 28 (1995): 131–53; and Gallagher, 203–55.

19. See J. G. A. Pocock, 'The Political Economy of Burke's Analysis of the French Revolution,' *Virtue, Commerce, and History* (Cambridge University Press, 1985), pp. 193–213.

20. Jane Austen, *Pride and Prejudice*, ed. Pat Rogers (Cambridge University Press, 2006).

21. On the relative status of Austen's characters see J. A. Downie, 'Who Says She's a Bourgeois Writer? Reconsidering the Social and Political Contexts of Jane Austen's Novels,' *Eighteenth-Century Studies* 40 (2006): 69–84.

22. Marilyn Butler, *Jane Austen and the War of Ideas* (Clarendon Press, 1976), pp. 214–15.

23. In Herodotus, Gyges is taunted by Candaules, the King of Lydia, into watching his wife undress. When she catches him, she makes him hide again in the same place to murder the king and take his place. Gyges becomes a tyrant himself, debasing coin to fund his own callous and violent regime. The secret of the myth is that the value of money is based purely on speculation and computation. See M. Shell, *The Economy of Literature* (Johns Hopkins University Press, 1978), pp. 11–62.

24. See F. Fetter, *The Development of British Monetary Orthodoxy 1797–1875* (Harvard University Press, 1965); B. Hilton, *Corn, Cash, and Commerce: The Economic Policies of the Tory Governments 1815–1830* (Oxford University Press, 1977); J. W. Houghton, *Culture and Currency: Cultural Bias in Monetary Theory and Policy* (Westview Press, 1991); Patrick Brantlinger, *Fictions of State: Culture and Credit in Britain, 1694–1994* (Cornell University Press, 1996); Robert Mitchell, *Sympathy and the State in the Romantic Era: Systems, State Finance, and the Shadows of Futurity* (Routledge, 2007); A. J. Dick, 'The Ghost of Gold: Forgery Trials and the Standard of Value in Shelley's *The Mask of Anarchy*,' *European Romantic Review* 18 (2007): 381–400.

25. F. Easton, 'The Political Economy of Mansfield Park: Fanny Price and the Atlantic Working Class,' *Textual Practice* 12 (1998): 470.

26. Jane Austen, *Mansfield Park*, ed. John Wiltshire (Cambridge University Press, 2005), pp. 443, 453. Hereafter cited as *MP*.

27. See L. Erickson, 'The Economy of Novel Reading: Jane Austen and the Circulating Library,' *The Economy of Literary Form* (Johns Hopkins University Press, 1996), pp. 125–41.

28. See A. Mellor, *Mothers of the Nation: Women's Political Writing in England 1780–1832* (Indiana University Press, 1996), pp. 32–4. See also T. Haskell, 'Capitalism and the Origins of the Humanitarian Sensibility,' *The Antislavery Debate: Capitalism and Abolitionism as a Problem in Historical Interpretation*, ed. T. Bender (University of California Press, 1992).

29. Hannah More, *Coelebs in Search of a Wife: Comprehending Observations of Domestic Habits and Manners, Religion and Morals* (Cadell, 1809), pp. 191–2.

30. See E. Rene-Dozier, 'Hannah More and the Invention of Narrative Authority,' *ELH* 71 (2004): 209–27.

31. On Absenteeism, see G. D. V. White, *Jane Austen in the Context of Abolition: 'A Fling at the Slave Trade'* (Palgrave Macmillan, 2006), pp. 22–7.
32. See Jane Austen, *Jane Austen's Letters*, ed. R. W. Chapman (Oxford University Press, 1964), pp. 256, 410. See also. P. Gardside and E. McDonald, 'Evangelicalism and *Mansfield Park*,' *Trivium* 10 (1975): 34–50; D. Monoghan, '*Mansfield Park* and Evangelicalism: A Reassessment,' *Nineteenth-Century Fiction* 3 (1978): 215–30; M. Waldron, 'The Frailties of Fanny: *Mansfield Park* and the Evangelical Movement,' *Eighteenth-Century Fiction* 6 (1994): 259–81.
33. See C. Jager, '*Mansfield Park* and the End of Natural Theology,' *MLQ* 63 (2002): 31–63.
34. T. Clarkson, *History of the Progress and Accomplishment of the Abolition of the Slave Trade* (Parke, 1808).
35. See G. E. Boulukos, 'The Politics of Silence: *Mansfield Park* and the Amelioration of Slavery,' *Novel: A Forum on Fiction* 39 (2006): 361–83. See also R. Allen, 'The British Nation and the Colonies: *Mansfield Park*' in *Literature and Nation: Britain and India 1800–1900*, eds. Richard Allen and Harish Trivedi (Routledge, 2000), pp. 43–54 and Christopher Leslie Brown, *Moral Capital: Foundations of British Abolitionism* (University of North Carolina Press, 2006).
36. For Austen's reading of these two writers, see W. Galperin, *The Historical Austen* (University of Pennsylvania Press, 2003), pp. 161–6.
37. C. W. Pasley, *Essay on the Military Policy and Institutions of the British Empire* (Edmund Lloyd, 1811).
38. C. Buchanan, *Christian Researches in Asia with Notices of the Translation of the Scriptures* (New York, 1812). For context, see K. Chancey, 'The Star in the East: The Controversy over Christian Missions to India 1805–1813,' *Historian* 60 (1998): 507–23.
39. For an explanation of why the gold standard was legislated, see A. Redish, 'The Evolution of the Gold Standard in England,' *Journal of Economic History* 50 (1990): 789–805, and Houghton, 136–43.
40. See B. Fontana, *Rethinking the Politics of Commercial Society: the Edinburgh Review 1802–1832* (Cambridge University Press, 1985), pp. 118–25.
41. D. Ricardo, *Principles of Political Economy and Taxation*, vol. 1 of *The Works and Correspondence of David Ricardo*, ed. P. Sraffa (Cambridge University Press, 1951–5), p. 46.
42. See Alex Dick, 'Romanticism, Liberalism, Criticism,' *European Romantic Review* 19 (2008): 125–30.
43. Austen, *Letters*, p. 292.
44. See T. Fulford, 'Sighing for a Solider,' *Nineteenth-Century Literature* 57 (2002): 153–78.
45. For the power of paper to produce its own standards and systems as well as the concomitant intersection between 'bank-paper' and 'book-paper,' see K. McLaughlin, *Paperwork: Fiction and Mass Mediacy in the Paper Age* (University of Pennsylvania Press, 2005).

11
'Facts are Such Horrible Things!': The Question of Authentic Femininity in Jane Austen

Ashley Tauchert

> The aim of all commentary on art now should be to make works of art – and, by analogy, our own experience – more, rather than less, real to us. The function of criticism should be to show *how it is what it is*, even *that it is what it is*, rather than to show what *it means*. In place of a hermeneutics we need an erotics of art.
>
> (Susan Sontag)[1]

> Sincerity in the proper sense of the word, meaning authenticity, is ... or ought to be, a writer's chief preoccupation. No writer can ever judge exactly how good or bad a work of his may be, but he can always know, not immediately perhaps, but certainly in a short while, whether something he has written is authentic – in his handwriting – or a forgery ... Some writers confuse authenticity, which they ought always to aim at, with originality, which they should never bother about.
>
> (W. H. Auden)[2]

Jane Austen may now be canonized for her six important novels but that's not all she wrote. Her early narrative work is available in various editions (now including some excellent and easily accessible e-texts) but it is rarely approached with the kind of critical seriousness long circulating around her more mature works. For Margaret Anne Doody, this is because we have been misreading Austen's 'short fiction' as 'chaotic and childish', mere 'prentice-hand attempts to perform what will be done properly in the six novels'.[3] While the mature novels have long been used as examples of a defining stage in the maturation of the English literary tradition, Austen's shorter narrative works resist and expose claims to 'mature' novelistic realism at a number of different levels. This chapter will explore the critical significance of this apparent division between early and late Austen as it divides on the works' claims to realism, where realism is understood as a sincere claim to represent an authentic vision of reality. Literary realism is always a construct, but for the realist claim to hold we have to be persuaded that the author is sincere enough in her representation and not just larking around.

Authenticity is a difficult concept to define without opposition to a forged or faked version of the real thing. It refers to nothing directly. Something can be said to be authentic if it relates sincerely to the truth. The authenticity of an object or a statement (or a work of art) also relates to its uniqueness, as Susan Sontag reminds us:

> a novel is the creation not simply of a voice but of a world. It mimics the essential structures by which we experience ourselves as living in time, and inhabiting a world, and attempting to make sense of our experience … This is possible because narration is possible, because there are norms of narration that are as constitutive of thinking and feeling and experiencing as are, in Kant's account, the mental categories of space and time.[4]

In what sense can we describe Austen's work as authentic then? Hegel defined great art as that which:

> liberates the real import of appearances from the semblance and deception of this bad and fleeting world, and imparts to phenomenal semblances a higher reality, born of mind. The appearances of art, therefore, far from being mere semblances, have the higher reality and the more genuine existence in comparison with the realities of common life.[5]

In Hegel's aesthetics, literature can only be authentic if it is also art. In this sense it can claim an authentic relationship to reality; rather than one based on false appearances or – in Marxian terms – false relations to the real forces of production.

The story with which we have reassured ourselves about Austen's development from an immature writer of anarchic short stories to a mature writer intervening in the aesthetic of the English novel is analogous to the critical argument made for the development of the novel itself: emerging from earlier, immature, unrealistic instances of fictional prose to become the appropriate mode of narrative representation under conditions of modernity.[6] Writers seem to have become simply better and more accurate in their representation of reality over the course of the development of the novel. Austen simply became *better* at and *more accurate* in her representation of reality in the course of growing up into the mature novelist we know and love. Doody has rather brilliantly challenged this teleology, arguing that if we stopped treating Austen's early short fictions as 'childish effusions' they might

> begin to loom very large indeed in Austen's *oeuvre*, pointing to the alternative Austen who might have been a different writer, who might have figured in our calendar more like Diderot or Borges.[7]

Another Austen may be out there then, one who created a world centred on 'libidinous pressures only fictively constrained by conceptual structures imposed as order.' This is a representation of the world as experienced by the girl rather than the woman, and as such a world in which the laws which constrain girlish desires (whether those governing marriage or the new form of novelistic realism) 'are alike revealed as pseudo-orderly and slightly crazed structures'.[8] Is this evidence of a more *authentic* Austen, then? This is the implication of Doody's argument: that Austen's aesthetic maturation is achieved through artificial restraint of her more authentic libidinal tendencies by the restrictive codes of 'Regency' dress: 'Her movements became constricted and she spoke in an altered tone'.[9] The important implication is that the shift between early and late Austen marks an adaptation to regulatory codes, a process of increasing insincerity, and an increasing diminishment of the earlier, anarchic voice into the later narratives of ordered restraint. I want to work out from Doody's important argument to explore Austen's early work in terms of a more thorough investigation of the language of realism she comes to define.

Austen's mode of authenticity is characterized by the irony that is never fully resolved in the work. Our appreciation of the authenticity of Austen's literary vision depends on the extent to which we can take account of the critical distance she builds between her representation and the reality to which it refers and on which it offers a (Sontag would say 'moral') judgement. How does Austen's manifest irony square with her otherwise insistent attention to authentic realism? Austen's six mature novels are at one level taken to be meticulous representations of Regency England, albeit representations from a limited viewpoint deploying a particular cluster of reference points: daughters, sisters, desire, economics, marriage, family, estate, clergy, interiority, love. Their continuing fascination lies in their capacity to induce in the reader a definable sense of pre-industrial England, endlessly reconstructed in visual adaptations and Austen tourist sites such as the Jane Austen Centre in Bath, which focuses particularly on the detail of Regency dress. They are also more properly considered authentic moral realism in that Austen's literary achievement marks a transcendent moment in the narrative tradition. Her work is considered artistically authentic in its attention to the constraints of English realism: aiming to capture in literary representation the immediate context for the action (mimesis) alongside a model of reasonable causality (verisimilitude) that remains plausible (if a little romanticized) today. She is also traditionally considered properly authentic in Lionel Trilling's careful delineation:

> In Jane Austen's novels, as in Shakespeare's late plays, the character of the heroines is shaped by their spirited acquiescence in the societal mode that Hegel called 'noble' and represented as the definitive circumstance of the 'honest soul'. Its visionary norm of life is the order, peace, honour, and beauty which inhere in a happy and (as used to be said) prosperous marriage, in the sufficiency and decorum of fortunate domestic arrangements.[10]

Austen's work is also caught up with the authentic at the level of characterization: the narrative anxiety that centres her novels is the anxiety centred on the uncertainty of the heroine's happy ending in the form of a providential marriage. The heroine's happy ending is directly correlated to the question of authenticity concerning her desire and its object: Emma realizes the quantum difference between *believing* she is in love with Frank Churchill and *experiencing* the transformative (and ultimately painful) truth of loving Mr. Knightley; Marianne suffers to the extreme from the final inauthenticity of Willoughby's love, contrasted with the quieter, more sincere affection of Colonel Brandon. The reality of desire and its possible outcomes demands an authentic object: Elizabeth has to discover that Darcy's honour is sincere rather than mere pride before she can recognize and fully experience a desire that leads her to her own happy ending premised securely on £10,000 a year and her status as mistress of Pemberley. We as readers believe the happy ending to be authentic (realistically plausible) rather than pure fantasy (mythic or romantic) as long as we understand that this is the happiest this heroine could possibly be within the material conditions from which she emerges and as long as we recognize the truly liberating effects of £10,000 a year at this point in English history. Finally the reader is invited to at least suspend a conventional disbelief in the romantic 'love' that organizes the union on which her happiness depends.

But is Austen sincere in these depictions of romantic triumph? This is a more difficult question, given the slipperiness of her tone, the resistance of her narrative outcomes to final critical interpretation, the range of ways in which she can be comfortably received: considered the first 'Mills and Boon' feminine romancer as well as the first of the English novelists to establish free indirect discourse as a defining realist possibility. Yet this Austen-the-realist is also Austen-the-romancer, who knowingly weaves the available desires of feminine false consciousness into a plausible and recognizable narrative that can still be taken as authentic by post-industrial readers. The Austen who taunts her readers with the 'compression of the pages' before them[11] and who leaves them wondering at the extent to which they also were taken in by the charms of Willoughby, and caught in the act of finding Brandon an unreasonable compromise, or wishing Fanny had said 'yes' to Henry Crawford, is only sincere if we accept sincerity to be the unveiling of false desires in the face of truth.

Austen is finally romantic of course, both in the sense of clinching the happy ending in an insistence on 'love' and in the way her narratives partake of a review of Enlightenment instrumental materialism. The difference between Elizabeth and Mary Bennet is perhaps the difference between authentic and artificially bookish femininity. Elizabeth's famous wilfulness is all the more interesting for the way it finally capitulates to Darcy's will; Emma's emotional and economic independence allows for a more powerful experience of the loss of her precious self in Knightley. Austen's artistic sincerity is sharp to the point of drawing blood from her feminist readers. This mode of realism is highly particular and purposive: achieving a sincere vision through the vicissitudes of irony. Socratic realism then, which forces a crisis of perception in the reader to provoke a clearer sense of what might in fact be possible in spite of what is still considered after all to be the 'truth universally acknowledged'.

I am going to focus this discussion on three examples of Austen's early narrative work: *Jack and Alice*, *Love and Freindship* (sic), and finally *Lady Susan*. Most of Austen's juvenilia was finished by 1793, and *Lady Susan* probably finished by 1794. *Jack and Alice* was produced by the time she was 17; *Love and Freindship* by the time she was 15 (over the period that Wollstonecraft would have been conceiving, writing and publishing her arguments for the *Vindication of the Rights of Woman*). Fay Weldon has claimed that we can find Austen 'trapped in these pages as a girl'.[12] I'm more inclined to say that something of the girl who created the great novelist is expressed in this early work.

Let's start with Austen's own depiction of a heroine turning from girl into young woman: 'No one who had ever seen Catherine Morland in her infancy would have supposed her born to be an heroine'.[13] The ungainly girl who becomes the romantic heroine of Austen's early fiction is unsuited to the role from the beginning: 'noisy and wild, hated confinement and cleanliness, and loved nothing so well as rolling down the green slope at the back of the house ... Such was Catherine Morland at ten.'[14] *Northanger Abbey* marks Catherine's transition from girlhood to young-womanhood, as this is centred on the narration of a feminine-romance quest for marriage. Catherine is caught in the transitional phase we would now call 'pre-adolescence'. At 14, she still prefers 'cricket, baseball, riding on horseback, and running about the country ... to books':

> At fifteen, appearances were mending; she began to curl her hair and long for balls; her complexion improved, her features were softened by plumpness and colour, her eyes gained more animation, and her figure more consequence. Her love of dirt gave way to an inclination for finery, and she grew clean as she grew smart.[15]

Her immersion in the material immediacy of 'dirt' gives way to the socialized 'finery' associated with femininity. She enters the realm of courtship in the course of the narrative, learning from culturally valued literary sources such as Shakespeare that:

> a young woman in love always looks
> – 'like Patience on a monument
> Smiling at Grief.'[16]

The girl-Austen would no doubt have practised this look for the benefit of her sister, mimicking the available tropes of womanhood. The transition from noisy, dirty, active, straightforwardly boyish girlhood to the significant and more arcane markers of young-womanhood are achieved through reading 'all such works as heroines must read to supply their memories with those quotations which are so serviceable and so soothing in the vicissitudes of their eventful lives'.[17] Novels teach the girl to become a young woman in their repeated performance of the romance quest that dominates young-womanhood. One of the functions of narrative is to record and transmit the process of becoming: Austen's particular material is in 'becoming woman'. She famously breaks through the narrative artifice of *Northanger Abbey* to make a caustic claim for the authenticity of novelistic truth:

> 'It is only Cecelia, or Camilla, or Belinda,' or, in short, only some work in which the greatest powers of the mind are displayed, in which the most thorough knowledge of human nature, the happiest delineation of its varieties, the liveliest effusions of wit and humour, are conveyed to the world in the best chosen language.[18]

Now at this point I am aware of over-generalizing inexcusably: not every young woman is subject to the romance quest, not every young woman identifies with the fictional heroines of romance, not every young woman makes this transition from androgynous 'girlhood' to the cramping self-consciousness of 'womanhood'. But most do. Those who escape the confining determinants of romance heroine in their life narrative are still marked by its absence in one way or the other.[19] What is significant here is Austen's close analysis of the way novels offer a paradigm for the transition into womanhood via the romance quest: the novels she claims as displaying the 'greatest powers of the mind' are named for their heroines. Yes, this is lampooned in *Northanger Abbey*, but at the same time the romance narrative is followed through to a self-conscious and satisfying conclusion. Catherine's quest ends happily in her narratively stage-managed marriage to the romantic hero she encounters on first arriving in Bath: when the narrator remarks on the 'compression' of the pages left in her narrative, she reassures her readers that 'we are all hastening together to perfect felicity'.[20] The narrative felicity of harmonious completion is analogous to the heroine's 'completion' of her feminine-romance quest. When it works on the reader, the Austenian happy ending makes us conscious that we always wanted it this way. Austen emphasizes the sheer artifice at work in the ending (there is nothing in the least accidental about it) while also relying on the yearning for its possibility its representation inspires.

Jack and Alice: A Novel, written by the adolescent Austen, is by contrast a direct assault on realist narrative. It opens with a description of the 'persons and Characters' of the tale in terms that, while lifted from the stock of available novelistic character descriptors, combine to make no sense at all:

> Mr. and Mrs. Jones were both rather tall & very passionate, but were in other respects good tempered, well-behaved People. Charles Adams was an amiable, accomplished, & bewitching young Man; of so dazzling a Beauty that none but Eagles could look him in the Face ... In Lady Williams every virtue met. She was a widow with a handsome Jointure & the remains of a very handsome face. (Chapter the first)[21]

The 'Alice' of the title is the eldest daughter of the Johnson family: in love with Charles Adams, and of a family defined by their tendency to drink too much. The characters reassemble almost immediately at a 'Masquerade', in costumes expressing the allegorical essence of each:

> Of the Males, a Mask representing the Sun was the most universally admired. The Beams that darted from his Eyes were like those of that glorious Luminary, tho' infinitely superior. So strong were they that no one dared venture within half a mile of them; he had therefore the best part of the Room to himself, its size not amounting to more than 3 quarters of a mile in length & half a one in breadth. The Gentleman at last finding the fierceness of his beams to be very inconvenient to the concourse, by obliging them to croud together in one corner of the room, half shut his eyes, by which means the Company discovered him to be Charles Adams in his plain green Coat, without any mask at all. (Chapter the first)

In a clear breach of novelistic convention, Charles *is* the sun he is supposed to represent: a superluminous example of his metaphoric reference. He outshines the object to which he has been compared, in a remarkable literalization of conventional character-building references: 'his Eyes were like those of that glorious Luminary, tho' infinitely superior.' The precise measurements of the room add to the effect of creative impossibility.

Character dialogue is also subject to violent distortion of writerly conventions – in this case rather tending to be *too* realistic to stand for the formalities of literary realism. This example comes from a conversation between Lady Williams and Alice Johnson:

> 'I was invited the following year by a distant relation of my Father's to spend the Winter with her in town. Mrs. Watkins was a Lady of Fashion,

Family, & fortune; she was in general esteemed a pretty Woman, but I never thought her very handsome, for my part. She has too high a forehead, her eyes were too small, & she had too much colour.'
'How can that be?' interrupted Miss Johnson, reddening with anger;
'Do you think that any one can have too much colour?' ...
The Dispute at length grew so hot on the part of Alice that, 'From Words she almost came to Blows', when Mr. Johnson luckily entered, & with some difficulty forced her away from Lady Williams, Mrs. Watkins, & her red cheeks. (Chapter the third)[22]

The characters make up their disagreement over a walk to Charles Adams' 'horse-pond', but Lady Williams soon returns to her former subject, and 'Alice had already begun to colour up':

'I will now pursue my story; but I must insist upon not giving you any description of Mrs. Watkins; it would only be reviving old stories & as you never saw her, it can be nothing to you, if her forehead was too high, her eyes were too small, or if she had too much colour' ...
So provoked was poor Alice at this renewal of the old story, that I know not what might have been the consequence of it, had not their attention been engaged by another object ... (Chapter the fourth)

The 'object' which prevents a full-blown fight between Alice and Lady Williams is a new character – Lucy – found lying beneath a tree, who proceeds to tell a life story that recurs as the structural origin of Fanny Price's life at *Mansfield Park*:

Having a numerous family [my father] was easily prevailed upon by a sister of my Mother's, who is a widow in good circumstances & keeps an alehouse in the next Village to ours, to let her take me & breed me up at her own expence.' (Chapter the fifth)

Lucy is also in love with Charles Adams, and has made her way to his grounds in Pamydiddle to pursue her suit of his hand in marriage. She had already 'made a bold push' and written 'a very kind letter, offering him with great tenderness [her] hand and heart' but received in reply 'an angry and peremptory refusal'. She puts his refusal down to 'modesty' and – in a vertiginous inversion of Mr Collins' persistence following Elizabeth Bennet's clear refusal – follows him to his home estate where she is caught in 'one of the steel traps so common in gentleman's grounds'. This long and unbelievable story is given while she remains with a leg 'entirely broken', and produces the best line of the piece:

> At this melancholy recital, the fair eyes of Lady Williams were suf-fused in tears & Alice could not help exclaiming, 'Oh! cruel Charles, to wound the hearts & legs of all the fair.' (Chapter the sixth)

Austen's intensification of novelistic absurdity is built on a rather pre-cise understanding of how language works: the extreme zeugma here exposes the metaphoric tendencies of the verb 'wound', and is then twisted further through the generalization of the claim ('all the fair'). We are shunted dizzyingly from the figurative to the literal (wounding hearts is one thing, wounding legs quite another). It is not that she does not know how to construct plausible fiction: rather that she knows why such a thing is in itself a linguistic deceit (insincere) and has the confi-dence to expose the trick.

Lady Williams then, after examining the fracture, 'immediately began & performed the operation with great skill, which was the more wonder-full on account of her having never performed such a one before'. More wonderful still, 'Lucy then arose from the ground, & finding that she could walk with the greatest ease, accompanied them to Lady Williams's House at her Ladyship's particular request' (Chapter the sixth). Language allows miraculous things to happen by the conjunction of subject and verb: these things may or may not be possible in the material world, but they are imaginatively possible. Austen's language play is very serious: it indicates a consciousness that things may be constructed differently, different kinds of causality can be imagined, and may be possible. The laughter is not only at the absurdity of the actions described, but at the limited sense of possibility these conjunctions expose in the mind of the reader. This is not realism as we have come to know it: it is a mode of conscious play that acknowledges the descriptive construction of objects and their transformative relations.

The 'Jack' of the title is dealt with in the short space of one brutal paragraph:

> It may now be proper to return to the Hero of this Novel, the brother of Alice, of whom I beleive I have scarcely ever had occasion to speak; which may perhaps be partly oweing to his unfortunate propensity to Liquor, which so completely deprived him of the use of those faculties Nature had endowed him with, that he never did anything worth mentioning. His Death happened a short time after Lucy's

departure & was the natural Consequence of this pernicious practice. By his decease, his sister became the sole inheritress of a very
large fortune, which as it gave her fresh Hopes of rendering herself
acceptable as a wife to Charles Adams, could not fail of being most
pleasing to her – & as the effect was Joyfull, the Cause could scarcely
be lamented. (Chapter the seventh)

Alice sends her father to 'propose a union' with Charles Adams. Her
father complies and is rejected. Alice takes to the bottle and Charles
ends up marrying Lady Williams. Lucy's fate is the strangest of all: she
goes to Bath and is courted by an 'elderly Man of noble fortune whose
ill health was the chief inducement of his Journey to Bath'. She writes
to lady Williams for advice, which is given in contradictory terms, but
Lucy is suddenly murdered by the otherwise forgotten character Sukey,
who had been earlier introduced as suffering from 'Envy and Malice':
'jealous of her superior charms, took her by poison from an admiring
World at the age of seventeen' (Chapter the ninth). The Duke marries
Sukey's ambitious sister, and Sukey herself is 'shortly after exalted in a
manner she truly deserved, & by her actions appeared to have always
desired. Her barbarous Murder was discovered, & in spite of every
interceding friend she was speedily raised to the Gallows' (Chapter the
ninth). The striking pressure on 'exalted' in its relation to 'raised' again
presents a conscious pun between figurative and descriptive language.

The anarchic narrative shifts available in *Jack and Alice* may be read for
a random and incoherent pastiche of the glut of frothy fiction Austen
had been exposed to as a growing heroine herself. The acceptable strains
on plausibility available from the most ordinarily novel become heightened to the point of causal breakdown. It's a technique that draws attention to the slippery way in which chains of events are glued together in
narrative according to conventional causal mechanisms that have little
to do with experience and much to do with belief systems. Austen's best
narratives expose the fallacy of individual agency, and represent the most
beautiful causality working at a level beyond the individual. Austen recognized the futility of human attempts to control causality: this becomes
central to her later works, where narrative causality is shown repeatedly
to be out of the hands of the heroine, left to the higher consciousness of
the organizing author. *Emma* is the most explicit example of this awareness of 'higher' narrative causality, since it tells the story of a heroine who
comes to recognize that she is a heroine in a story, and not the author.
What is distinctive about the later works is that this recognition is itself
tied to the narrative terms for achievement of a happy ending.

Love and Friendship pushes even harder at the plausibility of narrative conventions to comic effect. The narrative in this case is presented in epistolary form, which adds a new layer of implausible recollection and representational distortion by the character engaged in the writing of the 'misfortunes and adventures' of her life. In this case the key interest to this argument is the way the narrative movement is established. 'Letter the First' is from Isabel to Laura, repeating her entreaties to give her daughter 'a regular detail' of the life of the latter. The second is from Laura to Isabel, agreeing to 'satisfy the curiosity of your daughter' in order to provide a 'useful lesson'. From the third letter to the fifteenth, Laura tells her absurd life story to Marianne in increasingly emotive terms. Each letter continues the story as if broken only by exhaustion in the arm of the writer, or the conventions of epistolarity. Little attention is paid to the presence of the reading mind of Marianne, until 'Letter the Fourteenth', where she is addressed directly:

> Arm yourself, my amiable young friend, with all the philosophy you are mistress of; summon up all the fortitude you possess, for alas! In the perusal of the following pages your sensibility will be most severely tried ... [23]

Laura's narrative is impossible to paraphrase with any coherence: events are piled upon each other, strung together only by Laura's bizarre narrative consciousness:

> In my mind, every virtue that could adorn it was centred; it was the rendezvous of every good quality and every noble sentiment.[24]

References are scrambled from the beginning, in such a way as to make it impossible to try to unravel them:

> My father was a native of Ireland and an inhabitant of Wales; my mother was the natural daughter of a Scotch peer by an Italian opera-girl – I was born in Spain, and received my education at a convent in France.[25]

Unlike Catherine Moreland, who understood nothing until it was taught, Laura is an impossibly accomplished heroine: 'my progress had always exceeded my instructions ... I had shortly surpassed my masters.'[26] She lives quietly with only her parents and Isabel until one night there is a knock at the door:

Mary, instantly entering the room, informed us that a young gentleman and his servant were at the door, who had lost their way, were
very cold, and begged to let them warm themselves by our fire.
'Won't you admit them?' said I.
'You have no objection, my dear?' said my father.
'None in the world,' replied my mother.
Mary, without waiting for any further commands, immediately
left the room and quickly returned, introducing the most beaute-
ous and amiable youth I had ever beheld. The servant she kept to
herself.[27]

The similarly miraculous arrival of 'the most charming young man in
the world' in *Northanger Abbey* provides Eleanor Tilney with a conven-
ient husband, and her father with 'a fit of good-homour' at just the right
moment to allow for the happy union of our heroine and her man.[28]
Laura's 'natural sensibility' is 'greatly affected by the sufferings of the
unfortunate stranger', and she falls in love with him instantly. He is
called 'Lindsay', but our bizarre narrator decides 'for particular reasons'
to 'conceal it under that of Talbot' but immediately begins to refer to
him as 'Edward'. He tells his life story in terms of a young hero who has
been oppressed by his powerful father, and defines himself by his bold
and unflinching transgression of his father's rule:

'My father, seduced by the false glare of fortune and the deluding
pomp of title, insisted on my giving my hand to Lady Dorothea.
"No, never!" exclaimed I. "Lady Dorothea is lovely and engaging –
I prefer no woman to her – but know, sir, that I scorn to marry her in
compliance with your wishes. No! Never shall it be said that I obliged
my father."'[29]

His father identifies the 'unmeaning gibberish' of his son's language as
the result of 'studying novels', at which point Lindsay-Talbot-Edward
leaves to find his fortune. If it is about anything, this narrative is about
the possibility of relationship between narrative representation and
reality. In the narrative models readily available to Austen's developing mind, heroes defy the oppressive rule of their fathers, heroines
live only by their sensibility, and causality is imposed on random
events to produce an illusion of coherence. The narratives that Austen
produces take these elements to an extreme that exposes the artifice.
Novels help their readers to construct, and to position themselves as
agents of reality.

Laura marries Lindsay on the basis of her instantaneous feelings, they travel to visit Edward's aunt in Middlesex, who had 'not only been totally ignorant of my marriage with her nephew, but had never even had the slightest idea of there being such a person in the world.'[30] Lindsay-Talbot-Edward's sister – Augusta – is visiting her aunt at the time and an interesting dialogue occurs between brother and sister:

'But do you think that my father will ever be reconciled to this imprudent connection?' said Augusta.

'Augusta,' replied the noble youth, 'I thought you had a better opinion of me than to imagine I would so abjectly degrade myself as to consider my father's concurrence in any of my affairs either of consequence or concern to me. Tell me, Augusta, with sincerity: did you ever know me consult his inclinations or follow his advice in the least trifling particular since the age of fifteen?'

'Edward,' replied she, 'you are surely too diffident in your own praise. Since you were five years old, I entirely acquit you of ever having willingly contributed to the satisfaction of your father. But still I am not without apprehension of your being shortly obliged to degrade yourself in your own eyes by seeking a support for your wife in the generosity of Sir Edward.'

'Never, never, Augusta, will I so demean myself,' said Edward. 'Support! What support will Laura want which she can receive from him?'

'Only those very insignificant ones of victuals and drink,' answered she.

'Victuals and drink!' replied my husband, in a most nobly contemptuous manner. 'And dost thou then imagine that there is no other support for an exalted mind (such as my Laura's), than the mean and indelicate employment of eating and drinking?'

'None that I know of, so efficacious,' returned Augusta.[31]

In contrast to the novelistic tendency to centre the lives of characters on 'love', Augusta raises the problem of material subsistence. The ridiculous Lyndsay-Talbot-Edward asks if it is so impossible to his sister's 'vile and corrupted palate to exist on love' or 'conceive of the luxury of living in every distress that poverty can inflict, with the object of your tenderest affection'. This tension between the material needs of living characters and the ideational drive towards narrative culmination in 'love' is always at the centre of Austen's work. Materiality and ideality are shown to be thoroughly interpenetrating in the later works: here the mix is more of oil and water. Material needs are laughed out of court, since we are knowingly in a world of the girl-writer's imagination, where anything can (and does) happen according to her random whims.

Lady Susan is my concluding example. The most serious of the three early works, it projects a more secure and reasonable epistolary realism, which only gives way to its framing narrative consciousness in the 'conclusion'. This is the same concluding voice that we find at work in the closure of the 'mature' works, breaking the conventions of fictionality with a highly conscious reference to the strenuous credulity of the epistolary form:

> This correspondence, by a meeting between some of the parties and a separation between the others, could not, to the great detriment of the Post Office revenue, be continued longer.[32]

She simply can't quite maintain the solemnity of the fiction and bursts with laughter its claim to a simple authenticity. This is an early attempt at serious fiction, the only one that considers the moral dilemma of a bad mother. Lady Susan – the central consciousness of the narrative – is a duplicitous and powerful figure, and the layering of letters through which we hear her voice allow us to judge her as a manipulative and dishonest character who betrays the feelings and fortune of her own daughter to gain her wilful ends. It is a narrative about a libidinous woman: one who failed to sublimate her girlish desires in spite of marriage and motherhood. We are clearly not supposed to identify with Lady Susan, but the work fails to resolve the problem that she is by far the most dynamic and attractive character available, and the one whose command of language, while deceptive and inauthentic, is the most seductive. Austen's early narrative work is steeped in explorations of the unstable relationship between representation and truth; art and nature; representation and the real. Narrative fiction in general is marked by a questioning of the possibility of truth *in* representation. For Susan Sontag the truth that novels can provide are moral truths:

> Serious fiction writers think about moral problems *practically*. They tell stories. They narrate. They evoke our common humanity in narratives with which we can identify, even though the lives may be remote from our own. They stimulate our imagination. The stories they tell enlarge and complicate – and, therefore, improve – our sympathies. They educate our capacity for moral judgment.[33]

Novels are tricky objects to define, but in their self-definitions, the writers of early novels had to make decisions about whether they were creating history or romance. Think of Aphra Behn's *Oroonoko* which boasts of itself as a true history, or Defoe's *Robinson Crusoe* which goes out of its way to assure its readers it is not mere fiction. Samuel Richardson's petticoated subjectivity-in-writing is another example of the extraordinary measures taken by early novelists to construct an aura of authenticity in their creative fictions. Realism offers a particular (rather than universal) claim to truth within the terms of historical determinants. The fault line between 'history' and 'romance' is colonized by the novel, and this is in Austen's work shown to mark a fault line between perception and truth.

There are innumerable modes of realism in narrative, since narrative is the act of telling stories about how things are, what makes things happen, what's there and how it works. Austen's 'mature' works are steeped in consciousness of the material processes of narrative, drawing attention to the fictiveness of her constructed reality, to the book in the lap of the reader, to the 'compression of the pages before us'. *Lady Susan* works through this problem of the authenticity of representative language in a surprisingly explicit way that records something important about the development of novelistic consciousness and the heroine. It is a something Austen seems to have put behind her when she became the 'mature' novelist, but I am now close to claiming that it is more likely to be what fuelled her becoming-in-writing and her subsequent canonization and cultural memorialization. We still love Austen's narratives because they provide a literary coral reef which holds the shape of girlish laughter at the absurd claims of serious representational realism, even while they perform the seriousness of representation before our eyes.

The tone of Lady Susan's first letter is polite and gracious. This letter constructs a character from implied tone of voice, addressing Charles Vernon as '[m]y dear brother'.[34] The second letter, to her friend Mrs Johnson, performs a complete overturning of the expectations established in the first: 'Charles Vernon is my aversion'.[35] Where the first letter speaks of Lady Susan's impatience as she 'look[s] forward to the hour when [she] shall be admitted into your delightful retirement',[36] the second speaks to a third party of this move as her 'last resource. Were there another place in England open to me, I would prefer it'.[37] The first letter is addressed to her recently deceased husband's brother, and speaks of her need for 'fortitude' in the face of her 'separation' from her daughter (Frederica).[38] The second shows a different face to her accomplice, Mrs Johnson: 'Frederica, who was born to be the torment of my life ... I shall deposit her under the care of Miss Summers in Wigmore Street, till she becomes a little more reasonable'.[39] To her brother-in-law she tells a tale of her current hosts inviting her to prolong her stay; to her friend she tells that she must leave because 'only four months a widow' she had caused chaos in the household by flirting with her host *and* his daughter's fiancé. The story unfolds in conflicting layers of self-representation, emphasizing the gaps between Lady Susan's protestations of innocence and her manifest desire to realize her own will in all things. She is the most sexually active and explicit of all Austen's heroines, actively working to seduce the man her daughter is falling in love with. At the same time, she uncannily prefigures Emma, with her grey eyes and good figure, her wilfulness and unwillingness to conform to social conventions, her sheer determination to turn the narrative to her own desires.

Perhaps the most interesting aspect of *Lady Susan* as a narrative is its insistence on the deceitfulness of language. Letter 3 (from Mrs. Vernon to Lady de Courcy) describes Lady Susan's projected arrival at Churchill:

> Mr Vernon ... [d]isposed as he always is to think the best of every one, her display of grief, and professions of regret, and general resolutions of prudence were sufficient to soften his heart, and make him really confide in her sincerity. But as for myself, I am still unconvinced; and plausibly as her ladyship has now written, I cannot make up my mind, till I better understand her real meaning in coming to us you may guess therefore my dear Madam, with what feelings I look forward to her arrival.[40]

We are immediately in a world where 'plausibility' is under question and the 'real meaning' has to be discovered beneath surface appearances beyond the explicit performance of language. Reginald de Courcy writes to Mrs Vernon: 'by all that I can gather, Lady Susan possesses a degree of captivating deceit which must be pleasing to witness and detect'.[41] Lady Susan writes to her confidant, Mrs Johnson, that it is 'better to deceive [her husband] entirely; since he will be stubborn he must be tricked'.[42] Mrs Vernon comments on the delusive appearance of Lady Susan:

> I have seldom seen so lovely a woman as Lady Susan. She is delicately fair, with fine grey eyes and dark eyelashes; and from her appearance one would not suppose her more than five and twenty, though she must in fact be ten years older.[43]

Reginald de Courcy becomes entangled in Lady Susan's web of misrepresentation, and begins to fall in love with her, while her daughter

Frederica is falling in love with him. Sir Reginald de Courcy writes to warn his son of the danger of 'a match, which deep art only could render probable.'⁴⁴ Lady de Courcy describes Lady Susan as 'artful', and Mrs Vernon notices her 'pathetic representation' and 'artful display'.⁴⁵ Lady Susan is conscious that she is able to 'make a story' to hold up against any that is told about her, and is vain of her 'eloquence': 'Consideration and esteem as surely follow command of language, as admiration waits on beauty'.⁴⁶ She also decries 'artlessness' in 'love matters', and calls any girl a 'simpleton' who 'has it either by nature or affectation'.⁴⁷ She is, by her own testimony, 'tired of submitting my will to the caprices of others – of resigning my own judgement in deference to those, to whom I own no duty, and for whom I feel no respect.'⁴⁸

Lady Susan's striking libidinal energies push hard against social conventions into which women (and especially mothers) are supposed to fit. She does not sublimate, even in the face of a maturing daughter coming forward with legitimate desires of her own. At one level this makes her a figure for nascent female liberation. It is not a figure Austen foregrounded again. Her later work is more concerned to find modes of female libidinal satisfaction that can transform, rather than simply rub up against, the social order. Doody deserves the last word on this aspect of Austen's early narrative work:

> Austen proposes that libidinous desire is prior to the economic system, although constantly getting attached to it. Libidinous desire gets attached, for instance, to the feudal system of inheritance, creating a greed that cheerfully witnesses the removal of parents and siblings. Desire is officially attached to the system of monogamy. In attaching itself to any such systems, however, the libido proves itself capable of evading or transforming them – in Austen's world.
>
> This is a very frightening philosophic production on the part of a young woman. The disconcerting elements in Austen's fiction (even in the six novels) are sometimes very palpable obstacles to our smooth approbation. But these elements in her early fiction can be redefined as a lack of skill doing the accepted thing.⁴⁹

Rather than reading *Lady Susan* as a failed and immature novel, then, we might rather read it as a representation of the peculiar qualities of novelistic realism itself. Lady Susan is not real. She is a narrative experiment, an experiment with narrative, after which Austen turned her eye to the fate of the emergent consciousness of the daughter over that of the mother. Mothers are always present in the Austenian narrative, even, or perhaps most so, when they are also absent or dead. Mothers shape the heroine's journey towards a happy ending. Lady Susan is an odd narrative mother, neither sentimental nor maternal. As a figure of representation she also represents figurative language: cunning, eloquent, deceptive. *Lady Susan* can be read for an experimental figure of the problem of narrative realism itself: raising the question of the duplicity of language, the illusory nature of the representational mode of the novel, and the creative chaos that transpires when female agents take control of their narrative destiny.

These examples of Austen's pre-novelistic narratives offer two parallel ways to understand her transition from juvenile to mature novelist. Doody has noted the first, in which objective-historical forces perform a shift in writing context from Enlightenment to Regency, one which constrains the early, more philosophical and experimental Austen, but one which also makes her publishable as the writer of longer, safer and more 'respectable' works that could match 'Fielding and Richardson'.[50] Doody finds Eliza Haywood subject to the same literary narrative of increasing constraint. I want to propose a second model, one which does not preclude the first. This is the subjective aspect of narrative writing, which foregrounds the life of the writing subject. Along this line we can understand Austen's narrative work itself performing the trajectory of becoming-woman, analogous to the fictional development of her heroines. This process involves a harnessing of the kind of libidinal energies that run riot in Austen's early narratives to produce the aesthetic transcendence of the later works. Yes, this is a kind of Regency refashioning according to the more constrained codes at the turn of the eighteenth into the nineteenth centuries. It is a productive constraint, which benefits in ways that are difficult to fathom from the tightening of the fictional stays. There is perhaps as much secret pleasure in a well-tightened stay as there is in the freedom to roll down grassy hills and climb trees.

Finally the problem of representation in realism leads me to consider Austen's heroines as allegorical figures of 'History' itself. This would explain the deep irony that hovers around Catherine Moreland's distaste for history:

> the men all so good for nothing, and hardly any women at all it is very tiresome: and yet I often think it odd that it should be so dull, for a great deal of it must be invention.[51]

If we set aside Anne Elliot, Austen's heroines have a tendency to be between 17 and 19. We might consider receiving them as representational figures for 'History' as she unfolds in the mind of the writer. The two parallel interpretive series outlined above coincide to offer a figuring of narrative female subjectivity *as* a mode of history unfolding or becoming. The heroines' various narrative performances of 'becoming-woman' are also incarnations of the transition of the writing subject from girl into woman. They capture something of the development of women's writing through the eighteenth and into the nineteenth centuries. History as the objective narrative of facts and causality is not taken seriously by Austen, who has a stronger belief in history in the sense of inner experience. The centrality of shifts in perception to the narrative outcomes of her later heroines captures the perceptual-subjective working its way into the objective-correlative. While her early heroines are in no way constrained by narrative conventions, her later heroines are taught by their author how to find the object of their desire according to narrative conventions. Realist fiction may be insincere history, but it can also offer ways to think about the historicity of narrative itself as the unfolding of inner experience.

Notes

1. Susan Sontag, *Against Interpretation* (London: Vintage, 2001), p. 14.
2. W. H. Auden, *The Dyer's Hand and Other Essays* (London: Faber & Faber, 1987), pp. 18–19.
3. Margaret Ann Doody, 'The Short Fiction' in *The Cambridge Companion to Jane Austen*, eds. Edward Copeland and Julie McMaster (Cambridge: Cambridge University Press, 1997), p. 92.
4. Susan Sontag, 'At the Same Time: The Novelist and Moral Reasoning', in *At the Same Time: Essays and Speeches* (London: Hamish Hamilton, 2007), p. 215.
5. Georg Wilhelm Hegel, *Introductory Lectures on Aesthetics*, tr. Bernard Bosanquet (London: Penguin, 2004), pp. 10–11.
6. This argument emerges primarily from Ian Watt's famous analysis in *The Rise of the Novel*. It has been challenged in interesting ways that have influenced this argument: I would note, in particular, that works of Margaret Ann Doody, and Jane Spencer. However, the notion of the English novel maturing out of the inchoate effusion of narrative forms of the late seventeenth and early eighteenth centuries remains largely unshaken.
7. Doody, p. 92.
8. Ibid., p. 92.
9. Ibid., p. 98. Austen left behind three unpublished notebooks which have been collected and published by R. W. Chapman and also made available in Margaret Anne Doody and Douglas Murray's OUP edition (1993).
10. Lionel Trilling, *Sincerity and Authenticity* (Oxford: Oxford University Press, 1972), p. 73.

11. Jane Austen, *Northanger Abbey*, ed. Claire Grogan (Toronto: Broadview, 2002), p. 238.
12. Fay Weldon in Foreword to Jane Austen's, *Love and Friendship*, (Hesperus Press: London, 2003), p. viii.
13. Austen, *Northanger Abbey*, p. 37.
14. Ibid., p. 39. The excellent Broadview edition of *Northanger Abbey* (2002) offers a footnote reference from this description of Catherine to Locke's *Some Thoughts Concerning Education* (1693), which discusses the benefits of 'open air' and exercise to the development of daughters. Wollstonecraft certainly picked up this idea from Locke and made it a central tenet of her *Vindication of the Rights of Woman* (1792), but while I have no doubt that Austen would have read Locke, I am inclined to think that her understanding of the effects of the 'noisy and wild' enjoyments of childhood are drawn primarily from experience rather than theory.
15. Austen, *Northanger Abbey*, p. 39.
16. Ibid., p. 41.
17. Ibid., p. 40.
18. Ibid., p. 60.
19. See Iris Young, 'Throwing Like a Girl', *Body and Flesh: A Philosophical Reader* (Oxford: Blackwell, 1998), p. 269. Young's definition of 'femininity' as a 'defining mode' is in the background to this argument, as it was to an earlier essay for *Critical Quarterly* called 'writing like a girl'. Even in those cases where particular women do not identify with typically feminine behaviour, as defined within a particular social epoch, a relatively coherent mode of femininity is still 'definitive in a negative mode – as that which she has escaped, through accident or good fortune, or, more often, as that which she has had to overcome'.
20. Austen, *Northanger Abbey*, p. 238.
21. All quotations from *Jack and Alice: A Novel* are taken from, http://oddlots. digitalspace.net/austen/jack_alice.html.
22. Austen may have been thinking of Sterne's marvellous description of Tristram Shandy's father reaching for his handkerchief: 'Any man, madam, reasoning upwards and observing the prodigious suffusion of blood in my father's countenance, (as all the blood in his body seemed to rush up into his face, as I told you) he must have redden'd, pictorially and scientinctically speaking, six whole tints and a half, if not a full octave above his natural colour', p. 146. The editors note that Sterne was probably thinking through Hogarth's *Analysis of Beauty*, which grades colouring on a scale of 1–7.
23. Austen, *Love and Friendship*, p. 30.
24. Ibid., p. 4.
25. Ibid., p. 4.
26. Ibid., p. 4.
27. Ibid., p. 7.
28. Austen, *Northanger Abbey*, p. 239.
29. Austen, *Love and Friendship*, p. 8.
30. Ibid., p. 9.
31. Ibid., p. 10–11.
32. Austen, *Lady Susan*, p. 101.
33. Sontag, 'At the Same Time', p. 213.

34. Austen, *Lady Susan*, p. 43.
35. Ibid., p. 45.
36. Ibid., p. 43.
37. Ibid., p. 45.
38. Ibid., p. 43.
39. Ibid., p. 43.
40. Ibid., p. 46.
41. Ibid., p. 47.
42. Ibid., p. 48.
43. Ibid., p. 49.
44. Ibid., p. 58.
45. Ibid., p. 66.
46. Ibid., p. 64.
47. Ibid., p. 69.
48. Ibid., p. 98.
49. Doody, p. 93.
50. Ibid., p. 90.
51. Austen, *Northanger Abbey*, p. 122.

Select Secondary Reading

Theodor Adorno, *The Jargon of Authenticity*, trans. Knut Tarnowski and Frederic Will (1964, London: Routledge, 2003).

Donald Davie, 'Sincerity and Poetry' (delivered as a Hopwood Lecture in 1965, and re-published as 'On Sincerity: From Wordsworth to Ginsberg' in *Encounter* 31.4 (1968): 61–6).

—— 'On Sincerity: From Wordsworth to Ginsberg,' *Encounter* 31.4 (1968).

Paul De Man 'Autobiography as Defacement,' *Modern Language Notes* XCIV (1979): 923.

Nick Groom, ed., *Thomas Chatterton and Romantic Culture*, (Basingstoke: Macmillan – now Palgrave Macmillan, 1999).

—— *The Forger's Shadow: How Forgery Changed the Course of Literature* (London: Picador, 2002).

Charles Guignon, *On Being Authentic* (London: Routledge, 2004).

Leon Guilhamet, *The Sincere Ideal* (McGill-Queens University Press, 1974).

Jürgen Habermas, *Knowledge and Human Interests*, trans. Jeremy J. Shapiro (1968, London: Heinemann, 1972).

—— *The Philosophical Discourse of Modernity: Twelve Lectures*, trans. Frederick Lawrence (1985, The MIT Press, 1987).

Stuart Hampshire, 'Sincerity and Single-Mindedness,' *Freedom of Mind and Other Essays*, (Oxford University Press, 1972), pp. 232–50.

Geoffrey Hartman, *Wordsworth's Poetry 1787–1814* (Yale University Press, 1964).

—— *Scars of the Spirit: The Struggle against Inauthenticity* (Palgrave Macmillan, 2002).

Martin Heidegger, *Being and Time*, trans. John Macquarrie and Edward Robinson (Malden, MA: Basil Blackwell, 1962).

Fredric Jameson, *The Political Unconscious: Narrative as a Socially Symbolic Act* (1981, London: Routledge, 2002).

Marjorie Levinson, *The Romantic Fragment Poem: A Critique of a Form* (Chapel Hill: University of North Carolina Press, 1986).

Jerome J. McGann, *The Beauty of Inflections: Literary Investigations in Historical Method and Theory* (Oxford University Press, 1985).

—— *The Poetics of Sensibility: A Revolution in Literary Style* (Oxford: Clarendon Press, 1996).

—— *Byron and Romanticism*, ed. James Solderholm (Cambridge University Press, 2002).

Pam Morris, *Imagining Inclusive Society in Nineteenth-Century Novels: The Code of Sincerity in the Public Sphere* (Johns Hopkins University Press, 2004).

David Perkins, *Wordsworth and the Poetry of Sincerity* (Harvard University Press, 1964).

Henri Peyre, *Literature and Sincerity* (Yale University Press, 1963).

Herbert Read, 'The Cult of Sincerity,' *Hudson Review* 21 (1968): 53–74.

Fiona Robertson, *Legitimate Histories: Scott, Gothic and the Authorities of Fiction* (Oxford University Press, 1994).

Margaret Russett, *Fictions and Fakes: Forging Romantic Authenticity* 1760–1845 (Cambridge University Press, 2006).

Patricia M. Spacks, 'In Search of Sincerity,' *College English* 29 (1968).

Charles Taylor, *Sources of the Self: The Making of Modern Identity* (Cambridge University Press, 1989).

—— *The Ethics of Authenticity*, (Harvard University Press, 1991).

Lionel Trilling, *Sincerity and Authenticity: The Charles Eliot Norton Lectures*, 1969–1970 (Oxford University Press, 1972).

Dror Wahrman *The Making of the Modern Self. Identity and Culture in Eighteenth-Century England* (Yale University Press, 2004).

Bernard Williams, *Truth and Truthfulness: An Essay in Genealogy* (Princeton University Press, 2002).

Index